NEVER TEMPT A SCOT

The League of Rogues - Book 12

LAUREN SMITH

ISBN: 978-1-952063-00-8 (ebook)

ISBN: 978-1-952063-01-5 (trade print)

For all my bodice ripper fans out there. You aren't alone!

AUGUST 1821- BATH, ENGLAND

"Lydia, is that your sister?"

Lydia's friend Lysandra Russell pointed to a group of young men hovering around a delicate, petite figure in the middle of the crowded assembly room. Even at this distance, Lydia recognized her younger sister's fine-boned face and far too pretty features: the flaxen hair, the cornflower-blue eyes, and the lovely rosebud mouth that left every man she met ready to come to blows over her attention and her honor.

"Oh heavens, what has Portia gone and done now?" Lydia muttered. She stepped closer to Lysandra, who chuckled and waved her dark-blue silk fan patterned with silver stars.

"I believe she's convinced the men to wager for spots on her dance card. If anyone discovers that, she might

be cast out of the assembly rooms by the master of ceremonies. You know that sort of behavior is strictly
taboo." Lysandra tucked a stray strand of her bright-red
hair behind her ear and rolled her eyes. "Well, at least
she's having fun. You and I have been growing petals
over here against this wall."

Lydia giggled at Lysandra's artful description of them
as wallflowers. "Yes, Portia always seems to find friends
and aspiring beaux wherever she goes. My father tells me
our mother was much the same. A true beauty."

Lydia's heart sank a little as she said this. She wasn't
beautiful the way Portia was or their mother had been.
She was only a few inches above five feet, and though
she had the same flaxen hair as her sister, it lacked her
sister's elegant shine. Her blue eyes were not so bright a
blue. Her features, while not unattractive, did not have
the same irresistible beauty as Portia's.

So it came as no surprise that Portia was their
father's favorite. But she could not complain. Her father
did love her, and she was not treated as some princess of
cinders by her family. She was simply *not* the favorite. It
was no more complicated than that.

"I suppose I ought to free her of the horde she's
collected." Lydia squared her shoulders, knowing how
difficult it was going to be to get her sister away from
her group of admirers. They had been in Bath only one
week, yet the entire male population was already infatuated with Portia.

"I shall help you." Lysandra joined her, chin set firmly, as though she was facing down the French army all alone. Lydia adored her friend's loyalty. When things became serious, Lysandra could always be counted on to help.

They crossed the vast floor of the assembly room, careful to sidestep whenever twirling couples threatened to come into their path. They were also careful to dodge the numerous ostrich plumes that dipped low over the turbans of the older ladies. More than once they were nearly knocked over by an oblivious gentleman making an elegant bow.

Bath was ever a place to see and be seen by the fashionable set and the wealthy in England. Not that Lydia was much concerned with any of that. She had not much desire to marry. Not after her first serious suitor, a gentleman named Frank Ensley, had abandoned her to marry an heiress. The pangs of disappointment had been enough to set Lydia against marriage entirely.

"Look out!" Lysandra gripped her arm and pulled her out of the way of two handsome but clearly foxed gentlemen stumbling past them. They didn't even stop to apologize.

"Lord, it's a frightful exercise in patience and perseverance to cross a ballroom." Lydia collapsed her fan and held it up like a fencer would his foil. It might prove necessary to wallop a few gentlemen in order to arrive at their intended destination.

"Blast. I lost sight of her," Lysandra hissed. "The men have dispersed, but I cannot see her."

Lydia swallowed back a lump of panic. She and Portia had both come here under the watchful eye of their great-aunt, Cornelia Wilcox. She would be blamed if Portia were to be compromised.

"Try the corridor just beyond!" Lydia nodded frantically toward a darkened corridor that led to the retiring rooms, a place where ladies and gentlemen could see to their needs.

"Excellent thinking." Lysandra and Lydia parted around a pair of plump matronly ladies whose chins wobbled as they giggled over the latest on-dits.

"Ah-ha! She's here!" Lydia gasped in relief as she found Portia alone at the entrance to the corridor. She hugged her younger sister.

Portia raised her chin almost haughtily as she pushed Lydia away. "Lydia, what's come over you?"

Lydia reined in the frustrated response she wanted to give. It would do no good to snap at Portia, no matter how much she wished to. "You mustn't go places unaccompanied, especially here at the assembly rooms."

Portia's eyes flashed with a rebellious fire befitting her teenage years. "I know all the rules, Lydia. You need not lecture me."

"Oh? Because it appears that you enjoy breaking *all* the rules," Lydia replied levelly.

"You need not worry, dear sister. I have matters well in hand."

"Matters? What matters?" Lydia wanted to tell her sister that she was far too young to have *matters*, but she knew it would fall on deaf ears.

"I have made my decision as to whom I shall marry."

"Oh? You've chosen, then? Which gentleman?" Lydia ran through the list in her head of all the men who had offered for Portia in the last few months. There were at least a dozen. Portia had kept all of their calling cards in her bedchamber and would riffle them in her hands and giggle while she prepared for bed. To her, marriage was a game she wanted to win. She was too young to realize that a handsome buck she would marry now might grow into a cantankerous old man. Marriage was no game. It was serious business.

"Him!" Portia pointed an elegant hand toward a pair of men who were leaning against a column about twenty feet away. One was fair-haired, and one was dark. Both were tall, at least a few inches over six feet. She recognized only one of the gentleman, as Lysandra did, by the way she gasped. Portia did not however, since she did not spend much time in the company of Lydia's friends or their family.

"Rafe Lennox?" Lysandra shook her head. "Oh, Portia, you mustn't."

"No, not him, the dark-haired man next to him." Portia sighed dreamily as she gazed in his direction.

"I am not acquainted with that gentleman," Lydia said. "Who is he?"

"Haven't the faintest idea. I only know he shall be mine." Portia giggled and twirled where she stood, almost humming to herself. "Won't we make the most beautiful babies together?"

"Portia, that is ridiculous. You don't even know the gentleman's name," Lydia said.

Her sister laughed. "Oh, he's no gentleman. Lord, Lydia, look at how he holds himself, powerful, with little care to his clothes, his hair ruffled by the wind, and a hungry look in those gray eyes . . ."

"Those sound like fine qualities in a heartless seducer, not a husband," Lydia responded primly. But the more she dared to look at the gentleman in question, the more she saw exactly what her sister had described. He had a wild, barely restrained look that gave him an unmistakable air of danger. A flush rolled through her, and she had to spread her fan and whip it rapidly to dispel the sudden heat in her body. Her breath quickened as she saw the man break into a smile as a lovely woman walked past him.

Lord, that smile. It was the sort to break a woman's heart before she'd even been introduced to him.

"Maybe I *want* him to seduce me," Portia declared, a little too loudly, given the sudden stares of a few nearby ladies. Portia's words set their fans fluttering wildly, no doubt to cover the gossip the women would soon be spreading.

"Portia, please do not say such things."

"It's not *my* fault you aren't married, Lydia." Portia's unexpected insult stung more than Lydia wished it to. She loved her sister, but sometimes Portia was very difficult to like.

"Portia, that wasn't very nice," Lysandra said sternly.

"Well, it's true." Portia shoved between Lydia and Lysandra and started straight toward the pair of young men, who may well have been man-eating tigers as far as innocent young women were concerned.

"What on earth is she doing?" Lysandra asked. "Is she mad?"

Lydia sighed and rubbed her eyes. "Mad? No. Acting foolishly? Most certainly." Lydia rushed after her sister, but was too late. Portia was already talking to the dark-haired stranger. Lydia knew she should rush over and stop her, but she was frozen in place. The gentleman was one of the most handsome men she had ever seen. She had spent four seasons in London and had seen the best men in England, and none of them compared to him. Portia, for once, was right. He was a man a woman would be irresistibly drawn to, even at the cost of her innocence.

"Excuse me." Portia smiled as she stopped before Rafe Lennox and his dark-haired companion.

"Well, hello, my dear." Rafe grinned down at Portia, a

wolfish glint to his smile that would have sent a more intelligent woman sprinting toward the nearest chaperone.

"I know this is terribly forward, but I'm afraid I am not acquainted with either of you, and I should very much like to be." Portia's musical voice carried across the room. She sounded so sweetly innocent, but Lydia knew better.

"You hear that, Brodie? She would like to be better acquainted with us," Rafe said. The silent, dark-haired man next to Rafe grinned as well, and when he spoke, his Scottish accent was unmistakable. It was as though God had designed this man to make Lydia fall hopelessly in love with him.

The man named Brodie smiled at Portia in clear amusement. "Does she now? I believe we would as well, lass. What's your name?"

"I am Portia Hunt."

"Portia." Brodie rolled her name off his tongue, and Lydia could see her sister almost swoon. Lydia couldn't blame her—she was equally as affected. "My name is Brodie Kincade, and my companion here is Mr. Rafe Lennox."

"It's a pleasure to meet you both, Mr. Lennox and Mr. Kincade."

"How well acquainted do you wish to be, Miss Hunt?" Rafe inquired with a smile that spoke of dangerous intimacy.

Whatever Portia had planned to say was stopped when Great-Aunt Cornelia materialized next to her, snatching her away from the two gentlemen. She dragged Portia nearly a dozen feet away, creating a minor spectacle, which soon grew into a major one the moment she spoke.

"Portia Elizabeth Hunt, what on *earth* are you thinking?" Cornelia demanded sharply. "Eh, girl?"

Cornelia was a formidable creature, and despite her plumpness, she was a strong woman and not to be trifled with.

"I was thinking I was meeting my future bridegroom," Portia shot back as she pulled her hand free of Cornelia's grasp.

"You were doing no such thing!"

Rafe and Brodie watched with amusement while Portia argued with her great-aunt. Finally, Lydia found herself able to move, and she joined her sister and aunt in order to calm things down.

"Did you see your sister walk up to those young bucks and introduce herself? Mercy, I shall faint." Despite Cornelia's insistence that she would faint, she looked entirely unlikely to. "And where were you in all this, Lydia?"

"I . . . I'm sorry, Aunt Cornelia."

"Humph." Cornelia pointed an accusing finger at Portia. "I believe you've had quite enough for one night, young lady. It's time you went home for the evening."

"You never let me do anything. Father will hear about this!" Portia stormed off toward the entrance of the assembly rooms.

Cornelia shared a look with Lydia. "I'm sorry, my dear, but I'm afraid you must come home as well."

"Wait, Mrs. Wilcox," Lysandra said. "Would it be possible for Lydia to stay with me? I am here escorted by my brother Lawrence Russell and his wife, Zehra. They would be happy to chaperone Lydia and escort her home." Lysandra nodded toward her elder brother, another redheaded member of the infamous Russell family, who was currently dancing with his lovely new wife. "If you truly wish to punish Portia for her behavior, just imagine how she would feel knowing her sister is still here enjoying herself."

"I suppose . . ." Cornelia fluttered her fan as she thought it over. "Yes, all right, but I shall have to speak to them myself." She walked over to where Lawrence and Zehra had just finished the last dance.

Lydia sighed in relief. "Thank you, Lysandra, I should not wish to be in that coach tonight listening to Portia and Aunt Cornelia bicker."

"I agree." Lysandra put her arm in Lydia's, and they both trailed after Cornelia to see what the woman's decision would be. Lydia glanced over her shoulder at the two handsome men, who hadn't left their post against the pillar. They were not looking in her direction, nor did she expect them to. After all, she was, in comparison to Portia, utterly unremarkable.

The thought left a deep well of sadness within her, but she buried it with a cheery smile and laughter. Lydia was determined to have an enjoyable evening, now that she no longer had to watch over Portia and keep her out of trouble.

❧

PORTIA HUNT DRIFTED BACK INTO THE ASSEMBLY room, a light cloak draped about her shoulders. She spied her dreaded great-aunt Cornelia talking to Lawrence Russell and his beautiful new wife, who rivaled her in looks. Seeing that her great-aunt was sufficiently distracted, she caught the eye of the handsome Scotsman when his gaze swept the room in her direction. Once his eyes settled on hers, she tilted her head to one side and smiled invitingly at him. With a coquettish wink, she twirled and walked away to a more secluded part of the assembly room.

The Scotsman would come to her. All men came when she gave them that look. Sure enough, he came into the alcove off the main ballroom.

"Well now, we meet again, lass." He smiled down at her and stepped closer.

Portia was only too happy to lure him deeper into the private space. She wanted to kiss him, to see how he compared to the others. There hadn't been many, admittedly, but enough that Portia felt she was a good judge of kisses by now.

"Mr. Kincade," she said in a soft voice that held a hint of girlish innocence.

Brodie placed one large palm on the wall beside her head, effectively blocking her in. "So, are we to become . . . better acquainted?"

"I believe we are, but first . . ." She tiptoed her fingers up his chest to his cravat, toying with the perfectly folded fabric.

"Aye?" Brodie leaned down. Just a few more inches and his kissable lips would be against hers. Her pulse pounded with excitement.

"First, you must propose to me."

Brodie lifted his other hand to grasp her hip, and delicious tingles of excitement shot through her.

"Propose what?" he asked.

"Marriage, of course." She rolled her eyes, giggling at his silly teasing.

"Marriage?" He chuckled. "Oh, lass, I'll not be doing any such thing."

"What?" Her gaze sharpened on him.

"I'm of no mind to marry, but I willna say no to a kiss, if you wish to give me one."

Portia was infuriated. She slapped his cheek hard enough that his eyes widened, and his lips parted in shock.

"Well, I never," Portia growled. "Honestly. Without marriage." She glared up at him. "You *will* marry me, Mr. Kincade. Then you will have as many kisses as you wish."

Brodie stepped back, running a palm over his cheek. "Actually, lass, I think not. Good night to you." He turned and walked away, disappearing back into the assembly room.

Portia blinked. No man had ever said *no* to her before, for anything. But Brodie Kincade just did. That intrigued her. No, it excited her. A man who was not so easily won over by her charm and beauty. That was a man worth catching. But how to do it?

I shall have him compromise me, she thought. *There's no other way to it. He won't agree, otherwise, that much is quite clear.*

With a devious giggle, she pulled her hood up and returned to the foyer to wait for her dreadful great-aunt to return. Her sour mood had dissipated in the wake of her new plans. Brodie Kincade would be her husband within a week—she would bet her life on it.

2

Brodie rejoined his friend Rafe to watch the dancers swirl around the assembly room. "What the devil was that about?" Rafe asked.

Brodie tried not to scowl. He'd been in a good mood until a moment ago. Surely he wasn't that off his usual seduction methods, was he? He usually got slapped *after* a kiss, not before. His cheek stung faintly, but it was a strong reminder that English ladies weren't nearly so easily charmed as the ladies in Scotland. They clearly expected more to result from a bit of fun.

"The wee lass who introduced herself. She wanted to speak to me."

Rafe shot Brodie a sardonic grin. "Did she have anything interesting to say?"

"She wanted me to marry her." Brodie smiled ruefully. "Damned innocent creature."

Rafe's laugh held a hint of darkness. "Brodie, my friend, here is your first lesson of life in England. No one in this room is innocent, *especially* the young unmarried ladies. They are far more dangerous than anyone else here tonight."

Brodie took a glass of ratafia from a servant who passed them carrying a tray. "I'm not afraid of a wee hen."

"You should be. Even the most fire-breathing dragon of a chaperone should be less feared than a young unmarried lady. You see, *we* are the prey." Rafe tapped his own chest. "We're the ones being hunted."

"You let English lasses frighten you so?" Brodie chuckled. "My brother Brock wasna afraid of his bride. He simply ran off with her. Not even your brother and his fancy friends could stop him from claiming Joanna."

Rafe's eyes twinkled with mischief. "You don't understand. Your brother was doing what my sister *wanted* him to do. She was in charge of that adventure. Never assume otherwise. You forget, I stopped them on the road under the guise of a highwayman and caught your brother unaware. He stood no chance against us."

"There were three of you, and he was protecting your sister. If he hadna been with her, he would have easily taken you all," Brodie challenged. He would not let his friend speak ill of his brother. Brock had always looked after him and their younger siblings, Rosalind and Aiden.

"I seek no quarrel with you," Rafe cut in more amiably. "My point was to remind you that the unmarried ladies here in England treat marriage as a serious business. If that chit has marked you as hers, you had better watch your back."

"I thank you for the warning." Brodie swept his gaze over the ballroom with fresh eyes, searching for predators in pretty skirts.

Rafe continued his lesson. "Allow me to provide an example. You might think that an invitation to a dark alcove is a good idea. But unless you can be certain that the lady issuing the invitation is set on nothing more than a bit of fun, odds are you're walking into a trap." Rafe tapped his temple. "Best to keep a sharp eye until you are comfortable recognizing which ladies do not have marriage in mind. Widows are always good." Rafe nodded toward a curvaceous brunette dancing nearby.

"Widows?" Brodie repeated. "They dinna mourn their husbands?"

Rafe threw his head back and laughed.

"Depends on the widow, old boy. Many widows here are young and starved for a decent man's touch after having been married to men thirty or forty years their elder."

Brodie didn't like the sound of that. He knew that women most often married older men for practical or social reasons, but in Scotland the age difference usually did not exceed twenty years.

"Now spinsters are also an option, if they make it clear to you that they have given up on marriage. In fact, the ones with a bit of financial security often welcome romantic entanglements without marriage being offered. They have too much to lose if they marry."

Brodie listened to Rafe explain the various types of English ladies, from bluestockings down to cyprians.

"Now, these bluestockings, do they actually wear blue stockings?" Brodie asked. He was still foxed from their drinking earlier, and he was quite enjoying listening to his friend lecture about women. He was so foxed, in fact, that his vision was a bit blurred at times.

"Not that I've noticed," Rafe mused. "Honestly, I haven't the faintest idea where the name comes from. But you won't get far with one of those. Take Lysandra Russell." He discreetly pointed to a red-haired beauty in a green silk gown who had just been asked to dance.

"Aye, what of that one?" Brodie inquired curiously. He wouldn't mind bedding that lass.

"Complete bluestocking. She'll chatter to no end about science if you let her."

"Have you?" Brodie teased his companion.

Rafe flashed him a devil-may-care-grin. "I might have . . . in the hopes of a kiss. Half an hour later, all I had was some rather useless knowledge about comets."

"Comets?" That did mildly interest Brodie. While he was the most outgoing of his siblings, and by far the most scandalous, he did enjoy discussing things with women, at least when he wasn't kissing them. In Scotland, he spent much of his time at Castle Kincade and rarely in town, which meant his choice of ladies, especially ones who were well educated, was far lower than it was in Edinburgh, London, or even Bath.

"Perhaps the lass would like me," Brodie murmured as he watched her dance. She did have a pretty smile.

"Er . . . No. You must not have heard me say her name. She's a *Russell*."

Brodie still stared at him, having not a clue what the man was on about.

"As in *Lucien* Russell, the Marquess of Rochester. One of Ashton's friends?"

"Ah." Brodie nodded. "One of the League of Rogues, is he?" Not that he was worried. English gentlemen were no match for Scots in a bout of fisticuffs.

Rafe nudged him. "Whatever you're thinking about, forget it, my friend. Lucien won't fight you with his fists if you compromise his beloved baby sister. They would likely only find pieces of you in the Thames. Best not to risk it over a bluestocking."

"So, who am I to choose, then? I don't see anyone left," Brodie grumbled.

"Perhaps it's time to quit this place. We made a good show here. We pleased the master of ceremonies and have been on our best behavior, more or less. It's time to go to places more suited to our interests, wouldn't you say?"

Brodie felt like smiling again. "I would indeed."

"Are you any good at cards?" Rafe asked as they left.

"Quite good," Brodie assured him.

"Excellent. I know just the place."

🦋

LYDIA WAS IN THE MIDDLE OF ONE OF THE FEW DANCES she'd been asked for when she saw the handsome Scotsman and Rafe Lennox leave the assembly room. Disappointment stirred within her as the tall, dark-haired Brodie Kincade left her sight.

Lysandra joined her as the dance ended. "Are you all right?" Her face was flushed after that last quadrille.

"Yes." Lydia was not as exhausted from the dance as her friend. She adored dancing, and while she was rarely asked to dance at occasions like this, she danced at home whenever she was alone. While Portia was out paying calls, Lydia chose to enjoy that time either reading, gardening, or dancing.

"It seems your great-aunt has taken your sister home." Lysandra nodded toward the entryway, where they had last seen Portia and Cornelia.

"That's one small mercy." Lydia felt callous for saying that, but she had so few moments to enjoy herself in public without worrying about Portia and what fresh trouble she would stir up.

"Come and say hello to Lawrence and Zehra," Lysandra suggested.

As they made their way through the packed room, Lydia was relieved to be lost amongst the crowd for a spell. Being responsible for watching over her little sister meant there was always a chance she would end up at the center of attention, and not in a good way. It was a relief to be merely among the throng and not have to worry what Portia was up to.

"Lawrence, Zehra." Lysandra greeted her older brother and his new wife. Lawrence turned his attention to Lydia. "I've brought Lydia over, as promised," said Lysandra.

"Miss Hunt, a pleasure to see you again." Lawrence was a handsome red-haired devil and quite charming when he wasn't brooding. Since he'd married Zehra, he'd been brooding less and beaming more. The man was clearly infatuated with his wife, but that didn't stop him from being courteous. Lawrence bowed over Lydia's hand.

She smiled. "It is my pleasure as well, Mr. Russell."

He turned his attention to the woman at his side. "Please allow me to introduce you to my wife, Zehra. Zehra, this is Miss Lydia Hunt."

Lydia smiled warmly at the dark-haired, olive-skinned woman. She was exquisitely beautiful. It was no wonder that the last time she had met Lawrence he'd been preoccupied, because he'd already met his beloved

Zehra. There was quite a story behind it as Lysandra had informed her. Zehra had been captured in her father's homeland of Persia by a rival tribe and sold into slavery, only to be secretly bought by Lawrence. Zehra was in fact a Persian princess and a granddaughter to an English peer. Once Lawrence had freed Zehra, he had kept her at his home, in secret, until he could stop a Persian slave trader who had wished her harm.

"It is wonderful to meet you, Miss Hunt." Zehra curtsied, and Lydia did the same.

"Am I to understand we have rescued you from a bit of unpleasantness?" Lawrence asked.

"You have indeed, and I am most grateful. My sister, Portia, was quite determined to make a spectacle of herself. Our chaperone, Mrs. Wilcox, was quite upset. You spared me a long coach ride home, having to witness their duel of words."

"Ah, I understand. Quite glad to be of service." Lawrence shared a grin with his wife. "Well, we are ready to leave when you are. Or we can remain a bit longer."

"I am ready," Lydia assured him. In truth, she was tired enough to go home, knowing the moment her head hit her pillow she would be asleep. In London, balls could go into the early morning, when dawn turned everything a pale gray before the sun crested the horizon. But in Bath, balls ended promptly at eleven, and it was nearly eleven now.

"Then, shall we?" Lawrence waved a hand. The trio

of ladies fell in line behind him, and they walked outside together, where Lawrence summoned their coach home. During the ride to Lydia's residence, the women exchanged news of their mutual friends.

"We shall be attending the Pump Room tomorrow, if you would like to join our party," Zehra offered.

"I would like that very much," said Lydia.

"Wonderful. We will meet tomorrow after lunch, around two o'clock."

Lydia thanked Zehra again for the invitation before she exited the coach at her townhouse in Royal Crescent. "And thank you for the escort home, Mr. Russell." Lydia waved goodbye from the top step of the elegant home her father had recently purchased as their new residence.

Portia had convinced their father that Bath was the best place to find a husband, and so he had quickly purchased a home on the most fashionable street in Bath, the illustrious Royal Crescent. Lydia did enjoy living in the most elegant part of the city, but Bath was not as popular as it had once been. It seemed most of the younger crowd frequented other places, such as London or seaside resorts like Brighton. However, a wealth of older families still resided in Bath, and Portia was insistent she would find a handsome young man with a title and money here. Lydia knew that to find all three qualities of looks, good fortune, and a title wasn't easy, but she could not convince her sister otherwise.

As she entered their townhouse, their butler, Mr. Annis, met her at the door.

"Did you have a good evening, Miss Hunt?"

"I did." She'd certainly had fun with Lysandra, even if she hadn't been asked to dance as much as she would have liked.

Annis smiled warmly at her. "I'm glad to hear it. Mrs. Kloester has a glass of milk and a few biscuits for you in your room. We anticipated your arrival after Miss Portia arrived home."

"Thank you, Annis. Was Portia still upset? I hope she and Mrs. Wilcox did not quarrel too much during the ride home."

"Er, no. Quite the opposite, really. Miss Portia seemed rather pleased about something. She went to bed humming."

"Humming?" Lydia sensed impending doom, though she could not guess as to what form it would take. Her sister was up to something.

"If you need anything at all, I shall be awake another hour," the butler said.

"No, go on to bed, Annis." She started toward the stairs, then paused. "Annis? Is my father home, or did he go to his club this evening?"

"He's home, Miss Hunt. In his study, I believe."

Lydia changed course and headed for her father's study. The door was ajar, but she knocked anyway.

"Papa?"

"Yes, my child?"

Lydia nudged the door open and slipped inside.
Jackson Hunt was reading a book in one hand and
holding a glass of scotch in the other. Her father was tall
and fit and still quite attractive for a man in his early
fifties. He had a ready wit and indulgent kindness that
people often mistook for weakness, but he was in fact a
shrewd businessman. With a tidy fortune and a country
estate in Surrey, the Hunt family was well off enough
that most society doors opened to them. Especially the
homes where unmarried young men had caught a
glimpse of Portia.

"How are you, my dear?" Jackson set his book aside
and gestured to a chair across from his desk.

"Fine, Papa." She seated herself and tried to plan her
next words as best she could.

"Yes?"

"I am worried about Portia."

"Oh? What's the little bit gone and done now?" He
gave a smile he only reserved for Portia, and it pricked at
Lydia's heart like a thorn. He had no special smiles like
that reserved for her.

"She's taken a fancy to a Scotsman. He was in ques-
tionable company tonight at the assembly rooms, and
Lysandra Russell warned Portia not to take an interest
in him. I am worried she is going to do something
reckless in order to obtain a marriage to this
gentleman."

Jackson leaned forward, resting his elbows on his desk. "What kind of reckless?"

"Well, to start with, she walked up to this gentleman and introduced herself, rather than having the master of ceremonies introduce her. You know how strict the protocol is for the assembly rooms. She was lucky not to be cast out and banned from returning."

Lydia had always thought the position of master of ceremonies was silly, but it was derived from the royal courts and was designed to supervise public behavior and help maintain a level of decorum and manners at social functions. If one displeased or upset the master of ceremonies, one would likely be disgraced.

Jackson chuckled at Lydia's mention of Portia's outburst. "Well, at least she goes after what she desires. It reminds me of myself. I was about your age when I first saw your mother. There was nothing that could keep me away from her."

Lydia knew then that her request for Portia to be checked would go unanswered. Her father's gaze grew distant. He was lost in the mists of the past, where his beloved wife was still alive.

"Papa," Lydia said, trying to catch his attention.

"Oh, I'm sorry, Lydia. Never mind Portia for now. Did you enjoy the ball? Find any young man just up to scratch for you?"

"No." She ran her fingertips over her rather plain rose-colored silk gown. "Papa, please listen to me about

Portia. You and Great-Aunt Cornelia *must* keep a sharper eye on her."

"I know, I know. We depend on you far too much, don't we?" Her father sighed. "When your mother died, I was too quick to place so many duties upon your young shoulders." That was not something Lydia would disagree with him on, but she sensed he was gently changing the subject.

"What if I were to send you to Brighton? You may take that friend of yours, Miss Russell, along with you. What do you think? I could hire a chaperone for you and keep your great-aunt here in charge of Portia while she hunts for a husband."

The offer was far too tempting. She had been longing to visit a seaside resort and try her hand at bathing. But she knew her duty and couldn't leave.

"No, I should stay here and help you with Portia."

"Nonsense. Mrs. Wilcox and I can handle the child. Why don't you go on to bed? We can discuss this more in the morning."

That was the end of it. She would have no more luck tonight in convincing him. With a sigh, Lydia stood and nodded.

"Good night, Papa." She came around his desk and bent to kiss his cheek before she headed upstairs. As she walked past Portia's room, she saw a light on and was tempted to speak with her. Portia, while a vain creature often focused on gowns and balls, did enjoy staying up late to read, and Lydia thought it was best not to disturb her.

Lydia's lady's maid, Phyllis, stood waiting for her. They shared a tired smile as she helped Lydia undress.

"Would you like a bath tonight?"

"No, thank you, Phyllis. Go on to bed," she encouraged the maid, who gratefully left her bedchamber.

Lydia combed out her hair and climbed into bed. A small glass of fresh milk and a plate of biscuits rested on the table beside her. She ate her midnight snack and wondered what to do. She couldn't leave Portia alone. The trip to Brighton would have to be postponed.

She blew out the candle on her night table and settled into bed. But as sleep drifted near, her thoughts wandered back to the dark-haired Scotsman.

What if Portia were to successfully marry such a man? He would attend family dinners, father Portia's children . . . For some reason, the thought made Lydia's heart heavy. If anyone were to snare the attention of a handsome man like that, it would be her sister.

She was suddenly overcome with a foolish rush of tears, because she knew she would never have a chance to make a match with a man like that. She was too old, too uninspiring, and that knowledge crippled her with an unbearable loneliness that left her awake well past midnight.

❧ 3 ❧

Lydia had recovered some of her good spirits by the following morning when she sat down to breakfast. Her father was reading his paper, and her great-aunt was poring over a set of fashion plates. Portia made a late entrance, casting only a brief glance at Great-Aunt Cornelia, who arched a brow in return. It amused Lydia to know the two spent all their time antagonizing each other, while she was left quite alone.

"Ah, Portia, good morning," Jackson greeted his younger daughter.

"Morning, Papa." She kissed his cheek before she sashayed to her seat. She wore a gown of cerulean blue, and her hair was styled in the latest fashion, pulled back with artful curls framing her face. Lydia tried to ignore the sudden awareness of her own boring gown, a soft blue satin with fewer frills than her sister's gown. Portia always looked so perfect, while Lydia simply focused on being serviceable. She felt silly if she tried to look nice, rather like trying to decorate a simple country cottage with golden garland—a waste of time, money, and effort.

You cannot have fancy gowns, she reminded herself. *You're not a young girl fresh in her first season.*

"Morning, Portia," Lydia greeted.

Her sister smiled warmly at her. "Oh, Lydia, I'm sorry for being so cross with you last night."

"It's all right. I only wished to watch out for you," Lydia said.

Portia nodded as if to agree, then turned to their father. "Papa, I have found my future husband and should like very much for you to go and speak to him today."

Lydia froze in the act of buttering a muffin. Lord, if only she could strangle her little sister for her silliness. Aunt Cornelia squawked and tossed her fashion plates to the table so hard that her teacup toppled over, spilling tea. A footman rushed to clean it up. Jackson ruffled his paper and gazed at Portia, and what little of his expression that they could see over the top of his paper was slightly perplexed.

"What's all this?" Cornelia demanded. "You cannot have your father go speak to a man. That's not how it's done." She huffed and seemed to expect that to be the end of the matter.

"Now just a minute, Cornelia," their father said. "I may be willing to risk the scandal." He looked toward Portia again. "Has the man proposed to you, child?" Jackson inquired with a discreet look toward Lydia.

"No, but I believe he's too shy."

"*Shy?*" Jackson chuckled. "I did not think you would choose a shy man to be your husband. Are you quite sure this is the right fellow for you?"

"I would wager my life upon it." Portia's deadly serious reply had everyone at the table staring at her.

Cornelia huffed. "No man is worth such a wager, you silly creature." She leveled her hardest gaze at Portia. "Unless you've been up to things a young lady ought not to be."

"Oh, come now, Cornelia," Jackson said to his aunt. "My Portia is merely excited and in love, I daresay. She would not do anything to risk herself, would you, my child?" He looked to Portia, who shook her head, her eyes wide and guileless. Her expression was so innocent, she seemed a mere child rather than a young woman in that moment. Lydia rolled her eyes.

"There, you see?" Jackson folded his paper, and Lydia knew her father would turn a blind eye to this matter, despite her warning that Portia could not be trusted to behave. "Now, who is this fellow?"

"Mr. Brodie Kincade. He is staying with Mr. Rafe Lennox, only a few streets away. I have the address written down."

"Is he, now? Well, I shall pay a call later this morning."

"And *how* do you know where his lodging is?" Lydia asked quietly.

Cornelia pounced on the opening provided. "Yes, how *do* you know?"

"How do I know?" Portia still looked oh so innocent. "I overheard the two gentlemen conversing about it last evening."

Lydia had no idea how her sister had actually discovered this information, but she was fairly certain Portia was lying.

Jackson turned his focus on Lydia. "And what about you? Have you decided whether you are to go to Brighton?"

"As much as I would like to, I believe it would be best to stay here. I am to meet a few friends today at the Pump Room after luncheon."

"You're quite sure? I've heard the bracing sea breezes of the Sussex coast can be a tonic for all ills."

"Yes, Papa. I'm quite certain. Portia, would you like to go shopping on Milsom Street today after breakfast?"

"No. I'm afraid I have calls to make."

Lydia let it go. The days of her younger sister wishing to spend time with her were at an end. There was no point forcing the issue. "If you change your mind, I'll be leaving in an hour."

Lydia finished her breakfast and left the table. She

met her maid in the hall and informed her she was to leave for Milsom Street shortly. One of their young footmen, a man named Michael, met her as she put on her bonnet and collected her reticule.

"Ready to leave, Miss Hunt?" Michael asked.

"Yes, let's be off." She and the footman left the townhouse on Royal Crescent and headed toward the shops. Many women would have hired a sedan chair or hackney, but Lydia's penchant for dancing left her well suited to long and vigorous walks.

When she reached Milsom Street, she visited a haberdashery, with Michael trailing dutifully at her heels. Once inside the shop, she was perusing a display of kid gloves in a dozen colors on a table near a window when two gentlemen paused outside the shop. At first, she only glanced up out of habit, but when she realized who they were, her heart jolted in her chest. She was staring at Rafe Lennox and Brodie Kincade, who were talking quietly just inches away from her, separated only by the glass panes of the window.

Acting foolishly and entirely on instinct, Lydia dropped out of sight. Her footman did the same, crouching defensively beside her.

"Miss? What are we doing?"

"Hush, Michael. We are hiding," she whispered frantically, even though she knew the men outside could not hear her. She also knew that neither of them had seen her last night, which meant that hiding was absolutely pointless. But for some reason, she didn't want him to see her—maybe because once he did, he wouldn't even really notice her, and that would only hurt worse.

"Hiding? From whom, Miss?" Michael's features hardened as he hovered close to her.

"Oh . . . It doesn't matter. He's likely to not even notice me." She rose up from her hidden position and peeked out the window. The men were gone. She had acted like a ninny for no reason.

Then the haberdashery door opened, and in they walked. She was frozen for a moment before she hastily recovered herself. Turning away, she focused on a stand full of little ornaments and baubles as she tried to eavesdrop on the two men, who drifted nearer.

"What a night," Rafe snickered. "You really are excellent at cards, Kincade. Remind me never to play opposite you when real money is on the line."

"We certainly wore out our welcome last night. I dinna think they'll let us come back." Brodie grinned, and Lydia caught the full force of his smile in the reflection of the nearby mirror.

"They can't afford to. You fairly cleaned out the pockets of every man in the room. What was your secret, by the way?" Rafe casually examined a collection of ladies' gloves with mild interest.

"Every man has a tell," Brodie explained. "The trick is to watch a man before he plays the game. You will notice what he does differently once the pressure of the game is upon him."

"By Jove, you are a dangerous man, Kincade. I suppose that's why I like you." Rafe lifted up a pair of ivory silk gloves. "What do you think of these?"

"For you? A bit small." Brodie delivered this with a straight face.

Rafe snorted. "For a mistress. I recently parted from mine, but I am certainly looking for a new one. It's always nice to have a present on hand for when one finds a lady worth wooing."

"They are pretty enough." Brodie stared at the gloves. "Are all English ladies fixated on pretty bits of cloth? Or do they prefer jewels? I suppose I had better find out while I'm here."

Lydia couldn't help but wonder why that was. Was he also in the market for a mistress? Or did the charming Scot have marriage on his mind?

"Money, my dear fellow. That is what they like best. Lots of it." The way Rafe said this, with an edge to his tone, made Lydia wonder what sort of women Rafe usually consorted with.

Trying not to be seen, Lydia carefully dodged the two men. But her footman, intending to follow her, knocked over a display of hats.

"Oh!" She rushed to help collect the scattered bonnets, blushing wildly as she dared not look in the direction of Mr. Lennox and Mr. Kincade.

Only when she had fixed the display did she glance at them. Both of them had amused looks on their faces, and they quickly went back to their whispered conversation, no longer paying her any heed.

Lydia fled the haberdashery, her footman racing behind her. Even after all the ruckus she had caused, neither man had spared her more than a glance. It was both a blessing and a curse to not be pretty enough to catch a man's attention. Portia would have had them tripping over each other, trying to help.

Lydia shuddered at the thought that her father would likely be able to buy Mr. Kincade off as a husband for Portia, but he would no doubt acquire a mistress the moment he was in possession of Portia's inheritance. As unpleasant as that thought was, it would serve Portia right for buying a man's affections.

Perhaps it was time for Lydia to appeal to her great-aunt to help her search for a husband. There must be a few pleasant gentlemen in England who wouldn't mind a plain woman for a wife. She was quite certain that if her sister married Mr. Kincade, she could not live under the same roof as him for holidays. Not when she felt a dreadful and irresistible attraction to him.

Yes, she would speak to Great-Aunt Cornelia this afternoon about suitable options for a husband. She needed to escape the tall, dark-haired Scotsman and any wicked dreams he gave her.

BRODIE HAD ONLY BEEN HOME FOR HALF AN HOUR when Rafe's butler, Mr. Chase, informed him that he had a visitor.

"A visitor?" Brodie stood in his bedchamber, tugging on his cuffs, while his valet, a young man named Alan, adjusted his coat at the shoulders. Unused to having a man dress him, Brodie was still adjusting to the close relationship between a man and his valet.

After his older brother, Brock, had married Rafe's sister, Joanna, she had brought a large income into the Kincade family and had insisted that Brodie and Aiden also benefit from the joyful union by having valets hired for them. Alan was quiet and pleasant enough . . . for an Englishman.

"Yes, Mr. Kincade. He says his name is Mr. Jackson Hunt." The butler passed Brodie an elegant calling card.

"Hunt . . ." The name sounded familiar, but he couldn't recall where he'd met the man. "I suppose I ought to see him."

"Very good, sir. I shall have him shown to the drawing room."

"Thank you, Chase," Brodie called over his shoulder as he turned halfway to let Alan brush dust off his jacket. He had changed after his walk with Rafe. He wasn't used to lounging about so much and had asked Rafe to show him more of the city. As a Scot, he loved the land and liked to be familiar with any terrain he was on, especially while in English territory.

"All done, sir," Alan said. Brodie nodded his thanks, and then he proceeded to the drawing room.

His visitor, Jackson Hunt, was a tall man in his fifties. He stood by the fireplace and took in the measure of Brodie as he entered the room. Hunt offered a polite and hopeful smile that Brodie didn't quite understand, given that he didn't know the man and to the best of his knowledge he had no business with the fellow.

"Mr. Hunt?" Brodie nodded in greeting. "You'll have to excuse me. I canna recall the circumstances of our meeting."

"It's quite all right, Mr. Kincade, as we have not met before today." Hunt bowed to Brodie. "I apologize for the unannounced visit, given that we have no previous acquaintance, but I hope my business here today will be viewed favorably by you."

"And what is that?" Brodie inquired.

"My daughter, Miss Hunt, met you last evening at the assembly rooms and speaks highly of you. I came here as a messenger on a mission. I am a wealthy man, you see, and while I know the peers have their own way of doing things, I hope I may speak frankly with you."

"I wish you would." Brodie wasn't at all following what the man was saying.

"My daughter wishes to marry you. I am here on her behalf to inquire if you would like to court her with marriage in mind. I can promise her dowry would be an income of ten thousand a year."

Hunt delivered this with a gentle excitement that astounded Brodie, as though throwing large sums of money and daughters at a man was an everyday occurrence.

"What?" Brodie stared at the other man. "I don't even know your daughter, sir."

"But you do—she met you last evening. She's small, with flaxen hair and bright-blue eyes." Jackson mimed how short the girl in question was.

Brodie's half-drunk memory returned. The wee blonde who'd introduced herself and tried to exchange a vow of marriage for a kiss. He could barely recall her face.

"Ah . . . I ken who you speak of now. We met but briefly," he informed Mr. Hunt.

"Yes, well, she was very taken with you, and I hope that you and I can come to some sort of arrangement. If you were to marry her, it would be quite a large sum of money I would be willing to part with to make my child happy."

"I ken the bond of a father to his child, Mr. Hunt, but I barely know the lass, and I have no intention of marrying her or anyone at this time."

"I can pay you handsomely," Hunt insisted. "Name your price."

Brodie sighed. "Mr. Hunt, a man bought like a stallion to stud isna a good man for your daughter. I dinna want to upset the lass, but I dinna ken her, or love her."

"But she's a clever, humorous creature," Mr. Hunt insisted. "I'm sure you could learn to love her. She even caught the eye of the king himself in London two months ago."

Brodie had no doubt of that. Based on the vague details he remembered from the previous evening, she was more than pretty, but looks were not all that mattered to a man. Still, Brodie had no intention of marrying anyone. He was not the eldest son, nor the sole heir in the line of succession to the earldom. If Brock were to die without an heir, Aiden could easily carry on the title without Brodie ever having to have any children. He would be more than happy to let the title skip him and go straight to Aiden.

Brodie had no desire to pass on any of himself in the world, not when he feared his father's blood would be carried on as well. The last Earl of Kincade had been a heavy-handed, angry man whose greed had cost the lives of noble Scots more than a decade ago, and cost his father his soul. It was Brodie's deepest fear that any child born to him would inherit that blackhearted greed. He would leave such matters to his brothers, who were far better men than he was—Brock with his steadiness and infinite control, and Aiden with his endless compassion, especially for the wee beasties from the forest.

Brodie had no such qualities. He would always be the wildest of the Kincade brood.

"Is there nothing I can offer you to change your mind, Mr. Kincade?" Mr. Hunt persisted.

"I'm sure your daughter is a fine lass, but I'm afraid there isna a thing you could offer, Mr. Hunt. It would be best to convince the lass to turn her heart elsewhere."

Mr. Hunt's look of dejection surprised Brodie. The man truly did hope to secure a marriage for his daughter, and he wasn't just looking for a business transaction of some sort. It was obvious the man must dote upon her.

A fortunate lass, he thought.

Mr. Hunt soon recovered himself. "I am sorry to have troubled you, sir. I should take my leave." He collected his hat and departed.

Brodie left the drawing room and watched as the footman showed Hunt to the door.

Rafe came down the stairs from the upper rooms. "Who was that?"

"Mr. Hunt," Brodie replied.

"And who the bloody hell is that?" Rafe removed his jacket and waited for Brodie to follow him into the billiard room, where he set up a game.

"He's the father of the wee lass who so boldly came up to us last night."

"Oh?" Rafe laughed. "What did he want? Did she demand marriage?"

"As a matter of fact, she did." Brodie chuckled as Rafe's teasing turned into a stunned silence.

"The devil you say!" Rafe finally said. "All you did was speak with the chit."

"Aye, but apparently she fancies me. Her father just tried to buy me."

"Buy you?" Rafe's blue eyes sparkled with amusement. "Well, how much does a handsome Scot go for these days?"

"Ten thousand pounds a year, apparently, with room for negotiation." Brodie grinned and collected a pool cue from Rafe.

"Not bad, Scot, not bad at all."

PORTIA WAS PRACTICALLY BOUNCING AS SHE WAITED for her father to return that afternoon. When he did, the look on his face confirmed her worst fears. Jackson removed his hat and coat with a weary sigh before he took her hands, holding them clasped within his own.

"My dearest child, I fear I bear unhappy tidings."

"What did he say?" Portia demanded.

"I know you believed he had feelings for you, but for some reason, the gentleman would not have you. I offered ten thousand pounds a year, and he still would not accept."

Portia's heart sank. She wanted Brodie Kincade. Why could she not have him?

"Did you offer more?"

"I did, my dear. He was quite determined not to marry at all."

"Not marry at all? That seems rather silly. We must change his mind." Portia wasn't deterred by this setback.

Her father gazed at her in worry. "Well, I'm not sure that's possible."

An idea occurred to Portia. She knew that it was a wicked scheme, but she had few options left if she was to find a way to make Brodie hers.

"We must, because I carry his child, Papa."

"What?" Jackson stared at her, a horror-stricken expression upon his face. "But you said . . . How? How did he do it? When?"

"I'm sorry I was not honest with you, but we did not meet at the assembly. We met a fortnight ago, and he seduced me. I only discovered I was in the family way yesterday." She felt dreadful having to lie to her father, but she had to have Brodie as a husband.

A fierce light glowed in Jackson's eyes. "Did he force himself on you? I shall kill him."

"No! He didn't force himself on me. You know how passionate I am, Papa. Just as you and Mama were." Whenever she wanted to change her father's mind on something, it always helped to remind him of her mother.

"I do. You are so like me in that way." He cupped her face. "My darling child, soon to be a bride and mother." Worry creased his brow. "I will find a way to bring him here this evening, but I'm not sure how to convince him to marry you. I wish I could duel with him instead."

"No, Papa. I love him so much. You mustn't say such things."

"I suppose." Jackson stroked his chin. "If I could get him here, there are ways of convincing him. If I was able to bring a man of the church here too . . ."

"Yes, that's what we shall do," Portia agreed. "Bring him here tonight, and we will convince him that marriage is the best course of action."

Portia was certain that if she was able to get Brodie in bed she could change his mind about marriage. She was not ignorant of the ways of men and women. Her sister, Lydia, was far more innocent. Portia knew that in order to be effective with men, one ought to be acquainted with one's own body and how best to use it as a weapon. It was perhaps more mercenary than romantic, but she had watched her sister have three unsuccessful seasons living on romantic notions alone, and she would not follow her down that path.

It was a pity, for Lydia was very sweet and endearing —when she wasn't lecturing Portia about her behavior.

"I'm afraid I must go, my dear." Her father patted her shoulder affectionately. "Stay here and wait for me to return. Do you understand?"

"Yes, Papa."

"Good girl." He brushed her cheek with a fatherly kiss and was off again, leaving Portia alone.

She had only a little time to make plans, because she knew without a doubt that Lydia would put a stop to her scheme once she learned of it.

I must find a way to distract Lydia. Keep her away.

Portia rushed to her room to pen a letter. By tonight, Brodie Kincade would be here, and she would soon be married to the handsome Scot.

⁂

LYDIA RETURNED HOME LATE THAT AFTERNOON AFTER an enjoyable time at the Pump Room, where people sampled the healing waters in Bath. She found Portia most anxious at the door the moment she entered.

"Thank heavens, you've returned! You've received an urgent letter." Portia pressed the already opened letter into her hand.

"What? Who from?"

"Lysandra," Portia replied. "The messenger who delivered it said it was a matter of deep importance."

Puzzled, Lydia opened the letter and skimmed its contents. It was a short missive. Lysandra said she was returning to London immediately and needed Lydia to meet her there to discuss a personal matter.

"I've had a trunk and valise packed for you. I hope

you aren't angry with me for reading the letter ahead of time." Portia turned apologetic eyes to her sister.

"No, no, it's quite all right." Lydia noticed the two travel cases that were sitting by the stairs. A large trunk and a smaller valise. It was unusually thoughtful of her sister. Lydia had spent two hours at the Pump Room with Lysandra that very afternoon, and she'd made no mention of leaving. What had changed in the last few hours? Whatever it was, it must be serious.

"I shall ring for the coach." Portia rushed off, and Lydia thought she glimpsed a hint of a smile a moment before Portia turned her back and left.

Lydia was not devious like her little sister, but she was not without her own cleverness. She left the house again, walking on foot a short way before she hailed a hackney to take her to Lysandra's residence. Half an hour later she was ringing their doorbell, which was soon answered by the butler.

"Is Miss Russell at home?"

"She is. Shall I inform her that you are here?"

"Yes, please. I would very much like to speak with her."

"Of course."

Lydia toyed with the handles of her reticule while she wondered what Portia might be up to.

Lysandra came down the stairs, wearing a lovely walking dress of hunter green. She wore a light apron around her skirts, and it bore a few dark ink stains. "Lydia? Did you forget something at the Pump Room?"

"I . . . No . . . It's just a rather curious thing."

"What is?" Lysandra cleaned her hands on the cloth a footman discreetly passed to her so that she might remove some of the ink upon her fingers.

"When I returned home, Portia presented me with a letter, supposedly from you."

"From me? Well, I have been writing, as you can see, but not to you." Lysandra looked a little embarrassed. "I was writing to the Royal Astronomical Society."

"So you are not to leave for London on urgent business?"

Lysandra's brows rose. "What? No."

Lydia removed the letter Portia had given her and held it out to her friend. Lysandra read its contents, frowning.

"It looks like my handwriting, but I've written no such letter to you." Lysandra pointed to the letter. "If I had, there would be smudges on the letter, because I stained my forefinger. Whoever wrote this has made an excellent replica of my writing in hopes of tricking you."

"Portia," Lydia almost groaned. "What are you up to now?"

"Indeed, that is a good question." Lysandra's brows drew together. "She wants to lure you to London. Why?"

"Not to London, but away from our house. She even had my trunk packed. I suspect that she's obsessing over

Mr. Kincade and how to entice him into marriage, but I don't have the faintest idea why she would want me out of the way."

"She must be up to something rather serious, then." Lysandra bit her bottom lip as she thought the matter over. "You'd best hurry home and see what she's up to. Take our coach."

"Thank you." Lydia embraced her friend and rushed outside to wait for the Russell coach to be prepared. She had a sense that whatever her sister was up to, it had to do with Brodie Kincade and finding a way to entrap him in marriage. She could only hope that whatever scheme her younger sister had in mind had not yet been set in motion and that Lydia would be able to stop it.

4

Jem Webster and three of his men lingered in the shadows inside the tavern as they kept a careful eye on their intended target, a tall, dark-haired Scotsman who was drinking heavily with a blond-haired fellow who looked equally dangerous.

Harvey watched his boss carefully. "I don't know about this, Jem."

"We took the money, and there's more where that came from when we bring Mr. Hunt *that* man." Jem nodded subtly in the Scot's direction. He could understand the reservations his men had about tackling the fellow, given his size and muscled build, but he also knew that they would do just about anything for money. "I'll not pass up an opportunity for that kind of coin."

Jem stroked a hand along his scruffy jaw. It had been a lean few years working at various odd jobs, usually underappreciated and always underpaid. The best work only came when it was a bit out of the gaze of the law.

So when the fancy Mr. Hunt had presented his need for a group of men to bring him a Scotsman by the name of Brodie Kincade by this evening, Jem had accepted it without a second thought. Of course, that was before he had a chance to lay eyes on the man. Still, the money was too good to pass up. If he and his men got a bit bruised, it was worth it.

"There are four of us," Jem reminded Harvey. "He can't fight us all and win."

Harvey, a tall, burly fellow, rolled his shoulders and tried to look more menacing. "I hope you're right, Jem. My jaw is only just healed from the last job."

Jem rolled his eyes. "Well, that was your own fault for falling face-first onto that table."

"I was thrown by a bloke we tried to grab, Jem. You sure know how to pick 'em."

"Just be ready, Harvey." Jem ignored his second-in-command's complaints.

Jem and his three men moved deeper into the tavern, and at Jem's subtle direction, they all took seats at the table beside the Scotsman and his friend. It had taken the better part of the day to locate the man called Brodie Kincade, but they finally had. Now the challenge lay in how to catch the man.

A comely wench approached their table. He and his men ordered ale and stew, and the wench wandered off to check on the other patrons. Jem carefully strained his ears to listen to Kincade and his companion.

"You know," the blond man said, "I think we ought to return to London."

"Why's that?" Kincade asked.

"It's that business with the chit, the one whose father came to see you today. Damn if it doesn't strike me as odd." The Englishman played with his glass, contemplating.

Kincade leaned on the back two legs of his chair. "Odd? In what way?"

"If a man is bold enough to ask you to propose to his daughter . . . well, it's highly improper. And if a man has resigned himself to such conduct on behalf of his child, it makes one wonder what else he would resort to, with the proper motivation."

"Ah, I ken what you mean. You think he might try something else?"

"I do. I fear he might do something reckless. Not that I can say for sure, 'tis simply a feeling in my gut." The blond Englishman lowered his voice. "Or perhaps it is simply this ale. Still, I think we should go back to London."

Kincade reached for the empty pint glass the blond man held. "We can leave tomorrow, then. Bur first, another round?"

"Yes, yes." The Englishman passed his glass to Kincade, who stood.

Jem was struck with sudden inspiration.

"Harvey, pass me the bottle of laudanum," he whispered. Harvey discreetly passed Jem the dark-blue bottle from his coat pocket. Jem stood and walked toward the bar, standing close to Kincade while the man waited for his glasses to be filled. The man nodded when he received them, then returned to his table.

Jem bumped into him with the practiced ease of his cutpurse youth, draining half the bottle into the man's glass before muttering an apology and moving away. He returned to his table and signaled to his men to drink their ale, but they did not empty their glasses. After watching the Scotsman, they all knew he was still likely to put up a hell of a fight. Jem settled in to wait for his prey to weaken.

BRODIE WAS SECRETLY RATHER GLAD TO BE RETURNING to London. He did not, however, like to feel as though he was running away from Jackson Hunt and his troublesome daughter. A Kincade never backed down from a fight. He might choose not to fight, he might merely hold his ground, but to run with his tail between his legs? Over a girl with stars in her eyes? It was a bit much for a man to stomach. Nevertheless, Bath had proved to be far less entertaining than London. It was too . . . safe.

Taking a deep drink of his fresh ale, he listened to

Rafe talk about his exploits from his time as a high-wayman. His elder brother, Ashton, had been holding tight to the family's purse strings, and so Rafe had been robbing rich travelers in the fifty-mile radius around the Lennox family estate for the last two years. He was always careful to choose those who could afford such involuntary donations to his cause, or those who Rafe knew to be worthy of being brought down a bit. He also did it as much for the thrills as he did for the coin.

"So there I was, pistol aimed at this grumpy old chap, and he has the bloody nerve to tell me off when I'd only asked him for his gold pocket watch."

"What did you do?"

Rafe snickered. "Let him keep the watch, but I might have left him in his underthings and made off with his clothes."

"And what did you do with those?" Brodie asked.

"There was an old beggar who sits outside a traveling coach inn a few miles away. I gave him the lot."

"That's rather kind of you, for a highwayman." Brodie chuckled.

Rafe shrugged. "Yes, well, it's not always about the money." Rafe finished his ale and sighed. "Well, shall we head home? It's better to get an early start. I would like to give my valet a decent amount of time to pack. Otherwise, Timmons complains like a mother hen."

"Aye. I imagine Alan would like the same." Brodie

found it was a new experience to have his whereabouts and his plans affect the life of a servant.

Brodie and Rafe stood. "I'll be a moment, Brodie." Rafe nodded toward the door where he could go through and relieve himself.

Brodie leaned heavily against the chair back, his hands braced on the thick wood as he drew in a slow breath and wiped his mouth. Why had this last pint tasted a little bitter? Everything began to feel a tiny bit fuzzy. *Fuzzy* was a silly word, but his mind seemed suddenly full of wool. Warm, fuzzy wool. It was getting damn hard to string any thoughts together.

He looked about the tavern, but his throat felt sick, and his tongue was swollen. Something was wrong. He'd never been drunk like this on so little alcohol. He'd barely even had half of that fourth drink. He had to find Rafe.

Brodie stumbled across into the hall to search for his friend.

"Need some help?" A man appeared at his side.

"I'm fine," he growled. The man had the air of a cutpurse about him.

"Seems to me you're not. Christ, you're a big bloke, ain't you?" The man's hands barely closed around Brodie's upper arm.

"Let go of me." Brodie jerked free and turned away but stumbled into the wall, leaning heavily on it for support. Three more men filled the hallway, blocking his exit.

"You better get out of my way," Brodie warned, his hands curled into fists.

"Now, now, 'tis easier if you just come with us." The man behind him grabbed his arm again. Brodie didn't waste another second. He swung a fist, catching the man on the jaw. He went down like a rock, thudding on the floor.

"Bring him down!" someone shouted. An arm grabbed him around the neck, trying to choke him. Brodie tightened his neck muscles and slammed the man against the nearest wall. The other two men converged on him, striking every spot they could reach. To his horror and shame, Brodie sank to his knees, still gasping for breath as the world blacked out around him.

He came to minutes later it seemed—or maybe it was hours. His limbs were stretched out, and his body was being roughly handled as he was dragged down a darkened hallway. His vision tunneled in and out as he struggled to stay conscious, but it was no use. Whatever these men had done—and he knew they had indeed done something to him—he wasn't able to fight back.

HAVING FINISHED RELIEVING HIMSELF IN A CHAMBER pot, Rafe came out into the hall, only to see something

he'd never expected to see in Bath. Four men were dragging Brodie away like a stunned calf.

His friend hung limp as a sack of flour in their hold.
Another man might have run at them or cried for help,
but despite his reputation, Rafe was not so reckless as
many believed him to be. He followed the men into the
street, sticking to the shadows in order to remain
unseen. They lifted Brodie into a hackney.

"Bloody hell." This was no simple brawl Brodie had
somehow lost. This was an abduction. Rafe glanced
about and saw another passing coach. He waved it down
and instructed the driver to follow the abductors at a
discreet distance. Once settled inside, he wondered what
the devil Brodie had gotten himself into.

When the coach stopped, Rafe slipped out and
handed the driver his fare before he got his bearings.
They were at Royal Crescent, the most expensive and
exclusive area in Bath. Not at all the sort of place one
expected to see four rough men hauling an unconscious
Scotsman out of a coach. The men carried him up some
stairs and into one of the elegant homes on the curved
street.

Rafe waited several long minutes in the mews two
houses away while he decided what to do next. The
front door opened again, and the four men left. There
was no sign of Brodie, which meant he must still be
inside.

Rafe crept along the street until he was standing in

front of the residence. A few lamps were lit near the windows facing the street, but he could see no one inside. There had to be a way into the house. The servants' entrance, perhaps? He would find a way inside to rescue his friend. He could only hope that the bastard who'd taken the Scotsman had no immediate plans to harm him.

❧

BRODIE GROANED AS HE CAME AWAKE AND TRIED TO clear the fog in his head.

"How long will he be out?" a voice asked. A familiar voice.

"I'd say he'll be in and out for another half hour. Better give him a mouthful of this if he gets rough," a scratchy voice said. Brodie recognize that voice as well. It reminded him of dark halls and choking hands.

"Er . . . Right. Well, thank you, Mr. Webster. Here's the remainder of your payment."

"Thank you kindly, sir. You know where to find me, should you need my services again." Mr. Webster chuckled.

The shuffling of distant footsteps grew softer before the silence was punctuated by a heavy sigh a moment later.

"I see you are at least partially awake, Mr. Kincade. I did not mean for it to come to this, but I'm afraid

you've left me no choice." A man's face leaned over
Brodie.

Jackson Hunt. The little blonde lass's father. Rafe
had been right about the man acting desperately. Brodie
tried to speak, but he was too tired, too thick-tongued.
Damned Rafe. He was right about the girl, and her
father.

"Do not speak. I was told you've been given a heavy
dose of laudanum, and I suspect it has made it hard for
you to think. I'm sorry about that. I didn't wish for them
to drug you. Therefore, I will do the talking. You are to
remain here at my home, my guest as it were, while you
and I come to an understanding regarding my daughter.
She has told me the truth about your meeting. How you
seduced her, and how she is carrying your child."

Brodie stared at Jackson in a cold fury, wishing he
had the strength to shout every blasted curse that was
on the tip of his useless tongue.

"Now, as I have already told you, I will pay ten thousand a year to you for marrying my daughter so that she
might live in relative comfort, along with my
grandchild."

A snort of muffled laughter escaped Brodie. Ten
thousand pounds was enough for *relative* comfort? If
that was the case, then he had lived in abject poverty. If
Brock hadn't married Rafe's sister, their family castle
would have crumbled to gravel. Their family had lost
their fortune years ago after their mother had died.

"I shall let you rest and think on it." Jackson turned to leave, but he paused in the doorway. "I love my daughter, Mr. Kincade. She deserves the best in life. A man who loves her and her coming child. While I am sorely disappointed that you did not do the honorable thing with regards to her, I hope very much that you will see sense and become that man." Then he left the room and closed the door behind him.

Brodie waited until he had left before he tried to move. He jerked weakly, and his hands and legs moved only a few inches before abruptly halting. With a roll of his head to one side, he discovered that thick ropes bound his wrists and ankles to the bedposts.

They had tied him to a bloody bed. He felt like he was trapped in some blasted Gothic novel, only wasn't it the woman who was always in this position?

He pulled the ropes. They creaked slightly but did not yield. Soon he gave in to the effects of the laudanum and dozed off. He wasn't sure how long he was asleep, but he woke when he heard the door open and soft steps hurry across the room.

"Oh, my poor dear," a sweet voice breathed close to his ear.

Opening his eyes, he saw a petite blonde girl leaning over him. His vision was still cloudy with the drug, but he guessed it was Miss Hunt, the woman he had met at the ball last evening. The damned chit who'd gotten him into this nightmare, all because she'd taken a fancy to him. He knew he was good with women, but he'd never suspected he was *that* good.

The lass was pretty, of course, but looks weren't everything to Brodie. A woman could rival Helen of Troy, but if she dared restrain Brodie, he would never be hers. *Never.*

"I am sorry it must be like this," Miss Hunt gently cooed as she cupped his face. Her blue eyes burned bright as she leaned down and kissed him, as if that would somehow win him over.

"Untie me, now," he demanded.

"Papa says we mustn't, not until you calm down and agree to the marriage terms."

Miss Hunt kissed him again, flicking her tongue against his pursed lips. He refused to indulge her mad desires.

"You lied to your own father, you mad hag! Saying I bedded you."

"Don't think of it as lying. Think of it as . . . shifting around the order of events. Once we are married, I promise to let you bed me every day, Mr. Kincade. I will be a good wife, I will," she said earnestly.

"Why me? Why not another man?" He was finding it easier for his tongue to move. The laudanum was wearing off.

"Because you are *magnificent.*" The girl threaded her fingers through his hair. "That dark hair, those stormy gray eyes, those features cut from marble, and your body

. . ." Her eyes rolled down his chest to his legs. "You have a muscled physique not often seen among the gentlemen of England."

"It's because I have lived and worked on the land," Brodie said quietly. "I ken what it means to go hungry, to be poor, to have to work to stay alive. You ken none of this. We willna suit as man and wife."

"Oh, we will, I assure you. Would you like some water?"

"Aye. I'm damned thirsty." His voice was hoarse and his throat scratchy.

She poured him a glass, and he was indeed grateful, but the second he took that first bitter gulp, he recognized the taste and his heart hammered with panic.

"You drugged me, lassie . . . you . . ." He said no more as he sank into oblivion.

⚜

LYDIA CURSED IN A VERY UNLADYLIKE FASHION. SHE and the coach driver, as well as Tucker, the Russells' tiger, which was what they called the small boy who rode on the back of the coach, all stared at the broken carriage wheel in dismay.

"If it isna one thing, 'tis another," the burly Scottish driver muttered. "Well, there isna a thing we can do right now, Miss Hunt."

"Yes, Mr. Graham, you're quite right." She eyed the

darkening streets with a little trepidation but far more resolve. "I shall have to walk."

"Not alone you won't." The driver turned to the little boy who stood beside him. The lad couldn't have been more than ten. "Tucker, run home as fast as you can, fetch the grooms, and have them mend the wheel. Tell the mistress I'll be escorting Miss Hunt home."

"Yes, Mr. Graham." The boy ran off like a shot, racing back the way they'd come.

"Is it safe for him to be out alone?" Lydia didn't want the child endangered for her sake.

"This is Bath, miss, not London. 'Tis far safer. Tucker is a right quick lad, Miss Hunt. He willna do anything to call attention to himself."

Lydia hesitated a moment longer, then joined Mr. Graham as they walked along the pavement together. It would be a fairly long walk in the dark with only the streetlamps to guide them. But she was glad of the coach driver's company more than she could say, and she decided a bit of conversation would not be impolite.

"Mr. Graham, if it would not trouble you, might we converse a bit while we walk?"

The coach driver nodded. "If it pleases you, Miss Hunt."

"You're from Scotland?" It was more of a rhetorical question, but she was intrigued after seeing Brodie Kincade. She hadn't had too much interaction with

Scotsmen. They were a bit of a rarity in Bath, at least so far as her social circles went.

"Aye, I was born in Inverness, raised there as a lad before I moved to London with my family."

"What was it like? Scotland, I mean." She was curious to know more about a land that made handsome, brooding men like Brodie Kincade.

Mr. Graham was silent a moment, but she could sense he was thinking of his childhood there. "It is a place of nature and magic," he finally said. "The night sky is filled with stars, and a man can still see the old gods in the woods and hills."

"The old gods?" Lydia asked. "Do you mean the Greek or Roman gods?"

"No, lass, the Scottish ones. We have Beira, the most feared goddess of winter. She's a brutal old woman, that Beira, but she created the lochs and mountains. Then there's the kelpies, the water spirits—great horses made of kelp and seafoam—but you'd best be careful, lest they drown you." He reached up to show her that his fingers were covered with rings. "We wear silver to appease the old gods."

She marveled at the beautiful Celtic rings he wore and remembered that she had glimpsed a large ring on Mr. Kincade's right thumb. She hadn't thought much of it at the time, but now she was quite certain it was one of these pieces of silver.

"Do you miss Scotland?" she asked Mr. Graham.

"Aye. If you visit once, your heart willna leave it. Having been born there, I will always ache for home."

"But you won't return?"

He shook his head, a sad, forlorn look in his eyes. "There isna much work there. 'Tis better for my family to live here."

"I'm sorry, Mr. Graham. I cannot imagine how hard that must be." Yet in a way she could. Her father's business pursuits had left them in a constant state of upheaval. They might be in Bath for a few more months, but she would wager that by the end of the year they would move somewhere else in England. She had not had a proper home in a long time. She'd forgotten what it felt like to belong somewhere, to feel the call of a place that bore the name of *home*.

When she reached her family's townhouse, she offered Mr. Graham coin to get him home, but the Scottish driver's cheeks turned ruddy as he protested.

"Nay. It was my pleasure to walk with you, Miss Hunt." He bowed and waited at the foot of the stairs until she'd been shown inside. She waved goodbye to him before stepping into the house.

"Miss Hunt, I was told by Miss Portia that you had left for London," Mr. Annis said as he ushered her inside.

"I believed I was to go, but it seems I am to stay." She glanced around. "Is my sister at home?"

"No. Your father, sister, and aunt are attending a dinner party at Mr. Rochefort's home."

"Oh well, it is too late for me to join them. Please have Mrs. Kloester send a tray of cold cuts up to my bedchamber."

"Yes, Miss Hunt." She didn't miss the shadow of worry on Mr. Annis's face.

"Mr. Annis, is everything all right?"

"I . . ." The butler's gaze turned to the hallway, as if he was expecting to see someone.

"Please, Mr. Annis."

"I do not wish to speak ill of the master . . ."

Lydia placed a hand on his arm. "Of course not. Please, if it is important to you, you may confide in me without fear."

Annis hesitated. "I cannot even begin to . . ." He straightened his shoulders and sighed. "You must come and see for yourself." He led her upstairs to one of the empty bedchambers. He unlocked the door, which puzzled Lydia. They had never locked any doors in this house before.

Annis pushed the door open and stepped back. Lydia entered with no small amount of trepidation and gasped. Her hands flew to her mouth at the sight of a large form on the bed.

"Is that," she whispered to the butler, "a man?"

"Yes, Miss Hunt. He was delivered here two hours ago by four rather questionable-looking men."

"What? Why did they bring him here? Who is he?" She stepped deeper into the room, and the man stirred at the sound of her voice.

"They brought him here at your father's direction."

Lydia shuddered with sudden horror. "Papa did this?"

A rumbling growl came from the bed. "Let me go, foul wench!"

"Heavens! He's awake." Lydia rushed inside. "Annis, bring me a candle!" She stopped at the bedside. Annis handed her a candle, and she lifted it to the man's face.

"Mr. Kincade!" she almost screamed in shock.

He moved, but it was sluggish, and she soon realized why as she moved the candle over his body. His hands and feet were bound by rope to the bedposts, trapping him with his legs and arms spread wide to each of the four posts of the bed.

"Christ!" She turned to Annis. "Fetch me a sharp knife, quick!" Horror and shame at what had befallen the man under her roof nearly robbed her of her breath.

The butler left, and Lydia leaned close to the Scotsman, hoping he could more easily see her face.

"What happened, Mr. Kincade?" she asked him.

"What happened? You ken very well what happened, lass. You willna take me to the altar. I'll die first."

"Altar?" Suddenly it all made sense. A pit of dread formed in her stomach, so deep that it felt bottomless. Lydia had never imagined that Portia or her father would resort to this.

"I'll set you free at once," she promised. "Try to rest." She touched his face, and for a moment he leaned into the caress, but then his wild eyes flashed with rage, and he jerked his face away and groaned in pain.

The second Annis returned, Lydia carefully began to cut the ropes, but it seemed to take ages.

"Annis, have the coach brought round. I'll take him to the doctor. He seems quite ill."

The butler's face was pale. "I believe it is the laudanum, miss. He's been dosed heavily."

"What? By whom?"

"First by the men who brought him here, then again either by your sister or your father. Otherwise, he would have come out of it by now."

Lydia looked at Mr. Kincade, feeling helpless and ashamed at her family's treatment of him, but he was asleep again, his breathing soft and his eyes closed. She worked even more frantically to cut him loose until the last bit of rope frayed and broke. She gave his shoulder a gentle shake, hoping it would rouse him.

"Mr. Kincade, please try to stand. You are free. I wish to take you to the doctor at once."

He opened weary, bloodshot eyes and struggled to sit up. He kept his head in his palms, drawing in deep breaths. "I'm free?" he whispered hoarsely.

"Yes, but I believe you should see a doctor." Lydia set the knife down on the table by the bed as she sat beside him and pressed the back of one hand to his forehead.

"So gentle now," he murmured. "Such a sweet touch . . ." He struggled for words. "But it doesna matter. It won't change anything."

In one swift motion, he swiped the knife from the bedside table and pointed it at her heart while he gripped her throat with his other hand. Barely able to do more than gasp, Lydia held still as the tip of the blade pricked her through her silk gown.

"You had me kidnapped, and now I shall do the same." He stood from the bed on shaky legs but seemed in command of his body enough that he could spin her around and hold her captive against his chest. They stepped into the hall, and the knife now hovered at her throat as he held her in front of him like a shield.

Annis gasped at them from his position at the top of the stairs. "Miss Hunt!"

"You! Fetch her some clothes. I willna travel with a lass who looks unkempt," Mr. Kincade barked harshly.

"But" Annis began.

"Please, Annis," Lydia begged. The blade was resting against her skin. She feared that if she drew too deep a breath it would sink into her throat.

"Yes, miss." The butler fled to do her bidding, and Brodie led her down the stairs, but it was slow progress given that he relied heavily on her for support.

"Please, Mr. Kincade, let me go."

"After all you've done? No, I'll not fall for any more

NEVER TEMPT A SCOT

acts of false sweetness. You're as venomous and cunning as a viper, and I will have my revenge for it."

"But I didn't"

"Silence." Brodie's tone brooked no argument.

Lydia closed her mouth as they reached the bottom of the stairs. Annis held the small trunk and her valise, the ones Portia had packed for her supposed trip to London.

"You may tell Mr. Hunt that I have his daughter as my guest. And in exchange for his hospitality, I will send her back when I'm good and done with her."

Annis looked like he wanted to intervene, but the butler was no match for the angry Scotsman. She shook her head, and Annis kept his distance as he carried the two pieces of luggage down the stairs to the waiting coach.

"Get inside." Brodie smiled at Lydia as the driver rushed to open the door. Lydia stumbled into the waiting darkness of her family's coach, all too aware of the blade still held at her back.

5

L ydia collapsed into the seat opposite Brodie Kincade as he closed the coach door, and her heart raced as she tried not to panic. It felt as though her whole world was spinning. Her sister and father had done a terrible, wicked thing, and yet *she* had been the one abducted trying to undo their actions.

She jumped and gasped as the other door opened and Rafe Lennox ducked inside.

Brodie at first pointed his knife at the man, then stared, momentarily stunned. "Rafe?"

"Hello, old chap, thought you might need a hand with . . ." Rafe's words trailed away as he caught sight of Lydia. He grinned as the coach started to move. "Well, hello there."

Lydia shrank back as far away from the two men as she could get.

"I say, what's that sweet kitten doing here?" Rafe asked Brodie.

"Sweet? No, no, no. She's a viper, a *clever* one. She told her father that I compromised her and got her with child. The damned man *kidnapped* me. He thinks he can force me into marriage."

"Oh! But that wasn't me!" Lydia said quickly. "You mean my sister, Portia."

"Lies. You have no sister."

Brodie still held the knife, and Lydia couldn't keep her eyes off it. Rafe seemed to take pity on her.

"Right, well . . . I don't think the kitten here has claws enough to hurt you, man. So why not put the knife down? You're not in your right head."

A wild, feral look in Brodie's eyes warned them both that he was not yet ready to be reasonable.

"She drugged me, offered me water, but then she . . ." Brodie shook his head, as though trying to rid himself of the memory.

Lydia covered her mouth with a hand, unable to speak. Portia had drugged him? Her sister and father had done unspeakable harm to this man. As soon as he calmed down, she would have a rational discussion and explain to him that she'd had no part in any of this nonsense.

"Hand me that ribbon, kitten. The one in your hair." Rafe held out his hand to Lydia, who removed the ribbon and handed it to him. Rafe took a handkerchief from his waistcoat pocket and turned to Brodie, holding up the two items.

"Should you, or shall I?" Rafe asked.

Brodie slowly set the knife down on the seat and took the ribbon and handkerchief from Rafe. When Brodie looked her way, Lydia cringed at the look on his face.

"Dinna fight me, lass," he said, then lunged for her.

Lydia kicked and screamed as he came down on top of her. But the man was too large and too strong. He worked the handkerchief into her mouth, tying it behind her head so she was unable to spit it out, and then her wrists were bound together in front of her.

Lydia sat still, trying to calm her breathing so as not to panic or choke on the bit of cloth in her mouth. She was terrified and furious all at once, which had a crippling effect on her. Why couldn't Brodie tell her apart from Portia, and why wouldn't he listen to reason? Was he going to hurt her? Would Rafe stand by and let it happen? She forced her spinning thoughts to stop so she could focus on what the men were saying.

"When you left the tavern room, everything started to spin. I didna realize I'd been drugged until I was in the corridor and four men attacked me," Brodie said.

"Yes, I saw them carry you outside into a coach," Rafe interjected. "I thought at first that you were simply being ejected for starting a fight. Once I realized that wasn't what was going on, I followed at a distance."

"I wasna awake the entire time. I slipped in and out. It was the bloody laudanum. I woke to find the lass's father in the room, explaining how I would have to marry her. To do the right thing. Then I drifted off again and woke to find her kissing me and boasting of how she'd please me as a wife." Brodie shot Lydia a glare of purest loathing. "Then she offered me water, and when I drank, I tasted more laudanum."

"Bloody hell." Rafe shot a fiery look at Lydia. "You are a heartless wench." He focused back on Brodie. "So what is your plan for her? I shall have your back, regardless."

"Thank you." Brodie seemed to relax a bit as he settled back in his seat. "I want this lass to feel as used as I have. Oh, she will get what she wished—*me* in her bed. But she'll not have the courtesy of the title *wife*."

"That's a rather bold move, Kincade," Rafe murmured.

"You still have my back?"

"No. I do not hold with rape, and I sincerely doubt she would willingly go to your bed now."

"You underestimate me," Brodie replied quietly.

"Do I, now? You believe you can convince her to join you in bed, without coercion? That's a rather bold claim. Care to wager on it?"

Brodie's eyes glinted. "Why? You'd only lose."

"We'll see."

Damn Portia and her blasted schemes, Lydia thought. She

was going to be ruined. Her already slim chances of a respectable marriage were to be dashed on the rocks of Brodie Kincade's rage.

"I suppose that means we are leaving Bath?" Rafe asked the same way one might discuss the weather.

"Yes."

"And our destination?"

"Edinburgh. I canna take her to Kincade lands—my brothers would disapprove."

Rafe snorted. "Naturally."

Lydia made a sound of pleading and tried to lift her hands, but after a sharp look from the men, she fell silent again.

"Life really is more interesting with you Scots. No wonder Ash married your sister. The lure of scandal and adventure with you lot is irresistible. Very well, I shall come with you and help where I can. If this wench is as dangerous as you say, you'll need another set of eyes watching her."

"Thank you. I welcome your company, then." Brodie rubbed wearily at his eyes. "I canna stay awake. The laudanum keeps trying to pull me down."

"Not to worry. I'll handle everything. Rest."

Brodie closed his eyes, and Lydia relaxed for a brief moment, until she noticed that Rafe was watching her with a frightening intensity.

"It seems someone has swung a very large stick at a very angry Scottish bear," Rafe said.

Lydia knew pleading would not help. She was at the mercy of two dangerous men who thought she was her scheming younger sister.

What a bloody rotten mess.

❦

BRODIE WAS TRAPPED—CORNERED IN THE HALLWAY AS HIS father bore down on him in a rage.

"You think your mother would have cared about you?" Montgomery Kincade snarled. "You spineless brat!"

Brodie covered his head with his hands, waiting for the blows to rain down on him.

"Or perhaps I'll give your sister the thrashing you are too cowardly to take," his father taunted. This drew Brodie up from his crouched position.

"Do not harm her!" he shouted at his father.

"You can't stop me!" Montgomery turned toward Rosalind's bedchamber. Brodie rushed him, leaping onto the older man's back. The man howled in rage and swung around, throwing Brodie into the stone wall of the corridor like a rag doll.

Brodie woke with a start, his hands balled into fists as he instinctively prepared for an attack, but his father was not there. He wasn't a child anymore. He was a grown man in a crowded coach, which had just stopped moving.

It took him a moment to orient himself, and he was relieved to see Rafe. For a moment he was puzzled by the sight of the pretty lass bound and gagged sitting across from him, her eyes full of fear yet defiant. That was when the night's awful events came back to him.

"Ah, good, you're awake," Rafe said.

"Where are we?" Brodie asked.

"My townhouse. We still need to prepare before we head off. You'll be able to carry the kitten inside?"

"Aye." Brodie still felt weak, but not nearly so much as he had before.

"Good. Carry her inside if you must. I'll tell Mr. Chase to have a bedchamber prepared."

"No need. She'll share mine."

Rafe's lips twitched. "Remember our wager, Brodie."

"Aye. I have no intention of bedding her. I also have no intention of letting her out of my sight."

"Very well. I recommend you sleep off the laudanum before you woo her. We'll leave at first light."

Brodie reached for her hand. "Come without a fight and I willna carry you. If I must carry you, I willna be gentle about it."

The girl nodded in agreement, so he let her stand as he exited the coach first. When she started to step out, he grasped her waist and lifted her down. She was lovely, but not quite the same as he remembered from the previous night. Of course, the first time they'd met he'd been deep in his cups, and the second he'd been out of his mind on laudanum.

She was a pleasant enough weight and felt bloody

good in his arms, which only blackened his mood. He did not want to enjoy holding or touching her. Yet having the manipulative lass under his control seemed to have heightened his arousal. He had never been one for controlling women in sensual situations, but the thought of *this* woman under his control made his body burn with hunger. Or perhaps it was more a matter of satisfaction. He gripped her bound wrists and led her up to Rafe's townhouse.

"My good man," Rafe said to the driver. "A hundred pounds for your silence on where you took us this night. If asked, tell your master that we headed to the docks."

"But I did take you to the docks," the man said with a wink as he took the money. "Dropped you there myself."

"That's a good man." Rafe jogged up the steps to join Brodie and his quiet, wide-eyed abductee as they entered the townhouse.

"A hundred pounds? That's a bit much, isn't it?" Brodie asked.

"For his silence? Not at all, but I daresay a devilishly handsome highwayman will relieve him of half of it sooner or later."

"Good evening, sir," Mr. Chase greeted them, but when he saw the woman Brodie pulled into the house behind him, still gagged with a handkerchief and her wrists bound, the butler paled.

"Not again, sir. You know his lordship doesn't approve of this sort of activity."

"Again?" Brodie shot a look at Rafe. "You have a habit of bringing bound and gagged women to your home?"

"That's a story for another night, old chap," Rafe said with a laugh. "Now, Mr. Chase, as you can see, we have a guest. There are two pieces of luggage that belong to her that need to be brought inside."

"Yes, Mr. Lennox."

Brodie headed up the stairs, pulling the girl behind him. When he reached the door to his bedchamber he paused, looking her over. Her eyes were half-closed and glistening with tears.

"Oh, aye, maybe now you ken how I was feeling just a few hours ago." This whole bloody mess was a far cry from how he usually acted with women. He was the charmer of the family, the rake who'd never met a woman he didn't desire. Yet with this girl, he'd been turned on his head and had become an angry beast.

He heaved a great sigh as he opened the door and ushered her inside. She halted a few feet within the chamber, her eyes darting around the room, looking for escape, he presumed. She would find none except the way they'd entered.

"Here." He removed the makeshift gag and tossed it to the floor. She licked her lips, nervously eyeing him the way one would a wild boar staring at her across a clearing.

"Dry your eyes. I'll not touch you tonight, even if you were to tempt me." He pressed a fresh handkerchief into her hand, and she raised her bound hands to wipe her eyes.

"Please, Mr. Kincade, I must be allowed to explain."

He shook his head. "I'm not interested in your lies, lass. You've spread enough of them for one night. I may have been too deep in my cups to remember you clearly, but I would have remembered if I had bedded you."

Miss Hunt shook her head. "That's just it—you didn't meet me. You met my younger sister. My name is Lydia, not Portia. Portia introduced herself to you last night."

Brodie began to unbutton his waistcoat, which brought a pretty blush to her face.

"Your father spoke of only one daughter. And given how you acted when you found me bound to a bed, I canna trust you."

"How I acted? I was trying to free you!"

"You were trying to tie me back up after I managed to loosen my ropes," he growled.

"Loosen? I cut your ropes with a knife. The knife *you* then held against me! You were in too much of a stupor to know what you were doing."

"Because of the laudanum *you* gave me!" He curled his fists at his sides to control himself.

"I keep telling you, that was my sister!" she snapped.

"Oh, aye, a convenient sister she is too. There to take the blame for everything."

"My God, I have heard how stubborn the Scots are, but this is madness!"

The woman—she was more woman than girl, he noticed—slumped into the nearest chair, a remarkable actress right down to the way her fingers tied knots in the fabric of her gown. He wanted a better look at his unexpected prize. She was lovely, as he'd first thought, but her beauty was somehow muted by a sorrowful gaze, one that he sensed had been there longer than just tonight.

"Come here." He pointed to a spot right in front of him.

She stayed where she was, hesitant, which made him frown. At the sight of his frown, she relented and came to the spot he'd pointed at.

"I shall play your game then, Lydia, but you ken, I am the one making the rules."

Brodie unfastened her wrists and let the ribbon drop to the floor. He held her hands a moment too long. Shyly, or perhaps coyly, she pulled them away, her gaze avoiding his. The woman knew how to play the affronted innocent better than any woman he'd ever met. He felt a tug of sympathy, but he banished. It was something he'd learned to do at a young age.

"Now, turn around so I may free you of this dress."

His tone was gruff as he plucked at the sleeves of her gown.

"What?" She shrank away from him, but he curled an arm around her waist, pulling her flush against his body. She felt soft and warm against him, the way he loved a woman to feel—it was welcoming. But she was trembling from fear, and he didn't like that.

"Save your false modesty for another day when I'm ready to play."

Her hands fluttered a moment before settling on his chest. Her eyes seemed a softer blue than he remembered, and her face held a gentleness that did not match her previous actions. She was clever, far too clever for him to give an inch.

Brodie spun her around to begin unlacing the back of her gown, perhaps a little too roughly. She clutched at the bedpost, her breath coming fast as her body jerked with his motions. He soon had her gown open down the back. The satin fabric gaped open, revealing her figure beneath a set of stays. He unfastened those too, his captive remaining completely still until he released her.

"Strip down and get into bed. Or sleep in them and chafe, for all I care."

Miss Hunt spun to face him as her dress and stays fell to the floor. She hugged herself and half hid behind the bedpost, fear darkening her eyes. It confused Brodie. He knew true fear when he saw it. This lass had kissed him—she had *wanted* him. Why was she afraid of him now? It made no sense. He knew he hadn't dreamed her kissing him earlier, insisting she would be a good wife. What the devil had changed for her to not want him?

"Lass, I meant it. I'll not hurt you." He stepped closer, catching her around the waist before she could retreat farther.

"How can I trust you?" Her breasts rose and fell beneath her thin chemise. She gazed at him with all the fear of a wild lark finding itself in a cage for the first time.

"You're a fine one to talk about trust," said Brodie. "But unlike you, my word is my bond, and I do not lie to get what I want." He lifted his other hand to her face and brushed the pad of his thumb over her lips. The more he looked upon Miss Hunt, the more he preferred the reality in front of him to the alcohol-altered version of her in his memories. She was shapely, with a swanlike neck and a melting sweetness to her features that drew him in. But he knew that she was also the devil in disguise.

"Please," she whispered, her lips teasing his thumb, which still shaped her mouth.

"Please what?"

"Don't do whatever it is you are planning, Mr. Kincade. Please, let me go home. I shall not tell anyone what my sister did, and no one will force you to marry her."

"Sister," he chuckled. "Your pretense wears thin. I

remember you. I remember how you taste, how you smell, that hint of perfume." He leaned in to inhale, but the scent of expensive French perfume wasn't there. What he did smell was more like wildflowers blooming on a distant hill in the midst of a spring storm. She must have had a bath after she'd drugged him the second time. It was intoxicating and natural. Her breath hitched, and she squirmed in his hold, setting fire to his blood, but he held fast to his promise. He would not kiss her until she begged him to. Although resisting her soft, flowery pink lips would likely kill him.

"Bed, lass. Now." He dropped his arm from her lower back. She scrambled away, putting the bed between them. The girl pulled at the covers and climbed underneath the sheets.

He resumed undressing. He pulled his shirt over his head and tossed it over the back of a chair. Then he removed his boots with some effort, given that his balance still wasn't fully restored. He left his trousers on, however. It would be uncomfortable, but he had a suspicion his little captive would make a run for it in the middle of the night, and he wanted to be able to leap from the bed and capture her if she tried.

Weary now, he crossed to the opposite side of the bed and blew out the candle on the small table by the bed. Darkness fell around them, and he heard her shift restlessly.

"Dinna try to run off, *buaireadair*. I sleep lightly. I will catch you."

"What is a *buaireadair*?"

"A troublemaker, which is what you are, lass."

There was a moment's silence before she spoke. "I once thought you were such a handsome gentleman, possibly even kind when I first saw you at the ball. But now I know differently. You are a brute. A bully."

The almost prissy response brought a smile to his lips.

"Aye. You would know, seeing as how you are one as well. Good night, lass." He rolled over to face away from her shadowy outline. Yet he had a feeling he would dream about her, and that scent of wildflowers that made him think of home.

6

Lydia giggled softly as something tickled her cheek. She brushed a hand against her face, trying to make it stop. She stilled, her laughter dying as her hand felt warm flesh. Her eyes flew open, and she saw the pale morning light illuminate a hand close to her face. Brodie had been brushing the backs of his knuckles over her skin ever so lightly.

"Time to wake, lass. You need to dress so we may leave." He gripped the covers and tugged them off her body, which made her shriek and cover herself with her hands. The filmy chemise felt far less protective of her body in the light of day. She nearly toppled over in her attempt to escape the bed, lest he decide to remove her from it himself.

"Bathe and change. I'll have Rafe send a maid." Brodie left the room abruptly after that announcement.

Lydia scowled at the closed door. Then her angry expression turned to a worried frown. She had slept in Brodie's bed all night. Even though he had not touched her, if the fact were ever revealed, she would be completely and totally compromised. Even if she managed to escape and return to her family, she knew what her great-aunt would say. She was unmarriageable. Whatever life she might have dreamed of was now impossible.

Grief and longing for a life she'd never have came swift and sudden, like a violent storm, drowning her. Lydia covered her face with trembling hands as she gave in to silent sobs. It was a long while before she was able to collect herself. She straightened her shoulders, a look of resigned acceptance upon her face.

As she gazed into the mirror, seeing her pallor and the lost look in her eyes, she felt homesick for the safety of her own bed, her own family, even if they did drive her mad at times. To be trapped with this brute of a Scot who wouldn't believe her when she said she wasn't Portia —it was enough to turn her stomach.

But she wasn't going to let him use her as a carpet to walk all over. She still had some backbone, and she would find a way to make this work to her advantage somehow. If Brodie wanted a mistress, he would have one.

Her reasoning was simple: if the damage could not be undone, then she might as well enjoy what pleasures the man could offer. Brodie was incredibly handsome, and she could not deny that she had imagined belonging to him after first seeing him at the ball. And now he would be hers.

More importantly, he would not be Portia's.

There was some bitter amusement to be had at that particular fact. Her scheming sister had sought to entrap Brodie, but all Portia had done was drive him to abduct the wrong sister. Once Portia discovered this, she would no doubt be outraged at the notion of Lydia being mistaken for her, which also gave her some satisfaction.

A young upstairs maid, a shy girl by the name of Jane, came to the bedchamber to help her bathe and dress. They reviewed the gowns that Portia had packed in the two travel cases. At least her sister had thought to pack the prettier of her gowns.

Lydia chose a dark rose-colored satin gown with gold netting on the skirts. Pink silk peonies had been sewn around the hem, with delicate green satin vines and pale pink buds decorating the sleeves and bodice. It was one of her more extravagant day gowns.

At Lydia's request, Jane styled her hair in a simple Grecian fashion rather than the current vogue of ringlets about her face. When she was ready, she thanked the shy girl and exited the bedchamber. She half expected her abductor to be waiting outside the door to grab her, but the corridor was empty.

She headed for the stairs, noting the layout of this

fashionable townhouse, which was much like the one her father had purchased. This must be Rafe Lennox's home, as her sister had said. Lydia couldn't help but wonder *how* Portia had discovered this bit of information in so short a time. It worried her how her sister's cleverness could get everyone around her into trouble, and yet somehow never Portia herself.

She reached the bottom of the stairs and heard Rafe and Brodie chatting quietly in the dining room. She approached the open door with apprehension.

"What's your plan with the kitten? You'll soon tire of her in Edinburgh, I imagine," Rafe said.

"Possibly," Brodie said.

"No doubt she sees all this as some game."

"Aye. She's playing a game with me, I'm sure of it. So sweet and blushing like a wee bride, but damned if it isna attractive."

Rafe laughed. "She has you captivated already? A crafty creature indeed."

Lydia, her face flaming at being discussed so boldly by two men who didn't even know her, coughed politely as she entered the room.

"Good morning." Rafe bowed his head as he and Brodie stood. At least they had enough manners between them to know to rise when she came into a room.

"Good morning." Lydia glanced at the sideboard laden with chafing dishes, her stomach growling. She hadn't eaten a thing since yesterday afternoon at the Pump Room.

"Please, help yourself," Rafe insisted.

"Thank you, Mr. Lennox." She collected a plate from the table and served herself a breakfast of kippers, hard-boiled eggs, and buttered toast.

When she was ready to sit down, Brodie pulled her chair back and pushed her in. Again, it was a gentlemanly act, so out of place after he had brought her here against her will.

"No cries of innocence this morning?" Brodie asked.

"I have told you the truth a number of times already," Lydia said evenly. "Continuing to do so will not change a stubborn mind that's already made up. Instead, I will make do the best I can until you are willing to listen to reason."

"Then you're in for a long wait, lass," Brodie said, his tone a little curt. "Eat quickly if you can. We are to leave once you've finished."

Rafe lounged in his seat, perusing a paper, idly turning the pages as though he wasn't really reading. Every now and then his gaze would drift lazily between her and Brodie, his lips curved as though he was resisting the urge to smile at some private joke.

The devil take handsome men! Lydia decided she would ignore them both while she had her breakfast.

Lydia drank a cup of hot chocolate, hastily ate her breakfast, and then followed the gentlemen into the hall.

"Where are we bound?" she asked. She'd heard mention of Edinburgh twice now, but she wasn't quite sure if she believed that or not.

"Scotland," Brodie replied.

"Oh . . ." They really were headed to Edinburgh. She'd never been outside of England before.

Rafe's coach was already waiting for them, and she was handed up into it by Brodie. Thankfully, the coach was designed for long travel, with comfortable seats and a fair amount of cushions.

A footman loaded their luggage at the back, while their two valets assisted them before climbing on top of the coach into the seats above. Brodie and Rafe joined Lydia inside the coach. She couldn't help but wonder how they were to pass the time during the journey, but Brodie produced a small pile of books as one of the last things loaded inside.

"Oh, might I trouble you for a book, Mr. Kincade?" she asked, mindful to keep her tone polite and hopeful. "Otherwise, I might tire you with protestations of my innocence." This came out a little more sarcastic than she wished it to, but the man had a way of trying her patience.

He scowled at her, but after a second he handed her a book. The spine of the brown leather volume read *Park's Travels in Africa*.

"Park? Who is Park?" she asked as she examined the

title page. The author seemed to be a man named Mungo Park.

"'Tis a biography of sorts," Brodie explained. "The man ventured into the heart of Africa and wrote about his adventures and discoveries."

"Oh, thank you." Lydia turned the page to see an engraved drawing of a very attractive young man in a powdered wig. She settled in to read Mr. Park's story and was lost for a few hours in his retelling of his visit to Africa and what he thought of the lands, languages, and the lives of the inhabitants.

At their first stop, Lydia was escorted by Brodie into the coaching inn, where she could use the facilities and the men could see to acquiring a bit of food. Rafe caught the eye of a pretty barmaid and took the girl by the hand, leading her upstairs. They were absent an hour, and when Lydia realized what they must be up to, she blushed wildly.

"Pretending again?" Brodie asked. "I admit, I am curious—how can a woman so knowledgeable of men and their needs conjure a blush like that?"

"I remind you once again, you speak of Portia, not myself. But I doubt she knows much more about men than I do. She is young and full of girlish bravado." Lydia turned away, watching the men and women in the taproom rather than the brooding Scot beside her. She could still feel him looking at her, which only deepened her blush. One of his hands settled upon her knee, sliding up her thigh, over her gown, but the touch was so scandalous and unexpected that she nearly leapt from the table and had to fight to stay still.

"Do you wish for me to take you upstairs, lass? Have I denied you what you've been hoping for?" He caught her chin, the touch gentle despite his taunting tone. His gray-blue eyes were like a pool of water reflecting clear skies over gray stones. To Lydia's fury and shame, she felt a spark of fire in her body each time he touched her, yet his very words insulted her.

"Mr. Kincade. I would prefer not to be treated like that. If you wish to bed me, treat me like a proper mistress." She summoned her courage and looked him squarely in the eye as she spoke, letting him hear the steel in her voice. Maybe challenging him back would gain her some ground.

"A *proper* mistress? What would you know of that?" Brodie's sour mood seemed to fade, and a boyish grin replaced it. It reminded her of the way she'd felt when she'd first seen him at the ball, and her heart began to pound wildly all over again.

"Everyone knows that mistresses receive gowns, jewels, townhouses . . . I suppose other things." She honestly didn't know how mistresses were treated. Her guess was based on what she'd overheard from various rumors by other ladies at balls.

"Aye, they might, in exchange for being at the beck and call of their lord and master," Brodie said in a seductively sweet tone. "Would you like that? For me to *master* you, lass?"

He stroked his fingertips down her neck to the tops of her breasts above her gown. It was a modestly cut dress, yet his exploring touch made her feel naked. Her breath quickened, and her body burned along every inch that his fingers caressed.

Heavens, it was positively suffocating to be so close to him when he was touching her, yet deep down she didn't want him to stop.

She shook her head and scooted away. "No, I think not."

He dropped his hand from her bodice but leaned in to whisper in her ear, "Oh, I think you do, lass. I think you want me to trap those pretty wrists behind your back, so I may kiss you as long and hard as I like."

His lips feathered against her cheek as he spoke, and it sent bolts of excitement down her body. She didn't argue, didn't contradict him. It would be pointless. Her breath came quickly, and her entire body flushed with a heat so hot and thick that she had no way of hiding the effect his words had on her.

"Finish your lunch," Brodie said as he leaned back. "We have a ways to go before we reach the next inn."

Lydia did as he asked, but only because she was quite famished. It would be a long day indeed if she were to remain trapped with Brodie in the tight confines of the coach with a growling stomach. At least having Mr. Lennox present would lend some propriety to the trip.

At least, she hoped it would.

※

LYSANDRA RUSSELL EXAMINED HER NEWLY BUILT telescope. She'd just received the remaining parts from London. The chance to stargaze was something that always brought her joy and stilled her thoughts of other worries while she focused on her academic papers.

But her mind kept straying to Lydia. She'd expected a message at least by this morning, where Lydia would have explained whatever wild scheme Portia had been up to and she had managed to foil. Yet no letter had arrived. It was not at all like Lydia not to write to her.

Retrieving a clean cloth from a nearby table covered with books, Lysandra wiped her hands clean of a little bit of grease. Then she untied her work apron and tossed it over a nearby chair. She exited her upstairs study and went in search of their butler, Mr. Raikes. She found him belowstairs arranging the silver in the cupboards. It was something the butler took seriously, and he spent hours at it when the house was quiet.

"Raikes? Are there any messages for me?"

The butler shook his head. "I'm sorry, Miss Russell. We received no letters this morning, except for a few for Lord Rochester."

"Ah, best to forward those to London. My brother won't be in Bath for a few months."

"Already done, Miss Russell."

"Raikes, are Lawrence and Zehra still here?" She'd been so consumed with the telescope she'd quite forgotten to ask her older brother and sister-in-law what they had planned for the day. Lawrence was determined to allow his wife time to enjoy traveling around England before they started having children.

"I believe they are to attend the assembly rooms this evening after the dowager marchioness arrives."

Lysandra bit her bottom lip in thought. "Oh, is Mama coming today?"

Her mother was often an ally, but on occasion she was also a nuisance, especially when she was in a mood to make a match. Jane Russell was a serious woman when it came to marriage. She'd claimed credit for matching two of her brood—Lucien, the eldest, and then Lawrence, the second eldest. But Avery, Linus, and Lysandra were still unmarried, which meant they were increasingly under her watchful eye.

"I believe she will arrive this afternoon." Mr. Raikes held a large silver serving spoon up to the light, and then he pulled a polishing cloth out and began to wipe at some smudge that was likely too small to be seen even with her telescope.

"If any messages arrive for me, will you call for me at once?"

97

"Of course, Miss Russell," Raikes promised.

Lysandra left the servants' quarters. She had only just stepped into the hall when her mother burst into the townhouse in a flutter of colorful skirts and high spirits. She was laughing at something a footman had said, and the young man's face turned a ruddy red as he accepted Jane's hat and her spencer. Jane was still a stunning beauty, even in her early fifties, which made Lysandra quite proud. Her dark-red hair was only just beginning to show a hint of silver, and if anything it only enhanced her looks. Because she had forgone face paints in her younger years, her face was still smooth and her complexion clearer than most women of her age. And with a curvy figure but a slender waist, Jane looked more maidenly than matronly, which kept many a man on his best behavior around her. She was, as many men had learned, a force of nature.

"Lysa, dear." Her mother caught sight of her. "Why aren't you riding in the park? The weather is wonderful for husband catching." Her mother's teasing only made her smile. She made it sound like she should carry a butterfly net with her.

"Hello, Mama," she said as they embraced. "I was just finishing building my telescope. The last parts arrived this morning."

Jane held her tongue a moment. It wasn't that she disapproved—her mother believed in women pursuing education in all its forms. But she also wanted her children married, especially Lysandra.

"Have you spoken to Mr. Cavendish? I understand he is a member of the Royal Astronomical Society. Wouldn't he be glad to help you?"

Lysandra blushed. "Perhaps. Mr. Cavendish is rather occupied these days."

"Oh? With what? He's a gentleman with land and money. What else could occupy him besides pleasurable pursuits?"

"Mama," Lysandra said in warning, though she kept her tone gentle. She didn't want to think about Gregory Cavendish or the kiss he'd stolen from her last Christmas. Nothing had changed between them. He'd returned to London, she remained unmarried, and they both pursued their love of the stars . . *separately*. That was all there was to it.

"Very well, I shall move you down the list. Avery is next. I had better find him a wife, but he's always away on the Continent with that spy business. One can only imagine the sort of women he's forced to consort with."

Lysandra winced at her mother's casual attitude toward her brother's very dangerous lifestyle. "Mama, I was planning to go out. Would you mind terribly if I left you for the day?"

"Left me? Why? What happened?"

"Nothing. At least, I think it's nothing."

Jane caught the eye of her shy footman. "Tea in the drawing room, if you please."

The young man nodded and rushed off.

"Come. Tell me all of it over tea." Jane escorted Lysandra into the drawing room, where they both sat down. "Now, what's the matter?"

"It's my friend Lydia," Lysandra began, and then she told her mother the entire story, from the ball to Portia's inappropriate behavior and finally Lydia's mysterious letter that Lysandra had not written. By the time she was done, Jane's good spirits were gone.

"Poor Miss Hunt. We must investigate this business. I've always cared for the poor girl. I had even once hoped that she and Lawrence . . . But we all find love in our own way, don't we? And Zehra is a wonderful woman for my boy. But Lydia is a sweet child, and she needs a mother. Her father spends too much time fawning over Portia and neglecting Lydia. I know that parents have favorites, but they ought to do their best not to."

Lysandra smiled at her mother. "We all know *your* favorite."

"I do not have a favorite. I love you all equally."

"Perhaps," Lysandra said. "But Avery will always have a special place in your heart. He looks just like Papa."

Jane's eyes shimmered. "He does, but that does not mean I love any of you less. Do you understand?"

Jane had lost her husband when Lysandra was only ten, and she had grown up her whole life knowing that her parents had a love match. Yet despite having lost the other half of her heart, Jane had not withdrawn from life. Rather, she had been more determined than ever not to miss a minute of it.

"Now, we must focus on poor Lydia." Jane cleared her throat as the tea was brought in, and then she poured them each a cup. "I suggest we go and pay a call on her."

"I agree," Lysandra said. "The sooner the better." She was starting to have a feeling in her gut that something was wrong and her friend needed her.

❦

"WHERE DID HE GO?" PORTIA DEMANDED FOR THE hundredth time. After returning home late last evening after dinner at Mr. Rochefort's, she had gone straight to bed, only to have her father and Cornelia wake her up an hour later to tell her that Brodie Kincade was gone and he taken Lydia with him at knifepoint. Their butler, Mr. Annis, had recounted the story half a dozen times by now for all three of them.

Portia still couldn't believe it. Lydia and Brodie. *Together.* Why had he taken Lydia, though? Surely he would have wanted to take *her.* She was the prettier sister, after all. Portia hated herself for the selfish thought, but it was true. She was far lovelier than Lydia. Did that not matter to a man like Brodie?

"I don't know, my child. I returned to Mr. Lennox's

house last night but could not gain entrance. He was not at home this morning and neither was Mr. Kincade. The staff would not tell me when they planned to return. The coachman said that he was forced to take them to the docks, but no one there has said they were seen boarding any ships."

Aunt Cornelia scowled at both Portia and her father. "Jackson, you've made a royal mess of this."

"I don't know why Lydia would have freed him," Portia said with a pout.

"Because it was the decent thing to do," Cornelia snapped. "I would have done it myself had I known you had the young buck tied up like some poor animal." Cornelia huffed, and the feather in her turban quivered in response.

Portia wanted to smash every breakable object in their drawing room. It wasn't fair. Brodie was supposed to be *her* husband. Yes, tying him down did seem a bit silly now, as well as that whole drugging nonsense, but she'd been so desperate to have him. She'd thought giving him a bit more of the laudanum would have calmed him enough so that she could show him just how good a wife she would make.

"*Portia,*" her great-aunt snapped, and Portia stopped her restless pacing by the window.

"Yes, Aunt Cornelia?" she replied frostily.

Her great-aunt narrowed her eyes, not at all cowed by Portia's icy tone. "I know you told your father you are with child, but I have it confirmed this morning with your lady's maid that you most certainly are not."

"What?" Jackson looked to Portia, his face pale. "You . . .You lied to me?"

The way her father was looking at her now, it was like she was a stranger. It created an empty cavern within her chest. Was this shame she was feeling? "I . . ."

"The truth, girl," Cornelia barked.

"He never touched me, Papa. But I so wanted him for a husband, and . . ."

"Portia, I *kidnapped* and injured an innocent man based on the strength of your word. I thought I was protecting your virtue. He could have me arrested. I could face time in prison for this. How could you be so . . ."

"Foolish?" Cornelia supplied.

Portia was torn between tears and rage. "But . . . I love him, Papa, like you loved Mama. All the stories you told us of her . . . I wanted what you had."

Her father shook his head. "Then I have taught you all the wrong lessons. Clearly, you don't know the first thing about love. Love isn't about getting what you desire on a whim. It's about sharing your life with another person. A person you trust, someone who trusts you in kind. It's about sacrifice and loyalty and friendship and . . ." Jackson dragged a hand over his face and let out a weary sigh Portia had never heard before. It was a sound that broke part of her armor of self-indulgence and self-centeredness.

"Papa, I'm very sorry I lied to you." She threw herself next to him on the settee, and her eyes filled with tears. She reached for his hands, but Jackson pulled away and stood, putting distance between them.

"Cornelia, I think Portia should partake of the ocean air in Brighton. Would you be willing to escort her there? I will have the arrangements made in a few hours."

"I would be glad to, but what will you do?" Cornelia asked.

"Find and rescue my daughter, even if it means facing down a very large and rightfully angry Scotsman."

7

Brodie was in a black mood that afternoon as they journeyed toward the next coaching inn. He'd gone from loathing her, to desiring revenge against her, to simply desiring her, all in the span of a single night and day. He didn't know if it was because Rafe's blasted wager had made her a forbidden temptation or if her pleas of innocence straddled the line between believable and intolerable. The link between anger and arousal was a strange but real one, and he needed to be careful that he did not act in poor judgment because of it.

Yet all he wanted now was to take Lydia to bed and give in to his mad desires. But he'd kept his restraint, not only because of the wager, but because it was right. Yet here she was resisting his suggestions, and she even dared to demand fair treatment as a proper mistress.

The nerve. Given what she and her father had done to him, she didn't deserve fairness, yet he would give it to her, and that made him feel fairly disagreeable. Neither Rafe nor either of their valets had volunteered to accompany him inside after they saw Brodie's thunderous expression. So now Brodie and his captive were trapped inside the coach alone. After half an hour, he noted she wasn't reading her book.

"Miss Hunt," he said. She'd been frozen on the same page all this time, her gaze distant. He was curious to know what she was thinking about and what manipulations she was planning next.

She finally looked his way, and those soft blue eyes held him, calmed him in a way he hadn't expected. "Yes?"

"You've not been reading."

"Yes, I have." She held up *Park's Travels in Africa*.

"You havena turned a page in quite a while."

A faint shade of rose tinged her cheeks. "I was just thinking . . ."

"About what?"

"Mr. Park was Scottish. Did you know that?" she asked suddenly.

"Was he?" Brodie leaned forward a little. He hadn't had a chance to read the book yet. He had only purchased it recently. He loved to read, and it had always haunted him that he hadn't been able to rescue the books from their library back in Castle Kincade when his father began selling everything they owned to keep the castle. When he had seen Park's book in the book-shop, he'd desperately wanted to read it. Yet part of him had felt rather unsatisfied knowing he would never have adventures like Park. He would never see the world or live a remarkable life. The book seemed to haunt him with the promise of a life he couldn't live.

"Well, he was Scottish." Lydia turned a few pages, as if reviewing them. "He writes dispassionately about all that he sees, yet beneath that there is an undeniable curiosity about Africa, its lands and its people. He offers a beautiful glimpse into Africa's complexity and human-ity. He even details hundreds of languages and the customs of many tribes who live there."

Lydia was almost smiling as she spoke. For a minute, Brodie forgot about the gulf that lay between them. He forgot that he did not trust her or she him and that they were linked by scandal.

"Would you ever go to Africa?" he asked her.

"I believe I would, actually." Her sudden, unguarded smile made his pulse quicken. "I would sail from Portsmouth to Gambia and venture into the wilds there. It would be dangerous, especially for a woman, but if I could find an exploration party who would let me come, I would join it."

"Really?" Brodie pictured Lydia wearing breeches, her hair pulled into a tail at the nape of her neck as she sailed into the Congo in a shallow boat while watching a red-gold horizon. It was a breathtaking vision.

"Would you?" she asked.

"Aye," he said. "If I was able."

"Are you not able?" Lydia tilted her head as she closed the book and set it on her lap.

"I wasn't, not for a long time. Until recently, my family faced difficult days. We struggled to keep our home. It's only now that we are more able to do the things we longed to do for years."

"Your brother married Joanna Lennox, didn't he?" She was being polite by asking, even though she knew the answer. "I've heard it was a bit scandalous. There was talk of Gretna Green and a mad chase by Joanna's older brother and his friends, the League of Rogues."

"Aye, Brock did marry Joanna. Do you know her?"

"Yes, we're friends. But I admit I've not seen her in some months."

"I don't think she would be friends with the likes of you." Brodie leaned back and stroked his chin. He wanted to push her, to test her limits.

"What do you mean by that?"

"Joanna is a sweet, kind woman. She doesna make friends with scheming vipers such as you."

"Oh, stop it! Just stop being such a bully," Lydia hissed.

"In this coach, only one of us has been kidnapped." He reconsidered his words when she cocked an eyebrow. "That is, only one of us has been bound and . . ." The eyebrow arched higher. "Well, only one of us has been drugged with laudanum."

"And only one of us has been held at knifepoint," Lydia countered.

"You seem to be mistaking revenge for being wronged," Brodie shot back as he leaned forward to talk to her. "Never forget, lass, that you started all this." The air tensed between them in that instant, and Lydia reacted instinctively to his aggressive invasion of her space.

Lydia struck, not with an open palm, but a balled fist to his jaw. The blow stung, to be sure, but his hard face had met with harder blows over many years of boxing and brawls. He touched his face, puzzled. At the ball, she'd given him a delicate, even childish slap. Now he was facing a woman who was upset, truly lashing out.

"Ouch." She clutched her hand against her chest. "I think I broke my hand on your hard head!"

"Serves you right," he muttered, expecting her to continue to bemoan an exaggerated injury. But her face continued to be lined with pain. A sinking feeling in his chest quickly deflated his temper.

"All right, let me see, lass." He waved a hand at her.

"I'm fine."

He could see clearly how much she was hurting now. He joined her on the other seat and reached for her hand. She flinched as he pulled her arm toward him, examining her wrist and hand.

"Does this hurt?" He rotated her wrist, and she bit her lip and nodded.

"And this?" He flexed her delicate pale fingers, trying not to let his mind run away with images of her slender hands touching his body.

"That doesn't hurt too much," she whispered. "It's more my wrist, I think."

Brodie moved his fingers back to her wrist, gently massaging, but she would need to rest it for it to fully heal.

"You've likely sprained it, lass. It is an easy mistake. When you mean to punch a man, never let your wrist bend." He raised up her good arm and balled her fingers into a fist. "Swing slow, at my jaw," he commanded. She stared at him in disbelief. He sighed. "Do it."

She slowly swung her uninjured hand at him. He caught her fist in his palm and used his other hand to show her where her wrist was bent incorrectly—just a little force caused it to bend even farther.

"See? That's how you hurt yourself. Keep it straight."

"Oh, I see." Lydia straightened her wrist and pushed forward. Though he still held her fist, it was easy to see how much more stable this position was, locking right up to her elbow. "Why are you teaching me to hit you?"

Brodie chuckled, his anger fading. "I suppose because it is adorable to see you attempt to be feisty, lass." He sobered. "Though if you truly want to hurt a man who means you harm, lift your skirts high and kick him in the bollocks."

"His . . . Oh, good heavens, I could never—"

Brodie cupped her chin. "If a man means to harm you, you must not hesitate to defend yourself. Men talk about fighting fair, but men who win fights keep their mouths shut and do what they have to. Remember that."

Lydia bit her lip, and Brodie wanted more than anything to sweep her onto his lap and nibble that lip himself. Brodie took in her dainty nose, the heavy fall of lashes that swept down over her cheeks each time she blinked, and the soft natural rose in her cheeks that blended with her creamy skin.

It brought back a dim memory that seemed more like a dream to him. It was of his mother in the kitchens, dipping fresh strawberries into clotted cream. She would hand each of her children a strawberry, and he, his brothers, and Rosalind would enjoy the treat with her. It was one of the few happy memories he had of his mother before she died.

Brodie wondered if Lydia's mouth would remind him of strawberries and cream. He reached up to touch her again, and her breath came swifter, her face flushed as he leaned in.

"If you dinna want me to kiss you, you'd best hit me now like I showed you, lass," he warned and gave her but a handful of heartbeats to decide.

No blow came. Instead, her lashes closed, her lips

parted, and in one quick motion, Brodie cornered her against the coach wall and swept her into his arms. His body jolted with heat the second he claimed her mouth. Her lips were warm and trembling beneath his.

This was no bold kiss like the one she'd given him when he'd been tied down. This was the very opposite. She shivered, and her hands fluttered against his body before they settled on top of his chest. Her fingertips dug into the cloth of his bottle-green silk waistcoat. He flicked his tongue against her lips, and she startled, opening to him further. Her sweet taste did indeed remind him of cream and strawberries.

Brodie coaxed her to be bold, and he showed her with his mouth what he wanted most.

"Give in to me, sweetness," he whispered seductively. "Let me *master* you, my wild beauty." He had never wanted so much to control a woman's passion like he wanted to control Lydia's. Perhaps it was due to his frustration over the brief time she had been his master, or maybe it was simply that seeing her play a wanton innocent now was bringing out a primal part of him that wanted to own every part of her and teach her all the sensual delights he knew.

He groaned in agonized pleasure and cupped the back of her head, deepening the kiss. Her startled little sounds drew his baser instincts to the surface. He grasped her uninjured wrist and pinned it to the padded wall of the coach beside her head, holding her prisoner while he claimed his revenge in kisses.

She was panting, her fast breaths creating a rise and fall of her breasts, and he moved his mouth down to those tempting mounds. Her skin was smooth, and the creamy mounds were as flushed as her face. He wondered if her nipples were the same soft, sweet pink as her lips or a duskier color. He pressed hot kisses to her breasts, wishing her gown wasn't so tight, so that he might free her breasts completely.

She moaned as he flicked his tongue in the sensitive space between her breasts, and he laughed softly against her skin.

"Ach, there's so much a man can do with breasts like these," he murmured, and she only breathed harder.

"What things?" she asked, her words breathy as she wriggled against him.

"Oh, grand, wicked things. Things a lass like you once claimed to ken." He repeated the flick of his tongue, this time along the edge of her bodice, mere inches from her nipples.

"Mr. Kincade . . . Please, I can't . . ."

He glanced up at her face. A light layer of sweat dewed her skin, and he couldn't resist giving her what he knew she needed.

"Let me touch you, lass. I can ease the ache."

"Yes, please, I need you to touch me," she insisted breathlessly.

Brodie released her wrist and slid one hand up her leg, beneath her skirts, gently questing through the frothy lace of her underpinnings until he discovered her mound. She nearly shrieked with apparent surprise, but he silenced her with a long, hot kiss.

"Easy, lass, let me continue." He stroked his fingertips down her mound and to the bud of arousal that he wanted to see but couldn't, given the tight confines of the coach. He would have to content himself with working the pad of his thumb over it, pressing and brushing until Lydia screamed with pleasure against his mouth.

Brodie drank down her cry of startled pleasure, relishing his victory. She was going to be well and truly his soon enough, and she would never be satisfied with any other man again. Then, once she was hopelessly ruined and desperately in love with him, he would cast her off and send her home to her bastard of a father.

Lydia's struggles ceased, and she settled more deeply into his hold. He removed his hands from beneath her skirts and pulled her even closer to him.

"I . . ." She paused and tried again. "I've never felt . . . Was that . . . ?"

"Passion," he answered. "You've truly never felt it before?" That stunned him. The woman had professed her knowledge of passion. Had it all been bravado and lies? Was she truly an innocent? Completely untouched by a man? He supposed he would have his answer soon enough.

"Do men feel the same?" Her wide, guileless gaze should have been familiar. He dimly, *drunkenly* recalled she'd given him a wide-eyed, guileless look before, but this one seemed truer somehow than what his memory recalled.

"Of course we do. 'Tis what makes tupping so pleasurable."

"Tupping?"

He couldn't resist laughing. "Yes, lass, tupping, coupling, making love, fu—"

"Oh please, no more." She covered his mouth with one of her hands.

He caught her wrist and placed a kiss to her open palm before he drew her hand away from his mouth.

"You really mustn't say such things, Mr. Kincade."

"Brodie," he corrected. "If you're going to be my mistress, Brodie will do."

"Yes . . . Your mistress," she said, looking away from him, her expression suddenly distracted. She then turned back to him and squared her shoulders. "Well, if that is to be my fate, shall we settle upon some rules?"

"Rules?" He cocked his head. "We have no need of rules."

"I must insist." Lydia crossed her arms, no doubt an attempt to look in control, but all it did was render the lass more adorable. He kept having to remind himself that he should despise her for what she had done to him.

"Very well, name your rules. I'll decide if I agree."

"You must act respectable toward me in public. Do not mistreat me in the presence of others. I know you will not treat me as a wife, but a little respect is all I ask."

He blinked in surprise. He'd never intended to mistreat her. "I agree to that. What else?"

"If you must continue to hold me against my will, allow me to have food, suitable clothes, and decent accommodations."

"Ach, so you thought my plans were to leave you naked, starving, and sleeping in the stables? I may not think highly of you, lass, but I certainly never thought of treating you that low." He couldn't help his sharp reply, but she was insulting him by assuming he'd subject her to such wretched treatment. His only intent from the beginning was to ruin her reputation, not her life.

Lydia blushed but continued. "And please do not hurt me, if you understand my meaning."

He was no longer in the mood to tease her. Brodie held her gaze evenly. "I willna force you, lass." He kept his tone gentle as he addressed the deepest fear she seemed to have about him. "But be warned, I canna help it if you decide you want me. There are only so many times I will be able to resist you."

"You think I would try to seduce *you?*"

He chuckled. "I think in time you will be begging me to bed you, lass. You willna be able to help wanting me."

Her eyes narrowed. "You think far too highly of yourself if you assume I would ever beg you for anything."

"You just did, lass. You begged me to touch you, and I surrendered to your pretty plea."

She stared at him, lips trembling, and he felt like a cad.

"Rest, lass. We have a while to go before we stop again to rest. I'll not touch you again . . . for now. You may sleep without fear." He moved back to his seat across from her, and she began to relax. In a few moments, she fell asleep, and he simply watched her.

That sense of something being off continued to bother him. He had every reason to believe that this was the woman who'd ordered his abduction. It had to be pity he felt. She was reaping the consequences of her actions, and she was terrified, as she should be.

His instincts rarely failed him, yet right now those same instincts warned him that there was something wrong about Miss Hunt. Something he was missing and couldn't understand. It bothered him more than he wanted to admit.

JANE RUSSELL HURRIED UP THE STEPS OF THE

townhouse that Lysandra said was being rented by Rafe Lennox. They'd only just left Lydia Hunt's townhouse. No one had been at home, but Lysandra had begged the butler, Mr. Annis, to tell them what he knew about Lydia. A horrifying story had been related in whispers.

"I wouldn't tell a soul, Miss Russell, but as you are a close friend of my lady, and I know you have her best interests at heart, I must tell you the whole affair," the butler had said to Lysandra.

Jane could barely believe what she'd heard. Mr. Kincade's drugging and abduction. Lydia's discovery of Kincade and her attempt to rescue him. The drugged Scotsman stealing Lydia away into the night at knifepoint. It was almost too incredible to believe.

The crucial bit of information lay in that Kincade had taken Lydia to Rafe Lennox's residence. The driver had, after being questioned by Jane, admitted that he had lied about where the coach had taken Lydia and Kincade.

"Oh, Mama, I hope she is here," Lysandra said as Jane tapped the knocker under the door.

"As do I." Jane didn't want her daughter to know how truly worried she was about Lydia Hunt. Abducted. Held at knifepoint. Taken away in the night. The child was ruined if word ever came out about this, and she was in grave danger. Jane was determined to help her.

The door to Mr. Lennox's house opened.

"We are here to pay a call on Mr. Kincade," Jane said to the butler.

"I'm terribly sorry, madam, but Mr. Kincade is not home at present."

"When shall he return?" she asked quickly. Time was of the essence if she was to bring Lydia home. She might then be able to concoct a story that would explain Lydia's disappearance and thereby save her reputation.

"He has left Bath, madam," the butler replied uncertainly.

"And Mr. Lennox? Is he at home?"

"No, the master is also abroad."

"Abroad?" Jane asked. "What the devil do you mean, *abroad*? Did they run for France? Did they take that poor girl with them?"

The butler held up his hands. "Madam, please calm yourself. Please, do not upset yourself. The master would not wish anyone to suffer a fit of hysterics."

"*Hysterics?*" Jane pushed her way past the butler and into the foyer. "You would perish on the spot if I ever succumbed to hysterics. Bah!" She spun and jabbed a gloved finger into the butler's chest. "Where have they gone, and do they have that poor girl with them?" Jane narrowed her eyes. "And should you even contemplate trying to deceive me, know this—my son is Lucien Russell, the Marquess of Rochester, dearest friend to Ashton Lennox, the older brother of your master and the person who pays to keep this house running and staffed. Think wisely about your next words."

The butler's face was ashen. "I have no intention of deception, my lady. The master and Mr. Kincade, along with their female guest, departed for Scotland."

"Scotland?" Lysandra gasped. "Do you think they've gone to Gretna Green? Is Lydia to be married to Mr. Kincade?"

The butler swallowed hard before he answered Lysandra's inquiry. "No, miss, they are bound for Edinburgh."

"Not Gretna Green? But it is so much closer. Surely the inconvenience would—"

"Lysandra, dear, what I believe the man is trying to say is that Mr. Kincade does not have marriage in mind. Am I correct?"

Again, the butler nodded, his face pale.

"Oh heavens. Poor Lydia," Lysandra whispered.

"Where in Edinburgh are they bound?" Jane asked firmly.

"I do not truly know, madam. Lord Lennox has a residence there, a modest townhouse, but it would likely be closed up this time of year."

"Write down the address, please," Jane said, though it was not a request. As they waited for the butler to return, a handsome man about Jane's age rushed up the steps. He removed his hat before he knocked on the open door.

"Hello? I'm sorry to intrude, but is Mr. Kincade home?"

Jane sized up the man and at once saw some likeness to Lydia. This had to be the girl's reckless father. "Mr. Kincade is not here. Are you Mr. Hunt?"

"Er . . . Yes, madam." He eyed her more curiously now. "Are we acquainted?"

"Indeed we are not, but now is the least appropriate time to bother with formalities. I am Lady Rochester, Dowager Marchioness of Rochester."

"It is a pleasure to meet you, Lady Rochester, but I am on a most urgent mission." His apologetic expression softened Jane's temper a bit.

"Yes, we know, Mr. Hunt. You may know my daughter, Lysandra Russell." Jane stepped aside to allow Mr. Hunt into the foyer with them.

Mr. Hunt bowed again. "Miss Russell." The rigidity in his form no doubt came from the stress of the situation, and Jane felt compelled to put him at ease.

"Lysandra and I are going to help you find Lydia. It is why we are here."

"You know what happened?" He kept his tone quiet as his gaze darted around to search for servants who might be listening.

"Unfortunately, we do. We have learned that Mr. Kincade, Mr. Lennox, and your daughter are bound for Edinburgh."

"Edinburgh? Why there?"

"Mr. Lennox lives off the means of his older brother, Lord Lennox. Lord Lennox has a townhouse there that is currently closed and therefore empty except perhaps for a handful of servants. It is the perfect place for men who are up to no good to hide."

"Indeed." Mr. Hunt's face darkened. "Do you know the address?"

"We are waiting for it now," Jane said, and then the butler returned and presented her with a piece of paper.

"Thank you. Good day." She spun, leaving the poor servant to stand there gawking at her as she exited the house. Lysandra and Mr. Hunt followed on her heels.

"I thank you most graciously for your assistance, Lady Rochester, but I should handle the matter now." Mr. Hunt reached for the slip of paper, but she snapped it out of his reach.

"Nonsense. You and I shall be handling this together. Lysandra, you are to return home and stay there. Mr. Hunt and I shall find Lydia and return with her."

"We're going to what?" Mr. Hunt blustered.

"You heard me. You and I shall go together. You still have much to explain. In the meantime, my daughter will spread word that you have taken Lydia on a trip in the countryside."

Jane tugged her white kid gloves tight and fixed the gentleman with a stern look. His brown hair was fashionably cut, with hints of silver at the temples. Jane had to admit that she liked his face, the proportions of his well-formed features. He was tall, with a muscular build. Had it not been for what this man had recently done, she would have found him attractive. As it was, he was due a lengthy lecture on good behavior, and she was just the person to provide it.

"But we . . . We have only just met, Lady Rochester."

"And?" she challenged. "I am a widow, you are a widower, and we have far more important matters to attend to than worrying about gossip. I care not one whit what anyone says. Why should you?"

"Well, it's just . . ." Mr. Hunt's cheeks turned red, and he looked suddenly bashful.

"Come now, Mr. Hunt, we're both respectable adults, and we are wasting precious time as it is if we are to find your Lydia."

"Right. Then we shall take my coach." He gestured toward his conveyance, which was standing behind theirs.

"Not yet. First, follow us to my residence. I will pack quickly, and then we may be off."

"Very good, very good," Mr. Hunt murmured, apparently still in a bit of shock at the sudden turn of events.

Jane almost smiled. Even at her age, she still had the ability to surprise good-looking gentlemen. Her heart twinged as she remembered how she'd run away to Scotland to marry her late husband all those years ago.

She missed him every day, but over time the wound of his passing had begun to heal. She found pleasure

LAUREN SMITH

with her friends and in pursuing interests outside of the home, but a part of her deeply missed other forms of companionship.

Were there ever second chances for a widowed woman in her fifties? When she glanced one last time at Mr. Hunt before climbing into her coach, she couldn't help but wonder.

8

Lydia was surprised that she had managed to sleep at all in the jostling coach after what had happened between her and Brodie. When a particularly hard bump in the road jostled her awake, she found that Brodie had wrapped her in his coat. The enticing scent of man and woods drifted up from the heavy dark-blue fabric.

She shifted beneath it, testing her injured wrist. It felt stiff but no longer painful. That was a small relief. The last thing she needed was to be hurt while traveling so far from her family. And after what had happened a few hours ago, she would need every bit of strength to deal with Brodie. She wasn't sure if she was grateful that Mr. Lennox chose to ride on top of the coach with the servants, leaving her alone with Brodie, or if it would be worse to have him inside the coach, watching Brodie seduce her. She was quite certain Brodie wouldn't mind letting a rake like Lennox watch him kiss her.

She trembled as she remembered how Brodie's commanding mouth and wicked hands had set her body on fire. She'd been afraid—not of him, but what he made her feel. He'd sent riots of wild, frightening pleasure through her. All he'd had to do was touch her and she'd practically exploded.

Lydia had touched herself between her legs once or twice, during bathing, but she'd always been confused and a little scared of the sensations those few brief touches had given her.

Yet Brodie had boldly explored her and seemed to know just where and how to caress her to make that excitement build and finally create a wild release that had made her scream, though he had dampened much of her cries with that kiss. It was likely that Rafe and the valets riding outside on the top of the coach would have heard her, and her face burned with mortification that she had indeed begged him to touch her.

At least she had convinced Brodie to agree to a few rules when it came to his treatment of her, though he had danced around actually saying yes to her rules during their discussion. Still, she was confident—or hopeful, at any rate—that he would see fit to treat her with some modicum of respect and provide her with some necessities while she belonged to him.

Lord, the word *belong* seemed to carry such a weight

to it now, a sensual promise that worried her as much as it excited her.

Peeping at Brodie from beneath her lashes, she tried to imagine what life as a mistress would be like, and more importantly, what her life would be like afterward. Once he became bored with her and she returned home in disgrace, what then? It was a good thing she liked the countryside, seeing as how she would likely be relegated to a quiet life in some quaint cottage after her father had married Portia to whatever man she desired next.

"I can hear you thinking, lass." Brodie's voice rumbled as he stirred in the corner of the coach opposite her. He stretched out his long, lean, muscled legs toward her, his booted feet nestled beneath the shelter of her skirts, touching her own. It was an oddly intimate thing for two veritable strangers. Their feet touching under the concealment of her clothing. It made her aware of every little move he made as he shifted in his seat from time to time to become more comfortable.

"Are we to stop soon?" She pushed back one of the curtains on the carriage windows. The green landscape was dark with shadows. "The sun is setting."

"Aye, soon," Brodie replied as he continued to watch her with an unsettling half smile.

"You really must stop looking at me like that, Mr. Kincade," she warned.

He gave her a full smile now. "Like what?"

"Like you are thinking of terrible, wicked things."

"I hate to tell you this, lass, but I am a terrible, wicked man. It is in my nature to think of such things."

"Oh!" she huffed. "Your brothers did not seem so uncouth as you when I met them." She hadn't realized until she discovered Brodie's identity that she had glimpsed Brock and Aiden once at a ball, but she hadn't really known much about them, nor had she seen Brodie that night.

"What do you know of my brothers?" he demanded, smile vanishing.

"Not much, but I saw them at the ball where Joanna Lennox . . ."

"Slapped my brother?" He was grinning again. "Why do you think she slapped him? It wasna because he was kind and gentle."

Lydia didn't believe him. Joanna would never have run off to Gretna Green with a terrible man. She was all kindness and compassion, and only the best of men could have ever won her heart. Brock Kincade had to be a paragon of virtue compared to Brodie, whom she was growing more upset with every passing hour. Yes, he was attractive, but his handling of her had proved he was a terrible man, and that was not an opinion that would change soon, no matter how much she liked how he kissed.

"If you are bored, you may come over and sit on my lap." He patted his strong thigh with one hand. "I promise to find a way to entertain you."

NEVER TEMPT A SCOT

"You would like that, wouldn't you?" she shot back and let the coat he had put around her fall to her lap. His gaze swept over her body, and she had to fight the urge to cover herself with it again.

"I would indeed. When a man suffers frustrations, there is nothing better than to take a lass to bed and"— he let his eyes fall to her breasts and hips before he continued—"satisfy his needs in the roughest, most enjoyable ways possible. I could make you scream my name, Miss Hunt, and you would beg me for more."

Lydia threw the coat at him, which he easily caught with one hand. She wished she had heavier, harder things to throw. Of course, she suspected anything thrown at his block head would likely break instead. She finally sighed. "Are you going to be like this always?"

"Like what?"

"Exasperating." She waved a hand at him. "You will drive me mad."

"Then yes, I will always be this way. You know, I think I like you angry at me, lass. An angry woman has no place for fear, and I don't want you to fear me."

"You don't?" she asked. She hadn't expected that.

"No. And besides, you flush so prettily when you're raging at me."

"I do not rage," she huffed in protest.

"Aye, you do, and I find it appealing. You don't scare me—you amuse me."

Lydia wanted to scream. "I'm not here to amuse you, you cad!"

His tone changed to one far more serious. "No, you are here to please me."

She was suddenly exhausted with dealing with this stubborn man, and her rare show of a temper was returning.

"I'm here because you are a stubborn fool. I told you I'm not the woman who bound you to a bed and drugged you. That was Portia, my younger sister." Lord, if she ever laid eyes upon her sister again, Portia would have a great deal to answer for.

"And I believe you are clever enough to lie and invent a sister who does not exist to engender my sympathies. It will not work."

"If only that were true," Lydia muttered. "Someday when you realize how you've been mistaken as to my identity and character, I pray that you will suffer dearly for it," Lydia growled. She was done being polite. It had gotten her nowhere with this man. To think that she had been jealous of Portia when she'd assumed her sister's beauty and their father's money would win this man over. No, this man was odious, controlling, and a bully. He was everything she despised in a person. Yet when he kissed her, she seemed to forget all of her qualms and complaints.

I must endeavor to avoid such things whenever possible. He may turn me into his mistress, but I do not have to make it easy for him.

The coach came to a stop, and a few voices outside came closer. The door nearest Brodie opened, and Rafe peered inside. The sun had fully set now, and lamplight from a nearby coaching inn silhouetted him from behind.

"You two all right in there? I thought I heard shouting," Rafe said with a smirk.

Lydia stood, collected her reticule, and made to leave the coach. Rafe reached for her waist, lifting her down to the ground. Brodie leapt down behind her, his boots crunching on the stony road beneath him.

"See if you can acquire three rooms," Brodie said to Rafe.

"Three? My heavens, you do work fast. Well done, old chap." Rafe turned and walked into the inn.

"Why did he say that? Why three rooms?" Lydia paused as she counted in her head. A room for Rafe and Brodie, a room for the valets, and a room for her. Well . . . that was thoughtful. So why did that make Rafe laugh? Did he find it amusing that Brodie would let her have her own room?

She followed Rafe into the inn and tried to ignore the heat of Brodie's body as he stayed close behind her. The inn was busy, and nearly every table was full. Rafe leaned against the bar, one leg bent casually as he leaned in to speak to a man at the bar. The man handed Rafe three sets of keys.

Brodie put a possessive arm around her waist. "Over here, lass." They wound their way around the tables to one of the few empty ones left. Rafe passed by them on his way toward the door and tossed Brodie a key.

"Where is he going?" Lydia asked.

"To see to the coach and horses. We'll be resting the horses rather than changing them."

"Oh." She took a seat, and Brodie joined her, pulling her tight to him, his arm staying around her waist. "Mr. Kincade, please, do not"

"Hush. This is one of *my* rules. You are never to leave my side in a place such as this. And before you argue, 'tis not my pride but your safety I'm thinking of."

Lydia did not disagree with that. The men around her eyed her with open interest. One rather frightening looking man even leered at her.

"Pretty piece of muslin you have there," he said to Brodie. "How much for a quick taste?"

Brodie's hand on her waist tightened. "She is, isn't she? But I canna share her. She's my wife, you ken. No good Scot ever shares his woman, especially his wife."

If Lydia hadn't already been controlling her expression, she would have jolted at Brodie calling her his wife. It was only for the sake of dissuading the interest of the other men, but it still startled her.

"Ah, some men aren't so picky where coin is involved.

If'n you change your mind, I'll be here." The man winked at Lydia.

She scooted closer to Brodie, a wave of panic making it hard to breathe. What if he changed his mind about her? What if he became upset with her and tossed her to dreadful men such as these? She had no money, no way to get home. She was not brave like Joanna, nor was she clever or inventive like Lysandra. She was a woman with little choice but to throw herself at the mercy of Brodie Kincade.

"You're trembling," Brodie whispered in her ear as two glasses of wine were brought over.

"Please, Mr. Kincade, do not give me to those men." She expected him to laugh and say he might just do that if she didn't please him. Instead, he seemed quite furious, but not with her.

"I wouldna do that. I'll not let a man lay a hand on you, you ken? You're safe with me, lass."

She hated that *lass* sounded wonderful on his lips. She placed one of her hands on his. "You mean that? You swear it?"

"I do." He nudged her glass of wine. "Now, drink up. I'll have some food brought over." He waved the serving maid down and ordered three bowls of soup. Rafe joined them a few minutes later.

"Not the safest crowd here tonight. Quite a number of ruffians outside." Rafe said this calmly to Brodie, like he was reporting on the weather.

"Aye. Someone offered to pay me for time with Miss Hunt."

"Oh, that's famous," Rafe chuckled. "Did you kill him?" He glanced around. "Should I ask where you hid the body?"

"I thought it best not to rip off any arms before we had our dinner."

"Quite right. Wouldn't do to spoil our appetite." Rafe grinned at Lydia, as if she were somehow in on the joke.

When they had finished their meal, Brodie reached for her hand. "You had better get some rest. The horses will be fresh tomorrow morning." He led her upstairs, stopping at one of the rooms and handing her the key Rafe had given him.

"Lock yourself in," Brodie counseled.

"Oh, but I need a maid," she whispered. "Could you send one of the young ladies from downstairs up to see me?"

"What for?" He looked her over critically.

"My dress. I cannot undo it on my own."

"Is that all?" He shouldered his way into her room. She gasped in protest, but before she could stop him, he had turned her around and was unlacing her gown and stays. He did it far more gently this time than he had the night before, and for that she was grateful.

"There. Now, to bed with you," he ordered.

Lydia waited until he had left the room before she removed her loosened gown and the stays, along with her stockings and slippers. She retrieved a dark-red shawl embroidered with green vines and draped it around her shoulders to stay warm. It was not overly chilly for a June evening, but after everything that had happened, she felt very small, very alone, and very cold.

What was her family up to? Surely they'd tracked Brodie's movements back to Rafe's home, but then what? Did her father even suspect that they'd left Bath? Would Cornelia be shouting the roof down about scandal and wildly fluttering her ostrich feather fan to keep from pretending to faint?

A smile pulled at Lydia's lips. Hadn't she longed for a change of pace? For her life to have a bit of adventure? Well, she certainly had it now. More than she could handle. Abduction by a Scottish scoundrel, scandalous passion with said scoundrel, and a wild ride to Scotland. Only what her fate would be once they reached Edinburgh she couldn't know. That was part of the risk of having an adventure—one did not know if one would ever return.

She thought back to the book *Park's Travels in Africa* with a heavy heart and wondered if her fate would match that of Mungo Park. He had traveled up the Niger River and drowned after trying to escape an attack from natives. All of his journals, his maps, and his observations during his second journey into the heart of Africa had washed away in the jungle river. Adventure had cost him his life, as well as that of his sons, who had dared to follow in his footsteps. Only his daughter had survived to continue his legacy, but she'd had no chance for adventure . . . being a woman. That was just as tragic in a different way.

"What will be my legacy?" she asked herself as she sat down on the edge of the bed.

With her reputation ripped to shreds and her virtue soon to follow, she would have nothing left on which to survive. A woman's value in society lay in her virtue, cruel and unfair though that was. Lydia desperately wished the more fanciful articles that Lady Society penned in the *Quizzing Glass Gazette* would come true, that women would one day be given a chance to have value in trade or employment.

She had no head for figures or sciences like Lysandra, but she was diligent and organized. She understood everything about efficiency in one's household. She had taken control of her father's home and run it for the last five years, better even than most married women would have.

Lydia had a talent for hiring servants to certain positions and training others so they might improve their situations. The servants of the Hunt family were incredibly loyal because of that. They knew that Lydia valued them and, more importantly, that she sought to help them better themselves. She insisted that everyone, right down to the scullery maids, learn to read and write.

Consequently, productivity in the Hunt household increased dramatically.

If for whatever reason she could not live at home with her family, perhaps she could offer those services to her friends. Yes. Joanna, Lysandra, and the others of her close-knit group of friends would not abandon her after this, yet they would not be allowed to publicly be seen spending time with her. But if they hired her to consult on the running of households in a more efficient manner, that would give her an opportunity to see her friends. Clinging to that small bit of hope, she smiled.

And then, unexpectedly, strains of music began to come from below, a jaunty beat that soon had her feet tapping. She was unable to resist, and in a matter of moments, she found herself standing up in her bare feet and beginning to dance.

BRODIE REJOINED HIS FRIEND AT THE TABLE. "WHERE'S your kitten?" Rafe asked.

"In bed." Brodie waved for a pint of ale.

"I don't suppose she realizes you will be joining her tonight?" Rafe's blue eyes glinted with mischief.

"I dinna think so." Brodie smiled. "She will be surprised later on."

"Indeed she will." Rafe watched a man hang a circular wooden board on the wall, and several men stood, pulling knives out as they formed a line. The men began to take turns throwing the knives, trying to hit the bull's-eye that had been painted in the center.

"You bloody English canna throw to save your lives." Brodie drank his ale, watching in amusement as more than one man threw his knife too limply or too widely. A few maids screeched and ducked behind the bar when a knife would bounce off the board entirely, careening overhead.

"Care to show off your skills?" Rafe challenged.

"Aye. I'd be happy for the distraction." Brodie finished his drink in one deep swallow and pulled a slim blade that had been tucked inside his boot.

"With that tiny thing?" Rafe eyed the blade. Its handle was flat rather than rounded, to better fit against Brodie's leg in his boot.

"Size doesna matter. 'Tis how you use it," Brodie said.

"Not to the ladies it doesn't." Rafe snorted, and a few of the men around them chuckled with him.

Brodie took his place far away from the target. He gripped the knife by the blade and closed his eyes, which caused some people close to its path to take cover. He threw the blade hard and fast.

There was a thud and a carousing cheer.

"Bravo, well done—for a Scot," Rafe joked.

Brodie arched a brow. "For a Scot? Think you can do better, *Sassenach*?"

NEVER TEMPT A SCOT

"Well, certainly." Rafe's smile did not waver. "Everyone knows my brother is a master boxer, but while he learned to box, I learned . . . more practical things." Rafe snapped his fingers at a comely barmaid and held up a gold coin. "Love, please stand by the target and hold up this card by your face." He handed her a playing card he'd plucked from one of the tables nearby.

The girl, trembling, did as Rafe asked.

"Good, now don't move." Rafe winked at the girl as he pulled a dagger out of his coat. He grinned widely at the crowd and then became very still and quiet. His eyes hardened as he pulled his arm back, then with lightning speed threw the blade. It sang in the air for a mere second before it was embedded into the wood just beside the girl's cheek, right in the center of the playing card.

The girl drew in a deep breath and then crumpled to the floor in a dead faint, though completely unharmed.

"All right, I'll give you that," Brodie conceded. But throwing the blade was not a parlor trick for him. It was something he had learned out of necessity. He had caught rabbits to feed tenant farmers who were staying on their lands when his father raised taxes. A man only learned blade work like that of necessity. It made him wonder what had driven Rafe to learn such a thing.

Appreciating Rafe's skill with a blade, a few men near them ordered a round of drinks for everyone. Someone started playing a tune on a fiddle, and more than one maid began to dance for the onlookers, who cheered and clapped. Though Brodie could hold his ale well enough, he was perhaps a little too relaxed by the time he climbed the stairs and unlocked the door to the room he would share with Lydia.

What he saw startled him speechless.

9

Lydia was dancing.

Dancing in nothing but her pale chemise that clung to her skin as she moved provocatively. She curtsied to an invisible partner and then began to sweep a pointed foot across the floor as she gently waved her arms in a slow, prancing sort of dance. She was exquisite. Her hair came down in flaxen waves that gleamed in the candlelight. What he wouldn't give to be dancing with her right now.

A breath caught in his throat; Brodie was spellbound. She reminded him of the old stories of the fairy folk back in Scotland. Lydia could have passed for a princess. He leaned against the door, watching her with an ache in his chest that he had never felt before. It wasn't lust. It was . . . something else, as if her very dance symbolized something he'd always wanted but could not put a name to.

She spun on one foot, her arms above her head like a fine ballerina, and his heart continued to pound with boyish excitement. He wanted to catch her before she disappeared back to her royal realm, hold her close and breathe in that soft scent of wildflowers as he pressed his lips to her hair. But he couldn't. She was no fae creature. She was a woman, one who thought him a horrible scoundrel and feared him.

It was a sobering thought. Whether his anger was justified or not, he'd still let his temper get the better of him. Brock often feared becoming like their father, but Brodie knew better of his older brother. Brock had mastered self-control and was too compassionate to hurt anyone undeserving.

But not me, he thought. *I am more like our father than either of my brothers.*

Brodie was quick to judge, quick to throw a punch. He would never hurt a woman, not with his body, but with his words? He might. He had seen what harsh words could do. His father had never once laid a hand on their mother, but he had said unforgivable things to her. It had broken her heart, and she died so early in her young life, leaving four children to face their father's wrath.

"Oh!" Lydia finally caught sight of Brodie in the

doorway. She gasped and stumbled over a footrest she'd moved to one side. He moved fast, catching her in his arms and steadying her.

"Easy. I wouldna like it if you were to sprain a pretty ankle."

She tried to pull free, and he let her so he could close the door. When he turned back to her, she was reaching for the shawl she had draped across the bed, red-faced.

"I didna mean to startle you, lass. You looked quite fetching, dancing as you were."

Lydia's blush deepened. "I did not know anyone would be watching or I wouldn't have."

He stepped closer, but carefully, so as not to spook her. "Why not?" He moved like he was stalking a deer.

"I . . . well, it's rather silly to dance alone in one's sleeping clothes, isn't it?"

"There's nothing silly about doing something that one loves. Name any activity you like, and someone somewhere will consider it a silly pursuit, even reading in one's own library. So I pay no mind to what others consider silly, nor should you. Do you dance often?"

"Oh . . . some. I don't get asked to dance much at balls. There are far prettier women, like Portia, and" She stopped short and recovered. "I prefer to dance alone in my chambers. It's freeing."

He hadn't missed her comment about her sister. It had been delivered so easily, without thought. Was she

LAUREN SMITH

truly that good a liar? He supposed she might have been dancing for the exact purpose of dropping such a casual remark, but such a level of deception seemed unbelievable. Still, he would have to find a way to draw more details from her, either to learn the truth or to catch her in a lie. But that could wait. Right now he wanted answers about her love of dancing.

"Why don't men ask you to dance?"

"Why?" She stared at him. "I . . . I already said. I'm not in my first season, nor am I that beautiful."

Brodie drifted another step closer. "Not beautiful?"

She rolled her eyes, as if it was obvious. "My chin is too pert, my nose too buttonlike, my mouth too thin, my hair without luster . . ."

Brodie chuckled and gently caught her chin, turning her face this way and that, pretending to examine her.

"Oh, aye. I see the flaws now. Flaws everywhere."

Her soft blue eyes filled and began to glisten with tears.

"Your mouth is far too kissable. Men detest that. And your hair . . . it looks too silky. A wretched thing to have. And your throat, far too elegant and swanlike. I canna abide looking at it. Nor can I stand the soft flush of color on your cheeks or the way your eyes make a man think of warm spring days by a cool loch. Aye, you're too bloody attractive for my tastes, lass. I like my women to be pinch-faced with a meanness in their eyes and a sourness to their rosebud mouths."

144

Lydia started to laugh. "You really don't want all those things, do you?"

He rolled his eyes. "No, lass. I certainly do not. Do you not ken sarcasm when you hear it? I canna speak for those bloody English fools, but you are beautiful. Why you should think otherwise is beyond me."

He could see the disbelief still in her eyes. "I think I understand sarcasm better than you realize," she said defiantly.

"I mean it, lass. Call yourself unattractive again and I will put you over my knee. A spanking would set that mind of yours to rights."

She flushed deeply, much to his delight.

"You can't do that. I am a grown woman."

He trailed his fingers down her throat, his lashes lowering as he gazed at her parted lips. "I can and I will, lass. And afterward you will beg me to take you to bed."

"For striking me?" She arched a brow. "I'm quite certain I would not."

"You misunderstand me. It wouldna hurt much. It would ease into a burn that would make you desire me." Her breathing hitched, and he held in a laugh. "Now, I remember telling you to go to bed."

"I'm sorry. I was dancing because the music downstairs was so lively." She turned away from him to approach the bed. "Good night, Mr. Kincade. I hope you and Mr. Lennox sleep well."

"Thank you, lass. I'm sure we will." He began

undressing, and when she noticed, she halted midway through pulling the covers back on the bed.

"But you aren't sleeping here!"

"I certainly am." He smirked recklessly at her, and she wrapped her shawl tighter around her shoulders.

"But there are three rooms. One for me, the valets, and then you and Mr. Lennox."

"Oh, no. I'm not about to share a room with Rafe—not when I can share a bed with you."

That fear sparked in her eyes again, and he knew it was genuine. "I'll not touch you, lass, no matter how you tempt me with your dancing." He unbuttoned his waistcoat before he continued. "But you and I will share a bed. After all the misery you put me through, I am owed a few nights of feeling your sweet curves pressed against my body."

He tossed his waistcoat over a chair and pulled his long white shirt over his head.

"Now, in bed, Lydia," he commanded, though he kept his tone gentle. He gripped her shawl and slowly drew it away from her body, before letting it fall to the floor. Then he scooped Lydia up in his arms and tossed her onto the bed. She gave a little gasp of surprise at being plopped on the bed, before she scrambled under the blankets.

"I still think you should be staying with Mr. Lennox. It's not like I can escape. Where would I go?"

"I've underestimated your cunning once too often,

lass. Besides, I have no interest in watching him take a tavern maid to bed a few feet from me." He removed his boots, stockings, and trousers. Lydia stared at him like she'd never seen a man before, but perhaps she hadn't. Not like this, at any rate. He couldn't deny he was starting to think she was more innocent than she'd first led him to believe. But then, she wouldn't be the first lass to profess more carnal knowledge than she actually possessed.

He slid into bed beside her, wearing nothing but his smallclothes. The candle on the table beside him flickered, casting shadows over her face.

"Don't be scared, lass." He reached up to cup her face, and she closed her eyes but didn't pull away.

"I'm sorry, it's just that last evening you were still calmed by the laudanum, and tonight you are not hampered by it. I fear you will . . ."

"I will not," he vowed. "No matter how you tempt me."

Her eyes opened, and a spark of fire flashed in them. "Tempt *you*? By simply being here? It isn't a woman's fault if a man is tempted by her mere presence. That is your fault and yours to control."

"Aye, true. But you do tempt me, and I willna say otherwise."

Her eyes cooled a little, and he saw a return to a reasonable expression now that she felt less threatened.

"Why don't we talk a bit?" she asked. "Conversation

will help you focus on being a gentleman." Her tone sounded so calm, as though she were sitting with him in some drawing room and he'd come courting her with a bouquet of flowers like some lovestruck lad.

He chuckled. "Gentleman? You do say the most amusing things." But she was right, talking would distract him, at least for a little while, from his fantasies of the pleasurable things he would like to do to her.

"Very well. What should we talk about?"

"Well, what about your home, or Scotland? I've never been and would like very much to hear you tell me about it."

"You wish to hear about my home?" He hadn't expected her to care about such things, but she'd enjoyed the Mungo Park expedition book he'd given her.

He rolled onto his back, his gaze fixed on the timbers above their heads.

"I come from the clan Kincade. We live in the southern part of Scotland. Some would call us Lowlanders, but we aren't. Lowlanders are more English in their way of thinking. To a true scot, he can be a highlander even if he lives in the lowlands. All clans are different too, many would argue with the point I made just now."

"What does that mean, to be in a clan?" Lydia asked. "It's more than just a family, isn't it?"

"In the old days, before the Battle of Culloden, it did mean one's family. The word *clan* itself is from the Gaelic word *clann*, which means children."

"Children?"

"Aye. A man in a distant time began a family, and his name was carried on in the lives of all of his family members. And the people of Scotland, even as divided as we are by names, are all like the wild deer herds that roam the remote glens and mountain passes. We, like the deer, appear and disappear, vanishing into the dense forests, only to reemerge whenever we wish. We are the *Clann a' Cheò*."

"What does that mean, *Clann a' Cheò?*" Lydia moved a little closer, and he placed his hands beneath his head.

"It means 'children of the mist.'"

A soft sigh came from her side of the bed. "It's rather lovely, and it sounds fitting." Her tone was filled with a quiet wonder that stirred a strange feeling within his chest.

"Scotland is lovely," he agreed, and a sudden, undeniable need to be home filled him, making his chest tight. "Some call it a harsh land, because it has so few soft edges like England. But what is there—the cold lochs, the rocky mountains, the wooded glens and primeval forests—'tis stunning. All that is strong lives and grows in Scotland. There is a beauty to that."

He closed his eyes, picturing the lands around Castle Kincade, the way the light gleamed upon the green hills where the castle perched and the way the sky reflected upon the still waters of the loch nearby.

"That does sound rather wonderful."

"The land changes with the seasons. In spring, the fields are covered with wildflowers. In the summer, a heat settles thick upon the meadows until the storms come off the coast and carry away the humid air. And in the fall, as the leaves change and Samhuinn approaches . . ."

"What is Samhuinn?"

"Samhuinn signals the end of summer. We slaughter our fat cattle and preserve the meat for our long winter ahead. We also light bonfires to remember the old ways. Samhuinn Eve is the night when the shadow bodies of the dead walk once more amongst the living. That night, the veil between the worlds becomes as thin as gossamer. Many hills and ridges have special places where we set pyres ablaze to signal the start to a new year. It is said that this is where the living and the dead dance and sing in the flickering shadows together."

Lydia turned on her side to face him. "Do you believe the dead rise again during Samhuinn?"

"I do," Brodie replied, his tone quiet. "The first Samhuinn after my mother died, I was in the library. There was no candlelight—only moonlight filled the room. I saw a figure by the window. Her gown seemed to . . . I don't know how to describe it, but it seemed to be blurred at the edges, like smudges or the tendrils of black smoke crawling up from a dying fire. I didna know who the woman was until I approached her. She turned toward me, only to vanish in silvery mist. But as she did, I saw her face as clearly as I see yours now. It was my mother."

Lydia's eyes widened. "Were you frightened?"

"Of my mother? Never. She was a woman who held only love in her heart. But now I fear that someday my father will come back as she did. I doubt that reunion will be as pleasant."

"Your father is gone as well?"

"Aye, he is, and thank bloody Christ too."

"You didn't like your father?"

"No. I didna like him, and I certainly didna love the man. He was a cruel bastard. We buried him not too long ago, and I fear every approaching Samhuinn now that he will return. He would not be kind if he did. He would be angry and spiteful, and I dinna wish to see that."

"I can understand that." Lydia sighed, the sound so sorrowful it piqued his curiosity.

"I ken your father is alive, but what of your mother?"

"She's been gone six years. I lost her when I was fourteen. Portia was only twelve, and it was very hard on her and Papa."

Brodie kept still as he listened to her. He didn't want her to know that he was trying to detect any hint of deception in her story.

"You loved her, then?"

"Very much." Lydia's smile was soft and bittersweet. "She was an exquisite beauty, like my sister. I look a little more like . . . well, a faded watercolor version of her, at least according to my great-aunt Cornelia. You might remember meeting her at the ball."

"The old dragon who dragged you away at the ball?"

"Yes, but as I said, that wasn't *me*." Lydia's eyes met his solemnly. "I know you don't believe that, but I'm telling the truth. It was my sister. She's only eighteen and so very young and innocent, at least in some respects. I didn't know she would be so reckless, let alone that she would convince my father to do what he did."

There was a genuine earnestness in her eyes, but he wasn't convinced. "Even if I began to believe you, lass, your stories would do no good now. You are ruined, and you belong to me."

Though the truth was, even if she was as innocent as she claimed, he would not let her go. Not anymore. She was *his* woman, and he simply had to convince her of that.

"Please . . . I know you don't care about me. Let me go home, and I might still be able to find someone who would overlook my being compromised."

Brodie didn't want to hear another word. "No, lass. Ask me that again and I will silence you with a kiss, and if we kiss, I cannot promise that we willna do other things."

Lydia's eyes widened, and she rolled away from him. A moment later he heard sniffling as she wiped her face.

Bloody Christ, the woman was crying. He reached out and gripped her waist, pulling her against his body. She struggled for a moment but then surrendered when she realized she wouldn't get her way. He kissed her ear and then the crown of her hair, not to seduce but to soothe.

"You'll be fine. I promise. I will care for you. You'll have fine gowns, jewels, even a dainty white horse to ride. Whatever you wish."

She trembled in his hold, still refusing to look at him.

"I want my life, my freedom, my family, and a husband to love me."

Brodie was in that moment truly sorry, for he could give her none of those.

JANE RUSSELL WAS GLAD TO FINALLY BE OUT OF THE carriage after five hours. They needed to rest the horses before they could continue, and because night had fallen, it was best to stop and spend the night. Mr. Hunt exited the coach first and assisted her down. She stumbled on the uneven ground and fell against him. He caught her easily, and Jane's breath caught in her throat. She'd forgotten what it was like to be held by a man like this, the feeling for a moment of being young and . . .

She stopped the foolish thought before it could continue.

"Let's get inside. I'm sure you're hungry." Mr. Hunt offered her his arm, and they walked into the coaching inn.

Once their rooms were secured and luggage seen to, they retired to a private room for supper.

"I spoke with the innkeeper. He said he saw two men fitting Mr. Lennox and Mr. Kincade's description earlier. A young lady was seen with them. It must be Lydia."

Mr. Hunt sighed, the sound world-weary, as he took a seat opposite Jane. "Thank heavens. It seems we guessed the right road to take."

"It seems we did."

He raked a hand through his light-brown hair and gave Jane a thoughtful look. "I want to thank you for accompanying me, Lady Rochester. I'm not sure I could have handled this on my own."

Jane knew what he meant. He could have easily made the journey, but the worry for his child's safety would weigh upon him. No doubt he'd have second-guessed his actions until he was driving in circles.

"I am not one to be idle, and Lydia is a sweet girl."

Mr. Hunt nodded. "That she is. It's something I fear I did not remind her of enough."

Jane smiled. "You know . . . I had hoped earlier this spring of a match between her and my Lawrence."

"Really? What happened?"

"I'm afraid my son's affections were otherwise engaged. But I found myself exceedingly fond of your daughter."

Mr. Hunt smiled sadly. "I fear I have been a terrible father. Ever since I lost my Marianna, I let myself behave blindly, favoring my youngest because she resembles her so. I have spoiled Portia and disadvantaged Lydia most unfairly."

Jane reached across the table and covered his hand with hers. "It's easy to favor a child who resembles someone you love. Of all my children, Avery . . . he is so like my husband. I strive every day to give all of my children equal attention, but I admit it isn't easy. My two youngest seem to slip through my fingers at times."

Mr. Hunt relaxed, his eyes crinkling with a broader smile. "I admit, it gives me a small measure of peace to know I'm not the only parent who struggles with these issues."

"Indeed you are not." Jane suddenly grinned. "Perhaps we ought to start a society, one for single parents who need support in the raising of their children."

Mr. Hunt laughed, his good humor restored for the moment. "I would certainly join."

A maid entered the private room and laid out a supper of roast lamb and truffle soup. The two conversed for nearly an hour, long after the candles had burned low and the empty dishes had been carried away.

"We should rest. We will have another long chase tomorrow," Jane said finally.

Mr. Hunt stood and offered his arm to her and escorted her up the stairs and down the long corridor of rooms until they reached hers.

"I want to thank you again, Lady Rochester. Not only for your support in this affair, but for the amiable company you've provided. I had forgotten what it was like to spend time in the company of a lovely, charming woman."

Jane felt a sudden unexpected flush of heat roll through her. "I . . ." For the first time in years, she was speechless.

"I'm sorry if I have spoken out of turn," Mr. Hunt added hastily.

"No, it was just . . . I am shocked that I feel the same way. I hadn't realized I had missed the company of a man until now." She ducked her head, feeling shy in a way she hadn't in a very long time.

Mr. Hunt gently lifted her chin as he stayed close to her. "Would you do me the honor of calling me Jackson?"

He was close enough to kiss her, and for a wild moment Jane pictured him doing so. It was a wonderful image.

"Jackson . . ." She found herself smiling. "Then you must call me Jane. We seem to be bound in this quest, so it is only fitting."

"Indeed. Well, I shall bid you good night." Jackson

slowly stepped back and made a formal bow as she slipped into her room.

She closed the door, leaning back against it, her heart racing. It had been far too long since she had felt like a young woman. Far too long indeed.

❧ 10 ❧

Lydia was still not used to waking up next to a huge, muscled body, or *any* body, for that matter. The feel of Brodie behind her, one arm resting under her breast, made her body tense, though not necessarily in the ways she would have imagined. She was thankful that a layer of fabric, however thin, lay between his long, elegant fingers and her bare skin.

She began to carefully peel his fingers off her breast. With the last finger freed, she slowly moved his hand back to his own body. He suddenly sighed and shifted, placing his hand on her hip as he found a new position.

Blast the man!

She had a desperate need to use the chamber pot, and he wouldn't release his hold on her. There was nothing for it but to speak to him.

"Mr. Kincade, if you please, I need to use the chamber pot." She pinched his arm and repeated her demand when he still showed no signs of responding.

After the third time, Brodie groaned dramatically and rolled over.

"Fine, go," he grumbled.

She scrambled from the bed and had just crouched over the pot when she realized he would hear her.

"Could . . . Could you leave the room for a minute?" she asked.

He started to sit up, and she dropped her chemise back down to cover her legs. "Leave the room?"

"I can't go when you're *listening*."

He started to laugh but then choked down the sound. "I was sleeping, lass, not listening."

"Well, you're awake now."

"I dinna care if you fill the pot and the vase on the dresser. Just go and be done with it."

"Now I truly can't go with you here," she almost growled in frustration.

"I willna leave the room," Brodie's tone was just as gruff. "Go or not, 'tis your choice."

Lydia glowered at him, not that he could see her. She needed so badly to go, but she couldn't go as long as he was here. Tears pricked her eyes. Never had anyone made her feel so weak or helpless before.

"Fine. I'll sing for you, lass. I swear, I willna be able to hear a thing."

He then broke into a Scottish ballad as he rolled onto his side facing away from her. He even chuckled at his own bawdy lyrics, not that Lydia understood them, such was the heavy brogue he used in the song. Soon Lydia relaxed, and she was able to see to her needs and then wash up on the washstand. Only when she was done did his voice die away.

"You have a lovely singing voice, Mr. Kincade," she said, trying to fill the silence. When she looked toward the bed through the reflection of the mirror on the washstand, she saw that he was watching her again. He was propped up on one elbow, his gray-blue eyes drifting over her body.

"I'm no songbird, not like my brother Aiden. He sings to his wee beasties when he thinks no one is around."

"His wee beasties?" Lydia retrieved her wrap and covered her shoulders—and especially her breasts—as best she could. She'd never been concerned about the thinness of her chemises before, but then, she'd never been so close to a man in what she was now convinced was the thinnest fabric ever created.

"Aye. He has an affinity with animals. Ever since he was a wee tyke, he's been able to gain any animal's trust and companionship."

"What sort of animals do you mean?" Lydia drew closer to the bed and sat down on the edge closest to him.

"Well, he has a badger. That one tends to sleep in Joanna's bedroom, which is fine with her, since she and Brock always share his bed."

Lydia flushed at the mention of her friend sharing a bed with a man, even if that man was her husband.

"We have an owl, a tawny one about the size of a pigeon. It made a nest in one of the taller bookshelves in our library. He's a pretty fellow, very friendly. And then Aiden has a pair of otters, a pine marten, and a hedgehog."

Lydia couldn't resist smiling. "My, that is a lot of beasties."

"They give him comfort. Our father" Brodie stopped speaking abruptly.

"What about your father?" Lydia scooted closer, sensing that whatever he had been about to say was a deep confession of something.

"My father was a brutal man, especially after our mother died." He turned his shoulder to show her the scars on his back.

Lydia covered her mouth with one hand and reached out with the other to touch his skin. He didn't flinch, but instead held very still while her fingers traced the knotted scars along his otherwise perfect, muscular back.

"How did he . . . ?" The words died on her tongue as she imagined how a man would make these marks, but she couldn't fathom how any father could do that to his child.

"I was a fair bit younger, and he was strong. All of us felt his wrath at one point or another, but Aiden bore the worst. He was the smallest, aside from our sister, Rosalind. We all took as many beatings as we could to protect her. I managed to escape most days, but not Brock and Aiden. They wouldna leave Rosalind." He looked down at his feet. "I was a *coward*."

"Surviving doesn't make you a coward, Brodie."

Brodie dragged a hand through his hair and looked at her. "You called me Brodie."

"Yes, I shouldn't have, Mr. Kin"

"No," he said, cutting her off. "You must call me Brodie. I insist." He fixed her with a possessive stare.

"Really, I cannot"

"You can and will. You have shared my bed, and you belong to me. You will call me Brodie." There was a warning in his tone that she was not foolish enough to ignore.

"Very well . . . Brodie."

"Now, 'tis time to bathe. I'll have them bring the bath-water up." He left the bed, and Lydia covered her eyes. Well, she tried to. It was hard not to at least risk a peek at him. She parted her fingers and stared at his mostly naked body. His legs were thick and muscled, but also long enough with his great height to look perfectly proportioned.

She knew some men would actually put sawdust or other fillers in their stockings to make their calves bigger. In fact, at a ball once she'd seen an older man who had stuffed his stockings in such a way. She only learned this because the sawdust had come loose onto the floor around him as he walked, and it had become obvious to everyone what he had done. Lydia had helped conceal his legs with her skirts while she escorted him to one of the withdrawing rooms, where he had a chance to fix his appearance. But the gentleman had been so embarrassed that he had decided to go home.

Brodie interrupted her thoughts. "What are you thinking about?" He'd put on a pair of buckskin trousers and his dressing gown.

"Oh, it's nothing."

He raised a brow but didn't demand any answers. He left the room, and she took a moment to search her own luggage for a dressing gown. Thankfully, Portia had thought of that—or more likely, her maid had.

Poor Phyllis. She must be so afraid. Mr. Annis would have told the entire household what had happened by now. She couldn't help but wonder what her father had done in response. Had he gone to the local magistrate? Had he pursued her himself? She hoped so, but what if he caught up to them and challenged Brodie to a duel? *He might die.* The thought made her sick, and she bent over, trying to quell the sudden unease of her stomach.

The door to their room opened, and Brodie

returned, followed by a pretty young maid, who set a tray down on the table in the center of the room. "A bit of breakfast, miss?"

Lydia wasn't exactly hungry now, but the buttered toast and muffins did look good. Brodie watched her take one and nibble on it. The maid soon returned with a fresh pot of tea, and after an admiring look at Brodie, she left them alone.

Brodie nodded at the tray. "Eat."

"I am." Lydia held up the half-eaten muffin.

"Eat *more*. You're too thin, lass. A man likes a bit to hold on to when he makes love."

Lydia frowned at him, then at the muffin she was just starting to enjoy. Her temper, which so rarely flared, now erupted. She threw the muffin straight at his head. Unlike her punches, she was a far better thrower, and he caught the muffin right in the face.

"You shouldna do that, lass. I have a temper to match your own," he warned as he wiped crumbs off his cheek.

"Don't say such things! You keep reminding me that I am some common woman for you to use."

Brodie's eyes twinkled. "You're wrong, lass. I wouldna treat a common woman this way."

"So you admit to treating me *worse*?"

"No," he said and stomped over to her. His bare chest was visible as his dressing gown was open.

"Then what?" she demanded. "What am I to you?"

"You asked to be treated like my mistress. Well, a man *cares* for his mistress. He treats her well, clothes her, feeds her, makes love to her when he bloody well wants to, and she doesna get upset when he teases her."

"If this is your idea of teasing, you are a cold and heartless monster."

Brodie's eyes widened momentarily and then narrowed. "Cold and heartless, am I? You dinna know what you are saying. I am neither."

He grabbed her roughly and hauled her to him, slanting his mouth over hers, possessive and angry as he claimed what was his.

"I am a man who treats his woman with respect and affection," he said silkily in that rich Scottish brogue. "He kisses away her anger and reminds her that he cares for her and her pleasure."

Somehow when he said this, it held less of a threat and more of a gentle promise that made her heart race. As much as she hated him for kidnapping her, she didn't want to fight him. And as much as she hated herself for admitting it, she enjoyed these moments of heated passion. She was beginning to wonder if she had tried to anger him just to make him do this.

He carried Lydia to the nearest chair and sat her down upon his lap so he could continue to kiss her at his own leisurely pace. Brodie lifted a hand to her face, gently pressing at the corners of her mouth, and she opened her lips at his gentle but firm demand. The sinful, wicked way that his tongue plunged in between her lips and the way he played with her body left her breathless and excited.

He stroked his fingertips along her neck and rested his forehead against hers as they caught their breath. Lydia put a hand to his chest beneath the dressing gown, not to push him away but to simply touch him. His skin was warm and hard, yet smooth to the touch. Brodie Kincade was a hot-blooded specimen of a man. As terrible as her situation was, she had to admit that she was glad she would learn the pleasures of the bedroom with this man and not someone she wasn't attracted to.

"Better now, lass?" he asked in a soft, intimate tone.

"Yes." She couldn't leave, not when she could feel his heart beating so steady and firm beneath her palm. "I do wish you would just ask to kiss me," she mumbled. Although she was, against her own good sense, starting to like when he stole kisses from her like this.

"Good." He let her up off his lap.

She was still recovering herself when there was a knock at the door. Brodie called for whoever it was to enter. A trio of boys came in, each with big wooden buckets of steaming water. They poured them into the copper tub in one corner of the room. After two more trips the tub was full enough, and Brodie nodded at her.

He sat down at the table to eat with his back to her. "Time to bathe."

"I don't suppose it's worth asking you to afford me some small measure of privacy?"

"No. I will keep my back turned. That's all you get, Lydia." He caressed her name in a way that sounded far too scandalous.

She stood there a full minute before he spoke again. "Better hurry or the water will go cold," he warned.

Stripping out of her dressing gown and chemise, she climbed into the tub and sighed as the hot water enveloped her. She wanted to stay longer, but Brodie's presence made her far too self-conscious to do more than the essentials. She washed her hair using a bit of rosewater and then stepped out and wrapped herself in a large clean cloth. She then searched her luggage for a fresh chemise and thankfully found one. Only when she was safely in her dressing gown again did she face Brodie. He still had his back to her.

"Finished?" he asked.

"Yes."

"Good, 'Tis my turn now." He stood and removed his dressing gown. Before she realized what was happening, he had removed his smallclothes and was striding toward the tub completely naked.

"Mr. Kincade!" she gasped.

"I respected your modesty, but I never claimed to have any of my own to be concerned about."

She knew she had to turn away but was still too

stunned to do so, seeing first his front and then his backside.

"Paint a picture, lass, if you wish to gaze upon me longer," he chuckled. "Or you can join me. The tub is large enough."

Lydia turned away, aroused in a way that only added to her mortification. "No, I think not."

She kept her back turned and listened to him splashing about. Even that was enough to give her plenty of fantasies, however. She busied herself, or at least tried to, by focusing on what she would wear. Without a lady's maid to assist her, it was rather difficult to decide. Perhaps she could have one of the maids who worked at the inn to assist her. She would need some help, at any rate, especially with her hair.

She heard the water splash again as Brodie exited the bathtub, but she didn't dare risk turning around. "Better ring for a maid," he advised. "And have my valet come and attend me as soon as you are dressed."

Lydia shuffled over to the cord with her back to Brodie at all times and pulled it. A nice young woman answered the call. It was the girl who'd brought them breakfast.

"Yes, miss?"

"Would you mind helping me dress?" she asked, thinking quickly. "My maid has been delayed on another coach."

"Of course." The girl came into the room but froze.

Unable to contain her curiosity any longer, Lydia turned and saw Brodie seated in the chair wearing only his dressing gown. His dark hair was wet and curling at the ends, which only made Lydia's heart race.

"Please, don't mind him," she told the girl. "He's only my"

"Husband," Brodie replied. "Forgive us if we are enjoying our honeymoon a bit too much."

Lydia couldn't believe him. Why had he said they were married? Did he actually care about her reputation, despite all his statements to the contrary?

"Oh, never, sir. You make a lovely couple. I'm sure your children will be beautiful," the girl said, her cheeks a dark red as she assisted Lydia into a bright bishop's-blue day gown. The hem of the skirt and her bodice had been embroidered with red swallows. It was not a fancy gown, but it made her hair and skin shine more. After she took a moment to style Lydia's hair, the maid quickly curtsied and left.

"Why did you do it?" Lydia demanded as she whirled to face Brodie.

"Do what?"

"Call yourself my husband?"

Brodie sauntered up to her, placing his palms on her shoulders and peering down at her. "I suppose that's a fair question." He tilted his head to one side. "Maybe I don't wish for the innkeeper to think you are a lightskirt and toss us both out. It is better to appear as though all is proper between us, you ken."

Lydia couldn't deny his words had a ring of truth to them.

"Well . . . That does make sense," she agreed.

"And 'tis easy enough to say we are married when we aren't," he added with a wink. "Now, you do look bonnie, lass. Will you run and fetch Alan for me?"

"But"

"Go on, he's only three doors down to the left. I would go, but I think I might cause a scandal." He waved at his obvious state of dishabille.

"I thought you said you had no modesty to worry about."

"I don't. I'm only concerned about yours."

Lydia smiled. "Very well." She left the room and walked down the hall. She froze at the sounds of a man grunting and a woman gasping coming from a few doors down. As soon as it registered what must be going on inside, she blushed. It was the middle of the morning. She'd always thought such things were to be done only at night under darkness and with the protection of bedclothes. At least, that's what she'd been told by Cornelia when she'd gone out for her first season. She could still hear the woman's lecture now.

"You must never be alone with a man, even one who seems kind. You must never go walking with a man . . . riding with a man . . ."

Essentially, Cornelia's advice was to do nothing with a man until she was married. And after she was married: *"Never lie with a man without your nightdress on, or let him take you to bed before nightfall. And you must never let him see you bare-skinned."*

The list had been almost endless. Portia had tittered at all this, but Lydia had wanted to believe her aunt. She was starting to wonder if Aunt Cornelia might know far less about men—and even women—than she claimed she did. Lydia reached the door Brodie had indicated and knocked.

Alan, Brodie's valet, answered the door. The young man looked startled as he realized who had disturbed him and Rafe's valet in the midst of polishing boots for their masters.

"Good morning, Alan. Mr. Kincade has need of you, when you have a moment."

Alan nodded. "Of course, miss. Thank you." He closed the door behind him and headed for his master's room. Lydia lingered outside the door to give Brodie the privacy he had denied her. The energetic sounds from the other room had stopped, and Lydia wondered what was going on now. The door suddenly opened, and she leapt back. The young maid who had helped her dress that morning exited the room, fixing her hair and skirts.

"Oh, pardon me, miss." She blushed as Lydia stared at her. The girl muttered something about tea before she rushed away, leaving the door wide open. Rafe Lennox lounged in a chair by a small table in the middle of the room, grinning at Lydia.

"Morning, kitten. Did the mean old Scot toss you out?" He rose from the chair and waved for her to come inside.

"I don't think I should," Lydia said. If he had just made love to that maid, he might want another to take her place, and she certainly did not want that.

"I won't bite, kitten. I've had enough pleasure for a few hours. I promise on what little honor I have left that I won't touch you."

Lydia was still hesitant when she entered the room, so she left the door open.

"By all means, leave yourself an escape route. I will not stop you. Besides, Brodie seems quite possessive of you. We've shared women before, but he won't share *you*."

Lydia wasn't sure what shocked her more, his mention of sharing women or hearing that Brodie would refuse to do so with her.

"He won't even let me ride in the coach that often, and certainly not alone with you. You honestly think I want to stay on horseback for hours at a time or ride on that bloody top seat with the servants? Christ." He grinned. "And then I miss all the fun of him raging at you when he won't see the truth sitting in front of his face."

Lydia's heart sped up as she wondered what he was talking about. "What truth?"

"Who you are, of course. You see, I was not nearly so foxed as he was the night of the ball. I remember the little chit who introduced herself, and it certainly wasn't you. You are not Portia Hunt, but Lydia—friend to my sister, Joanna." He was chuckling now. "Kincade kidnapped the wrong sister. How bloody marvelous."

Brodie paused with his hand inches from Rafe's door. He heard voices inside. Moments ago, he'd finished dressing and had gone looking for his wayward abductee, but having seen his friend's door ajar, he'd wanted to see what the man was doing. Then he recognized Lydia's voice inside. For a moment he was stirred to panic and even rage. Was his friend trying to seduce Lydia? Or was Lydia in fact the seducer? Either scenario seemed possible.

He'd already come to the conclusion that his little beauty, his secret dancer, was not all that she seemed, but what had made her seek Rafe out rather than Brodie? Perhaps she intended to manipulate Rafe now that she realized her tricks did not work on Brodie.

He scowled as he fought to contain his temper, the temper that haunted him like a curse. But it wasn't only anger that churned within his gut. He felt . . . betrayed. Betrayed by both his friend and Lydia.

Brodie took a deep breath, trying to rationalize his overreactions, as Brock had always tried to teach him to do. He wasn't a brute, no matter how much Lydia insisted he was. Yes, his temper could be a fierce thing, but he would never direct it at her in a physical manner.

Rafe, however, was another matter. Damned if he didn't want to throttle Rafe at this moment. He took a step closer, leaning in to better hear their voices and to figure out just what he'd stumbled upon. If he didn't like what he heard, he'd barge into the room and deal with it.

"And then I miss all the fun of him raging at you when he can't see the truth sitting in front of his face." Rafe laughed.

"What truth?" Lydia asked in an angry voice. That made Brodie almost pleased. His little captive certainly wasn't happy with Rafe.

"Who you are, of course. You see, I was not nearly so foxed as he was the night of the ball. I remember who the chit was who introduced herself, and it certainly wasn't you. You are not Portia Hunt, but Lydia—friend to my sister, Joanna." Another laugh escaped Rafe. "Kincade kidnapped the wrong sister. How bloody marvelous."

Brodie's heart stopped. That couldn't be true. If it was, it made him a blackguard of the worst kind. It meant he'd kidnapped an innocent woman and held a knife to her throat, and . . . she'd been telling the truth all along. All of his actions toward Lydia had hinged upon his belief in her guilt, and now he was the guilty one. He was a monster. He was no better than his father.

"I tried to tell him that, but he won't listen." She sounded frustrated, almost to the point of shouting—or perhaps crying with rage.

"Of course not, kitten. He's a Scot. Stubborn and tempestuous is their nature. It cannot be helped." Rafe's tone was conciliatory, as if he completely understood Lydia's anger and frustration.

"Why didn't you tell him?" Lydia pleaded. "He would listen if you were to tell him the truth. I tried to free him, and he has ruined me forever. *Please*, convince him to send me home."

Brodie winced as the truth sank in like a pugilist's left hook to his head. She had been telling the truth. She was Lydia, and Lydia was the elder sister, innocent of the other sister's acts. She had been trying to save him from the start, and all he'd done was abduct her at knifepoint, abuse her tender sensibilities with his temper, and force his attentions on her more than once.

Shame, an emotion that Brodie rarely felt, overpowered him in that moment. He'd ruined her life. She'd tried to help him that night, and he'd devastated her with his actions.

"Sorry, kitten, I am no gentleman, regardless of how I present myself in society. I am enjoying this little battle of wills between you two far too much." Rafe chuckled in clear delight.

"Then you are worse than Mr. Kincade. At least he's honest about his ill intentions," Lydia accused. It was backhanded praise that was not at all deserved. Honest about his ill intentions? It only made Brodie's guilt deepen until it felt like a great weight pulling down on his stomach.

He was a bastard. When his brothers found out, he would take a beating to be sure. Perhaps it was not too late to send her back? No. Her father was likely on their trail as it was, and given what he'd been capable of before, Brodie fully expected the man to be prepared to put a bullet through his heart.

He rushed back to his chamber to have Alan pack at once. He needed to reach Edinburgh, fast. He had to find a way to fix things. Not that he was sure that was even possible. The ways of English society were like a deep bog covered in reeds to provide the illusion of stable ground. It was more likely that he'd make matters worse somehow.

Perhaps he should take her to Castle Kincade instead? Let Joanna and Brock take care of her? They could escort her home and perhaps concoct some kind of story explaining her absence. At least then he could escape facing the girl's father on the dueling field.

The one thing he could not do was let Lydia know he had learned the truth. She would want to go home to Bath, and he wasn't ready to let her go. It was selfish, but he had to admit it. In the last two days, he had grown accustomed to waking with her in bed beside him. He was also completely addicted to kissing her. The innocence he had believed she feigned was already luring him in like a siren did a sailor to perilous rocks. He was hopelessly infatuated with her. And knowing that she was not the heartless chit who'd had him abducted, but rather that she was the sweet woman she'd appeared to be . . . It made him even more protective and possessive. He wouldn't share her with anyone. Perhaps he truly should turn her into his official mistress and treat her as such, with all the pleasures and things that would see to her every comfort and desire.

If he did that, things would have to change, of course. She couldn't travel unaccompanied any further. She needed a proper maid to look after her.

He called to his valet as he was finishing folding up a shirt to pack away. "Alan."

"Yes, sir?" the young man answered.

"Run downstairs and inquire whether one of the more decent maids would be willing to work as a lady's maid. Offer a proper wage."

"Yes, sir. Right away." The lad left the room, and Brodie paced back and forth, considering his options.

He would take Lydia to Edinburgh, and he would keep moving as long as he thought her father was still on their trail. Perhaps her father would give up before too long. Unlikely, but still a possibility.

"Mr. Kincade? I found a woman to be the lady's maid," Alan announced.

Brodie looked up to see the comely maid who had brought them breakfast.

"You agree to serve as a maid to my wife?" Brodie asked the girl. Behind her, Alan's eyes widened when Brodie said *my wife*, but the young man made no other betrayal in his features.

"Yes, sir. I have been wanting to leave my employment at the inn for some time. My mother was a lady's maid to a gentlewoman. I know what is expected." The young woman bowed her head respectfully. "I also know that anything that I learn while in service will be kept a secret. I wouldn't wish to endanger my ability to have a future reference should I leave your employment."

"Ah.." Brodie sighed. "So you know then that the woman isna my wife?"

"It wasn't hard to guess, sir. I've seen a few trysts under this roof since I've started working here."

Brodie stared hard at the maid but he saw no hint of dishonesty in her.

"Very well, the woman is Miss Hunt...er...my mistress."

"Understood, sir. I will address her however you wish."

"Miss Hunt is fine. Thank you for your discretion.

Alan, pay the lass an advance on her wages so she may start the journey with us at once."

Alan retrieved Brodie's coin purse and paid the young woman, who flushed and offered Brodie and Alan a smile of thanks.

"What is your name?" Brodie asked her.

"Fanny Mullins, sir."

"Thank you for joining us, Fanny. Miss Hunt will be pleased to have you helping her." He glanced toward his valet. "Alan, have Miss Hunt's luggage put aboard the coach, then see that Miss Mullins has what she needs as well."

"Yes, sir." Alan collected the valises and the heavy trunk full of Lydia's fine gowns. As the valet and the maid left the room a moment later, Lydia returned, no doubt upset over Rafe's blatant refusal to come to her aid.

"I have been thinking, lass," Brodie said carefully. "It wasna right for me to make you journey without a maid. I have found a suitable one here, the girl who brought us breakfast. She is trained and has agreed to help us. She and Alan are packing up the coach."

"Oh . . ." Lydia blushed. "Thank you, I appreciate that."

Brodie looked upon her with a new light. Rafe was right—he had missed the truth that had been right in front of him this entire time. Of course, last night he'd admitted to himself that he no longer cared if she was the clever, scheming little creature he had thought her to be. He wanted her in his bed, no matter what. That desire hadn't changed, only now he knew full well that he would be seducing an innocent. Granted, she had professed an interest in what he had to offer, but it didn't make what he was thinking any more right.

But perhaps, if he did it correctly, he could sate his desires and hers. If he offered her a true position as his mistress with her willingness, they could find their enjoyment in each other for a while to come.

He knew he was a selfish bastard to want her like this. Maybe he should reconsider. Perhaps when they reached Edinburgh, he would find someone else to tempt him before he succumbed to his desire for her again.

He shook himself out of his conflicting thoughts. "I had better go see that Rafe is prepared to leave. You may wait outside for us."

Lydia lingered a moment longer, blocking his exit.

"You have need of something?" he asked.

The rosewater scent from her bath wafted between them. He had shared the bathwater, but where the rose scent had faded on his skin, it still clung to hers. He knew that if he closed his eyes, he would feel like he was at Castle Kincade once again.

He could almost picture it—Brock and Rosalind sprinting ahead of him, Aiden lagging behind, clutching a wee beastie in his hands. They used to chase each other between the towering hedgerows and around the blossoming rhododendrons that grew so tall and thick in the spring and summer that they blocked entire paths of the garden.

"I . . ." Lydia hesitated. He saw clearly in her eyes that whatever she'd been about to say she had chosen to bury instead. "Thank you for the maid."

"You already thanked me," he replied with a crooked smile. Her face warmed with another blush.

"Right, yes. I'm sorry." She stepped out of his way, and he passed by her, their bodies brushing in a way he enjoyed far too much. He stepped over to Rafe's room and knocked.

"Come in," Rafe called out.

Brodie entered and saw with relief that Rafe's valet was already packing away his things.

"Good, you're nearly ready. I wish to be off at once."

"Oh?" Rafe eyed him with curiosity. "What's the rush, old boy?"

"I wish for us to be there sooner," was all he would say. If Rafe planned to continue to hide the truth about Lydia from him to amuse himself, then Brodie had no desire to share his plans.

"Still haven't bedded the wee lass?" Rafe said, imitating Brodie's Scottish accent.

"No, I havena and willna until we reach Edinburgh."

"Why the wait?" Rafe asked. "It is easy enough to

manage in a coach or bed in some cozy little inn like this."

Brodie continued to keep up the pretense that he still thought Lydia was guilty. "She may be a conniving creature, but I believe her when she says she is a virgin. I won't take a virgin in a coach or some inn. She will have a first time in a fine bed in a fine house."

"Nice to see you do have some gentleness about you, old boy," Rafe said.

Brodie snorted. "I have a little, but my temper often covers that up." He left Rafe and his man to finish packing and headed downstairs to wait with Lydia.

The stable yard was full of coaches, some finely painted, some adorned with family crests or shields of heraldry, while others were red-and-gold Royal Mail coaches. The rest were public or private stagecoaches but far less fancy.

Rafe's coach was blue and silver, with the Lennox crest emblazoned on the side. They were lucky to ride in such a fine conveyance. It had plenty of room on top for luggage and for servants to sit facing each other in pairs on the perched seats. Alan and Fanny climbed up to their seats, and Lydia stood beside the coach talking to them. The morning sun created a halo of gold light around her flaxen hair and a slight breeze played with her skirts which displayed hints of her curves. She was a bonnie lass. *A bloody innocent lass,* he reminded himself.

Rafe and his valet joined Brodie in the yard a minute later.

Brodie came over to her by the coach. "Ready to leave?"

"Yes." Lydia peeped up at him before looking away.

The coach driver lowered the step for her, and Brodie offered her his hand rather than shoving her inside as he had been doing. She placed her hand in his, that small sign of trust making him proud. She took a seat opposite him, and Rafe joined them inside, chuckling as he did so.

"So, you hired a maid for our guest?"

"I did," Brodie replied warningly as he saw Rafe smile.

"Excellent choice," Rafe said. "Very nice girl, Fanny." He winked at Lydia, who blushed. Brodie was no fool—he assumed that Rafe must have bedded the maid.

The coach driver closed the door, sealing the three of them in, and a moment later they were off. It was another six hours to Edinburgh, but Brodie would find some way to amuse himself, since he couldn't very well toss Rafe out of his own coach, though right now Brodie was tempted. He pulled out the stack of books and saw Lydia's eyes brighten with interest.

Brodie studied the books he had recently purchased in Bath and passed her one.

Lydia looked at the title. "*The Spy?*"

"Aye, 'tis a new book by an American, James Fenimore Cooper. It is about a good man who is wrongly accused, and even the men closest to him doubt his innocence."

Lydia's eyes grew frosty. "My, how could I ever relate to such a story? It's so beyond my limited experience in the world."

Brodie realized what he'd just said, and he felt the weight of his guilt grow. "Well, things work out for him. In the end, he shows through his actions that he is innocent. It is a lesson that one should be judged by one's actions, not by one's class or reputation."

Lydia returned her gaze to the book and turned to the first page. He liked the fact that she was a reader. Some men scorned reading when they could afford other entertainments, and women were expected to read only if they were unmarried and had no children. Both views seemed ridiculous to him. Brodie's mother had raised him to love books, to see the value in every printed page, and the words of wisdom each held.

He spent the next three hours watching every small movement she made as she read. Her blonde hair, artfully styled by Fanny that morning, had a few loose curls framing her face. They weren't the tight, perfect kind of curls most ladies wore. These held a gentle but wild look about them. The way they caressed her cheeks made him envious. He wanted to touch her. He wanted his lips to kiss that creamy skin while she blissfully sighed his name.

At one point, Lydia noticed his attention and tried to distract him by asking questions about Scotland now that they were over the border. Her interest in his country was a surprising and pleasant thing, so he told her as much about his homeland as he could.

After some time, Rafe spoke up. "I say, as fascinating as this lecture is about . . . misty mountains, lochs and whatnot . . . do you mind if we stop? I need to attend to my needs."

"Of course." He opened the coach window and told the driver to stop at the next bit of woods. Rafe popped out of the carriage before it even stopped rolling and headed straight into the nearby woods.

"Would you like to stretch your legs?" Brodie asked Lydia.

"Oh yes, please. I would appreciate that." She set the book aside, and he assisted her out of the coach. "I do believe I may need to see to my needs as well," Lydia admitted quietly, her face flushed.

"Are you able to do it in the woods?" Brodie was surprised. She seemed unlikely to be comfortable with that.

"Yes, I'll be quite fine, so long as you're not listening." Lydia actually smiled, amused at his reaction.

"Don't go too far, lass. I wouldna want you to get lost."

"I won't. I shall keep a straight path in this direction," she assured him as she pointed.

He kept a close eye on her figure as she disappeared into the woods. If she didn't return in ten minutes, he would go after her to make sure she was all right. He wasn't worried about her escaping. Where would she go? But it was all too easy to become lost in the thick woods of Scotland and lose one's way.

LYDIA CAREFULLY PICKED HER WAY THROUGH THE woods, keeping in mind to maintain a path back as straight as possible. If she yelled, she was certain Brodie would be able to hear her and come running.

When she finished, she spotted a nearby stream, where she washed her hands in the cool water. The stream babbled over sandy-colored stones, smoothed by centuries of water rushing over their surfaces. She picked up one of the smooth stones and brushed her thumb over the almost glass-like surface. It was lovely here in Scotland. Brodie had explained how the Highlands and Lowlands varied and how all the northern lands above England had a harsh beauty to them.

She slipped the stone into a pocket of her skirts to have as a keepsake, but then she froze at the sight of a tall, red-haired man staring at her from twenty feet away. He wore a leather coat and dark trousers, and he looked to be in his late forties. Harsh living had taken its toll on his once-handsome features, leaving a series of craggy lines as he scowled at her.

Uncertain of what to do, she tried to smile at the man, but something warned her that he was dangerous. Why else would he be silently watching her in the woods with no one else about? She had no choice but to walk in his general direction, as he blocked her path back to the coach, but she was careful to make a wide arc to avoid him. He turned only his head as she started to pass by him, and she was so focused on him that she never saw the true danger coming.

Someone jumped at her from behind, clamping a dirty hand over her mouth and silencing the shout that rushed to her lips. Another man grabbed her from the front, binding her wrists and gagging her with a cloth. Lydia thrashed about as one man lifted her into the air. Her feet struck the man in front of her in his groin. He doubled over, grunting as he cursed.

"Little shite!" He got to his feet and slapped her hard across the face. Pain exploded through her with a force that left her ears ringing.

"Bind her legs!" the man holding her from behind growled. He squeezed her ribs, making it hard to breathe. Terror ripped through Lydia as she fought for her life, but when a third man joined them, she had exhausted herself. She was pushed to the ground and her legs bound with rope. The red-haired man lifted her up and tossed her over his shoulder. She struggled to lift her head as the three men took off at a run, but she was jostled so much she couldn't see where she was.

They stopped a short while later, and she was set down on her feet for a brief moment while the men mounted horses they had tied in a copse of trees. Then she was hoisted up and laid facedown over the lap of the red-haired man, his hand holding her back still over the horse. She dared not move, barely dared to breathe, lest she fall and be trampled as the horse took off in a mad gallop.

They rode for what felt like hours. The sun was perched on the horizon when the men finally slowed to a stop. Their leader, the red-haired man, stopped his horse at a dense clump of woods. Lydia was dropped unceremoniously to the ground, where she fell to her knees and gagged. One of the men noticed and removed the cloth from her mouth so she could vomit.

"Christ, Willie, she's sick," the man who'd helped her complained to the red-haired man.

"Get her up and walking a bit. It will clear her head," Willie said. Then he nodded at the third man. "Fergus, let's set up camp here."

Lydia's legs were freed but not her wrists. The man behind her gripped one of her arms roughly and pulled her into motion.

"You heard him. Walk, lass," he growled.

Stumbling over the rocky ground, she tried to calm her panicked breath in hopes that it would ease her upset stomach. She licked at her chapped lips and winced as she tasted blood. Her lip was split, probably from the blow she had been dealt earlier. Her face and neck hurt, but she could handle the pain.

Her stomach finally settled, and when she and the third man returned to the camp that they set up, a new set of fears replaced her nausea. What did these men want with her? What were they going to do with her?

"Sit." Willie pointed to the ground, and she did as he ordered. The three men faced her as they sat by the small fire, which was contained by a ring of stones.

"Give her the flask," Willie told Fergus. Fergus passed her a leather flask, scowling as he did so. She recognized him as the one who had slapped her.

Hands shaking, she accepted it, taking a large drink. She gasped, choking. It was not water but whiskey. The men laughed at her reaction as she tried to catch her breath and returned the flask to Fergus. He took it back and handed her a flagon.

"This is water," he said.

"Thank you," she replied, her voice raspy. She gulped down the water until Fergus snatched the flagon from her.

"That's enough. We dinna want you to become sick again."

Lydia touched her wrists, which had been rubbed raw by the thick ropes.

"May I please have these removed? I won't run away. I haven't the faintest idea where I am."

"See, Reggie?" Fergus snorted. "I told you she was a proper English lady."

"Cut her loose," Willie commanded in a deep, curt tone that sent chills down her spine. "You canna run. And if you do, we *will* find you, and you willna like us when we bring you back."

Lydia nodded. She was not a fool. Running away would only get her killed, or exposed to the elements with no ready source of food, water, or shelter.

Reggie pulled a small but dangerously sharp blade from his boot and cut the ropes around her wrists. Her skin was raw and bleeding in a few places. Lydia bit her lip to hold back a whimper. These men had very little kindness in them, and they would have no sympathy for her pains, but she needed to find out what she could about them.

"Excuse me, but why did you take me?"

"For a pretty English bird like you, those fancy gents you were traveling with would do anything to get you back. They'll pay a hefty price for you," Willie explained.

"But how will they find me?" she asked.

"We left a note where we snatched you. It tells them where to meet us tomorrow and how much we want for you."

They must have been prepared to take the first traveler they came upon that they could snatch up from amongst a party who dared to stop at the side of the road. It was a clever enough plan, but they had chosen poorly. She wasn't entirely sure that Rafe and Brodie would come after her. She hoped they would, but now that Brodie was rid of her, perhaps he would be glad she was gone and think nothing more of her. What then? Would these men let her go, or would they kill her?

"Go ahead and sleep," Willie ordered. "We'll wake you when it's time."

Lydia lay down on the ground, shifting to find a position that was somewhat comfortable, which she soon learned was impossible. As she lay there, she listened to the men whisper in the dark, their words little more than the soft hisses and clicks of a language she didn't understand. It must be Gaelic. She finally drifted to sleep, dreaming of Brodie and wondering whether or not he would come after her.

BRODIE SCANNED THE EDGE OF THE FOREST. IT HAD been nearly fifteen minutes, and there was still no sign of Lydia.

"Rafe, I'm going after her," he called out.

Rafe waved a hand at him to indicate he had heard. Brodie, his hand on the knife in his coat, started toward the woods. He moved slowly, studying the way the branches had broken as he followed the trail Lydia had left. He paused at a clearing near a small stream. Dozens of footprints were imprinted deep in the soaked grass, and one of Lydia's blue hair ribbons lay on the ground, ravaged with mud. Beside it lay a folded bit of paper. A hasty note had been scrawled on the paper.

We have your woman. Meet us at noon tomorrow at the Boar's Head Inn on the main road. Bring two hundred pounds or she dies.

Brodie crushed the note in his fist. A blood rage swept through him, so powerful that if the men who had taken her had stood before him at that moment, he would have swung a broadsword as his ancestors had in the past and taken their heads clean off. Instead, he drew a steadying breath and made his way back to the coach.

"Rafe!" he bellowed. Rafe was leaning against the coach, his arms folded.

Rafe pushed away from the coach, his lazy, sardonic manner vanishing. "What? Didn't you find her?"

He pushed the crumpled note into Rafe's hand. "She was taken." Rafe smoothed out the note and read the message aloud.

"Bloody Christ," he growled. "So, do we meet them?"

Brodie stared at the four horses for a moment. "No. Here's what we'll do. Free one of the horses. I will follow their trail. You will continue down the road to the Boar's Head and wait for me. If they arrive and I dinna come, you pay whatever they ask and wait for me to join you."

"I'll go with you," Rafe said.

"No, you can't. I need to ken that you will protect Lydia and free her from those men if they reach the inn before I can catch up to them."

"You don't think there's any chance they'll be on the road ahead of us?" Rafe asked.

"Would you, if this was your plan?"

"No, I wouldn't. I would stay off the main road and hide a safe distance away, somewhere I felt comfortable I wouldn't be attacked, or where I felt I would have a decent chance of seeing anyone coming."

"They willna see me coming," Brodie said in a dark tone that matched his rage. If they harmed her, he would kill every one of them.

"Are you sure you don't want me to come?" Rafe asked. "You know I like the kitten, and if they hurt her . . ."

"They'll be dead," Brodie vowed.

"So long as we agree on that." Rafe's voice was as cold as a loch in winter.

"Take a pistol." Rafe reached into the coach and pulled out a pistol from underneath the coach cushions, which Brodie accepted with a frown. He would have preferred at least two pistols so he wouldn't have to take the time to reload in the midst of a fight. "Mr. Withers, release one of the front horses. We have need of it."

As soon as a horse was made ready, Brodie mounted it without a saddle and took off into the evening light.

He could follow her trail even in darkness as long as the moon was out.

Once he found her, he would deal with those bastards who had taken her. He whipped the long reins over his body to strike the horse's flanks and urged it onward, leaning forward as he rode into the growing gloom.

❀ 12 ❀

Lydia stirred just before dawn, her entire body aching, as though she had slept on a bed of rocks. She rubbed her cheek against her pillow, only to wince as something hard and cold dug into her face. She came awake with a start and stifled a moan as she found she had indeed slept on a bed of rocks.

The sky overhead was a murky gray that still bore hints of the passing night. The campfire was nearly dead, with bits of logs aglow with burning embers and the smell of the smoke teasing her nose. On the opposite side of the fire, the three Scottish bandits were lying on thin pallets on the ground, seemingly asleep.

Rubbing her eyes, Lydia sat up. The movement caught Willie's attention.

"Don't move, lass," he warned.

"Would you prefer I relieve myself here?" she whispered.

Willie kicked Fergus's stomach. "Wake up, you arse. She needs to piss."

Fergus rolled over and scowled up at the sky. "So?"

"I said *git!*" Willie kicked him again. Fergus got to his feet, grumbling as he grabbed Lydia by the arm and dragged her to the nearby woods.

"Go and piss," he grunted.

"I'm sorry, but I cannot go with you watching me," she said, meeting him stubborn stare to stubborn stare.

"If ye really need to go, you'll go, me watchin' ye or not."

Lydia crossed her arms. "Are you so backward that seeing me would arouse you?" It was completely uncouth to say that, but she wanted him to know how foul he was being.

"Fine. I'll turn my back, but don' do anything stupid like try an' run. Ye willna get far, and I'll take more'n a might of pleasure dragging ye back."

Lydia wanted to tell him exactly what she thought of him, but she had a feeling it would end with another slap. Instead, she turned and headed for the nearest clump of bushes. She saw to her needs quickly, and when she returned she held out a hand. "Your flagon, please."

"What for?"

"I wish to wash my hands."

He passed her the flagon from his hip, and she

poured water over her palms before drying them upon her dress. She didn't feel as clean as she wished, but it was better than nothing. She plucked a few larger leaves and twigs off of her gown.

"Let's be getting back," Fergus snapped.

Just as they returned to the small clearing, Fergus tensed and stopped dead in his tracks. Lydia, who'd been focused on the ground so as not to trip over a root or rock, walked right into him.

"Oof!"

"*Shush!*" he hissed, and slowly pulled out a long dagger from his coat.

"What is it?" Lydia asked in a whisper. Fergus ignored her, and his head swiveled back and forth as he surveyed the campsite, where the other two men were still sleeping.

Smoke billowed up from the dying fire as a fresh breeze stirred the embers to life. Suddenly, through the haze, she saw a man running toward her. Lydia's heart leapt into her throat as she saw Brodie bound from the trees opposite her and Fergus. He was sprinting, his feet a blur as he charged the sleeping men on the ground between them.

"Willie! Watch out!" Fergus bellowed. Willie and Reggie bolted up, pulling daggers from their boots.

Brodie skidded to a stop, raised a pistol, and fired a shot. Reggie sank to his knees and toppled over.

"You bastard!" Willie rushed at Brodie, and the two clashed in a clang of knives and fists.

Both she and Fergus stood their ground as the two brawny Scots fought like ancient Celtic warriors. But Fergus soon shook off his shock and grabbed Lydia from behind, pressing a dagger to her throat.

"Not a sound," he warned in a deadly tone. "Or I'll cut your pretty neck to ribbons." He dragged her back deeper into the woods. She was still able to watch Brodie battle the other man through the trees.

Willie dealt a glancing blow to Brodie's shoulder. Blood soon stained the fabric of his clothes, but he didn't stop. He kept fighting, pushing Willie back toward the fire. He caught Willie's fist in one hand, and the other held the blade now aimed at his heart.

Holding Willie's wrists, he forced the man back through sheer brute strength. When Willie's feet touched the burning fire, stirring up sparks, he hissed and tripped. Brodie fell with him, both men rolling until they came to a sudden halt, with Brodie lying beneath the other man. Lydia nearly screamed, but the knife at her throat kept her silent.

"Ha! Willie got him!" Fergus hooted.

"No, please no . . ." Brodie couldn't be dead. Not because of her. He couldn't be.

Tears blurred her eyes as Willie shifted and rolled off Brodie. As she blinked the tears away, she realized that it wasn't *Willie* who had moved, but Brodie. Willie fell onto his side, and she saw that a dagger was buried in Willie's chest, hilt deep.

"No!" Fergus yelled.

Brodie scrambled to his feet, pulling his own dagger again as he searched for the source of the cry. When he spotted them, he started forward slowly, his blade at the ready.

"Not another step!" Fergus shouted, and he pushed the knife deeper into Lydia's throat. She couldn't help it —she yelped at the prick of pain, and Brodie froze.

"Release the lass and I willna kill you," Brodie called out.

"No!" Fergus snapped. "Ye killed my brother!"

Brodie retrieved the pistol he had dropped and calmly began to reload it in the clearing. "You wish to join him?" His movements were slow and eerily calm as his gaze moved between them and the pistol as he worked to reload it.

Fergus took another few steps into the woods, keeping her in front of him. After a tense minute of her and Fergus watching Brodie, he faced them again.

"Let her go, man. Or I'll put a bullet between your eyes." He calmly raised the pistol level with their faces.

"You'd better let me go. He's a crack shot." Lydia honestly had no clue how good of a shot Brodie was. Likely he was good, but she did not wish to test that by risking her own life.

"All right!" Fergus hollered. "I'm letting her go." He

released his hold and pulled his knife away from her throat. Lydia took a few tentative steps forward before she was sure she was free. She dashed toward Brodie, who opened his arms, and she leapt into them without a thought. He swept her up and spun her behind him, putting himself between her and Fergus. She clutched Brodie with relief, but when she glanced over her shoulder, she saw Fergus running toward Brodie, his dagger raised.

Without thinking, Lydia shoved Brodie out of the way. Fergus crashed into her, and she felt a blinding pain in her left arm.

Brodie stabbed his blade into the other man, sinking it deep into Fergus's chest. The man stumbled, caught the blade, and pulled it out. The look of surprise on his face lasted a few seconds before he fell to his knees and collapsed.

Lydia stared down at the knife wound on her arm.

"Are you hurt?" Brodie saw the bloody gash on her upper arm.

She raised her eyes to his and tried not to gasp with the pain.

"Christ, hold still, lass. You're bleeding." He pulled a handkerchief from his coat and lifted her arm.

Lydia gasped as he pulled the fabric of her sleeve away.

"I'm sorry. I wish you didna have to feel that, but there's no time for gentleness." He examined the wound and then wrapped a handkerchief around her arm. "Hold that tight." He knelt at her feet and lifted her skirts. She was in too much pain and shock to question what he was doing. He cut part of her petticoat off and used it to wrap around the handkerchief and cinch it tight.

"That should do for now, but we need to find a doctor." He glanced at her body. "Can you walk? I have a horse waiting. It isna far."

"Yes." She gladly followed him when he offered her a hand, placing her good hand in his outstretched one.

By the time they reached the horse hidden a good distance away, her legs were trembling and she was beginning to stumble. Brodie caught her just before she collapsed in his arms.

"Hold on to me, lass."

"I'm so—sorry." She buried her face against his chest as tears flowed down her face.

"You have nothing to apologize for, lass, you hear?" He brushed a kiss to her hair and then against her forehead. "It is I who should apologize. I shouldna have let you go off alone, modesty or no. I kept telling you how beautiful Scotland is, lass. But I forgot to remind you that it's dangerous." He held her for a long moment in the thicket, until she found her panicked breathing had eased.

"Now, can you ride?" he asked.

"Yes, I think so."

"Good." He grasped her by the waist and lifted her onto the horse's back before climbing on behind her.

"Sorry there's no saddle. Lean back against me. You can rest while we ride."

She leaned back as he suggested and started to close her eyes. "How far are we from the coach?"

"Quite far, lass, but we aren't going that way. Those men meant to trade you at an inn farther up the road. I dinna know how far away it is. Rafe wanted to come with me, but I feared I wouldna find you in the dark and might be too late. So I sent him to the inn with the coach to pay your ransom if I couldna catch up to you first."

Lydia hadn't realized how exhausted she had been until she was safe in Brodie's arms. Funny that she would think of being with him as safe, given that he had *also* abducted her. Yet here she was, resting against him, grateful that he was the one who'd found her.

She tried not to think about the men he had killed. She did not mourn them, yet at the same time she couldn't help but see them as desperate men doing what they felt they must to survive. She felt oddly guilty that Brodie had taken their lives to save hers. Would he hate her for it? Perhaps he didn't care at all. Perhaps that was life in Scotland.

During the ride, she somehow managed to drift in and out of a light sleep. The horse's quick canter was at first jostling, but it soon became a soothing rhythm. At one point she thought she was dreaming, but she realized she was half-awake as Brodie sang a song to her in Gaelic. The language was soft, seductive, and exotic in a way that made her feel homesick for a land that wasn't even hers.

"We're here, lass." Brodie gently stirred her awake as they neared a small coaching inn, with a faded painted sign that read "The Boar's Head Inn."

Rafe, who had been standing outside the door, rushed toward them. "Bloody Christ!"

"Take her inside and find a doctor," Brodie said.

"Come on, kitten." Rafe carefully helped Lydia to dismount. "Who is the doctor for?"

"I got stabbed . . . but only a little," Lydia replied, raising her wounded arm, giggling at the absurdity of it all.

"Only a little? Hell's teeth, you're in shock, my dear," Rafe muttered. "Best to get you some warm food, a bed by a fire, and a stout glass of brandy."

"That sounds lovely," she agreed, and let him escort her inside the inn.

⚜

BRODIE DISMOUNTED AND WALKED HIS HORSE OVER TO the stables, where a young groom took charge of his beast.

"Give him a few sugar lumps when you're done brushing him down. The horse has earned it."

"Yes, sir." The lad clicked his tongue and led the horse away to be looked after. Brodie remained inside the stables a moment, and when he looked down, he noticed that his clothes were covered with blood and dirt, as were his hands. He turned his hands over, and they suddenly trembled.

He had *killed* three men. Killed them with so little thought except that they had taken Lydia from him.

Was he truly a monster to kill without hesitation like that? Lydia would fear and despise him now, he was certain of it. She would always look at him and see a man who took lives, brutally and bloodily. What she thought shouldn't matter. But it did—it mattered far too much.

He remained in the stables contemplating his actions another ten minutes before he returned to the inn. The valets were downstairs, but Rafe and Fanny were missing.

"Alan, where is Lennox and the maid?"

"With Miss Hunt, sir. She was in a bad way, all shaky and sort of laughing, like she'd gone mad."

Brodie sighed and dragged a hand down his face. He supposed he'd been facing the same thing, though in a different way.

"Do you need anything, sir?" Alan looked politely at Brodie's bloody attire.

"Aye, clean clothes."

"Of course, sir. Let me show you to your room."

Brodie followed the valet upstairs. "Has Lennox sent for a doctor yet?"

"Yes, sir. Apparently there's one not too far from here."

"Good." Brodie began to strip out of his clothes, while Alan unpacked a fresh set of stockings, trousers, shirt, and waistcoat for him.

Once undressed, he asked Alan which room Lydia had been taken to.

"She's next door on the right. There were plenty of rooms, so Mr. Lennox chose separate rooms for you, him, and Miss Hunt. Fanny will stay with her."

Brodie didn't like the idea of staying a full day and night, in case those highwaymen had friends, but Lydia was in no condition to travel today. Besides, he would need a doctor to assess her injuries.

He stepped into the hall and knocked on Lydia's door. Rafe opened it and sighed. "There you are, I've been wondering if you ran off."

He stepped back to allow Brodie to enter.

"How is she?" he asked in a quiet tone.

Rafe nodded toward Lydia, who lay curled up on one of the two beds in the room, covered in blankets. "Better now." Fanny was watching her eat a bowl of stew.

Rafe and Brodie moved to the opposite corner of the room, so as not to be overheard by the women. "What happened to her?"

"I'm not entirely sure," Brodie admitted. "I found their camp just before dawn, but I canna tell what they did to her before I arrived."

"And the men?"

"Dead. There were three men. Two were sleeping, but Lydia and one man were in the woods. I shot one. Your pistol is in my room. And I used a blade on the other two." He wondered if Rafe would judge him for killing the men.

"I'm glad you killed them," Rafe said. "If I'd been there, I certainly would have." He glanced toward the bed. "We'll likely know more when the doctor arrives. She's been asking for you, by the way," Rafe added.

Brodie stole another glance toward Lydia. "She has?"

"Yes, I don't think she wanted you out of her sight." Rafe's easy smile was softer than usual. The rakehell normally didn't show his gentle side, but it was quite visible now.

"I thought she wouldna want to see me again after I killed those men in front of her."

"I don't think she's worried about that, old boy. She's worried about you. She said you were hurt."

"Only a scratch. I barely even bled. But she caught a knife to her arm, and she didn't scream or cry. The lass is both bonnie and brave."

Lydia had finished the bowl of soup and was now speaking quietly to Fanny. She still looked pale, but her expressions were animated.

"Why don't you go over to her, Kincade? I'll watch for the doctor's arrival downstairs." Rafe patted Brodie's shoulder as he left.

Brodie drew in a deep breath and walked over to the bed. Fanny turned at his approach. "You may sit if you wish to stay, or you may tend to anything you need to," he told her.

"Thank you, sir." Fanny looked to Lydia. "Do you need anything, miss?"

"Not for now. Thank you, Fanny."

The maid excused herself and left them alone.

Brodie sat down beside her on the bed. "Rafe has sent for a doctor."

Lydia reached across the blankets, her fingers brushing against his. He turned his palm over, inviting her to touch him. It felt good to have her caress him, even in the smallest ways.

"Lydia, I hope . . ." He choked down his fear and continued. "I hope you can forgive me for killing those men. I shouldna have done that."

She continued to move her fingertips over his palm in soothing patterns as her lovely blue eyes fixed on him.

"You were trying to rescue me. They would have killed you, Brodie. I don't need to forgive you. I only hope you can forgive *me* for putting you in such a position. You came for me. You didn't have to."

The brave, bonnie lass.

"The men who took you brought their fates upon

themselves, lass. You have no blame for that." His gaze drifted down to her arm. "Does it hurt much?"

She blinked, as if he had broken some spell. "Does what hurt?"

"Your arm."

"Oh." She shook her head. "Not too much. Mr. Lennox gave me a stout glass of brandy." The sight of her smile fairly stole his breath. "And I do mean *stout*." She opened her other hand to indicate the size of the glass, and he couldn't resist chuckling.

"Rafe's answer to everything is a good drink."

"I think he's quite right in this case." Lydia lay back and winced.

"What's the matter?"

"I think I have some twigs in my hair from sleeping on the ground last night." She brushed at it with her good arm a little. "Brodie, could you . . . ? That is to say, would you mind very much if I asked you to comb my hair out? I meant to have Fanny do it, but I forgot."

Brodie had never been asked by a woman to brush her hair before, and if any other woman had made the request, he would have thrown back his head and laughed. But for Lydia? At that moment, he would've done anything she asked.

"Aye. Where's your brush?" He looked around the room until he found her luggage.

"In the smaller valise." She pointed to the case next to the large trunk.

He dug through the contents until he found the hair-brush and a mother-of-pearl-handle comb. He held them both up to her, utterly baffled as to where to start.

"The comb first, and go gently, please. I suspect it's in quite a mess." Lydia sat up and turned her back to him. She searched for pins, removing them before he started. Brodie carefully began to use the comb to thread the tangles loose. He did find a surprising number of twigs and bits of leaves in the silken strands.

"Lass, I think you hid half the forest in your hair." He added another twig to a growing pile on the table beside the bed.

"It was a very bad night of sleep."

"I imagine it was. Cold ground, no blankets or pillows, no feather-tick mattress. Just hard, unforgiving earth," he said.

"It sounds like you've slept like that before." She looked over her shoulder at him, and he was entranced by her profile. She was lovely beyond measure. Lovely in a way her sister would never be, and it was only partially to do with her looks.

"My father used to be rough with me and my siblings. I spent many a night sleeping in the woods. If he couldna find me, he couldna hurt me." It was one of the things he did often back then. Run away and hide from anything that could hurt him. His father's abuse had made him a coward, and he would always hate his father for that.

"Oh, that's awful." Lydia tried to turn around to face him. He gently urged her to stay still so he could brush more tangles out. Her hair was smoothing out into a glossy golden waterfall down her back.

"The old man is dead. I no longer need to fear him," he said quietly.

Lydia did turn then. "That doesn't mean that what he did to you didn't leave a scar. Our hearts carry scars as much as our bodies."

She was wise for one so young, and he realized more than ever that he had ruined this good young woman's life all because of his temper and his pride. Now she was giving him compassion when he least deserved it. His face heated, and when she noticed, her head tilted to the side as though she was puzzled by his reaction.

"Lydia . . ." He started to speak, but the door opened and Rafe entered with a doctor behind him. Brodie wasn't sure whether he was frustrated or glad for the interruption.

"This is Dr. Jacobs."

"I was told this young lady is my patient?" The Scottish gentleman raised a pair of pince-nez to his nose and approached the bed.

"Aye. This is Miss Lydia Hunt," Brodie introduced her.

"A pleasure, Miss Hunt." The doctor made a short bow, and Lydia thanked him. "Though I do hate to meet lovely young ladies under such circumstances. Gentle-

NEVER TEMPT A SCOT

men, you may go, unless the lady wishes for you to stay. But I urge you to leave, in case I must make delicate inquiries."

Brodie and Rafe stepped into the corridor, where Fanny was already waiting. She was nervously twining her fingers in her apron and watching their faces for news.

"Fanny, would you go and keep the lass company?" he asked the maid. "I dinna want her to be alone."

"Of course, sir." The maid rushed inside and closed the door. Brodie wanted to be in that room with her, but if he learned of any other injuries that he hadn't noticed, it might bloody well kill him.

"I think you're the one in need of a brandy now." Rafe nodded his head to a door across the hall.

"I certainly am." Brodie followed his friend, but his mind and thoughts were still with Lydia.

❦ 13 ❦

Lydia held still while Dr. Jacobs unwound the bandage from her arm. He made a face as he saw the thick, clotted blood in the oozing wound.

Fanny put a hand to her lips. "Heavens."

"Heavens indeed," the doctor said as he began to dab a cloth soaked in alcohol around the wound. Lydia hissed as the alcohol stung.

The doctor cleared his throat. "Miss Hunt, I'm afraid I must inquire about the nature of these injuries and how you came by them."

As Lydia told him the story of her abduction, the doctor nodded.

"We've had trouble recently with a pack of brigands in the area. They search for travelers, especially English ones, who they believe are easy prey." The doctor rebandaged her wound and cinched it tight. "You must change this bandage daily. Clean it with alcohol. I didn't stitch you up, but if the wound doesn't begin healing by the time you reach Edinburgh, have a doctor do it there. You're lucky the blade was sharp and the cut was shallow and clean." He carefully examined her face in the light. "Did those men hit you as well?"

"Yes, only once." She touched her still tender cheek.

"Did they injure you anywhere else? I know the subject may seem impolite, but you must tell me if they forced themselves upon you." He paused before speaking in an even more gentle tone. "Sexual violation can do great damage to one's body and one's mind." The doctor's words made Lydia want to cry for some reason.

"No, they did not. I was fortunate." She wiped away tears. "I'm sorry, I'm not usually so silly."

The doctor patted her hands. "There is nothing silly about being upset and scared. You have been through a terrible ordeal. Many ladies would be understandably upset, as would many men. Let your maid take good care of you. No heroics, eh? I know ladies hide their hurts far better than men." He chuckled. "You may be the fairer sex, but you're also far braver when it comes to managing pain."

"Thank you, Doctor." Lydia managed a smile for him.

"No traveling today. I'll tell the gentleman you are traveling with that you'd better rest until tomorrow." He collected his tools and tucked them back into his worn black leather bag before he left the room.

"What can I do, my lady?" Fanny asked. "Would you like a hot bath?"

"A hot bath would be nice. I feel dirty." *Dirty all over.* She hadn't been truly hurt by those men, not in the way the doctor meant, but she still felt damaged in some way, and she needed to scrub her skin until she was pink from it.

"I'll have a bath made ready, then." Fanny moved the changing screen to cover the copper tub in the corner of the room and left to have water brought up.

Lydia had only just settled back into the bed when Brodie entered.

"I've spoken to Dr. Jacobs. He told me you need to rest today."

"I'm sorry. I know you had plans to arrive in Scotland sooner."

He waved a hand. "'Tis no matter." He paced the room slowly, every now and then his gaze turning back to her on the bed. "Fanny says you wish to bathe."

"Yes." Lydia wondered what was bothering him.

"Good. A bath would be good for you."

Fanny soon returned and supervised two lads bringing in buckets of steaming water. When they were done, Brodie gently but firmly pushed the maid out the door.

"Thank you, Fanny. I shall help her."

"Oh, Brodie, really, you mustn't," Lydia sighed.

"Why not? I put you in this mess, lass. Have you forgotten?" He came over and helped her out of the bed. She could walk—at least she thought so—but her legs suddenly gave way, and she crumpled in his arms.

"Why can't I walk?" she asked in a frightened whisper.

"It is a surge of blood. It can take a while to happen. You feel fear and you escape, and then when you are safe, the fear catches up to your body and you are weak for some time."

"How do you know that?"

"Because the day my father gave me those scars on my back, I ran away from home. I managed nearly two hours before I stopped running. When I realized I was safe, I collapsed. My legs couldn't hold me up. Every part of me was shaking like an autumn leaf. One stiff breeze could have plucked me from the branch and carried me away."

He spoke softly about such a violent pain from his past as he walked her to the tub behind the screen. Before she could protest, he removed the chemise from her body and set her down in the tub as though she were a child. He knelt down beside her; his eyes were fixed on her face as he helped her bathe. She scrubbed vigorously until her skin reddened. Brodie caught her hand that held the bathing cloth and stopped her.

"You can't wash away bad memories," he said.

"I know," she murmured.

"Close your eyes."

She hesitated but then did as he asked.

"Picture those men, see them on the ground. Now see them vanish. See the clearing vanish, but the land remains. Imagine rolling green hills and diamond-bright skies. Wee sheep bouncing over the grass, a frisky collie chasing them, birds singing in the woods . . ."

She saw all of it. It was like that moment this morning when she'd seen Brodie emerge from the mist into the brigands' camp, just like he had said before when he'd spoken of the deer in the Highlands. He was a child of the mist, vanishing and appearing as he wished, only this time he'd emerged from the fog to save her. And that was truly all she'd ever wish to see again of this morning's events. Brodie Kincade, coming to save her like an ancient warrior.

Oh heavens. Was she falling in love with him?

"Feel better, lass?" His hand cupped her chin, and she opened her eyes. She was lost. There was no other word for it. A knot rose in her throat, and she couldn't speak. She merely implored him with her eyes to give her what she needed most in that moment. *Him.*

He leaned in over the tub, his fingers tickling her throat as he touched her. Her body hummed, and soon the hum turned to a passionate throb of need that she'd never experienced before in her life.

"Yes . . ."

"Yes?" He seemed confused.

"I feel better when you touch me. Please don't stop." She slowly rose from the bath, and he moved at the same time, reaching for a long cloth to wrap around her. She stepped from the copper tub and into his arms. He pulled her to him, almost roughly, but he seemed to catch himself, and his hands gentled.

"I'm sorry, lass, I dinna mean to be rough like this. 'Tis just that I want you so much." His face turned a little red, and he pressed his forehead to hers. She closed her eyes, inhaling deeply.

"I want you too," she admitted. "So much it hurts."

He exhaled a shaky breath. "I shouldna take you, lass. I've done nothing but put you in danger and hold you against your will. You canna want me or this . . . not now."

"Shouldn't I decide that?" she challenged in a whisper. "You haven't been a gentleman, and now is certainly not the time to start. You promised me wicked things," she reminded him. His gray-blue eyes darkened with passion, and she was lost all over again to this devastating man.

"I did promise that." His lips curved in the slow smile that undid her.

"Then you had best deliver it, Scot," she teased. "I'm here . . . I'm *willing* and *begging* you."

"Never tempt a Scot, lass," he warned. His eyes glowed like diamonds submerged in dark pools.

"Oh?" She slowly pulled the cloth away from her body, and he swept her up into his arms and carried her to the bed. He laid her down upon it with surprising tenderness, and she did her best to resist the urge to cover her body. She had never been fully naked with a man before. She'd never been *anything* with a man before, and this was exciting and frightening.

Brodie swept his gaze over her body, bold and unapologetic. "You are more bonnie than I could've dreamed of, lass." He stared at her for a long moment, and her heart raced as he began to undress. She took pleasure as he bared his body to her, *for* her. His strong arms flexed as he stripped down to nothing but his bare skin. Then he came toward her again.

Lydia swallowed nervously. How could he seem bigger when he was naked? Surely it couldn't be possible, yet it was. He crawled onto the bed toward her and caged her beneath him. She melted in pleasure as he kissed her, long, slow, and deliciously open-mouthed. She adored the way he kissed, like he was hoping to get slapped for it. It was wicked, just as he was, and she couldn't get enough.

She raised one of her hands to his chest, wanting desperately to touch him. He didn't stop her. His skin was warm, and his muscles moved beneath her palms as he shifted his weight and settled on top of her. She parted her legs to allow him to settle into the cradle of her thighs. It was the oddest sensation to both want him inside her and to be afraid of it, but Brodie seemed to be in no hurry. He continued to kiss her leisurely, nibbling on her lips until she almost giggled. Somehow in that moment as they kissed and before he claimed her fully, a delicate invisible thread was spun between them by some ancient cosmic weaver.

"Please, Brodie. I need *more*," Lydia said with a sweet, aching desperation.

"Yes, my bonnie lass." He gently nipped her neck, and she moaned as he moved his hand down between their bodies. She tensed a little as he lifted his hips and gripped his shaft.

"Oh, lass, I hate to hurt you," he warned, and she bit her lip the second he breached her, hard and fast.

The sharp pinch would have brought tears to her eyes, but he was kissing her again, distracting her from everything but pleasure. His hard body eased deeper into hers, and she curled her arms around his neck, holding on to him as he began to rock against her in a slow, sweet rhythm. Soon, the slide of their bodies and the wet, hot connection between them became the single most exquisite thing she'd ever experienced. She felt pried open to this man, body and soul, and he to her. Nothing could hide between them as they joined each other into one beating heart, one fused soul.

Brodie's hands explored her body, but there was no violence in this, no wickedness. It was lovemaking, with painfully teasing touches of their lips and hands as he thrust in a timeless rhythm that seemed to go on forever.

She stroked her fingertips along the corded tendons of his neck and down the hard-sloping muscles of his shoulders. The moment her pleasure seemed to spike and then cascade over an invisible edge, she clung to him, calling his name over and over as the last of her defenses crumbled and she fell completely and irrevocably in love with Brodie Kincade. He cried out as he found his own pleasure, and she sank into sleep almost instantly beneath him.

◌◌◌

BRODIE RECOVERED HIS BREATH, HIS BODY QUAKING with the force of a climax that had rocked him to his core. Lydia's eyes closed, a hint of a smile hovering about her soft, kissable lips as she fell asleep.

All he could do was stare down at her in confusion. Lovemaking had never been like this before. Yes, he had been with women sweetly, gently, but this was different somehow. It was infinitely *more*. He had drowned in the blue of her eyes and was washed away by the sound of her sighs and moans, like listening to the sea endlessly crash upon the shore. In that instant, he had felt a reverent worship for her like no other.

He felt lost and yet also like some part of him had been found. A part he thought lost forever, the part that still believed in foolish dreams of love and hope. But that wasn't possible. There could be no hope for him, not with his father's violence in his blood. No matter how much he wanted Lydia, it would be wrong to subject her to a life with someone like him. He'd only be a greater monster if he did.

He disentangled his body from hers as gently as he could and tucked her beneath the covers to make sure she was warm. He dressed and walked down to the taproom, where he purchased an entire bottle of whiskey.

Rafe came down a few minutes later and pulled up a chair beside Brodie. "How's the kitten?"

Brodie refilled his glass from the bottle and took a deep, burning drink. "Sleeping."

"Well, was it that bad, or that good?" Rafe asked with an amused chuckle.

Brodie didn't pretend to mistake the man's meaning. "A little too good," he admitted.

"Oh? So the clever minx had practice, then?" Rafe waved a hand to a barmaid for a bottle of his own. *Smart man.* Brodie would have thrown a punch if he had dared to reach for his bottle.

"Not at all. She was as innocent as a babe, but of course you *knew* that, didn't you?" Brodie growled.

His companion merely shrugged. "Finally figured it out, did you? That one is the kitten. You left the viper in Bath."

"You should've told me, Rafe. I ruined a decent woman."

"You have ruined other innocent women, Brodie. She wasn't your first."

"She came with me at knifepoint. I have destroyed her life with my hunger for revenge."

"Not necessarily. You could marry the kitten."

"Marry her?" Brodie threw his glass back, downing another gulp of whiskey. "No, I canna marry anyone."

"Why not?"

"Because Lydia deserves a good man. A sweet, gentle fellow who will worship her every step and faint away at her every smile and cover her bedchamber with flowers."

"And that's not you?" Rafe asked quietly, his blue eyes burning intensely.

"No." He was a wicked man with wicked desires, yet he wanted with all his heart to be that man for Lydia, but he knew he would only be fooling himself.

"So now that you know the truth, are we still bound for Edinburgh? Or do we go back to Bath?" Rafe poured himself a glass of whiskey and sipped it.

"We keep going. We canna go back. I've taken her to my bed."

"Very well. To Edinburgh." Rafe raised his glass, but Brodie only grunted in response. He knew he should take the girl back to her family, but as he had said, he was a wicked man, and now that he had tasted her, been with her, he wasn't ready yet to let go of her. The only honest thing he could do now was take care of her as his mistress and make her as happy as he could.

JACKSON HUNT WAS IN A BLOODY ROTTEN MESS. THE last two days of riding with Jane Russell had confused him. The beautiful widow was fiery and full of life and unapologetic about anything she did.

She'd drawn him in and he wanted things he had resigned himself to never having again. This was the worst time to be facing feelings like this. He needed to be worrying about his daughters. This whole terrible affair had been an alarming call for him to wake up. He had let Portia get away with far too much, and he had neglected Lydia dreadfully. Until he rescued Lydia from that dangerous man, he could not rest, could not let himself be distracted—not even by the natural warmth and charm of someone like Jane Russell.

He risked a glance at her as his coach rolled through the streets of Edinburgh. She looked lovely in a dark-green gown, the bold color accenting her dark-red hair. She was twirling a pair of gloves between her fingers, and the soft tan kid material was as dainty as the hands that played with them.

"Jane . . ."

She turned to face him, her brows rising in silent question.

He wanted to tell her how lovely she looked. Part of him wanted to do something a younger, more reckless version of himself would have done, like kiss her, but he didn't dare. Instead, he sought her advice.

"I'm afraid for my daughter. I've angered this Kincade fellow, and rightly so. I hired men to abduct him. I kept him a prisoner in my home. If we find them today, he and I may come to blows or end up dueling. Should the worst happen, may I trust you to take Lydia to safety? You will take her home, away from him?"

"Yes, of course. I will protect her as if she were my own child." Jane's words were spoken with such honesty that it left no room for doubt. And from what he knew of Lady Russell, his daughter would be very well looked after. "But it need not come to that," Jane added. "I might be able to reason with the man. I've had years of practice dealing with stubborn men who have no desire to listen to reason."

He relaxed a little as she smiled. He believed she was capable of doing exactly what she said.

The coach finally came to a stop in front of a lovely townhouse near Edinburgh Castle on a long, sloping street called the Royal Mile.

"This must be it." Jackson opened the coach door, his stomach in knots at the thought of Lydia being held within the house. He gently grasped Jane by the waist and lowered her to the ground before they walked up the steps together. He rapped the iron knocker on the door and waited. After a moment, the door opened and a butler stood there, peering at them in surprise.

"May I help you?" the butler asked.

"We would like to pay a call on Mr. Rafe Lennox and Mr. Brodie Kincade."

The butler frowned in confusion. "I'm terribly sorry, sir, his lordship's brother has not been here for several months."

Jackson wasn't expecting that answer. He had been so certain that this was where the wild chase would end. That he would find his Lydia here and take her home.

"They aren't here," Jane murmured. "He looks as startled as we are."

The butler continued to stare at them in polite confusion, and Jackson saw a gleam of cunning in Jane's eye.

"We are friends of Lord Lennox and his brother, Mr. Lennox," Jane said quickly, her tone polite and gentle as she spoke to the butler. "We were told that Mr. Lennox was headed this way and that we must be here to meet him. But it seems we have arrived too early. Would you mind terribly sending a note to this address?" She handed the butler a crisp slip of paper. "Please let us know when Mr. Lennox and Mr. Kincade arrive."

The butler examined the address and nodded. "Of course, madam."

"Thank you." She took Jackson's arm, and he let her

lead him back to the coach. "I have an idea," she said as they climbed back into his coach.

"I'm listening."

"Either they did not reach Edinburgh before us, or they decided to go to Castle Kincade. I know that Brodie's brothers are there, and neither of them would let Brodie keep your daughter. We shall send a letter to Castle Kincade straightaway and see if they went there before we make our next plans. In the meanwhile, the Lennox butler will hopefully write to us at my address should they arrive here."

"You have a residence here?"

"My son does. A nice little house a few streets away. You and I shall go there and wait for some word."

Jackson stared out the window, frowning as the evening shadows started to fall. "I hope she's all right. It's the uncertainty that has me worried."

Jane leaned across the coach and placed a hand on his. "You will find her. *We* will," she said. "I promise you."

He turned his palm over and twined his fingers with hers. He hated himself for wanting to pull Jane into his arms when his sole focus should have been on his daughter's safety.

I'm a terrible man and an even worse father.

❦ 14 ❦

Lydia woke stiff and weary, her arm aching. She moved and then stilled as she realized she was completely naked. Memories came back to her in bits and pieces, but one thing was startlingly clear: she'd been completely naked last night and had made love with Brodie.

She shivered—not from embarrassment, but from the delicious memory of the overpowering pleasure that she'd shared with him.

That night had been infinitely more wonderful than she'd ever imagined it could be. The way her body had fit to his, how she'd felt as though she were a part of him and he of her. It had been incredible. She rolled over in bed, wishing to cuddle against him, but she found his spot empty. She swept a hand over the other pillow. A hint of warmth still lingered there, which meant he'd only recently left. It made her strangely giddy to think that he'd spent the night beside her. She buried her face in his pillow, breathing in the remnants of his scent.

Then she lay on her back and stared up at the ceiling. She was still lost in silly daydreams when the door opened and Fanny appeared.

"How are you feeling, miss?" the maid asked.

"Better. A little sore, though. My arm, I mean." She sat up, keeping the bedclothes pulled up around her body. "Do you know where Mr. Kincade is?"

Fanny retrieved bits of clothing from the floor. "Yes, he's downstairs with Mr. Lennox. They both wished to check on the horses after last night, to make sure no one stole them. After those brigands kidnapped you, he said he would be surprised if they didn't have men here who would steal their horses during the night."

"Oh dear, I hadn't thought of that." Lydia forced herself out of bed. She and Fanny searched for clean gowns in her trunk.

"Well, what about this one?" Fanny held up a fine bright-orange gown that had a blue silk sash and capped sleeves. Rosettes of white were patterned on the hem, but other than that, the gown's bold colors needed no additional ornamentation. She and the maid shared a smile.

"Excellent choice, Fanny."

Half an hour later, Lydia was dressed and ready to leave. As she entered the taproom, she glanced about. A tall, thin man was working at the bar, and he snapped his fingers at a maid, who bustled over to Lydia to see if she needed anything.

"What do you have for breakfast?"

"Just porridge, miss," the girl said with a little embarrassment.

"That would be fine, thank you." She sat alone in the room, wondering when the men would return from the stables and whether they had eaten already.

She was halfway through her porridge by the time they came in. Rafe and Brodie were laughing about something, and Lydia's stomach fluttered with excitement. Brodie seemed so happy and relaxed. He really was the most handsome man she'd ever seen, and his easy smile just now only deepened that belief.

Rafe, however, spotted her first. "Ah! Morning, kitten."

"Good morning, Mr. Lennox." She glanced between the two of them as they joined her at the table. Brodie's smile faded a little as he sat down beside her, but he didn't look angry.

"How is your arm?" he asked.

"A little sore. Fanny helped me clean and bandage it."

"Good. I'm glad the lass has a strong stomach."

"She does. There was a bit of blood, and she kept calm." Lydia imagined she would have been faint at the sight of blood, but she had been in such a state of shock last night that she hadn't gotten lightheaded, and now she'd become used to living with the injury.

"I wish we could remain longer to let you rest, but I would feel better if we reached Edinburgh soon, should you need to see a doctor."

Lydia didn't disagree. She didn't have the least bit of desire to stay here so close to where those men had taken her.

"Have you eaten?" she asked them.

"Aye, half an hour ago," Brodie confirmed. "If you finish up, we can pack and leave."

He stood and went upstairs, leaving her alone with Rafe.

Rafe propped his chin on his hand and flashed her a puckish grin. "Well, let's hear about it, kitten."

"I beg your pardon?" She set her spoon inside her empty bowl.

"Oh, come now," Rafe chuckled. "You and the Scot. You and he tangled the sheets. The walls aren't exactly thick here."

Her face flooded with a firestorm of heat. "Mr. Lennox! You cannot speak of such things."

"Why not? Despite my public façade, I've never claimed to be a gentleman. Besides, there's no one to overhear us." He waved a hand around the empty room.

"That may be the case, but I don't wish to speak of it."

"It was that bad? Such a pity. I should have gone after

you myself. I can promise you—you would have adored sharing my bed."

Lydia raised a brow. "Aren't you busy enough with Fanny?"

"Fanny?" he asked.

"My new maid? I saw her leave your room yesterday morning."

"Oh yes, her. That was just once. We had our fun, but she's taking her post as your maid far too seriously and won't come back to my bed now."

"You *poor* thing," Lydia retorted.

"Aha! So you do have claws!" He threw his head back and laughed. "Oh, kitten, you are too sweet. Well, because you delight me, I'll tell you this. You have the Scot tied up in knots. He thoroughly enjoyed last night, *a bit too much* even. Whatever you are doing, I suggest you keep it up, my dear. I want to see how the fellow handles it."

She crossed her arms over her chest. "Why does this amuse you? He is your friend. Shouldn't you be trying to help him?"

"Kitten, there is one thing you should know about me. The thing I take pleasure in, the *only* thing, is making this drab existence we call life more interesting. And so far, you and Brodie have been *most* entertaining." With a knowing smirk, Rafe got up to see to the coach.

"Are all men so blasted frustrating?" she muttered to herself.

"Only the best ones," Rafe answered over his shoulder, his ears far sharper than she'd realized.

Lydia left a few coins that Brodie had given her for the barmaid on the table and joined Rafe outside. She took her seat and waited for the gentlemen to join her, but only Brodie got into the coach.

"Is Mr. Lennox riding on the top seat or is he riding a horse alongside us?" she asked.

"He's up top for a little while. He doesn't mind sitting with his servants. We should be in Edinburgh in two hours, hopefully."

"Oh, that's a relief. I don't think I can stand much more of this coach." She shot a hopeful look at him. "I don't suppose you have any more books?"

"Aye." He reached under his seat, and she browsed the handful he held out, choosing a book on the history of Stuart England. She began to read, but after a short while she became aware of Brodie watching her.

"You aren't reading?" she asked. Her voice was huskier than she wished it to be.

"No, I'm afraid I'm too distracted, lass," he answered, his voice deep and almost silky.

She sighed and rolled her eyes. "I cannot understand you, Mr. Kincade. This morning you would barely speak to me at breakfast, you did not even stay in bed with me—"

She squeaked in surprise as he lunged for her. When he captured her in his arms, he pulled her onto his lap.

He was careful not to touch the arm where she'd been injured.

"Hush, lass, let a man have what he wants. Why do you think I was so ready to be off? The sooner we reach Edinburgh, the sooner I can have you all to myself in a proper bedchamber where no one will bother us for days, except to bring us food."

Lydia stared at him. "Days?"

"Days," he echoed as he cupped her neck and urged her to lean into him so he could brush his lips over hers.

She surrendered to his kiss, and he managed to distract her from all other thoughts. He moved his mouth to her neck, gently scraping his teeth along her skin before he nipped her. She jolted as a sharp pang of need shot straight to her womb.

"Be bad with me, Lydia. Let me show you a way to pass the hours ahead." He murmured the tempting words in her ear, and she found herself nodding eagerly before she could stop herself. He slid his hands up her skirts, teasing her calves and her thighs, and she wriggled on his lap. When he reached the apex of her thighs, she wanted to beg him to hurry, but he took his time. He unfastened his trousers and urged her to lift her hips. Then he was pulling her down on his erect shaft. The sudden sensation from this new angle was so very different than the previous night when he had lain on top of her. She felt fuller sitting on top of him like this.

"What's the matter, lass?" he whispered as he kissed her.

"This is different than the last time," she gasped before kissing him back.

"Different how?" He rocked her up and down on him. It was becoming harder and harder to think, with the building pleasure between them.

"It feels full . . . almost too much," she confessed in a whisper.

He smiled. "Lass, how you flatter me." He captured her lips again in a raw, open-mouthed kiss, and she buried her hands in his hair, fisting the thick, dark strands as she rolled her hips, feeling him move inside her at the same time.

The gentleness that had begun as an echo of last night gave way to a frantic coupling. Brodie grasped her bottom under her skirts as he lifted her and jerked her down onto him. She broke free of his kiss to gasp and clutch his shoulders as he used her in the most delicious way.

"That's it," he growled. "Take your pleasure from me."

And she did. She circled her hips in a way that felt good and hit all the small secret spots within her, until she reached a glorious peak where there was nothing left for her but to fall back to earth. He followed her over the cliff of ecstasy a moment later and buried his face against her neck.

She breathed his name and cradled his head as they held on to each other for a long while. She didn't want to pull away. She wanted to stay connected to him as long as she could. But she knew they couldn't, and when at last he separated them, he used a handkerchief to clean her before he helped fix her skirts. She was more than mortified when she came to her senses and realized what she had done. That she had made love in a coach like some wild, wanton creature.

"Don't be ashamed." Brodie pulled her into his side, curling an arm around her shoulders as he comforted her.

"But I am," she replied. "What we did was . . ."

"Was perfectly natural, lass. We just didna use a bed." He nuzzled her cheek, his soft laughter easing her embarrassment somewhat. She liked it when he was in a good mood. This was how she'd first pictured him that night of the ball, a charming rogue with no worries.

"Will you show me all the different ways to make love?" She pressed her head under his chin and burrowed into his welcoming warmth.

"Aye. I will," he promised with a silky chuckle.

"Good, because if I am to be your mistress, I wish to know what all the fuss is about."

His arms tightened around her body, and he kissed the crown of her hair. "I will make you happy."

She believed him, even though her heart worried

that it wouldn't last. Rationally, she couldn't see how it would be possible.

❦

JOANNA KINCADE WAS SITTING IN THE DRAWING ROOM at Castle Kincade with her mother and older brother Ashton, talking about London and all their mutual friends, when a clamor outside had her leaping to her feet in alarm. A young footman burst into the room, his eyes darting around until he found her.

"My lady! An urgent message just arrived from Edinburgh." He thrust a letter into her hands.

"What is it?" her mother, Regina, asked. She and Ashton came to stand on either side of Joanna.

"I honestly have no idea." She broke the wax seal and unfolded the urgent missive.

"Read it aloud, my dear," her mother prompted.

Joanna cleared her throat and began to read.

My dear Lady Kincade,

I write to you of the most dire and urgent of circumstances. I am in Edinburgh with a gentleman named Mr. Jackson Hunt. His eldest daughter, Lydia, has been abducted at knifepoint by Mr. Brodie Kincade, your husband's brother. We believe that they are bound for Edinburgh, accompanied by your brother, Mr. Rafe Lennox. However, upon our arrival, we found no trace of them at the Lennox residence in Edinburgh. It occurred to me that perhaps Mr. Kincade chanced going to Castle

Kincade, but I cannot be sure. Please send a response to the
address below as quickly as you can.

    Sincerely yours,

    Jane Russell

    Dowager Marchioness of Rochester

Joanna finished reading the letter and then looked to
her older brother and her mother in shock.

"Abducted?" Regina muttered. "But why would
Brodie take that poor girl? He is a little wild, perhaps,
but then again, he is a Kincade, and we've seen how
unpredictable they are."

Ashton scowled and took the letter from Joanna to
read it again. As a baron, Ashton should have had the
least influence among the League of Rogues, all of whom
were members of the peerage, but due to his clever work
in the financial markets, he had amassed wealth and
power far in excess of his title. And when necessary, he
had used that power and influence to do whatever was
needed, especially when it came to dealing with Rafe's
actions.

"That bloody fool," Ashton growled.

"Brodie?" Joanna asked.

"No, Rafe. I have a suspicion our brother is at the
root of whatever trouble this is. He's likely having a good
laugh at Brodie's expense."

"But why abduct Lydia Hunt? She's so sweet, and oh,
Ash, we *must* tell Brock and Rosalind. They will know
what to do about Brodie."

"Know what to do about whom?" Rosalind, Ashton's wife and Brock's sister, said as she appeared in the doorway.

"It's your brother, Brodie." Ashton passed the letter to his wife. Rosalind began to read, and then after a moment, she slid onto the nearest settee and gazed at Ashton in clear confusion.

"I . . . I don't understand. Who is this woman they say Brodie has taken? What could she have done to him?" Unlike her brothers, Rosalind's brogue was not nearly as thick. She had been married to an older English gentleman a few years ago and had done her best to assimilate with London society before she'd been widowed. Yet there was still enough of the Scot in her, especially when she was upset, for the brogue to become more pronounced.

"Done to *him*? Lydia Hunt is a friend of mine. She's the most wonderful girl. She wouldn't do anything to Brodie to make him do this," Joanna said.

Ashton spoke up. "Didn't you say a few weeks ago that Portia Hunt had set her cap for Brodie?"

"Yes, that's right," Rosalind said. "I met the young woman at a party. She had heard rumors of my brothers, and rather than being scared off, she was intrigued. She inquired whether they were unattached. I informed her that Brock is married and Aiden was returning here with me. Only Brodie was to stay behind in Bath."

Ashton began to pace around the drawing room. "I

didn't have a good feeling about Rafe leaving here so soon. I thought that a stay in the country would keep him out of mischief, but he was eager to return to Bath after just one week here. He must have had a hand in this somehow."

"Where do you suppose they would go?" Joanna asked.

Rosalind considered the question. "There's our townhouse in Edinburgh, but Lady Rochester said they had not arrived there. I'm certain they won't come here," Rosalind said. "Brodie wouldn't bring a woman home unless he was planning to marry her. Do you think they stopped at Gretna Green, Ash?" Rosalind asked.

Ashton shrugged. "You know him better than I do, love."

"I fear Brock and Aiden know him better than me," Rosalind admitted quietly. "He may have changed since I escaped to London."

Ashton took the letter back from Rosalind, reading it yet again, as though he could divine some secrets from the page. "Joanna, would you please go find your husband?"

Joanna left the drawing room in search of Brock. Instead, she found Aiden lounging on a window seat in the library, feeding tiny bits of meat to a small owl. Aiden was smiling as he stroked the backs of his fingers over the downy soft feathers of the tawny owl.

"Aiden, do you know where Brock is?"

The owl gave a disgruntled hoot at being disturbed. Aiden turned his attention toward her. "He's in his study, I think. What's wrong, Joanna?"

"It's Brodie. He's abducted a poor woman and run away with her. He's headed for Scotland."

"What?" Aiden stood, and with a click of Aiden's tongue, the owl hooted and took to the air, returning to its roost on the topmost shelf of the library.

"We received a letter from Lady Rochester, who is traveling with the woman's father, and they are searching for them. They believe Rafe is with them."

Aiden's gaze turned even more serious. "Rafe? Gah. Brodie shouldna be anywhere near him. I like your brother, Joanna, but he is . . ." Aiden was obviously trying to be diplomatic. "Trouble."

"He is," Joanna agreed. "But we must find them. They have my friend Lydia."

Aiden strode past her into the hall and loudly bellowed for Brock. She heard the bang of a distant door and running steps, and then her husband appeared at the top of the grand stairs.

"What is it? What's the matter?" Brock practically leapt down the stairs, only to stop and pull her into his arms. She melted into him, relishing the way he held her. They'd been through so much together, and she sensed he would never be less protective of her.

"I'm fine, Brock. But we have a problem."

He pulled back a little to look down at her. "A problem?"

"It's Brodie. He's kidnapped my friend Lydia Hunt from Bath. He and Rafe are in Scotland, supposedly headed to Edinburgh." She quickly filled in the rest of the details for him as Ashton, Regina, Aiden, and Rosalind all gathered around them in the hall.

"Where do you think he would go?" Joanna asked.

"He wouldna come here," Brock said with certainty. "Not if he knew what was good for him. I don't know what drove him to do this, but I'll box his ears for such foolishness."

"Then he'll be bound for Edinburgh," Ashton said. "To my townhouse on the Royal Mile. Lady Rochester and Mr. Hunt must have passed them on the road and arrived early."

"Perhaps." Brock was scowling now, enough to match Ashton's own. "We must leave at once," he finally said, then turned to his brother. "Aiden, would you remain here, should they choose to come this way?"

Aiden nodded. "I will."

Brock turned to Ashton. "Are you ready to leave, *Sassenach*?"

"Of course."

"Good. Joanna, you and Rosalind, as well as your mother, shall travel in the coach. Ash and I will ride on ahead. We may be able to catch them if there are only two of us."

"Very well." Joanna didn't like to be separated from Brock, but the situation was dire, and it would only mean a day or two of being apart.

She hadn't yet told him that she suspected she was with child and would not do so now. If she did, she would be left behind. She would wait to tell him, after they had rescued Lydia.

15

It was early in the evening when Lydia, Brodie, and Rafe finally arrived in Edinburgh. They'd taken care to travel more slowly after one of their horses threw a shoe and they'd had to stop halfway to Edinburgh to have a new one put on.

Now the coach rattled over the cobblestones of Edinburgh's Old Town, which jolted Lydia awake, much to Brodie's dismay. He had been enjoying holding her in his arms, perhaps too much. She was the perfect weight when settled on his lap, and he didn't want to let her go.

"Are we here?" she asked as she rubbed the sleep out of her eyes.

"Aye." He wondered how far away they were from Lennox's townhouse. Rafe had said it was on the Royal Mile, an ancient street that wound its way up to the old castle.

They came to a stop. Brodie climbed out and escorted Lydia from the coach. The row of expensive houses around them didn't really surprise Brodie. If Ashton Lennox owned a property, he would be sure to own a costly one.

"Home sweet home," Rafe joked as he headed up the steps. He knocked, and as soon as the door opened, he clapped a hand on the poor butler's shoulder.

"Evening, Shelton!" Rafe seemed in better spirits now that they had reached their destination. Lydia hoped that that was a good thing. She didn't want to know what mischief he could get up to when he was in a bad mood.

"Mr. Lennox." The startled butler let them all proceed into the hall. "We were not expecting you."

"Sorry, old chap, but here we are."

Rafe winked at Brodie, but Brodie wasn't in a good mood. He wanted to get Lydia settled into a bed. He was sick of traveling in coaches and wanted to make love to her all night.

"And how long will you and your guests be staying, Mr. Lennox?" Shelton inquired politely. "I should like to inform Mrs. Lewellen so she can stock the kitchens."

"Unsure. A while, I suppose." Rafe removed his coat, and Brodie did the same.

"Shall I send word to your friends that you have arrived?" the butler inquired as he waved a footman over to collect their coats.

Rafe's jovial smile thinned. "What friends, Shelton?"

The butler paled. "The gentleman and lady who came to inquire whether you had arrived yet. They said they were supposed to meet you here." Shelton now seemed to sense the dangerous waters he had entered. "Am I to assume that no such plans were arranged?"

"Yes, Shelton. I believe we would like to avoid *all* friends, for the time being. Isn't that right, Kincade?"

"Aye."

"Very good, sir."

Rafe snapped his fingers as the butler turned to leave. "Shelton?"

"Yes, sir?"

"Do you know anything else about these friends?"

"Only the address where they are staying and their names." The butler produced a slip of paper and handed it to Rafe, who glanced at it and snorted.

"The girl's father has somehow beat us here. And he's with Lady Rochester."

"Lady Rochester?" Brodie hadn't met the woman.

"Remember the pretty red-haired bluestocking at the ball? The one I warned you about? That was Lysandra Russell, sister to the Marquess of Rochester. This woman is Lysandra's mother."

"Lysandra's mother is here with my father?" Lydia said in excitement. She turned to Brodie and clasped one of his hands in hers. "Oh please, let me go and see them."

"No." The word slipped out before he had time to think it through. But now that it was said, he wouldn't change his mind.

"What? Why not?" Lydia demanded. "I can put them at ease, he can see that I'm safe, and he can take me home—"

"I said *no*, lass. I won't say it again."

Her lovely blue eyes filled with confusion. "Are you going to see him, then? Please be careful—my father may react poorly, and I do not wish either of you to be hurt."

"I will not see your father, and neither will you." Brodie didn't want Hunt taking his daughter back, for more reasons than his own selfishness.

Lydia didn't see what Brodie did. That she was too sweet, too compassionate to put her own needs and desires first, which meant she would never make demands on her father for the love and affection she needed. While Brodie could not say he loved her, he could give her all the attention and affection she needed.

He also had no desire to face down her angry father. The man would no doubt challenge him to a duel, and Brodie was still furious enough because of Hunt's actions toward him that he would no doubt accept. So it was far better if all parties kept their distance.

"Brodie, he's my *father*." Lydia's reply was quiet, but there was a dangerous edge of defiance to her tone that warned him she wasn't going to let this matter go.

"He's also the man who had me drugged and kidnapped and intended to drag me in front of a priest at the barrel of a pistol."

"You cannot keep me from him."

"I can, lass. You're mine, dinna forget that. I dinna want you to see that man, and I dinna want to see him either."

Rafe's brows rose in surprise as Brodie and Lydia squared off, but he did not intervene.

"You do not *own* me," Lydia warned. "If I wish to see him, I will." She snatched the paper from Rafe's hand and glanced at the address Lady Rochester had provided the butler. "I assume this is not too far from here, Mr. Lennox?"

"Er . . ." Rafe shot a glance at Brodie. "Not far, but—"

"Thank you. I will see you gentlemen in a few hours." She started toward the door, but Brodie caught her by the wrist, pulling her to a halt. "Let go!" she shouted.

"No," Brodie growled. "You will go and wait for me upstairs."

"I will see my father first. He must be worried sick about me."

"I doubt that, lass. I know that he cares little for you." The second his words registered with her, he saw the violent flash of pain it caused. He hadn't meant to. He wanted her to stay—he needed her to.

"He cares," Lydia insisted. "Why else would he be here?"

"To retrieve me again for your sister?"

She looked as though he had slapped her. He wished he could take the words back, but it was too late.

"You . . . You know the truth, then?" Her lips trembled, and she looked at Rafe. "Did you finally tell him?"

Rafe shrugged. "The old boy discovered it on his own. Imagine that."

"And even knowing that you've ruined an innocent woman, you still won't let me leave?" Lydia asked Brodie.

"It isna so simple as that, lass."

"Yes, it is *absolutely* that simple." She tried again to free herself from his unrelenting hold. "Let go of me, Mr. Kincade!"

Even as she rightfully raged at him, she was so bloody beautiful. And that was why he had to protect her, even if she hated him for it.

"Stop fussing. I don't have the patience for it tonight." He needed time to think. To sort things out.

She stomped her booted foot on his in an attempt to kick him, but he barely felt it through his thick boots.

"I will put you over my knee, you little hellion," Brodie warned. She stilled, her face red as she scowled at him.

"You do and I will hate you forever."

"Better that you hate me than get yourself hurt."

When she tried to hit him again, he ducked. In one

swift move, he threw her over his shoulder, catching her legs with one arm to hold her down so she couldn't kick and thereby fall and hurt herself.

"Careful, old boy," Rafe laughed. "The kitten has her claws out." Brodie ignored him as he marched upstairs, Shelton rushing up after them.

"Where is an empty bedchamber?" he bellowed at the poor man.

"Here, sir." Shelton rushed to open the nearest door.

"And the key for the lock?" Brodie held out his free hand, ignoring the tiny fists that beat at his back in desperation.

"Let go of me, you brute!" Lydia yelled. Brodie took the key from Shelton and carried his wriggling cargo inside. He headed straight for the settee at the foot of the bed and sat down. After a brief struggle with her, Brodie slid her down in front of him and over his lap. Then he brought his hand down on her bottom, just hard enough to catch her attention.

"Ouch!" Lydia shrieked, though in a way that spoke of indignity rather than pain.

"That is for fussing," he said and gave her a second whack. "That is for not listening to me." Another three smacks and she quieted her outbursts.

He stopped, his hand hovering above her bottom, before he hesitantly placed it on her lower back, hoping to soothe her. He hadn't spanked a woman as punishment in some time, and he wondered if he had gone too far. Lydia was a gentle-born woman and not used to such treatment. His intention wasn't to harm her, but to get her attention and remind her that he was in charge. He turned her over on his lap, and his heart clenched at the sight of tears streaming down her face.

"Please let me go," she said in a small voice.

"Did I hurt you?"

"Please, let me go," she said again, and he did. She almost fell trying to get off his lap. Lydia curled her arms around herself and rushed away from him to the corner of the room farthest from him.

"Lass, I'm sorry." He stood and came toward her, but she turned her back on him.

"Please leave me alone."

Brodie stopped. He stared at her back a moment before he nodded to himself and left the bedchamber. He locked her in and slipped the key into his pocket before he headed down the stairs. Rafe was waiting for him in the drawing room, drinking a whiskey and lounging in a chair by a freshly lit fire.

"That was quick." Rafe chuckled until he saw Brodie's face, and then he sobered. "What happened?"

"I spanked her," Brodie grumbled as he threw himself into a chair.

"Oh?" Rafe asked, a slight edge to his tone.

"Not hard, mind you. At least, I dinna think so. I just wanted her to stop and listen."

"Not the best way to open someone's ears, going through the derriere." Rafe snorted at his own comment.

"Aye, well, she wasn't going to listen to reason, was she?" The truth was he didn't know what he'd hoped to accomplish. Even with all his restraint, he felt like he had been channeling his father. He felt like a bloody bastard.

"Perhaps not. You are right, though—she cannot go see her father. He'll take her home, but only after he challenges you to a duel. Assuming you don't let your temper get the better of you and kill the man before that."

"Aye. I wouldna be able to refuse his challenge, not after what he's done."

"And he's just as honor-bound to offer the challenge for what you've done to Lydia." Rafe sipped his whiskey before he stood and walked over to the tray on a nearby table and poured Brodie a glass. Brodie downed it all in one gulp.

"You know, Kincade, that's a sipping whiskey."

Brodie snorted. "For a *Sassenach*, maybe." He held out his glass, and Rafe refilled it. "It's not just the threat of a duel, though."

"Oh? And what else is there?"

Brodie stared at the amber liquid in his glass. "I dinna rightly know. It's the way she's been treated by her own father. The man clearly favors his younger child over her, which makes not one bloody bit of sense. I want to show her that *I* care about her, even if he doesna care."

"So you admit that, do you?"

Brodie didn't look at his friend but nodded. "'Tis a bit hard not to. She's sweet, intelligent, passionate, kind, amusing . . ."

Rafe crossed his arms and frowned at the flames, still holding his own whiskey. "Well, now that our evening has been thoroughly spoiled, what are you going to do about Lady Rochester and Mr. Hunt?"

"We must put them off the scent," Brodie said.

"That might be manageable, but you don't know Lady Rochester. She is as clever as her children, perhaps more so. She won't fall for any trick for long."

"Well, unless you have any better ideas, I say we send her on a wild chase to the north while we leave Edinburgh."

"As a plan, it has the virtue of simplicity. I'll have Shelton send her a message tomorrow after we leave for your castle, that we arrived late and left early the next morning for the Isle of Skye. I have a friend there we can send them to. By the time they realize they were fooled, we will be far away."

"Good. I want to be off as soon as possible." He didn't want to run into Jackson Hunt, but he also didn't want to let Lydia go. At least, not yet.

LYDIA RUBBED A HAND OVER HER BOTTOM AND CURSED Brodie Kincade with every foul bit of language she knew —which, unfortunately, wasn't nearly enough to do justice to her feelings.

Her pride had been hurt far more than she had been physically. He had treated her like a misbehaving child, and he'd tried to make her feel to blame for resisting his commands. And on some bizarre level, she did. That made no sense whatsoever.

She should defy him at every turn, shouldn't she? He had no right to tell her that she could not see her own father. He was the one who'd kidnapped her. Her choosing to stay with him did not change that fact. She had believed him to be an honorable man who had taken drastic action to avenge a wrong made against him. She did not agree with such measures, but on some level could understand it. Even his stubbornness in not believing her was understandable, given Portia's talent for deception.

But now she'd learned he had known the *truth* about her and her sister, and still he would not let her go. How did he square that with his so-called honor?

Furious, Lydia paced the length of the bedchamber, scowling as she tried to figure out what to do. If Brodie returned here tonight expecting to bed her, he would be sorely disappointed. For the first time in her life, she wanted to behave as Portia would. She wanted to scream and throw expensive breakable things into the nearest wall.

Yet she checked that destructive urge. This was Lord Lennox's house, who was blameless in all this. She wouldn't damage his home, especially when he had no idea his brother and brother-in-law were using it for such nefarious purposes.

Lydia paused in her pacing to look at the window opposite the bed. She approached the sash window and pushed it open. The perfumed smells of a well-tended garden came from below. She peered into the gloom, seeing through the growing darkness to the ground below.

It was a decent fall, and she could not jump without severe injury. But there was a trellis covered in ivy directly below the window. Lydia retrieved her reticule that had been packed away in her luggage, which still contained a small bit of coin from Brodie, and secured it to her wrist before she lifted her skirts and hefted a foot over the edge of the window. She found the latticework of the trellis after a moment and started to put pressure on it to see if the thin wood would bear her weight. Then when she was satisfied that it was safe, she began her descent. It wasn't easy, because her arm was still quite sore, but she was able to favor her good arm as she climbed down.

It was slow work, but when she reached the bottom

with only minor scrapes, she grinned and tilted her head back to look at the window above.

"Lock me in, eh?" she muttered to herself. "That will show you, you stubborn Scot." She brushed dirt and leaves off her gown and then carefully tiptoed through the gardens until she met the tall wrought-iron gate that blocked her only exit. It was most likely locked. She tried the gate anyway and nearly stumbled as it swung open on rusty hinges.

That was certainly unexpected, but it was also to her advantage. She closed the gate behind her, wincing at the sound of it creaking again. But no alarm was raised, and no one came to investigate.

Lydia walked through the narrow passage between Lord Lennox's townhouse and the one next to it until she reached the street. Streetlamps illuminated only part of the walkways. Lydia was no fool. She knew she had to be vigilant and cautious here. She watched for any passing hackneys that she might be able to hire, but after walking a quarter of a mile, she'd found none.

Suddenly, she heard a small cry for help. She looked around. The street was quite deserted. When she heard the cry again, almost certainly that of a child, she crept toward it. The cries led her down one of the small passages that Brodie had told her were called "closes" and found a small girl of about five or six in a dirty, tattered dress, her eyes wide with terror.

"Miss! Please help me!" the little girl sobbed.

Lydia grasped the girl's hands in her own. "What's the matter? Where is your family? Do you need help finding your home?"

The girl sniffed and shook her head. "It's my mama! They took her!"

"Who?"

"Them . . ." The girl pointed into the darkness beyond. Lydia peered into the darkest parts of the close but could not see anything.

"Where's your father?"

"Dead." The girl started toward the darkness, but Lydia grasped her shoulders, halting her.

"You must stay here and hide. I will find your mother."

She helped the girl conceal herself in the shadows behind a few wooden crates stacked against the stone walls of the nearest building. Then she crept down the alley, uncertain of what awaited her.

Distant sounds echoed in the darkness. Something heavy was being dragged along the ground. A man cursed softly. Light blossomed as a candle was lit. The ghostly faces of two men, made grotesque by the flickering light, caused Lydia to halt and hold her breath.

"Here, move the light closer, Burke," one of the men said.

The candle lowered to illuminate the body of a young woman upon the ground next to a large trunk.

"Lucky us. We didn't even have to kill this one, she

was already dead," the first man said to the one he had called Burke.

"Oh, aye. The doc will pay the same. She's a fine one, in good condition."

"Set the candle down. Help me load 'er up," the first man ordered.

The light was put on the ground nearby, and the shadowy macabre dance of the two men was haunting as they lifted the poor deceased woman and folded her body into the trunk. "Now, grab the child. I'll smother her."

Lydia stifled a gasp. They were going to kill the child. Lydia had to protect the girl. She had to stop them. She tried to think, despite the terror rising inside her.

The two men left the candle on the ground and headed toward her in the dark. Fortunately, they didn't see her, because the passageway was nearly pitch-black. Lydia held her breath, her blood roaring in her ears. A moment later, their steps were close and the smell of their unwashed bodies filled her nose. Lydia stuck out a foot, and the man nearest her fell flat on his face. He grunted, and the other man tripped over him, landing on top. The two men started to fight, each snarling and hitting each other as they blamed the other for what had happened.

Lydia, still flattened against the wall, slid step by careful step down past them. She wanted to run, but if she did they would hear her.

"Oy, you smell that?" one of them growled. "Bleeding roses . . ."

"Maybe it was the woman."

"No, she didn't smell nice. She smelled dead."

Suddenly everything was dangerously quiet. Lydia halted, afraid to move. They were listening for her.

After an eternity, the two men moved again.

"Go back and fix the body in the trunk," one of them said.

Lydia sighed in quiet relief and started to move again. And that's when she was tackled to the ground.

"Gotcha!" one of them grunted in triumph as he crushed her beneath him. "Bring the light!"

A candle was brought around and held up to her face.

"Well now, what a pretty pigeon," the man holding her said with a chuckle. "Seen something ye shouldna, eh?" He nodded to Burke, and before she could scream, something struck the back of her head.

16

When Lydia came to, she lay on the floor of a wagon next to a large trunk. A heavy burlap covering lay over her body, almost smothering her. Her first instinct was to rip the covering off her face, but then she remembered the little girl, the woman in the trunk, and the two men who had attacked her. The wagon rolled to a stop. Burke and Hare's voices were muffled, yet she could still hear what they were saying.

"We'll have to go back for the child after we drop off these two." Hands grasped the burlap above her head, and Lydia went still as the covering was flung back.

"Get the trunk first." The trunk was dragged off the wagon, and the two men carried it toward a building nearby. She started to sit up, but then she heard voices as the men returned, so she lay limp again. Her heart was pounding so hard she couldn't imagine how the men didn't hear it.

"Doc says seven pounds for the first and another seven for this one."

Rough hands lifted her up and carried her toward the building. She tried to hold her breath again as she was set down on top of a table.

"Here's the other one, Doc."

A new voice replied to that announcement, one more cultured than either Burke or Hare.

"Well now, that is a beauty. And still flushed with her recent passing. See the blood still rosy beneath the skin? Quite lovely." The heat of a candle's flame near her face almost made her flinch.

"How did this one pass away? Do you know?"

"Er . . . a fall . . . Aye, that's right. She tripped and fell down the stairs," Burke said quickly.

"Really?" The doctor didn't sound convinced. "If that were the case, she would have bruises. Is that a bump on her temple?" The doctor suddenly was touching her, his cold hands methodically exploring her head and arms before he lifted her skirt to her knees to examine her legs. It took all of her resolve for Lydia not to move or make a sound, lest she betray she was alive to these men, who clearly would kill her.

"It only just happened, Doc," Hare added.

There was a moment of silence, and then the doctor sighed.

NEVER TEMPT A SCOT

"Very well. You know I never like to inquire where you find the bodies. I daresay my students will enjoy watching the dissections of these women tomorrow. Pretty bodies make it far more interesting, and this one is especially lovely. I might have to have my friend come and sketch her body the way I did that poor prostitute."

Burke chuckled. "That one was pretty."

"Here. Take your payment and be gone. I don't want anyone to see you or your wagon here if we can help it."

The sound of jingling coins and a chuckle from Hare and Burke was followed by their fading footsteps.

"Now my dears, it's just us three," the doctor said. Another wave of panic threatened to make her gasp for breath. She listened to him moving around nearby. At one point, cloth brushed against her bare arm, and she almost jerked away out of instinct. She strained to listen to every sound he made and when she was certain he'd walked away far enough, and hopefully wasn't facing her, she took a chance.

Lydia opened one eye a tiny bit and saw a bald man with glasses nearby. He was examining the other woman's body on a table, mumbling to himself. Lydia opened both eyes then, hastily taking in her surroundings. She was in a workshop of sorts, with medical instruments littering the various surfaces. She had to find a way out of here. Had she trusted the doctor to be honorable, she would have spoken up and let him know she was alive, but that wasn't something she was certain of. He was paying for bodies and didn't care much how Burke and Hare came across them. She did not want to take the chance.

She found a small knife on the table next to her, and an idea sprang to her mind. The doctor hummed as he stood next to the other table with the dead woman. Lydia seized the knife, curled her fingers around the cold metal of the instrument, and threw it as hard as she could. It clattered down the corridor. She closed her eyes as the doctor spun and headed in the direction of the sound, calling out to see if anyone was there.

The moment he was gone, Lydia flew off the table and scrambled for the door. She rushed out into the cool night, gasping as she took in a lungful of air. She ran, heedless of direction at first, just so long as it was away from there. Only when she knew she wasn't being followed did she finally slow down. Then she stopped, her feet aching from the sprint.

The street was dark and empty, and she felt suddenly small and afraid. She didn't know the city, didn't know where Brodie was, or her father, at least not from this part of town. Anyone outside at this time of night might not be safe to ask for directions. But as filled with fear as she was, she forced herself to keep moving until she found a tavern. She didn't dare go inside, but she waited for what felt like ages until she saw a barmaid come out of a side door and pour a bucket of dirty water upon the ground.

"Excuse me, miss, could you tell me where the Royal Mile is from here?" She gave the girl the address of Rafe's townhouse.

"Ooh. Fancy place, that. 'Tis about a half mile away. Ye can take this road 'ere and walk until ye see the weavin' mill. Then take a right and keep walkin' until ye see the townhouses on Royal Mile."

"Thank you, miss. I wish I could repay you for your kindness." Lydia would have given the girl money, but her reticule was missing. Likely Burke or Hare had stolen it off her body when they believed her to be dead.

"Not to worry," the maid said. "Be careful. Not too many will be friendly to a sweet *Sassenach* like ye at this time of night."

"I will be careful. Thank you."

She started in the direction the girl had pointed, her head throbbing, her feet sore, and her body aching from the fall when she'd been tackled to the ground. All she wanted was to be in Brodie's arms, to feel safe. No doubt he would rage at her for running off, but she didn't care. She just wanted to be with him. He was her only light in the dark streets of Edinburgh.

"IT'S AWFULLY QUIET UP THERE. I BET YOUR DARLING kitten is asleep. You can safely join her in bed now if you wish," Rafe teased.

Brodie was still weighed down with guilt as he stood. The whiskey he'd drunk tonight would have felled a lesser man, but not Brodie. He shook off the effects and started up the stairs, ignoring Rafe's laughter. When he unlocked the door to Lydia's room, he whispered her name.

"Lass? Are you there?" he whispered again when no sound greeted him. A single candle was lit in the darkened room, and there was an unmistakable sense of emptiness.

"Lydia?" His panic began to increase when she still didn't answer. He retrieved the candle and searched the room. The room was empty, and a sash window stood open at the opposite end from the door, a light breeze billowing the curtains out.

Brodie stormed out of the bedchamber. *"Lennox!"*

Rafe met him halfway up the stairs. "What is it?"

"She's gone! The daft lass climbed out the bloody window."

Rafe almost laughed, but Brodie shot him a black glare. "The only way out is through a gate on the left side of the house. We don't keep that locked."

"Show me," Brodie growled.

Neither of them bothered with coats as they rushed out the front door. Rafe showed him the gate, which was unlocked but closed. After a quick search of the gardens turned up nothing, they moved on to the streets.

"Which way would she go?" Rafe asked.

"Toward the light," Brodie reasoned. If he were a woman alone, he would choose a more lit direction with streetlamps. He led the way, seeking out any sign of her.

Lord knew how long she'd been gone. He and Rafe had been drinking and talking for at least an hour, which gave Lydia plenty of time to leave and get herself lost, hurt, or taken. It was hard not to dwell on all the things that went on in the night on the streets of Edinburgh. And if a bad group of men found an Englishwoman alone, especially a beautiful one . . .

"I expect she'd try to hire a hackney to reach Lady Rochester's home to see her father."

Brodie actually hoped that was the case. At least then she would be safe. But he didn't see any coaches around of any sort.

"Perhaps we ought to go there," Rafe suggested.

Brodie sighed. "Aye, if we must." He didn't look forward to what would happen if he did, but he had to know she was safe.

Someone called his name, and Brodie's heart leapt into his throat as he spotted Lydia at the end of the street. She was limping, but when she realized he'd seen her, she started a mad dash toward him.

"Bloody Christ," he grunted as he caught her in his arms, holding her tight. She started to cry and shake.

"There, lass. You're safe now."

"Oh heavens, we have to go. Now." She pushed at his shoulders.

"Go?"

"Yes! We must save her from them."

"What the devil are you on about, kitten?" Rafe asked.

"The girl. They're going to kill her. We have to go." Lydia broke free of Brodie's arms and sprinted up the street. Brodie was on her heels as they headed down a small passage and skidded to a stop as he saw her gently coaxing someone out from behind a stack of crates.

"Please come out, little one. You're safe," Lydia was saying. Brodie threw out an arm, stopping Rafe before he could barrel past him into the alley.

They waited with bated breath as a small child emerged from behind the crates, a filthy little creature Lydia scooped up in her arms without hesitation. But the child was a little too big for her, and she staggered under her weight. Brodie came over and relieved Lydia of her burden. The child panicked, crying out.

"Hush, it's all right. He's not one of those other men. He's come to help you." Lydia clasped one of the child's hands, and Brodie shifted the little girl in his arms. She quieted down and lifted her head to stare up at him with big blue eyes.

"We must leave before they come back," Lydia murmured, her tone holding a note of panic.

They started at once for Rafe's townhouse. Lydia was at his side, and Rafe trailed behind, keeping to the shadows in a dangerous way that relieved Brodie. He felt safer knowing Rafe was there to watch their backs. When they reached Rafe's home, Lydia collapsed on the settee and held her arms out for the child. Brodie set the girl down on the settee, and she instantly cuddled against Lydia.

"What happened to my mama?" the little girl asked in a soft, worried voice.

"She's gone. I'm so sorry," Lydia answered with heartbreaking honesty.

"Gone?"

Lydia stroked the straggly locks of the child's dirty brown hair. "Yes. Like your Papa."

"I . . . I knew she wouldn't wake up." The little girl's lip trembled, but she didn't cry. Something about that made Brodie's fists clench as he fought a wave of fury. That a child should suffer such loss so young and yet see it as just another part of life spoke of a childhood even worse than his own.

"What happened to you, lass?" he asked Lydia.

She continued to hold the little girl as she explained how she'd escaped out the window and gone in search of a coach, then how she'd heard this child cry for help and how she'd come upon the two men loading the dead mother into a trunk. Brodie's fists remained clenched as he heard her tell how the body snatchers had knocked her out and delivered her to a doctor, and her narrow escape from his dissection table.

"I heard them planning to come back and take the child to the doctor next."

Brodie glanced at Rafe, and Rafe's face was dark with storm clouds.

"Kill a child?" Rafe's growl was only slightly less menacing than the fury in his eyes. "I wish I could have run into them myself."

"And you, lass? Did they hurt you?" Brodie asked as he searched her for any signs of injury.

"Only my head," she admitted. "It hurts a little, but I'm feeling better already."

"Should I fetch a doctor?" Rafe asked.

"No, not for me." She looked to the child. "Are you hurt, little one?"

The girl shook her head.

"Can you tell me your name?" Lydia asked.

"Isla. Isla MacKenzie," the girl said.

"Isla, you're going to stay here with me. At least until we find your family," Lydia promised her.

"I don't have one," the girl said solemnly. "Mama was all I had." Her voice was so adult that it made Brodie's throat tighten. "Could you be my new family?" Isla asked in a hopeful voice.

"Well, um . . . ," Rafe stammered. "That is . . . you see . . . I'm sure we can find . . ."

It was the first time Brodie had ever seen his friend truly lost for words. But the look on Lydia's face made

Brodie do what he always seemed to do around her—act without thinking of the consequences.

"We will be, if you want us to, wee one," Brodie replied.

"Isla, would you like to get cleaned up and have something to eat?" Lydia asked.

The child nodded, her gaze still a little fearful.

"Um . . . I'll see to it," Rafe volunteered, beginning to recover his composure. "At least for a short while . . . so you two can talk." He approached the settee. "Would you like to come with me, sweetheart?"

The girl held out a tiny hand, and Rafe instead scooped her up and carried her from the room.

Alone, and the immediate concerns dealt with, Brodie stared at Lydia, who looked down at her feet.

"I'm not sorry I ran off," Lydia said, her defiance returning. "You were unreasonable, and you humiliated me."

"Aye, and I should do it again. You could have *died*, lass. You know that? Those men were resurrectionists."

"They're what?"

"Grave robbers. They sell bodies to doctors and professors for autopsies. But not all men rob only graves. I've heard tell of some who 'conveniently' find bodies, even if that means producing them themselves. They're damned dangerous."

Lydia bit her lip. "I'm sorry. I know you must be furious, Brodie."

"Furious?" he scoffed. "My anger is a distant second to the fear you caused me tonight, lass. This isn't like any city you are familiar with. There are all manner of dangers you could have fallen prey to tonight."

She didn't argue with him. She merely continued to stare at him. He moved toward her, and when she didn't flee, he sat down on the settee next to her.

"The truth is, I dinna want you to be hurt. I dinna want to face that fear again, you ken?" he said gently. Lydia nodded and closed her eyes. He cupped her face with one hand and pressed his forehead to hers. He took a deep breath. "And I'm sorry I disciplined you the way I did."

She pushed back to look him in the eye. "You're sorry? Did I hear you correctly?"

"I won't repeat myself," he said quickly. "What you dinna seem to realize is that any reunion with your father now will end with pistols at dawn. And there can be no positive outcome from that."

Lydia's brow creased as she thought about it, and then she nodded her understanding and kissed him on the forehead. No more needed to be said on the matter. She curled her arms around his neck and moved to bury her face against his throat. "Brodie?"

"Aye, lass?" He wrapped his arms around her and pulled her onto his lap.

"Are you truly all right with the child being here? I know what happens to children without parents. I don't know what the future holds for us . . . but I know that my father would let me raise her if you and I go our separate ways."

Brodie didn't want to think of that, not just yet. "Aye, the wee one can stay with us."

"You are softhearted," Lydia murmured sweetly, and he almost disagreed with her.

"Only for you, lass." It was the truth. With Lydia, his hardhearted self seemed to melt away. His usual charm and merciless seduction didn't matter now. All that mattered when Lydia was around was her safety and happiness.

"We should leave tomorrow. You may write to your father here in Edinburgh and tell him you are safe. We'll find a way to reunite you without bloodshed when he and I have both had time to let our tempers cool."

"Thank you." She moved her head up and brushed her mouth over his, leaving him almost trembling with the need for more of *everything* from this woman.

"We should go see to Isla. She must be so frightened."

Brodie lifted Lydia off his lap, and they went upstairs together. They found Rafe speaking to the housekeeper, Mrs. Llewellyn, who was holding a small nightgown.

"Ah, there you are," Rafe greeted them. "Fanny is washing the little scamp now, and she's had something to eat. Mrs. Llewellyn has a small nightgown she can make do with tonight. But she'll need proper clothes tomorrow."

"That shouldn't be too difficult," Brodie said.

"Excellent," Rafe said. "Well, I'm off to bed. Unlike you Scots, a full bottle of sipping whiskey leaves its mark on me." He grinned and left for his bedchamber.

"It's a good thing we were here," said the housekeeper. "The poor man had no idea what to do with the girl. Offered her a glass of that whiskey to calm her nerves!"

"Oh dear," Lydia said. "Mrs. Llewellyn, is there an empty bedchamber we could use for Isla?"

"Yes, Miss Hunt." The housekeeper bobbed a quick curtsy and went to attend to that task.

"Let me go see how the girls are faring." Lydia left Brodie in the corridor as she slipped into the bedchamber. He could hear Lydia gently teasing the girl and Fanny giggling inside. And after a few minutes, when he was allowed to enter, he was astonished by the sight of the small girl now robed in an overlong nightgown. Her big blue eyes seemed so ancient, and her dark-brown hair lay in wet tendrils over her shoulders. Fanny was gently running a comb through the tangles.

"Isla, this is Brodie Kincaid," Lydia said. The little girl blushed deeply and half hid behind Lydia's skirts.

Lydia looked down at Isla. "We have a lovely big bedroom for you, sweetheart. Would you like to see?"

"How many people will I have to share the bed with?" the girl asked in a whisper.

"No one, my darling. Just you," Fanny said. She and Lydia shared sympathetic glances.

"Aye, Isla. You have an entire room all to yourself. Come and let me show you." Brodie held out a hand, and she came to him after a coaxing push from Lydia. The child's hand was so small and soft that he felt like a giant as he curled his fingers around hers. He led her to the room next door, which Mrs. Llewellyn had informed him was ready for the child as she left.

Isla's eyes grew wide at the sight of the tall four-poster bed. Brodie lifted her up and set her on it, then retrieved a red velvet cushioned footstool and set it against one side of the bed.

"You can climb on this to get in and out of bed."

Isla stretched a dainty little foot toward the footstool and touched it. She smiled up at him shyly.

"Time for bed." He pulled the bedclothes back, and the child climbed beneath them. Brodie tucked her in and on impulse bent and kissed her forehead. "Sleep, wee one. Tomorrow will look brighter. I promise."

"Good night." Isla sighed, her eyes closed, and she surrendered to sleep.

Brodie blew out the candles in the room and stepped outside, where Lydia was waiting.

"Do you think she will be all right?" she asked.

"If not, we are nearby." Brodie reached for her hand.

Lydia laced her fingers through his as they walked to their bedchamber.

"Heavens, I am quite fatigued," she sighed as he closed the door.

He pulled her into his arms. "You have been through a lot tonight, lass." He simply held her at first, stroking his palms up and down her back. When she pressed her lips to his neck, the tension in him returned, only one caused by desire rather than fear.

"I'm not too tired to . . . you know," she confessed in a whisper.

"Neither am I," he reassured her. He was all too aware of where their bodies touched. He wanted, *needed*, to sink into her welcoming softness.

Brodie stole slow, sweet kisses as he moved her up against the wall. He trapped her wrists above her head with one hand, and his other hiked up her skirts as he wrapped one of her legs around his waist. Then he freed himself from his trousers and guided his shaft into her. She moaned at the deep penetration.

"That's it, lass. Tell me how it feels," he encouraged in a hoarse whisper.

"Oh," she gasped as he thrust in quicker and harder. For the next several minutes, they didn't speak as he took her hard against the door. There was a primal need he felt to claim her again, to feel connected to her after having almost lost her tonight. He released her wrists to cup her bottom and have more control over their movements. Lydia dug her fingers into his shoulders and arched her back as he made love to her.

A soft cry escaped her lips as she came, and her inner walls fluttered around his shaft, threatening to drown him in sweet ecstasy. He had never bedded a woman who had felt as good as Lydia, and it wasn't simply a physical reaction. When he joined his body with hers, it felt like there were no secrets in the space between them. It was just perfect, and nothing in his life had ever been perfect before.

"I love you," Lydia whispered suddenly.

He stilled as his own release began to fade, but the warm glow inside him didn't vanish. It only grew stronger as their gazes met.

"You don't have to say anything, Brodie. I just wanted you to know. I've always believed in speaking the truth of my heart." Her face flushed. "I honestly don't even know how I fell in love with you, but I did."

"I . . ." He carefully weighed his words. "I am honored, lass. You give me a great gift with your love." He couldn't return the words, but she deserved the truth. He *was* honored by her love. Once they were in bed, he settled her into his arms, and for one brief moment, he dared to dream. Dared to dream of saying the words back to her.

🎋 17 🎋

R afe Lennox awoke to the sensation of being watched. Long before he opened his eyes, he became convinced he was not alone in his bedchamber. Experience had honed his senses, and he felt that unmistakable tingling at the back of his neck. He cautiously opened one eye, resisting the urge to reach for the pistol under his pillow. He swept his gaze over the room and quickly found the spy.

Little Isla was at the foot of his bed, her large blue eyes fixed on him. Somehow, that made him jump worse than if it had been an actual intruder. He calmed himself, reminding himself she was no threat. In fact, she was a bloody adorable scamp, now that all the dirt and grease had been scrubbed off her. Her hair, which had been dark-brown last night, was now a softer, more lovely russet color.

Now wide awake, Rafe winked at Isla. "Morning, sweetheart." She smiled shyly back at him but said nothing. "Are you all right?" He hadn't been around a lot of children growing up, other than his youngest sister Joanna. To him, children were from another realm and difficult to comprehend.

"Please, sir, may I have something to eat?" Isla's sweet brogue was as pretty as she was. Well, hunger was an easy enough thing to relate to. Suddenly possessed by a paternal instinct, he nodded.

"Of course, pet. And please call me . . . er . . . Uncle Rafe." That sounded right. He suspected it wouldn't be long before Joanna made him one officially, so Isla would be good practice.

Isla waited by the window, her tiny palms pressed against the glass as she looked down into the gardens below. Rafe dragged himself out of bed. He gently urged the little creature into the corridor so he could dress. Once he was ready, he came out and led her downstairs. He informed a passing footman that they wished to eat as they entered the dining room. The child's eyes widened as she took in the expensive furnishings, the warm oak-paneled walls, and the portraits of his ancestors. The Lennox family had been half-Scottish even before they had joined with the Kincades by marriage.

"Here, sweetheart." Rafe pulled out a chair, and the child climbed onto it. She was not quite tall enough to reach the table comfortably.

Rafe stroked his chin thoughtfully. "Hmmm. That won't do, will it? Can't reach the muffins."

The girl stretched out a hand, trying to grasp the imaginary muffins, further demonstrating his point that she was too short.

"Well, I suppose you could eat on the floor . . ." That earned a little giggle from the far too serious child. "No, that won't do either. Ah! I have it!" He strode to a small settee that was backed against the wall overlooking the gardens and plucked two plush pillows from it. Isla slid out of the chair so Rafe could set the cushions down, and he hoisted her back onto the chair.

"Better?"

She grinned and nodded.

Satisfied, he pushed his little charge's chair close to the table and sat down beside her. A footman soon brought in the first wave of food. Muffins, kippers, hard-boiled eggs, toast, and a pot of marmalade were among the offerings.

He helped Isla prepare a heaping plate.

"Isla," he said once she began to eat, "would you mind if I asked about your family?"

She shook her head.

"You mentioned that your papa is gone. Do you know if he's still alive?"

"He's passed," Isla replied. "Fever."

"Oh." He had feared the father had simply abandoned his wife and child, though he wasn't sure which outcome was more tragic.

"Your mother . . . ?"

"Fever too. She wouldn't wake up. I . . ." Isla set the muffin down on her plate. "I was crying, and I went downstairs to find help. They heard me, and when I told them my mama wasn't moving, they came and took her away."

"They?"

"The men who took my mama."

Rafe frowned. "Was your mama still breathing when they took her?"

Isla shook her head. "She made a terrible sound, like a rattle, and then she was very quiet. I was so scared."

"Do you know who these men are?"

"They stay at the inn sometimes. They are bad men."

"That they are," Rafe agreed. He wished he had met them last evening. He had no deep-seated objections to grave robbing, per se. The dead didn't need any of their mortal baubles, and doctors made far better use of their corpses than the worms.

But Lydia had heard these men say that they intended to silence the girl to both cover their sins and line their pockets. And for that, he would have killed them.

Rafe put a hand on the child's head, brushing her hair back in an attempt to soothe her. "That's all I needed to know. I'm sorry, my dear. Finish your breakfast." He moved her plate closer in encouragement. After a moment, she reached for her muffin again.

Poor thing, Rafe thought. But the child was safe now. Brodie and Lydia would not let her go uncared for. But when those two parted ways, he wondered if there would be a battle for who would take the child. Brodie may bluster and growl as all Scots do, but he had a soft spot for helpless creatures as much as his brother Aiden did.

"Isla, have you ever had chocolate to drink?" Rafe asked.

"No," the girl replied.

Rafe chuckled and prepared her a cup of hot chocolate. "Well then, you are in for a treat." He added two scoops of sugar to it.

When Isla took a sip, her eyes widened and she licked her lips before she beamed up at him.

"Like it?"

She nodded vigorously.

"Then drink up and I might let you have a second cup." He felt he'd already proven himself to be an excellent uncle-in-training, but he wasn't sure what to do to keep her occupied after breakfast.

"Do you know how to play whist, by any chance?"

Isla shook her head, and he grinned wickedly.

"Excellent, I shall tutor you to fleece the richest men in His Majesty's kingdom without them ever knowing, through a simple game of cards."

❦

JANE RUSSELL BARELY HAD TIME TO THINK AS SHE rushed out of her bedchamber in nothing more than a chemise and a dressing gown, clutching the letter her maid had given her to her chest. She burst into the room next to hers, and in her surprise, the letter fluttered down to the floor.

Jackson Hunt stood facing a gilded mirror as he shaved himself, while his valet set out clothes on the bed. Both men paused in their activities to look at her, curious and surprised by her entrance.

But Jane's attention was solely on Jackson and the fact that he was bare-chested. He wore only a pair of lean, buff colored trousers, which clung to his narrow hips but displayed far too clearly his muscular thighs and bottom.

"Good heavens. I'm so sorry." Jane wasn't entirely sure she had said that aloud until Jackson nodded to his valet, who hastily slipped past Jane and left the room.

"I . . . should come back later," Jane murmured, yet she didn't move from the doorway.

Jackson finished shaving and wiped his face clean before he turned to face her. His hazel eyes looked at her intensely, and her body responded in a way she hadn't felt in a long time. Heat filled her face, as well as other parts of her.

"You dropped something," he said, nodding at her feet.

Jane looked down at her slippers and saw the item she had thought so important a moment ago.

"Oh . . . Right . . . Yes, how silly of me." She retrieved the letter and opened it. "The butler from the Lennox house has written to us."

"Oh?" Jackson came over, and she had to force herself to stare at the page, in order to not stare at Jackson's chest. The man looked fit enough to rival any of her sons in any sort of physical competition. It was enough to make a woman reach for the nearest bottle of smelling salts.

"He said that Mr. Lennox, Mr. Kincade, and their female guest spent last night at the townhouse but left before dawn. They have no plans to return to Edinburgh and are bound for the Isle of Skye to the enclosed address."

"The Isle of Skye?" Jackson groaned. "What the devil takes them all the way up there?"

"I haven't the faintest idea, but it is a rather pretty place. I went there once with my husband."

"I've never been," Jackson admitted. "I spent my younger years building a life and trade. It didn't lend much to traveling. At least, not to places that were pretty."

Jane folded the letter and finally looked his way again. There were faint lines around his eyes as he offered her a smile. Her heart gave a traitorous leap within her chest.

"So, we are bound for Skye?"

"It seems so." Jackson's deep chuckle melted through her.

"Well then, I should leave you to dress and . . ."

Lord, she was staring at his chest again, wasn't she? Since when had she become a blushing bride on her wedding night? A bare chest should not affect her so.

"You can touch me, Jane. I am not made of stone," Jackson teased.

"You could have fooled me—you look as hard as marble." She frowned. "How are you so sun-kissed?"

He laughed again. "By working in the gardens. I work alongside my gardener. He's an older fellow who I won't ever terminate, and he needs help with lifting and digging and so forth. I could hire one of the young lads to do it, but it feels good to stay active."

Jackson caught her wrist and placed her palm on his chest. His skin was smooth, except for the light-gold matting of hair on his chest, and he was wonderfully warm.

"Heavens . . ." Jane didn't seem to have any other word for what she felt. It was like heaven to remember how good it felt to be young and full of life's hungers. Tears suddenly welled in her eyes.

"Did I do something wrong?" He cupped her chin and lifted her face up when she tried to hide.

"No. It's silly." They stared at each other for a long, tense moment.

"Am I a fool to want something more with you?" Jackson asked. "Have we passed that point in our lives for second chances?"

"I don't know," she said. "But I admit, you make me feel young again. And I feel guilty in so many ways, especially for wanting . . ." She dared not finish her thought.

"For wanting love again?"

"It seems foolish to think it's possible," Jane said. "Youth is full of impulse and desire, and as one matures one replaces those feelings with more practical needs . . ."

"Until one sees those youthful feelings as misguided rather than important," Jackson finished.

"Yes, exactly. My life has been focused on duty, honor, and propriety for so long now. Even though I care little for the opinions of others, I have structured my life around the needs of my children and the stability of my family. I haven't thought about what I wanted in a long time."

"Nor have I. Perhaps it's time we started?" Jackson brushed his fingers down her neck in the most wonderful way, sending shivers of delight through her.

"Perhaps it is." Jane stared at his full lips. It made her rather giddy to imagine them exploring hers. He continued to stroke her neck, which mesmerized her and had her nodding before she could stop and think better of it. Jackson took control and pulled her into his arms.

Jane, a force of nature who had made even dukes tremble, melted in this man's arms as he kissed her. She had forgotten how she loved to be kissed, to be the sole focus of a man's passion.

"Good Lord," Jackson groaned as he buried his face in her neck.

"Yes?" she teased as her hands roamed over his chest and back.

He returned his mouth to hers, stealing little nibbling kisses. "I could kiss you for days." He parted her dressing gown to explore her curves. She was shy about her body, which was no longer as young and firm as it once had been.

"Would you let me look at you, my darling?" Jackson asked.

My darling. She could have swooned. It had been too long since a man had used such an endearment for her.

"Jackson . . ." She breathed his name as her senses spun.

"Yes?" He feathered kisses along her jaw as his heated body pressed against her own.

"Take me to bed," she commanded in a whisper.

He lifted her up, carrying her straight to his bed. She lay back as he closed the door to his room.

Heavens, he was a beautiful man. There was something to be said about a man who kept his physique. He was strong, sturdy in a way that most younger men were not. There was a promise that he knew his body and a woman's and she would not be disappointed with the outcome. He took his time, removing his trousers as she looked on.

"Your turn," he said as he approached the bed.

Jane sat up and removed her dressing gown. She loosened the ties of her chemise at her throat, and the fabric dropped off her shoulders. He reached up to stroke his fingertips over her skin just above the chemise, which still hung over her breasts, before he carefully pulled it down to her waist to expose her fully.

Jane was blushing as red as her hair. Her body was not that of a young girl's. Her breasts were larger, heavier with the passing of time and nursing children. She wondered if Jackson would find her disappointing, but she was stunned to find only heat in his eyes.

"Exquisite," he said as he brushed his thumb over one nipple. Jane's body came alive after years of being dormant.

He moved closer, laying her back on the bed so he could pull the chemise down the rest of her body and drop it to the floor.

"Jane, you are a vision." Jackson groaned as he leaned over her and stepped between her parted thighs.

"As are you." She gazed in admiration at his strong, muscled form and the boyish grin that covered his lips. "What is it?" Jane asked as he caressed her breasts before sliding a hand down her body to her folds. She hissed as he sank a fingertip into her, testing her readiness. She was ready—there was no doubt of that.

"I feel like an untried youth being allowed a night with a most beautiful buxom maid. I want to leap on you and take you fast, but I also wish to savor every moment. It's been a very long time since I felt that way." There was an undeniable softness behind the heat in his gaze. It made the moment between them so much sweeter.

"Let us savor it. It has been a long time for me as well, and I am honestly not sure I remember how to do it properly."

Jackson laughed and leaned over the bed to capture her mouth. Just like that, they rushed headlong into the moment together. He thrust into her body. He was slow and gentle at first, and Jane threw her head back on the bed. His eyes drifted over her as he withdrew and entered her again, making love to her at a leisurely pace, and she started to beg him for more. As the pleasure built between them, Jane let go of every thought and simply surrendered to her feminine needs.

She cried out Jackson's name as she came apart, and he followed her a heartbeat later, shouting her name. He held her hips as she trembled with the aftermath of pleasure.

If she was being honest, she hadn't gone without private moments of satisfaction all these years, but there was nothing better than a real man and real passion. The simple touches in the privacy of her bath were but a shadow compared to this.

Jackson joined her on the bed and pulled her into his arms. "Do you have regrets?"

Jane rested her chin on his chest, and he ran his fingers through the loose tumble of her red hair. "Regrets? With you? No." She was silent a moment as she collected her thoughts. "I do regret that I've gone so long without having a connection to a man again. I do regret that."

"It is rather strange," Jackson mused. "When I lost my Marianna, many women made it quite clear that they would happily marry me. But the thought of it, sharing my life with another woman, even a mistress . . . I couldn't imagine it."

"You've had no women, not even a mistress, after all this time?"

His face reddened. "There was one night exactly a year after my wife died. I was wandering around in a rather bad part of London. I found a tavern and was quite determined to drink or gamble away every coin in my purse, but I ended up meeting a maid working in the taproom. She was not a prostitute, but a barmaid. Still young, but not so young as the others, and I felt she was closer to me in age and might be a nice companion to talk to. I paid her to sit and talk with me between seeing to her tables. Molly was her name. She was a sweet woman, and at the end of the night, she offered me her hand and led me upstairs. We coupled in the dark, and she let me call her Marianna, and afterward I wept like a young boy. It was . . ." Jackson's throat closed. "That was the only time." His hazel eyes settled on Jane's face.

"This was different, wasn't it?" she asked. A wicked smile began to form on her lips. "You know, from the moment I saw you coming up the steps to Mr. Lennox's townhouse, I knew it would come to this."

"What?" Jackson looked at the two of them in bed. "*This?*" He scrunched the bedclothes up over his bare chest as though he was shocked. "Have I been taken advantage of?"

Jane laughed at that. "I believe that was a completely *mutual* part of the matter. No, it's just that, after all these years, I think in order to recapture my own life, I had to run away to Scotland again." She smiled, perhaps a little foolishly. "I make no demands on you, Jackson. Whatever you wish this to be, I will enjoy it for as long as it lasts."

He began to stroke her hair again, a thoughtful expression stealing across his handsome features. "I am yours, Jane, for as long as you desire me."

She slid up his body a few inches and lowered her head to kiss him. All thoughts outside of this room, this moment, were banished, if only for a little while.

✣ 18 ✣

Lydia giggled as she watched Isla stand on the small platform in the dressmaker's shop on the Royal Mile street in Edinburgh. Isla looked like a giant doll with her hair curled in long ringlets and her new dress on.

"Hold still, darling," Lydia said when Isla started to fidget. "Just a few more minutes, all right?"

Isla let out a long-suffering sigh, which made Brodie and Rafe laugh. The two gentlemen were somewhat uncomfortable in so feminine a shop, but they were bearing up well by letting little Isla amuse them with her antics.

The dressmaker knelt at Isla's feet, a set of pins in her mouth as she adjusted the hem of the pretty lilac gown Isla wore.

"Mrs. Giles, will you have the gowns for my daughter

and other items ready by this afternoon?" Lydia inquired. It had been a tad easier than she'd expected to claim Isla as her child in public, at least while they were purchasing items for her. Lydia was beginning to think she'd spent too much time around Rafe for lying to come so easily now.

"Certainly, ma'am. The gowns will be easy enough to modify. I have a good team of girls who can make the adjustments this afternoon."

"Excellent. Where can we find a shop to buy her shoes?"

"At the end of the street. There's an excellent one there with children's slippers and boots of all colors and sizes."

Lydia thanked the woman and helped Isla go behind the changing screen to put on the pale-blue ready-made gown that she could wear out today.

"Brodie, could you carry her again? I don't want her walking in those worn-out boots." Lydia knew that the girl had been well cared for by her mother, but it was clear from the state of the child's clothing that the last year hadn't been easy for the young mother and her child.

Rafe mumbled something under his breath about Brodie and Lydia acting like an old married couple, but Brodie cuffed him on the shoulder to quiet him. He lifted the child up and carried her out of the dressmaker's shop. Isla giggled, her arms curled around Brodie's neck as Rafe stuck his tongue out at Brodie's back the way a little boy would. Lydia's heart twisted with bittersweet pleasure. She was glad they were making the child happy, but she couldn't forget that the child's mother and father had both died, leaving her all alone. And this distraction for Isla was just that, a distraction. It would take more than new clothes and smiling faces to mend the wounds she no doubt kept hidden.

After acquiring appropriate boots and slippers in various colors, the group passed by a toy shop on the street.

"Do you mind if I take the little kitten in here?" Rafe asked.

"Not at all," Lydia said. "Perhaps Isla will find a toy in there as well."

Rafe smirked at her teasing and took Isla inside. Lydia watched them through the shop window.

"Brodie, do you think she will be all right? She's so shy and quiet."

Brodie took one of her hands and brought it to his lips, kissing the tops of her fingers.

"Can you blame her? We are strangers, and she's lost all of her family and doesna even have the comfort of her normal surroundings. It's a lot for a child to take in. But she is engaging with us, and that means she hasna given up. She's a strong child."

"We should return to that inn where her mother died. I want to ask the innkeeper some questions about her mother and collect any belongings, if they haven't gotten rid of them yet."

"We can, but you and the bairn will stay in the coach where 'tis safe."

Lydia decided it was not worth arguing the point with him, so she returned her focus to the child and Rafe. Isla was looking at two dolls, both lovely and wearing exquisite clothes. She slowly pointed to a flaxen-haired doll with a rose-colored dress like the one Lydia was currently wearing. Rafe seemed to be offering to buy both, but Isla shook her head and put the other doll back on the shelf. Rafe rolled his eyes and scooped up Isla and her new doll and paid for the toy before carrying her and the toy out of the shop.

"She's bloody hard to spoil," Rafe grumbled. "Who'd have thought mistresses were easier to please?"

Isla lifted up her new doll and made it kiss Rafe's cheek. The rakehell blushed and quickly handed her over to Brodie. Lydia couldn't help but tease him.

"What's the matter, Rafe? Afraid you'll want a child of your own if you hold her too long?"

"Perhaps," he admitted, his expression honest for a moment before he returned to his guarded look of amusement. "Where are we off to now?"

"The inn where we found her," Brodie said as they got into Rafe's coach.

Isla played silently with her doll, but when they stopped at the inn, her eyes grew wide with fear.

"Am I going back? I knew I couldna stay with you." She spoke in a very small voice filled with terror. She clutched the doll tightly to her chest, her tiny hands white-knuckled with her fierce little grip.

"No, my sweet one. You must stay here with Lydia. Rafe and I wish to ask some questions and retrieve your mother's belongings if they are still there."

Lydia pulled Isla close and kissed her forehead. "We'll stay here—don't worry." She nodded to Brodie that he and Rafe could leave.

BRODIE STEPPED OUT OF THE COACH, AND RAFE JOINED him. The inn, while not one of the nicer places to stay, was on a well-to-do street with decent shops and residences nearby.

"I wonder how the woman and her child ended up here?" Rafe wondered as his gaze ran over the edifice of the building.

"I don't know," said Brodie. They entered and found the innkeeper helping a maid clean up a table of dirty dishes. The innkeeper was a thin-faced woman who looked quite unpleasant. When she caught sight of Brodie and Rafe, her sour expression softened, likely because she recognized money when she saw it.

"What can I do for you fine gents?" She smoothed a few stray wisps of her hair back from her face and patted the tightly knotted bun at the back of her head to make sure her hair was in place.

"You had a woman staying here," Brodie said. "A Mrs. Mackenzie?"

The woman's eyes narrowed. "If you be wanting her, she's gone. Left in the middle of the night but left her belongings and didn't pay."

"We know she's gone. Mrs. Mackenzie passed away last evening," Rafe said as he reached into his coin purse. "We'll happily settle her bill. We would also like to see her room and take any belongings she had to return to her family."

The innkeeper's eyes widened. That much coin erased any hesitation.

"Aye, this way, sirs. She owed me for two nights. That'd be three pounds."

"Here's ten." Rafe handed the woman her coins. "That should cover two nights plus anything you can tell us about her."

They followed the woman upstairs and down a short hall, where she unlocked a room.

"She had a child with her. A little girl," the innkeeper said. "You ken what happened to her?"

"She's safe in our care," Brodie said as they stepped into the room.

"I havena touched her things," the woman assured him as she fingered the money Rafe had given her.

"How long did she stay here?" Brodie asked.

"Oh, Lord, might've been two weeks. She was quiet, the child too. I think she was looking for work. Seamstress, if I recall. But she was too pretty, if you ken my meaning. Looked more like a lady. She had soft hands, pretty dresses."

The innkeeper lingered at the doorway for a moment before telling them she would be downstairs if she was needed. Once they were alone, Brodie and Rafe carefully searched the room. There was a carpetbag full of elegant dresses that were a few years out of fashion. A child's doll and a pair of miniature portraits of a lovely woman and a handsome man.

Brodie examined the portraits. Isla had her mother's face but her father's eyes and coloring.

"I wish I knew what happened to her," Rafe said. The sorrow in his voice wasn't something Brodie had expected from the hardened rakehell.

"Aye, she must have been a good woman to have raised so sweet a child as Isla." They collected everything in the room, including some embroidery hoops with half-completed designs on them. Isla deserved to have whatever memories of her past they could give her.

Brodie shook his head. "Poor little scamp. To think she was all alone when her mother died, only to have those men take her mother's body away."

"I'm more concerned about how they planned to come back for Isla." Rafe met Brodie's stare. "They would have killed her if Lydia hadn't found her."

"Aye. They'll come to a bad end. I just wish I could be the one to deliver it." Brodie left the small bedchamber and headed downstairs. They thanked the innkeeper again before leaving. Brodie took care to load the carpetbag on the outside of the coach, giving it to the footman who had accompanied them. Then he and Rafe got back inside.

"What did you discover?" Lydia asked.

"Her mother had been looking for work as a seamstress. She may have been gentry, though. She had fine clothes. We have her belongings."

At this announcement, Isla spoke up. "Did you find Mama and Papa?"

"Their portraits?" Brodie clarified. Isla nodded. "Yes, wee one, we did. You may have them when we get home."

Isla went back to studying her doll, a pensive look far too old for one so young on her face.

"By the by," Rafe said to Lydia. "I sent Lady Rochester and your father a note sending them to the Isle of Skye so we might have a chance to leave Edinburgh without running into them."

"And where are we bound now?" Lydia didn't question the decision, and for that Brodie was thankful. After last night, she seemed to have given up on trying to see her father, at least for now.

"To Lennox House to rest and then pack. We'll leave for Castle Kincade," Brodie said.

"Is it very far?" Lydia asked.

"About a day's ride. We should pack and be off in a few hours after the rest of Isla's things arrive from the seamstress."

"Are you to accompany us, Mr. Lennox?" Lydia inquired. She played with a lock of Isla's hair, which had been pulled back with ribbons that matched the ready-made dress Isla had worn out of the modiste's shop. Brodie felt a strange tightening in his chest at the sight of them. She was a natural mother, so easy with children. It was one of a dozen mysteries he wanted to puzzle out about this woman.

"I imagine I will," Rafe said, his thoughtful gaze on Isla. "No doubt my brother has got wind of this mess by now and is on his way here. The last thing I need is to hear another one of his lectures. With luck, we'll miss him on the road. I have no doubt Lady Rochester wrote a letter to him, or perhaps even Joanna and Brock, telling them everything. I shudder to think what would happen if Brock and Ash joined forces to come after us." Rafe chuckled darkly. "I have absolutely no intention of being here when they arrive."

"You may have a point," Lydia agreed. "I shouldn't like to see either of those men upset."

"Am I going with you too?" Isla asked in a quiet voice.

"What? Of course." Lydia cuddled the girl close.

"Good." Isla yawned and laid her head on Lydia's shoulder.

By the time they reached the Lennox townhouse, Isla was fast asleep. Brodie carried the girl out of the coach and up the steps. Shelton greeted them at the door, and the housekeeper, Mrs. Llewellen, smiled fondly as she met them on the way upstairs.

"Tuckered the wee tyke out?" she asked, stroking Isla's hair.

"Aye. She'll have new clothes this afternoon. We wish to leave as soon as the clothes arrive. Could you see to having dinner prepared for us in a basket so we may eat in the coach?"

"Of course." The housekeeper hurried off, while they saw to their other preparations.

"Lass," Brodie said to Lydia. "You should write to your father. We can leave the letter here. Brock and Ashton will most likely arrive soon, and they can see it delivered to him."

"Thank you, Brodie." Lydia leaned in and stood up on her tiptoes to kiss him. "I only wish for him to know that I am safe."

Brodie wound his arms around her waist, holding her close. "You don't mind staying with me?" he asked.

"I know that *this*"—she gestured between them—"is not going to last forever, but I would like to be with you at least a little while longer."

"You mean that?" Brodie asked quietly.

"Yes. I've been thinking quite a bit in the last few days. This is an adventure for me. There's been danger, romance, excitement. I've never had the chance for anything like this in my life, and once I go home to Bath, I will have to leave it all behind." She hesitated as she met his gaze. "And I don't want to leave you or this adventure. I want to live in this moment, not plan my tedious, buttoned-up life five steps ahead. I want to enjoy every minute I'm with you."

Brodie's heart swelled, and he found he couldn't speak. He pulled her deeper into his arms and kissed her with a tenderness that came naturally to him now. She was, in her quiet, sweet way, taming the wildness in him, and he didn't mind that one bit. He would be whatever she wanted, so long as he could call her *his* for just a little longer.

RAFE PUT ISLA TO BED IN THE BEDCHAMBER THEY'D provided her and placed her new doll in the crook of her arm. He kissed her forehead, and she sighed, the sound melting his wicked heart in unfathomable ways. As he prepared to leave, Isla woke enough to reach out and catch his hand, her tiny fingers curling around his.

"Uncle Rafe?" she murmured.

"Yes, kitten?" he asked.

She looked toward the carpetbag that Rafe had set down on the table by the door. "May I see my parents?"

"Of course." He retrieved the gilded frames and sat on the edge of the bed as he held them out to Isla.

"Can you tell me their names?" Rafe asked.

"My mother was Ellie." Isla held up her mother's likeness, then her father's. "This is Angus."

"I wish I could have met them."

Isla glanced up at him, her wide-eyed innocence mixed with an ancient knowing. "You smile like Papa. I remember his smile." Rafe couldn't help but grin. "Like that." She set the miniature of her father down on her lap and placed a dainty hand to Rafe's cheek, exploring his smile with the sweet curiosity of a child. Her touch sent a flood of warmth through his chest, and in that moment, he knew he was lost to this child.

At that moment he did something he'd never done before in his life. He made a vow that he actually planned to keep. He would protect her from the world. He would slay her dragons. He would be a father to her in whatever way he could for as long as he was needed.

"Time for you to rest, scamp. We'll leave for Brodie's castle in a few hours." He pulled the blanket up to her chin and carefully set the portraits on the table beside her bed, facing her. "They'll be watching over you and bring you happy dreams."

Rafe kissed the girl's brow again before he stepped out and closed the door. His body shook as powerful waves of emotions rolled through him. Regret that he hadn't met Isla's mother, sorrow that the child was an orphan, and love . . . love for the child that was strong as any love he'd ever felt for his family members.

He wanted to take Isla home, to make her his daughter, but she needed proper parents and a stable life. He wasn't suited to raising a child. She was better off in the care of Brodie and Lydia, who knew just how to care for her. But right now? Right now he could be here for her. It would have to do. The grief in him was so raw and agonizing that it robbed him of his breath for a few seconds, and he clutched his chest, trying to regain control. He was a man cursed to never have a life that matched his siblings. Rafe didn't want to change, didn't want to become a normal gentleman with a normal lifestyle, but those desires meant that a stable life, with a wife and children, had always been unlikely for him. Could a man have familial happiness without sacrificing adventure and excitement?

<hr />

PORTIA STARED OUT AT THE SEA OFF BRIGHTON'S coast. Her face was devoid of emotion, even though she was experiencing a rush of thoughts and hurts. Aunt Cornelia held a parasol over her head while she and Portia stood off a mile away from the water. In the distance, men frolicked like boys in the waves. Farther down the shore, rolling bathhouses for the ladies backed slowly into the water. Women covered head to toe in bathing costumes tiptoed down the ladders into the shallows to experience the ocean. Their squeals of surprise at the brisk, cold water would have amused her at any other time, but all joy within her had withered away.

"Now, this is a lovely spot. Don't you think, my dear? An excellent place to distract us from worrying about your father or your poor dear sister." Cornelia, while genuinely concerned for Lydia's well-being, had taken the time to remind Portia frequently that the entire situation was her fault. Whatever terrible fate that befell Lydia was to be on Portia's head.

Well, if Lydia hadn't stuck her nose where it didn't belong, hadn't tried to free the man Portia had already laid claim to, then none of this would have happened, would it? So who was really the one to blame?

Despite the frequent dour reminders of Portia's bad behavior, her aunt seemed quite happy to be in Brighton. Cornelia's spirits had been lifted when she had run into an old love earlier that day, some tired old earl named Donald something or other, as they'd been waiting to enter the townhouse they'd rented.

"Portia, dear, are you listening to me?" Cornelia cut into Portia's wandering thoughts.

"Yes, the coast is quite lovely," Portia admitted.

The air was so different from the heavy smog of

London and even Bath. Somehow the clean air had helped her clear her head. Despite her admittedly self-centered thoughts of late, she was worried about her sister. She must have been terrified—might *still* be terrified. And in danger, with that Scotsman who was set on revenge. Surely he'd learned that Lydia had only been trying to help him escape. He must have taken mercy upon her and not harmed her, but Portia had no way of knowing until they heard from their father.

"Would you like to try your hand at bathing this afternoon?" Cornelia asked as they walked along the gravel path, far away from the sand, which would have gotten into their stockings and boots.

"Yes, I would," Portia lied. Her thoughts weren't on the beach, but were miles away in the wilds of Scotland.

"You know, in my youth, we were taught to fear nature, to fear the sea and the forests. But what I see of this now is quite picturesque. The sea is thrilling. It makes one stop and think, does it not?"

"Yes," Portia agreed. "There is an undeniable beauty to it." She looked to the cliffs that abutted the sandy shore and how they met the rolling surf and the cloudless bright-blue sky. She thought of something the poet Shelley once said: *The place is beautiful. All shows of sky and earth, of sea and valley are here.*

Cornelia smiled. "You know, child, when you aren't determined to be a spoiled little creature, you are rather delightful and intelligent."

Portia bit her lip to stop a vehement retort from slipping out. Instead, she simply replied with an old quote her father used to say about the ocean. *"Toward the close of a fine summer's evening, then the sun, declining in full splendor, tints the whole scene with a golden glow, the seashore becomes an object truly sublime."*

"Quite right, quite right," her aunt agreed.

"Hello!" A shout from behind had the ladies turning.

An older man was hurrying toward them at a brisk pace. Although he was around Cornelia's age, in his early seventies, he moved with the energy of a much younger man. It was the earl they'd met before. Donald . . . Rhyton, perhaps? Her mind had been elsewhere when the introductions were being made. For the life of her, she couldn't remember what he was the earl of.

"Oh, my lord. What a pleasure to see you here!" Cornelia beamed at the white-haired gentleman as he reached them.

"My fair Cornelia." The earl bowed over her hand, kissing it. And he smiled warmly at Portia.

"How are you, Lord Arundel?" Cornelia asked as he joined them on their walk.

Arundel, that was it. Donald Rhyton, the Earl of Arundel. She committed the name to memory now.

"Excellent, now that I have run into you. I was hoping to find you so that I may invite you and your niece to join me at my home for dinner this evening."

"We have no other engagements. We would be most delighted, wouldn't we, Portia?"

Portia replied that she would, but it wasn't as if she had much choice. Cornelia would not hesitate to jab the tip of her parasol into Portia's bottom if she dared to beg off.

"Wonderful. Wonderful. Are you bound for home?" Lord Arundel asked.

"We are," Cornelia confirmed.

"Then allow me the honor of escorting you back. We still have much to catch up on." The earl offered his arm to Cornelia, who blushed like a young lady and tucked her arm into his.

Portia followed behind, her mood darkening at the thought of a dinner with no young people and nothing to listen to but reminiscing about things that had happened in the previous century. For a moment, she almost envied Lydia's predicament.

During their dinner later that evening, her aunt and the earl became embroiled in a lengthy conversation about India and how his favorite grandson had just purchased a commission to serve in His Majesty's army and was bound for the subcontinent.

"Capital fellow, my grandson. He's engaged to the most splendid beauty, the daughter of the Duke of Suffolk, wouldn't you know? Never a better made match. We're all quite pleased."

"That is splendid, my lord!" Cornelia said.

Lydia knew that her great-aunt always loved to hear about well-placed matches in society, which was no doubt why Lydia and Portia had left her so disappointed.

"Excuse me." Portia stood, and the earl hastily rose to his feet. She waved a hand at him. "Oh please, do sit, my lord. I must excuse myself for a moment." She exited the dining room and inquired politely of a waiting footman where she might be able to relieve herself. He led her to a private room and handed her a small bourdaloue, a small piece of china that looked rather like a gravy boat, which she might hold under her dress. Portia closed the door of the room and glanced about with a sigh. She didn't actually need to use the bourdaloue. She simply wanted a moment alone to think.

Lydia was somewhere in Scotland. If Portia were an angry Scot on the run with an Englishwoman, she would not leave a trail of breadcrumbs so obvious, which meant they would not be in Edinburgh, so her father was headed in the wrong direction. It seemed more like he'd hide out at Castle Kincade.

A plan began to form in her mind. If she could be clever about it, which she felt she could, she could leave her aunt here in Brighton and sneak away to Scotland to rescue Lydia herself.

Portia was not one who dwelt on what was fair in life —other than for herself—but she owed it to her sister to rescue her. If she could find Lydia before their father did and return her safely to Bath, their father might never have to encounter Brodie and challenge him to a duel. She would never forgive herself if her father came to harm over all this.

She poked her head out of the private room she'd been shown to and glanced down the hall. Seeing no servants about, she began to peek into the nearest rooms until she found a room that would aid her plan. She ducked inside and closed the door. It looked like the Lord Arundel's private study.

Rubbing her hands together, Portia noticed a large case at the end of what looked like a study. The glass case held a dozen long rifles and just as many flintlock pistols. Portia approached the case and eased the glass door open. She removed the smallest of the pistols, and, searching the cabinet below the case, she found what she would need to load the gun. She wrapped it in her shawl, never more glad that she'd taken a large thick cotton one this evening. The pistol almost peeped out of the woven material.

With a grim little smile, she returned to the dining room.

Later that night, once they had returned to their lodgings, Portia waited for her aunt to head up to bed. Portia pulled out a carpetbag in the dark of her room and removed a set of clothes she had paid a young footman for.

Now dressed in a boy's togs, she covered her bound-up hair with a cap and hastily packed a set of dresses and other necessities for traveling. She slipped out of the servants' entrance and walked the short distance to a large coaching inn nearby. When she found a Royal Mail coach, she inquired about the quickest route to Scotland. She was glad that the royal mail coaches ran almost continuously and she would have a chance to travel overnight.

Within minutes, she was riding next to four other passengers crammed inside. The top of the coach was carrying more passengers and dozens of pieces of luggage. As the coach rattled off into the night, Portia fell asleep, dreaming of what she would do when she reached Castle Kincade, climbing in through an unbarred window, waving a pistol and rescuing her sister. She only hoped that her sister was all right, but there was no way to know until she reached the angry Scot's home.

shton and Brock came flying into the city of Edinburgh, their horses lathered and in desperate need of rest after the relentless pace the two men had set. Ashton led the way to his town-house on the Royal Mile. He left Brock holding the reins while he rushed up the steps and banged the knocker loudly. His trusted butler, Shelton, answered the door quickly, even though it was still early in the morning.

"My lord!" Shelton looked flustered and a little panicked. "We were not expecting you."

"I'm sorry I didn't have time to send word," Ashton said as he called for a groom to take the horses from Brock, who hastily joined Ashton in the hall. "Where is my brother, Shelton?"

Shelton paled. "Master Rafe?"

"Yes, I know he's staying here. Where is he?"

"Well, actually, sir, he left town last evening."

"What?" Brock cut in.

"Shelton, you had better explain everything, from the moment my brother arrived here," Ashton said grimly.

"Of course, my lord. It all started when the Dowager Marchioness of Rochester arrived with Mr. Hunt. They said they were to meet Master Rafe and his companion, Mr. Kincade." The butler proceeded to explain Rafe and Brodie's late arrival, thereby missing Lady Rochester and Mr. Hunt. "Master Rafe was most insistent that I send Lady Rochester a message telling her that Master Rafe and Mr. Kincade were bound for the Isle of Skye."

"Skye?" Brock muttered. "Why would he tell them his destination?"

"He wouldn't. It's a misdirection. Correct, Shelton?" Ashton asked.

"Aye, sir. Master Rafe, Mr. Kincade, Miss Hunt, and the wee one are bound for Castle Kincade."

"Yes, that makes sense. Wait, what *wee one*? They have a child with them?"

"Aye, sir. A little girl, no more than six years old."

Ashton groaned. "What fresh hell is this?"

"Did they kidnap her too?" Brock growled.

"No, my lords, you misunderstand. The child, Miss Mackenzie, is an orphan."

Ashton couldn't believe what he was hearing. "Why the devil would two rakehells take an orphan with them?"

"Well, it's because of the resurrectionists, you see. They couldn't let the poor child be killed and dissected by a doctor."

Ashton scrubbed a hand down his face. "Shelton, for the love of God, you are not making sense."

"Perhaps I'd better start over . . ."

"Perhaps you'd better."

By the time the butler had explained the wild series of events, Ashton was no closer to understanding what he had been told.

"Rafe has taken a fatherly fancy to an orphan? Shelton, are you quite certain it is *my brother* were talking about, not some other fellow? The last time he was left alone with a child he threw himself out a window and into a prickly patch of roses to escape the child . . . who couldn't even walk."

"Quite certain, my lord. Miss Isla is a darling child, and she has been through too much for one so young. Even the staff here adore her, and she was only here a day."

"And you're certain they are bound for Castle Kincade?" Brock asked. Shelton answered with a nod.

"How did we miss them on the road coming in last night?" Ashton asked his brother-in-law.

"It isna hard. Brodie knows many ways to reach the castle. They could have easily avoided the main roads."

"Just like you did when you stole Joanna away?" Ashton's tone was sardonic.

"I didna steal my wife, man. She came willingly. You know that as well as I do." Brock's expression turned into that thunderous look only the Kincades seemed to manage.

"Regardless, we'll have to wait for the women to arrive before we head off again. Damn Rafe and his cat-and-mouse nonsense."

"Well, taking the back roads will add time to their travel, which works in our favor. Still, I worry about Joanna and all this travel. She thinks I dinna ken her little secret, but I do."

"What secret?" Ashton said, worry suddenly knotting his stomach. If anything was wrong with his sister . . .

"She's in the family way. She's been sneaking out of bed in the morning and becoming sick each day in our bathing chamber. She's been hiding it from me, but I sleep lighter than she thinks I do."

Ashton stared at him. "Joanna is with child? Why, that's wonderful. I have the strangest urge to shoot you and then pour you a drink." Ashton grinned. "And so long as we are sharing secrets, Rosalind is two months along. We have been waiting until we are sure, but I might as well share the news with you."

Brock returned Ashton's smile. "Let's say we both forgo the pistols and find the whiskey instead."

"Excellent idea." Ashton led Brock into the drawing room, all thoughts of Brodie momentarily forgotten.

CASTLE KINCADE LOOKED LIKE SOMETHING OUT OF A fairytale to Lydia. As she and Isla stepped out of the coach, Lydia got her first true look at the tall, gray stone castle, which stood like a protective wolf on the sloping hill. A person could see it from miles around, since the castle was on high ground. A lovely lake lay in one direction and a vast forest in the other.

"It's lovely," Lydia told Brodie as he joined her next to the entrance. A tall wooden door covered with iron-mongery made the entrance look rather imposing. Brodie raised the heavy knocker and brought it down on the wood four times.

The door opened a minute later, and a man stared back at them.

"Master Brodie!" the man exclaimed. "We didn't know ye would be coming. His lordship just left for Edinburgh yesterday to find you."

Brodie winced a little. They got lucky missing them along the way, but how long would their luck hold out? "Morning, Tate. How about we keep my coming home a secret for a few days, eh?"

Lydia bit her lip nervously as the man called Tate nodded and called for two footmen to remove the luggage from their coach.

"I shall endeavor to do my best. Master Aiden will

wish to see you. He remained here, should you arrive," Tate said.

"Good to know. Oh, Tate, you must remember Mr. Rafe Lennox from a few weeks ago?"

"Indeed, sir. Welcome back, Mr. Lennox." Tate bowed to Rafe. He had been here only a few weeks ago to visit Joanna, something Lydia had learned while they rode here.

"This is Miss Lydia Hunt, and the wee one is Miss Isla Mackenzie."

Tate smiled at Lydia and blushed when Isla grinned up at him and held out a tiny hand, which the steward shook with great solemnity.

"Miss Hunt will stay with me. Please see that Isla has a room close to ours."

"Yes, Master Brodie." Tate did not question that Brodie and Lydia were to share a room, and Lydia was grateful for that. She had no desire to face the scandalized glares of servants.

"Where is Aiden, Tate? I might as well face him now."

"Out, sir. For his usual walk."

"Bloody hell," Brodie muttered.

"What's the matter?" Lydia asked in a whisper.

"He'll be gone a good three or four hours," Brodie replied with a frown.

"Why would he be gone so long?" Lydia asked.

"Aiden is the gentlest of the four of us. Our father

saw that gentleness as a weakness and hurt Aiden at every possible turn. My brother only feels safe when he's in the woods amongst his wee beasties."

Lydia put her arm through Brodie's and leaned into him, hugging him from the side. "I hate that you've all suffered so much."

Brodie gently shrugged free of her touch. He bent down and scooped up Isla and started telling the child all about the old lairds of the castle. Lydia tried to ignore the prick of pain in her chest as he walked away from her. It felt like a dismissal.

"Do not take it personally, kitten," Rafe said. "No man likes to share the darker parts of himself, especially with a woman he cares about."

"Why not?"

"Men think they must be impenetrable and without weakness. For one who has lived a charmed life, like myself, it's of little matter, but Kincade has a dark and painful side that he will never wish to share with you. It's best to leave it alone." Rafe gently patted her shoulder before he followed Brodie and Isla upstairs.

Lydia lingered in the grand hall for a time, looking over the woodland tapestries and a pair of portraits from the eighteenth century. She couldn't resist taking a closer look at those. She could see Brodie in the faces of the two Scottish lords who were proudly wearing their kilts with the unique Kincade plaid. She explored the corridors of the lower part of the castle and stopped at the library.

It was a grand room with shelves that went fifteen feet high. Tall ladders with wheels on the bottom could roll along the shelves to aid someone exploring the topmost parts of the library. Sunlight came into the room, illuminating the gilded spines of the books.

Lydia's heart stirred with excitement. Already this was her favorite room. She trailed a finger down a row of books that led to a cozy window seat. She heard a soft fluttering above her head and discovered a tiny owl that could fit in her hands was watching her from its nest.

"Hello there," she said, smiling up at the owl. It gave a soft series of hoots, as its head rotated toward the door.

"Ach, I see you found our resident librarian." Brodie stood in the doorway, relaxed with his arms crossed.

"Yes, he's quite a handsome one." Lydia turned her gaze back to the owl. The boundary of the sunlight from the tall windows just reached the base of his nest, making the loose feathers glint silver and gold.

Brodie joined her, winding one arm around her waist and kissing her cheek. He did not apologize or explain why he had pulled away earlier, but Lydia wasn't angry with him, only sad that he didn't wish to let her in.

"Where's Isla?"

"With her new favorite uncle. We have a dozen

beasties in the house, and they are currently trying to find them all."

Lydia turned in his arms and placed her palms on his chest, staring into his gray-blue eyes. They were so clear, like water in a shallow well with moonlight reflecting on it.

"Brodie . . . I meant what I said a few days ago. I should like to stay here with you—if you still want me."

He closed his eyes and held her close. "Aye, lass, I do. I'll keep you as long as I can." He left unsaid what would happen when everyone who was searching for them finally caught up to them.

"When they come, you will let me go, won't you?" She wanted him to say no. To argue that he was madly in love with her and would marry her and keep her always. But he did not, and she knew he would not. He was as Rafe said, impenetrable and wounded. He would never let her in. She was not the sort of woman to scream or cry and make demands. Brodie held an affection for her, she knew, but it was not love. If she had time, she felt she could get him to open up to her, maybe even open his heart, but time was not something they had.

"I dinna want to let you go, lass. I'll hold on to you for as long as I can before I must let you go." His eyes held such a wounded honesty that she knew he spoke the truth.

"Kiss me," she said.

He opened his eyes to look down at her, and she was

LAUREN SMITH

undone by the tenderness she saw in his face. He cupped her face with one hand, while the other explored the hollow of her back as his lips met hers. It was a whisper of a touch at first, as though he was holding back, making the need inside her build. He nibbled at her bottom lip as he parted her mouth, his tongue flicking slowly against hers. It was a kiss that spoke of unspoken promises and tender surrender.

Lydia pretended that he loved her, that he was using his lips to say what he could not with words. She told him back, kiss for kiss, *I love you.*

Brodie moaned, his kiss becoming hungrier. He gripped her bottom, pulling her tight to him. Would she always have this wild desire for him? Would it haunt her until the day she died?

"Lydia, let me take you to bed," he said huskily against her mouth.

The owl above them burst into a series of hoots, and someone called out from the library doorway, "Ach, Brodie, do you ken how much trouble you are in?"

Brodie's mouth left hers reluctantly. "Aiden. You're back sooner than I expected."

Lydia peered over Brodie's shoulder to see the youngest of the Kincade brothers. Like Brodie, he had dark hair and fathomless gray eyes. He was perhaps an inch taller and thinner too, well built but not quite the mountain of muscle his brother was. Around his shoulders a pine marten rested, its claws digging into the young man's coat as it held on. Aiden carefully unwound the long creature and set it on the floor. The creature glanced between the two men before scurrying away down the corridor.

"So, this is the lass who sent Brock and Ashton running off to Edinburgh?" Aiden's teasing smile set Lydia at ease. He was as Brodie had said, gentle, yet there was nothing weak about him. Rather, he seemed to radiate a quiet strength.

"Hello, I'm Lydia Hunt." She stepped around Brodie, but he kept a possessive arm around her waist.

"It's a pleasure, lass." Aiden smiled, and his humor shone through when he spoke next to his brother. "I willna steal her from you, brother, no matter how she might fall for me." Aiden batted his lashes in a silly way at Lydia.

"Hush, puppy," Brodie snapped, but he finished with a chuckle.

Aiden winked at Lydia again. "I hope you don't mind a few wee beasties about the castle," Aiden said.

"Not at all. Brodie told me all about your furry companions. I think it's quite charming. We were just admiring the little owl up there a moment ago."

Aiden gave his brother a surprised look. "I think you ought to marry this lass, brother."

Brodie pointedly ignored Aiden's comment. "We should go to dinner. You must be famished."

They left the library and met Rafe and their young

LAUREN SMITH

charge coming down the stairs. Isla sat astride the banister, and Rafe was aiding her balance as she slid down.

"Good Lord, we've been spotted, kitten. Run!" Rafe scooped her up, and they sprinted back up the stairs, where Rafe stopped and twirled around, making the child squeal with delight.

"Who is the child?" Aiden asked.

"She's an orphan we rescued in Edinburgh," said Brodie.

Aiden's eyes fixed on the child as Rafe carried the giggling girl back down the stairs. "An orphan?"

"Kitten, this is Aiden, Brodie's younger brother. Aiden, this is the kitten."

"I thought I was the kitten," Lydia teased Rafe.

"That you are. All sweet women are kittens. I shan't tell you what I call women who aren't so sweet."

Brodie snorted at that.

"It's a pleasure to meet you." Aiden bowed formally to Isla, who smiled shyly and half hid behind Rafe's legs.

"I'm Isla. Isla MacKenzie."

"She's my little Isla Mac." Rafe looked like a proud father. The little girl had already stolen his heart.

Rafe looked hopefully at the others. "Did I hear someone mention dinner?"

"Yes, we were just about to send someone to fetch you."

They all proceeded into the large dining room. It had been recently remodeled after a fire that had destroyed

326

much of the castle. Lydia had been stunned when Brodie told her the story during the ride here. How Brock and Joanna's cook, a woman who had been in love with their deceased and abusive father, had tried to poison Joanna and then attempted to burn down the castle.

Thankfully, no one but the mad cook had died, but the castle had been in ruins. The local townsfolk the brothers had supported for years came to help rebuild it. With the help of Joanna's fortune, they had recently finished the repairs.

The new dining room held a large oak table, and the cold stone walls had been softened with tapestries depicting Bonnie Prince Charlie and his Highland warriors preparing for battle. A few family portraits also hung by the fireplace at one end of the room. Brodie pointed them out to her.

"That's my mother and Rosalind."

"Your sister looks just like your mother."

"Aye, she does. It used to enrage my father to see Rosalind after our mother passed. It's why she fled home so young and married the first Englishman she came across. She was able to escape with him to London and have a good life, until he died and she married that bloody baron."

Brodie shot a look at Rafe, who laughed. "You won't hear me disagree."

Lydia sensed that Rafe and his older brother did not get along all that well.

Thankfully, Isla was a welcome distraction from these uncomfortable topics. She now told Aiden about how she and Rafe had explored the house.

"We found two otters in the large fountains in the gardens." Isla giggled. "They were hiding under lily pads."

Aiden's unguarded smile made Lydia grin as well. When she caught Brodie's eye, he was relaxed, watching his brother and Isla with open fondness.

He can love, if only I had time to win his heart. But Lydia had to be smart and not allow her desires and wishes to make the situation worse.

"Then we found a hedgehog," said Isla. "She was quite fussy. And the badger!" The girl was delighted to have the focus of the entire table on her. It wasn't because she needed attention, but she was hungry for affection. In a way, Lydia understood. Although her father was very much alive, he had never been fully alive for her, only Portia. Lydia had lived a half life when it came to her family.

Brodie leaned over to whisper in her ear. "What's the matter, lass? You look troubled."

Lydia wanted to unburden herself to him, but she didn't dare. He had used her emotional weaknesses against her in an argument before when he was angry, and she had no desire to ever allow him to do that again.

"It's nothing. I believe I am missing home." It wasn't a lie. Even in the midst of this adventure, she still longed for home. Not that Bath was truly home. Home was wherever her loved ones were. She loved the people at this table, but she also missed her father, her sister, and even Aunt Cornelia.

"Perhaps a bit of dancing will do you good?" Brodie suggested.

"Dancing?"

"Aye, dancing. Aiden, fetch your fiddle after dinner," Brodie told his younger brother.

Lydia brightened instantly, and her heart skipped a beat. Dancing? Here? How wonderful.

Brodie placed a hand on her thigh under the table, brushing his fingers over her leg, and it only heightened her excitement.

"Tonight, you willna be dancing alone. You will be dancing with me," Brodie promised.

20

Brodie escorted Lydia into the ballroom, which had been refinished with a new wooden dancing floor. Aidan retrieved his violin and stood in the corner of the room while servants rushed to light the wall lamps and the candles in the chandeliers. Rafe held Isla's hand and was explaining how men and women danced at balls, and then he executed a feminine curtsy to show the girl what to do next. Lydia's laughter at the sight had Brodie's heart skipping a few beats. She was so perfect, especially when she lowered her guard and could be herself, assuming that no one was paying attention to her.

Aiden finished tightening the strings and gave a nod to the dancers.

"Miss Hunt." Brodie grinned as he bowed to Lydia.

She curtsied, holding her gown away from her legs, and when she did, he caught a glimpse of her delicate ankles.

"Mr. Kincade," she answered with a teasing smile. Then they began to dance as Aiden played a lively tune.

Lydia was the best dancer he'd ever seen, both quick and sure-footed, with delicate, light steps. She pirouetted, hopped, twirled, and clapped in time to the country dance as though she danced every day of her life. Perhaps she did. She'd almost said as much at the inn they'd stayed at on the way to Edinburgh. The thought that she was a woman who quite literally danced her way through life, even in secret, filled his chest with an undeniable warmth.

He kept pace with her, laughing as they locked arms at the elbow and spun, before he caught her by the waist and twirled her in a dizzying circle.

So long as the music played and she was in his arms, he could forget all about the rest of the world, or the limited time they had together. There was only this dance and the perfect woman with him.

The music finally died, and Brodie clutched Lydia tightly to him, both of them breathing hard. She lowered her lashes, the exertion giving a healthy color to her cheeks. When their gazes locked again, he smiled at her, his body almost trembling with his joy.

"Has the music stopped?" she asked, her voice almost a whisper.

He lifted his head and looked about, but the ballroom was empty. There was no sign of Rafe, Isla, or Aiden. How long had they been gone?

"Never mind. I still hear music," Brodie said.

"Oh? You do?" She chuckled. "What does it sound like?"

"A slow waltz." He softly began to hum the melody of a waltz. Brodie held her hand with one hand and her waist with the other as he danced with her alone in the ballroom. He fell into her blue eyes as he sang an old song his mother used to sing when he was a boy.

OH THE SUMMERTIME IS COMING
And the trees are sweetly blooming
And the wild mountain thyme
Grows around the blooming heather.
Will ye go, lassie, go?

LYDIA CAUGHT ON TO THE MELODY AND HUMMED with him as he sang.

AND WE'LL ALL GO TOGETHER
To pluck wild mountain thyme
All around the blooming heather.
Will ye go, lassie, go?

. . .

I WILL BUILD MY LOVE A TOWER
  Near yon pure crystal fountain
  And on it I will build
  All the flowers of the mountain.
  Will ye go, lassie, go?

AND WE'LL ALL GO TOGETHER
  to pluck wild mountain thyme
  All around the blooming heather.
  Will ye go, lassie, go?
  Let us go, lassie, go.

BRODIE RAISED HER HAND HIGH SO LYDIA COULD twirl before coming back into his arms. Brodie held his breath as her body pressed against his.

For the first time in as long as he could remember, he was overcome by joy, pure and untainted. It filled him to bursting. It was both the best and worst of feelings.

"Thank you," Lydia said as she pressed her head to his chest.

"For what?" he asked.

"For letting me have an adventure with you. Ladies like me don't often have the chance to run off chasing the sunset. We stay home, sew, read, and pretend that we are content with a life with that and nothing more. Society allows a lady like me to live only a half life. But you've treated me like a whole person. You've cared for me in your way and shown me what it means to feel all the things a person ought to in life. That is what I'm thankful for."

Brodie couldn't speak. The lass had robbed him of all words. He gathered her in his arms, holding her long after the lamps burned low and moonlight covered the floor, lending a melancholy beauty to the two of them alone in the ballroom.

"Why don't we go to bed?" he suggested.

Lydia linked her fingers to his. "Show me the way."

❦

JOANNA, ROSALIND, AND REGINA ENTERED THE townhouse in Edinburgh late that night. The ladies were exhausted. Joanna's mood was sour after the journey, and her concern about her friend only increased when the Lennox butler informed her at the door that Lydia was not there.

"Where is my husband?"

"In the drawing room, my lady," Shelton said. "He and his lordship are in good spirits." The butler almost chuckled, as if it were somehow a joke.

"Good spirits?" Regina echoed suspiciously. "Come now, Shelton," she admonished.

The butler winced. "I meant to say they are foxed, my lady."

"Foxed?" Rosalind scowled. "My husband doesn't get foxed, especially when he is supposed to be on a rescue mission."

"You may wish to inform him of that, my lady."

Joanna scowled and led the other two women into the drawing room. They skidded to a stop at the sight of Brock and Ashton laughing in chairs by the fire, two empty bottles of whiskey between them.

"Lass!" Brock grinned, his eyes slightly glassy from his drinking.

"Sister!" Ashton chuckled unevenly and then raised an empty glass to Rosalind. "Wife, and mother." He gave a drunken cheer.

"Ashton!" his mother snapped. "What's gotten into you?"

"More a matter of what's gotten into *them*." Ashton pointed at the two younger women and then snorted in laughter. It took Brock a second to work it out, and then he started to laugh as well.

"Us?" Joanna shared a glance with Rosalind, who was equally confused.

"Explain yourself," Regina demanded.

"Bairns," said Ashton.

Regina shook herself. The word as it came from his lips made no sense. "Bay-urns?" Was he trying to say something Scottish?

"Aye," Brock cut in. "We began to talk about them, and the next thing we knew, we were celebrating, and then we just sort of . . . kept on celebrating." Brock had to explain slowly as he had trouble focusing on the words.

"Bairns . . . Oh! Babes!" Regina spun to face the other two women. "Wonderful! Which of you is going to have my first grandchild?"

Joanna sheepishly raised her hand, only to have Rosalind do the same.

"Both of you?" Regina cried out in delight and embraced both women at the same time.

Joanna hugged her mother back, but she was soon scowling at her husband and brother once again. "Why didn't you stop Rafe and Brodie?"

"Because they were already gone," Ashton said with a sigh. "Poor Lady Rochester and Mr. Hunt are bound for the Isle of Skye."

"What?" Rosalind gasped. "Why the Isle of Skye?"

Brock explained what Shelton had told him. By the end, the three women had formulated a plan.

"Once you sleep off the drink, you must go and chase down Lady Rochester and Mr. Hunt. We shall all escort them to Castle Kincade."

Ashton and Brock looked thoroughly displeased with the idea.

"I think it's time you two went to bed," Regina ordered the two drunken men.

Ashton and Brock both laughed at that, but when they looked toward their wives, they sobered a bit.

"I think they're serious," whispered Brock.

"Brock. Bed. Now," Joanna said, and Rosalind gave Ashton a pointed look that required no words.

Both men stood and moved on unsteady legs toward the women. Joanna put an arm around Brock's back as they allowed Shelton to escort them to an empty bedchamber. Brock collapsed onto the bed, and Joanna had to straddle each of his legs to pull his riding boots off.

"How did you know about the baby?" she asked as she dropped the second boot to the floor.

"I always ken when you leave our bed, *Sassenach*. It feels empty without you. When you kept leaving me, something felt wrong. So I followed you, my sweet brave lass, and I heard you toss your accounts into the chamber pot."

Joanna fell onto the bed beside Brock, and he pulled her close, kissing her.

"Are you upset about the baby? You and Ash were quite drunk this evening."

"Upset? Did we sound upset to you, lass? But I must admit, I am worried. I didna have a good father, nor did you and Ashton. He and I spoke, and we both fear we won't be good fathers."

Joanna smacked his chest. "Getting foxed is not what a good husband *or* father does. Talk to your wives next time. Rosalind and I know you will be good fathers."

"How can you be sure of that, *Sassenach?*" He looked so serious and troubled.

"Brock, who raised your siblings after your mother died?"

"I did."

"Exactly. And did they all turn out well?"

Brock looked suddenly sheepish. "Well, Brodie's gone and kidnapped a—"

"Besides that . . .admittedly complicated matter."

"Er . . ." He still looked doubtful.

"At the very least, Aiden and Rosalind are fine. *You* did that."

"So you're saying two out of three isn't bad?"

Joanna groaned. "*When* we learn the truth about Brodie, *then* we can decide whether we need to assess your parenting skills again. But the truth is, you took care of them. Three of them. And not only that, you had to protect them from the abuse and tyranny of your father. If you could manage that under such dire conditions, imagine what you'll be like raising a child without that fear and abuse looming over you."

The crease in his brow faded. "You truly believe that, lass? I will be a good father?"

"I do." She nuzzled his cheek and then cupped his face so she could press a lingering kiss to his lips.

Brock wound his arms around her waist. "You know, I'm not too foxed to make love to you."

"Is that so?" Joanna giggled. "Prove it to me, Scot."

And so he did.

JACKSON HUNT FACED A DECISION HE HAD NEVER expected to encounter again in his lifetime. It was close to midnight. They had finished a late dinner, and the candlelight made Jane's skin glow like smooth alabaster. She had removed the pins in her hair earlier that evening, and her dark-red hair tumbled down in silky waves. She smelled like the most exotic flowers in a well-tended hothouse.

"Jackson?" She spoke his name sweetly.

"Yes?" he replied, his throat a little hoarse with emotion.

"You're doing it again."

"Doing what?"

Jane's lips twitched with the ghost of a smile. "Staring at me." She cupped her chin in her hands and rested her elbows on their small dining table in the private room of the coaching inn.

"Oh." He chuckled and rubbed the back of his neck. "I was thinking."

"About what?" Jane moved her chair a few inches closer to his. The dark blue of her velvet gown was adorned with a diamond-and-pearl-studded brooch, which accented the swell of her perfect breasts. It was hard to think straight when she was tempting him like this.

"You might think me an old fool. But if I never tell you, I'll never face rejection."

He was surprised at his own honesty, but in the last few days he had grown to trust Jane with his thoughts. Now he was facing the test of whether he could trust her with his hopes and dreams. Jane reached across the table and covered one of his hands with hers.

"What is it, Jackson?" Worry drew her delicate dark-red brows together.

"I . . ." He realized he could not do what he wished to until he had committed to it properly. He pushed his chair back and then knelt on one knee before Jane, clasping her hands in his. "I know we've only known each other less than a week, and this may seem like utter madness, but I choose to believe in fate and second chances. Jane, will you give me that? A second chance at love and life? Be my wife, my lover, my treasured companion and dearest friend?"

He held his breath as he gazed at her. Her lovely lips parted in shock. He feared she would say no for so many reasons, including that it would mean she would no longer be a dowager marchioness, but a simple trades-man's wife. Would she pull away from him?

Her eyes welled with tears, and she slid out of her chair to join him on her knees. She cupped his face, her fingers soft and warm as she held him.

LAUREN SMITH

"Yes. Yes, my darling, yes." The words were spoken softly, but they reverberated down to his very soul, echoing like a sonorous choir of angels.

Yes. She had said yes.

His hands trembled, and he couldn't stop smiling as he hauled her into his arms and hugged her tight. He buried one hand in her hair and tried not to laugh at the wellspring of joy deep inside him as it threatened to bubble over.

"I vow to make you happy," Jackson said.

"I vow the same." Jane giggled. "Lord, what will we tell the children?"

"I don't care, as long as you are my wife." He stole a quick kiss. "Let's do it tonight."

Jane's eyes glowed. "What?"

"Let's marry tonight. There's a blacksmith in the village here."

Jane laughed and hugged him tighter. "You don't mind waking up an angry Scot who will be wielding a hammer?"

"I would face a thousand angry Scots if it meant I could marry you tonight." Jackson would risk anything for this woman. Since he'd met her, he had sparked to life like a raging fire, and he would not surrender her for anything.

He helped her to her feet, and they went to see the innkeeper, who told them where to find the blacksmith. They walked down the cobblestone street of the village to a small house next to a forge. Jackson pounded on the door. A lit lamp sat in the window, and he figured many couples had disturbed the blacksmith for hasty marriages at all times of the day and night.

"I'm coming!" the man bellowed a moment before he opened the door. A tall, dark-haired man, built like a brick house, glared at them.

"Would you mind marrying us, good sir?"

The blacksmith blinked and peered down at them from the porch of his cottage.

He scraped a hand over his beard. "You ain't that young, are ye?"

"Indeed we are not, both widower and widow by many years. Nevertheless, we would very much like to marry at once."

The man sighed. "Ach, fine. Come in." He opened his door wide. Jackson, holding Jane's hand, led her inside as they followed the Scotsman, who lit a few oil lamps and carried one to the forge next door. There was a cozy little enclosed room just off the main workshop. The blacksmith set the lamp on a table next to a symbolic anvil. The door to the room opened, and two people in dressing gowns entered. One was an older man, and the other was a middle-aged woman.

"This is my father and my wife. They will be the witnesses." The blacksmith produced a dark-blue ribbon, which he wrapped around Jackson's right hand and Jane's left.

Jackson only vaguely remembered the vows he spoke; his heart and mind were too excited to focus on much besides staring at Jane. It had been so long since he'd felt like this, like he had hope, that he had a full life once again to look forward to, and not just trying to find such a life for his daughters.

All the years since Marianna's death seemed to have a purpose now. They had kept him waiting for Jane to walk into his life. How strange that they had both been in London society for so long and yet had never crossed paths before now. If Lydia had never been taken by Brodie Kincade, they might never have met. It was ironic that he now had a reason to shake Kincade's hand —after he throttled him, of course.

"You are man and wife under the eyes of God and these here witnesses." The blacksmith lifted the hammer up and smashed it down on the anvil.

Jackson kissed his wife, and Jane smiled as she kissed him back.

"We'll have your papers ready tomorrow," the blacksmith said. He nodded to the woman, who took note of their full names on a piece of paper. "Now let me get some bloody sleep. Er . . . and congratulations."

"Thank you. We shall come by tomorrow." Jackson shook the blacksmith's hand, and then he escorted Jane back to their inn. When they reached their shared room, he grinned at her.

"Care to start our honeymoon tonight before we resume the chase for Kincade and Lydia?"

Jane began to undo his cravat, a coquettish smile on her lips that heated his blood.

"Absolutely, husband." She used his loosened cravat to pull his head down to hers for a long, deep kiss that was the beginning of one of the best nights of his life.

21

The following days passed in a blur of laughter, delight, and kisses. Lydia explored the lands around Castle Kincade, with Brodie as her guide. Half the time they had Rafe and Isla accompanying them, and the rest . . . well . . . They took advantage of their time alone.

This was one such moment. Lydia laid a large plaid blanket down on the ground by the lake, and then Brodie removed the food from a wicker basket. She lay back on the blanket while he prepared their plates. She took a moment to admire him without his being aware of it.

His dark hair, slightly too long to be considered fashionable, was tousled by the wind, and a shadow of a beard ghosted his jaw. He was the most handsome man she had ever known. She had met prettier men, certainly, but there was something about the hard-edged features of Brodie's face and form that made him seem invincible, untouchable, and that he was hers to surrender to. Hers to touch. Hers to love.

Brodie noticed her eyeing him and offered her a wolfish smile. "What are you thinking about, lass?"

"You." She smiled and rubbed her foot against his thigh. It was so easy now to be playful with him. Here she didn't have to worry about scandal, rumors, or ruination. She was free.

Brodie's eyes warmed as he caught her foot and tickled her ankle. She giggled and pulled free of him. He offered her a plate when she sat up, and they ate in pleasant silence.

The waters of the lake glinted in the bright late-summer sunlight. Ducks and swans floated on the surface, bobbing beneath the water to quest for food. It was all so blissfully peaceful.

"Lydia . . ."

She turned to look at him. "Yes?"

"I never apologized for taking you from Bath the way that I did. Although, I canna say I regret it. This last week has been . . ." He didn't finish, but his smile pulled at her heart.

"It has been wonderful," she said.

"I hate that I scared you." Brodie brushed a lock of

her hair behind her ear, his gaze impossibly tender. "I would never hurt you, lass."

She leaned into his palm as he cupped her cheek. "I know."

"'Tis funny, is it not? All this time, I thought I kidnapped the wrong sister. But as it turns out, I took the right one." He leaned in and kissed her. It was a sweet kiss, like one between two people who had been lovers and friends for years, not days.

Lydia moved her hand to the back of his neck to keep him close as she deepened the kiss. Their mouths broke apart briefly as she teased him.

"Never hold back with me, Scot."

Brodie chuckled and tumbled her backward on the blanket. He captured her wrists above her head with one of his hands, pinning them into the soft plaid blanket beneath them. He took his time kissing her, first sweetly, then more passionately until she was flushed with excitement.

"This is how I will remember us," he whispered in her ear between kisses. "Like this, in the sunshine, the breeze in your hair, and clear skies reflected in your eyes." Brodie nuzzled her neck, and Lydia's heart swelled within her chest.

She would remember *everything* about him when this was over, not just how he was with her, but how he was with those he cared about. How he sang Isla to sleep each night, how he teased Aiden into smiling, or how he would let his guard down over a game of cards and laugh with Rafe. There were a thousand things about Brodie Kincade that could make a woman fall in love. He believed he was cold and aloof, but he betrayed himself with every bit of love he gave others, even if he didn't realize it.

She captured his lips with hers, and he pulled her skirt up to her waist as he slid into the cradle of her thighs.

"Make love to me," she demanded. "Fast and hard."

His wicked grin made her moan as he pinned her hands above her head again so he could continue his tender assault at an agonizingly slow pace.

"You devil!" She gasped and fought against his imprisoning hold because she wanted to touch him, to grip him while he tortured her with his sinful mouth.

"Be still, my wee captive. I'll take you as I please." He laughed so mockingly she almost laughed as well, but she was too desperate for him now. The sudden sound of a footstep and a cold voice froze her and Brodie in place.

"Release my sister, or I swear I will kill you."

Brodie started to move.

"*Slowly*, or I'll shoot."

Lydia peered over Brodie's shoulder to see a bedraggled boy covered in dust, aiming a flintlock pistol at Brodie's back. Lydia recognized the face. It wasn't a boy at all. "Portia, no!"

Brodie spun, taking Portia to the ground just as the gun went off with a loud crack.

"What the bloody hell do you think you're doing, woman?" Brodie snarled at Portia. "You could have killed her!"

"You monster!" Portia screamed. "I was saving her from you!"

Lydia scrambled to her knees and pulled on Brodie's shoulder.

"Let her go, Brodie. She thought you were hurting me."

Brodie slowly released Portia. He got to his feet and helped Lydia up.

Portia was breathing hard as she stood. "Lydia, are you all right?"

"Yes, I'm fine, Portia. Why on earth are you wearing men's clothing? And where is Papa? Is he with you?"

"I'm alone," Portia replied sullenly. "After you were taken, Papa sent me to Brighton with Aunt Cornelia. I escaped, dressed like a boy, and traveled on the Royal Mail coaches to Edinburgh. Then I hired a coach to the village nearby and had to walk the rest of the way." She smacked her breeches, which were covered with dirt.

Lydia couldn't help but stare at her little sister. Gone was the perfect beauty. Her sister was bedraggled, filthy, and looked ready to collapse.

Brodie picked the pistol up from the ground and

tucked it behind his back in the waistband of his trousers.

"Portia, dear, you look exhausted."

"I am," Portia admitted. "But I had to save you." Her eyes shot to Brodie. "He truly wasn't trying to hurt you?"

"What? No." Lydia rushed to reassure her.

"But he kidnapped you with a knife to your throat. I couldn't stop thinking about how frightened you must have been. All because I was so foolish." Portia's voice shook, full of desperation and panic in a way Lydia had never heard before.

Lydia clasped her sister's hands in hers. "Yes, there was a bit of a misunderstanding at the beginning, but not anymore. We've both grown to care about each other."

Brodie crossed his arms over his chest, scowling at Portia. Lydia put herself between her lover and her sister, just in case things got out of hand.

"You have quite the nerve to come here acting like the injured party, lass," he said to Portia. "Let's not forget who kidnapped whom first. Who lied about being with child. You owe me one hell of an apology."

Portia's eyes narrowed. "I am *sorry* I thought you would be a good husband. I'm certainly *sorry* for convincing my father to catch you and bring you home to me. I'm *sorry* you were such a foolish man to mistake my sister for me."

Lydia covered her face with her hands. That wasn't an apology, and she was certain Brodie would be furious.

"*Fine.* I accept. Now, you can return to the castle with us, rest for a day, and we will see you to a coach and send you home to Bath."

"What?" Portia snapped. "Did you not hear the part of my story where I fled my aunt in Brighton? Papa isn't in Bath. He went after you! I have no one to return to."

"That isna my problem," Brodie snapped back. "You found your way here on your own—I'm certain you can survive alone in a fancy house in Bath."

Lydia grasped Brodie's arm. "Please don't send her away just yet. We need to discover where my father is on his way to the Isle of Skye and perhaps we can find a way to send her to him."

"Lydia!" Portia gasped. "You must come with me. You cannot stay here."

"Why not, Portia? I am happy here."

Portia pulled her away from Brodie to have a moment of privacy to converse.

"Lydia, you cannot stay, not unless you marry him," Portia said in a hushed tone.

"I don't see why you care. You haven't cared about me in any of this."

"Of course I have," Portia insisted.

Lydia stared hard at her little sister. "You didn't think of me that night you made a fool of yourself at the ball. You didn't think of me or Papa when you lied about

Brodie seducing you. You didn't think of Brodie when he was attacked and drugged, or when you drugged him yourself. I knew you were spoiled, Portia, but I never imagined you could also be cruel. If Mama were alive, you would have broken her heart."

Portia's lips parted, and her bottom lip quivered. She dropped her head.

"You're right. Mama would have been devastated. I never should have come here!" Portia suddenly dashed toward the distant woods, leaving Lydia staring after her in shock. It was just like her to run away without a thought as to where she was going.

With a heavy sigh, Brodie took off in the direction her sister had gone. He returned a few minutes later with a squirming Portia thrown over his shoulder. He dumped her onto the plaid picnic blanket.

"I wasna about to let the foolish child get killed by boars. We have many in the woods."

"A boar?" Portia gasped.

"*Boars*, plural. As I said, we have many, and they would have gored you with their tusks. 'Tis not a pretty way to die."

Portia scrambled to her feet again, and this time she grabbed Lydia's hand, trying to drag her toward the castle.

"We're safe out here by the lake, Portia, really," Lydia said, trying to reassure her panicked sister.

Brodie collected the plaid blanket and gathered the

dishes into the basket. They headed toward the castle, but it seemed as though luck wasn't with them today. As they reached the front doors of Castle Kincade, three riders were spotted on the road, headed straight for them.

Lydia had a terrible feeling one was her father.

22

Brodie ushered Lydia and Portia through the front door and turned to face the riders. As soon as they were close enough to recognize, he silently cursed. It was more or less as he'd expected. Brock, Ashton, and Jackson Hunt skidded to a stop and dismounted. Hunt moved the fastest, and Brodie didn't try to stop what happened next. He raised his arms open-handed and took the angry father's hard right hook to his jaw. Brodie stumbled back, catching himself against the doorframe.

"Where the bloody hell is my daughter?" Hunt threw another punch, and Brodie knew this one would blacken his eye. After a few more hits, Ashton and Brock dragged Hunt away from him.

Blood dripped down Brodie's chin, and his bottom lip stung. His whole face was a mass of pain as he got back to his feet. The old man was surprisingly strong. He would be lucky to see out of even one eye tomorrow.

"Brodie, where's the lass?" his older brother demanded.

"Inside. She is safe and well. As is her sister."

"What?" Hunt shouted. "Portia's here too? How the devil—?"

"Easy, man," Brodie said. "Your younger daughter only just arrived. She said she left her aunt in Brighton and traveled here alone. She thought she could rescue Lydia from me. She nearly killed me with a pistol."

"Where are they? I demand to see them at once." Hunt shoved past Brodie, who allowed him to storm the castle, as it were.

"Lydia! Portia!" Hunt called out as the door closed behind him.

Brodie sighed and winced. Ashton and Brock watched him solemnly.

"Christ, Brodie, do you have any idea of the trouble you've caused?" said his brother. "You'll be fortunate if Hunt doesn't challenge you to a duel."

"That doesna bother me." In truth, it did bother him, but after such a beating part of him would not mind shooting the old man in the leg just to even the score.

"It bloody well bothers me," Ashton growled. "Hunt has just married Lucien Russell's mother, which makes him practically family to me. If you kill him, it would not only break Lady Rochester's heart, it would enrage Lucien. And believe me, you do not want that man coming for your blood. And since Brock is married to Joanna, *you* are *my* family, which means some small part of my own honor demands I defend you against one of my dearest friends. Do you see the dilemma we all face?"

Brodie nodded, but deep down he no longer cared. The day he had dreaded had finally come. He was losing Lydia. As he entered the castle's grand hall, he found Hunt talking to his two daughters. He fiercely embraced them both, and then he berated Portia for leaving Brighton.

"You could have died!" Hunt exclaimed.

"Yes, I know, but . . ." Portia sighed dramatically and then gasped. "Papa, are you wearing a wedding band?"

Brodie felt strangely like an outsider in his own home as Hunt told his daughters about how he had married Jane Russell over an anvil.

"Oh, that's famous!" Portia exclaimed. "How romantic! I only wish we had been there. Right, Lydia?"

"Yes, I'm so sorry we missed it, Papa."

Lydia caught Brodie's eye, and her excited smile faded as she noticed his battered condition.

"Brodie!" She pulled free of her father's hand and rushed over to him, trying to touch his face.

Brodie caught her hands and gently held her at bay.

"Papa, did you do this?" Lydia demanded.

"I did. And I plan to do more once I see you and Portia safely away from here."

"No," Lydia said as she turned to look at her father. She was as beautiful as she was defiant in that moment. "You will not harm him ever again."

"There is a matter of honor that must be settled, not just for me, but for Mr. Kincade as well. I have wronged him, just as he has wronged me. And to each of us I'm sure the other's sin seems the greater. Isn't that right, Kincade?"

The proud Scot in him was prepared to meet Hunt on the field of honor. The odds that one of them would die were great. He was an excellent shot, and while he could fire into the air, he had no guarantee that Hunt would do the same. If he could shoot as well as he punched, the odds that Hunt would kill him were high.

The problem lay with Lydia. No matter who lived and who died, Lydia would be heartbroken and would in time grow to resent the survivor. For everyone's sake, he had to be a coward. He had to turn his back and walk away.

"Sorry to disappoint you, Hunt, but I have no honor. Take your daughters and go."

Brodie turned on his heel and left. As he stepped into the brilliant late afternoon sunlight, a dark violent storm ravaged his heart from within. He went to the stables, and as soon as he had a horse saddled, he rode away, leaving the castle and his bleeding heart far behind him.

❧

LYDIA STARED AT THE OPEN DOORWAY WHERE BRODIE had gone. A dull headache crept behind her eyes as she finally but unwillingly accepted that her time with Brodie was over. That the man she loved had not only walked away but in fact rode away as fast as he could.

She had run after him, but only as far as the tall oak doors. She had stopped there, stilled by an invisible force as she watched him flee. She wasn't a fool. She knew why he had left. He was too good of a shot to miss her father, and if he refused to fire, her father would most likely kill him. So he had done the only thing he could and left. She understood, she truly did, but it didn't mean that her heart hadn't shattered at his abandonment.

"Lydia?" Her father put a hand on her shoulder. She tore her eyes away from the Scottish landscape.

"Yes, Papa?"

"Forget him. It's time we both go home. Once the coach arrives with Jane, we'll go home to Bath. Jane has already been engaging people to help explain your absence from Bath. Your reputation may yet be intact."

She let him escort her into the drawing room, where he once again recounted his adventure with Jane and how after they had married, they had met up with Brock and Ashton on the road to the Isle of Skye. As Brock and Ashton's wives were both pregnant, the women had waited to take a coach with Jane, which was meant to arrive in a few hours.

"I'm happy for you, Papa," Lydia said, and she meant it. To have Jane as a mother would be wonderful. It meant Lysandra would be her sister, and all those charming Russells would be her protective brothers-in-law. But the joy she wished she could feel right now was impossible.

Portia joined her sister on the settee, while their father was momentarily distracted speaking to Brock. She reached over and clasped one of her hands.

"I'm sorry, I didn't know," Portia whispered.

"Know what?"

"That you fell in love with him. Heavens, I nearly shot the man."

Lydia did not deny it. What point was there now?

"How did it happen?" Portia asked. "How did you fall in love with him?" The interest in her little sister's eyes was unexpected. "It's just . . . I keep hoping to fall in love. I was so certain that if I willed it in my head, my heart would follow. It's been frustrating to find that I cannot do that. I thought I could make Brodie love me if he but stayed with me awhile, if he but kissed me . . ." Her sister's tone was tinged with desperation and confusion, enough so that much of Lydia's anger at her sister's foolish actions eased.

"You cannot make love out of nothing. It cannot be forced or willed into being," Lydia replied softly. "It comes on slowly, without one noticing. And when you do realize it, the feeling hits you like lightning. When I first saw Brodie at the ball, I thought he was the most handsome man I had ever seen, but I knew he was not meant for the likes of me. It was only after he took me north that things changed. Our anger with each other softened, and little by little as we got to know each other, I eventually realized I was in love with him."

She looked at her sister. "Love is not a splendid, wondrous thing, dear sister. It is a broken heart, a wrenching sob, a collection of dreams fading before your eyes. Pray that you never know love, Portia. I would not wish this fate upon anyone."

Her own words caused such pain that she could not stand to sit there and pretend to be fine, even amongst her family and friends.

Lydia rose from the settee and left the drawing room for her bedchamber. She threw herself onto the bed, unable to stop the sobs that came. She jolted as something grazed against her arm. She lifted her head and saw Aiden's pine marten watching her. It nuzzled her arm, and she reached out hesitantly to touch it, and it rubbed its cheek against her fingers.

A quiet exhaustion stole through Lydia as she lay

there. She could feel her hopes and dreams fading into dust as the sunlight gave way to shadows outside.

⁂

WHEN JANE, JOANNA, ROSALIND, AND REGINA finally reached Castle Kincade, the women were quite mad with fear, particularly Jane, who knew that a duel was very possible.

"Jackson!" Jane called out for her husband as she and the others rushed into the hall.

"Here, my love!" Jackson stepped out of a nearby room, and she all but flung herself at him.

"Are you hurt? Tell me it didn't come to a duel?"

"No and no, my darling. Rest easy. Lydia is safe, and Portia too."

"Portia? I thought she was in Brighton with your aunt?"

"She was," Jackson sighed. "She ran away and came here to try to rescue Lydia herself."

"Oh, good heavens." Jane glanced about. "But if you didn't duel with Mr. Kincade, then where is he?"

"Gone. He said he had no honor to defend, took a horse from the stables, and rode away. He hasn't returned since."

At this point, Rosalind spoke up. "My brother said he had no honor?"

"Yes. It quite puzzles me, but that's what he said."

Rosalind and Joanna exchanged glances.

"Where is Lydia?" Jane asked.

"Upstairs in her room. She was quite upset. I didn't wish to bother her."

"Oh dear, we had better go." As one, the four women headed up the grand staircase. A maid in the hallway indicated which room Lydia was staying in, and Jane knocked lightly on the door.

"Lydia? May we come in?"

There was a moment of silence before the door opened. Lydia peered at them with puffy red eyes. She had been crying. Jane's heart broke for the girl.

"Oh, sweetheart, come here." She took Lydia into her arms and held her close. She had wanted to be a mother to this young woman for so long, and now she was. She only hoped she could earn Lydia's trust now. Jane let the girl cry as she gently coaxed her to sit on the bed. Rosalind, Regina, and Joanna stepped outside to give them privacy.

"I'm so sorry, Lady Rochester. I mean, Mrs. Hunt. Heavens, I don't even know what to call you." Lydia sniffled and wiped her eyes with a handkerchief.

"It's all right. You may call me Jane, or even Mama, if you like."

Lydia managed a watery smile. "I've always thought of you like a mother whenever I spent time with you and Lysandra."

Jane brushed a lock of hair back from Lydia's face. "I

remember what it feels like to have a broken heart. Even all these years later, it's not something one forgets."

Lydia lifted her teary gaze to Jane's. "How did you know that I love him?"

Jane nodded. "I couldn't imagine you would be crying right now for any other reason."

Lydia nodded and wiped at her eyes again. "I don't normally cry. Yet I can't seem to stop now." Without further encouragement, Lydia told Jane everything, leaving out no details, except for when it came to moments of private passion.

Jane was stunned. How could Brodie Kincade not love this woman back? Was he truly that much of a rakehell that he was unmoved by Lydia? Or . . . Jane bit her lip in thought. Did he love her madly but yet didn't have the time to make things right with Jackson? It was quite possible that Brodie had chosen to leave rather than hurt Lydia by facing Jackson down, since it would be hard to calm the tempers of two men who had both wronged each other. Yet Brodie's attempt to avoid hurting Lydia by leaving had, in fact, hurt her anyway.

"Now that you are here, we should return to Bath." Lydia sat up, straightening her shoulders as she tried to mask her pain. "We have so much to do now that you and Papa . . ." Lydia embraced Jane again. "Lysandra and I are truly going to be sisters now, aren't we?"

"Yes, you are," Jane agreed as she stroked Lydia's hair. "You don't mind that I married your father?"

"Mind? No, you've always been so wonderful to me. If I had thought you and Papa could have made a match, I'd have introduced you to him myself."

Jane chuckled. "I am fortunate. Your father has given me something I never thought to find again."

"I'm so very happy for you both." Lydia's joy was genuine, though she was a bit shaky from crying.

"My children will certainly be surprised, but they know that I do not hesitate when my instincts tell me to do something. And spending time with your father while searching for you, I felt it, deep inside." Jane shook her head with a wry smile. "My first marriage was made just as quickly, and I had no doubts about my love then. I have no doubts here either."

Jane kept an arm around Lydia's shoulder. "Now, tell me about this little orphan, Isla."

AIDEN WATCHED THE HUNT FAMILY DEPART AS HE, Brock, Joanna, Ashton, Rosalind and Regina all waved goodbye. Being the quiet brother, Aiden saw and heard much from those around him.

He knew Isla's leaving was breaking Rafe's heart, the widening distance between the rake and the orphan making its mark on the man to the point where Aiden wondered how no one else could see it. It was as plain as the fact that Brodie, his wild and reckless brother, was making the worst mistake of his life by not going after Lydia.

Aiden was able to slip away unnoticed and went to the stables to have a horse prepared, and then he rode out into the twilight. There only a handful of places Brodie would go, and he knew them all.

Half an hour later, Aiden reined in his horse and dismounted near a small waterfall deep in the woods a few miles away from the castle. He looped the reins of his horse around a low-hanging branch once he spotted Brodie.

His older brother was sitting on a tall rock near the base of a shallow waterfall. His knees were bent, and he rested his forearms on them, looking very much like the young boy who used to hide here when their father was still alive. With stealthy steps, Aiden crept up behind him.

"I knew you would find me," Brodie replied without turning. "You always do."

Aiden climbed up on the rock beside him and watched the clear water cascade into the pool below before it joined the stream. "And I knew you would hear me. You always do."

"She's gone, isn't she?"

"Aye. And Isla with her."

Brodie dropped his head between his knees.

"Then all is as it should be."

"Is it?" Aiden asked. "I see only broken hearts and broken people."

"We've always been broken," Brodie replied. "That hasna changed."

Aiden cocked his head to one side. "Hasn't it, though? Rosalind ran away vowing never to return. Yet she's here, with a loving husband and a child on the way." Brodie continued to stare at the water, so Aiden continued. "Then there's Brock, so fearful of his temper, yet he's calm and happy with Joanna and soon to be a father as well."

"That doesna mean you and I will be the same," Brodie muttered.

"Maybe not me," Aiden agreed. "But you? That woman loves you. I know you all think me damaged and that I canna and willna ever be whole, but I see things more clearly than you ken. I see life all around me, see the way it pairs things together, the falcon and his mate, the otters in the river, the wee creatures in the ponds. Animals know their mates. Men are the ones who hesitate, who let clouds gather to cover what fate has shone a light on for us. You have a mate, brother, and you have no reason to turn away from her except for your own fears."

Brodie sighed. "I don't trust myself, Aiden. I fear everything about life, at least the parts that matter. I am a coward, and I am cruel."

At this Aiden laughed, but he felt a pang of guilt for

it given the dejected look on his brother's face. "Brodie, you are no coward. You leave when you know it's the only way to survive. Not every fight is worth using one's fists. You fled because it spared Lydia having to choose between you and her father. She knows that. And you are not cruel. You speak in haste and can say things that wound, but you are like a badger with an injured paw. You lash out with no true desire to hurt others, only to protect yourself. That can go away in time. And with love. Both of which you have within reach."

Aiden saw the light of understanding creep across his brother's face.

"You are a man who survives," Aiden added more quietly. "But you canna survive with a broken heart, and you canna survive without her in your life."

Brodie was quiet a long moment before he straightened his shoulders, and then he looked up at the glorious skies above them.

"You're right. Perhaps it is time I stopped running away from everything and started running toward something."

"*Someone,*" Aiden corrected as he and Brodie climbed off the rocks. "And you'd best start running now."

"Hush, pup!" Brodie laughed as he took off toward his horse.

Aiden took his time returning to his own horse and slipped the pretty mare a few bites of apple while he stroked his palm down her chestnut nose.

"It is just you and me now, I suppose," he told the horse. The mare nickered and bobbed her head before nudging her nose against his shoulder playfully. Aiden looked toward the horizon, watching the sun vanish and the purple hues gather in the woods to take its place.

"If I be so broken, then let me go in these twilight shadows," he murmured, thinking of an old story of a fairy princess who had rescued a brokenhearted High-lander. But a fairy princess could not stay a fairy forever in the realm of humans, and so she had to choose: her immortality or her love.

Aiden had often dreamed of a dark-haired fairy princess with eyes the color of warm honey. She haunted his waking moments almost as much as his dreams. But the fairies were lost to the world of men. Magic had faded from the earth, and there was little left to tether the two realms together.

Aiden hummed a sad song as he mounted his horse and rode home. He gave silent thanks to whatever crea-tures of myth still dwelt in the woods, and he saw once again the fairy princess in his mind, calling to him.

✵ 23 ✵

One Week Later...

Brodie walked up the steps to the Hunt townhouse in Bath, his pulse quickening as he pushed away hazy memories of dragging Lydia down these very steps at knifepoint. He was certain he would not be received here, but he had to try, and keep on trying until he succeeded.

He rapped the knocker, and the butler answered. Brodie remembered him from the night of the abduction as well. But rather than a look of recognition or surprise, there was only cold indifference.

"May I help you?"

"I need to speak with Mr. Hunt, please."

"Do you have an appointment?"

"Well, no. Can I make one?" Was this the point where English toffs left their calling card? He wasn't that familiar with these formalities. "I don't have a card, I'm afraid."

The butler sighed, his tolerance strained. "Your name?"

"Brodie Kincade."

"You will wait outside." The butler shut the door before Brodie could even acknowledge him.

Something odd was going on. Surely the butler knew who he was? If he did, he would have expected a more hostile reception, and if he didn't, then why was he being so rude? It made no sense.

In time the door opened again. "It seems Mr. Hunt is not currently engaged and is willing to see you. This way."

Brodie straightened and stepped into the hall. The butler closed the door behind him and led him toward the study.

"Personally, I am hesitant to allow a stranger into this house," the butler said. "One never knows what they might do if given the chance. A truly *unscrupulous* cad might even try to make off with one of the family's daughters at knifepoint."

Brodie looked at the butler when he said that, but the man's features were like stone. Still, his words said it all. He *did* know who Brodie was and what he had done. So why the game?

Inside the study, Hunt sat at his desk, but he wasn't alone. An older man sat in a chair across from him. Hunt was looking over a document, and when Brodie came in, he handed the document over to the older man. "See if this will do. I will tend to my guest while you examine the terms of the sale."

He got up and came over to Brodie. "Ah, Mr. Kincade, is it?"

Now this was ridiculous. The butler's ignorance he could understand, but this? He was about to vent his frustrations when Mr. Hunt spoke again.

"I believe I met some of your relations during my recent trip to Scotland. Lovely people. Most accommodating."

"Mr. Hunt, I do not ken why you are—"

Again, he was interrupted. "You see, I recently met the most wonderful woman, and we decided to get married in Scotland. A hasty thing, to be certain, but we both felt we'd waited long enough to find happiness again. We brought my daughters along with us. My eldest, Lydia, was already friends with my wife's family, and it would have been wrong not to include her. We stayed at your family's castle overnight on the way back. Your elder brother was most welcoming."

Brodie still had no clue what game Hunt was playing, but noting the sidelong glance Lydia's father gave to the old man reading the document, he decided to play along. "Sorry I missed you while you visited my brother. I was there recently myself."

"I've been informed that you met my eldest daughter once. Is that true?" he asked pointedly.

It then dawned on Brodie what was going on, at least in part.

"I . . . Yes. Briefly, at a ball held here in Bath. I was most taken with her. It is because of her that I have come to speak to you."

The man behind them in the chair who was reviewing the document Hunt had handed him glanced up at them both, clearly a willing audience for the charade that Hunt had concocted to protect Lydia's reputation from scandal. It was rather clever.

Mr. Hunt smiled at that and nodded in approval. "I see. Am I to understand that you would like to court my daughter?"

Brodie smiled back. "Aye. But of course, I wish to have your permission first."

The old man, satisfied with what he had read, set the document down on the desk and got up. "I see no problems with your terms, Mr. Hunt. My client will be most pleased. Now, will I be seeing you at the assembly room tonight? My granddaughter is debuting."

"I believe I will be there, yes. It will be a pleasure to see her again."

The door opened, and the butler led the man away. Once the door shut, Hunt's tone changed. "I understand why you did what you did at the castle, Mr. Kincade. Had our roles been reversed, I hope I would have made the same choice. But I need to understand why you're here now. We're alone—you can speak plainly."

"I wish to marry your daughter. I didna think I could, not after what happened between us. I ken that I ruined your daughter, but I wish to make things right."

"Make things right?" Hunt echoed the words with emphasis. "Haven't you heard? We've only just returned to town, and my daughter was with us the whole time."

"But surely word of what happened—"

"I think you underestimate my wife's ability to turn gossiping tongues against themselves. Even before she left Bath, she had her daughter establishing a story as to Lydia's whereabouts. One that only required slight clarification upon our return."

Brodie shouldn't have been surprised, but he'd secretly hoped that he would have had Lydia's ruination to help his cause for marrying her.

"I'm pleased to hear about your marriage," Brodie replied carefully, wondering what Hunt wanted him to say.

"I've been examining my role as Lydia's father of late, and I have found that I have been a terrible disappointment. I will not, therefore, be allowing just any gentleman to court my daughter. Any man who wishes to have that honor must therefore have only the purest of intentions toward her."

"I have the purest of intentions," Brodie assured him. His voice then roughened a little from a sudden rush of emotion. "I love her more than my own life, more than anything else."

"And if you love her enough to let her go, would you?" Hunt asked.

He kept his chin held high. "I already did. But now I realize that loving her the way she deserves means coming after her. I wanted to spare her the pain of seeing one of us hurt, or worse, but I didna give her the chance to tell me what she wants. Would you agree that she ought to make that choice?"

Lydia's father stroked his chin. "And if she does choose you?"

"I will honor and cherish her. I willna ever hurt her again."

"And how am I supposed to trust you?"

Brodie reached down to his boot and pulled out a small *sgian-dubh* blade and held it out hilt-first to Hunt.

"Then trust my word over this blade. It was a gift from my mother. This blade has been with me through the dark days and the days of splendor. I vow upon the steel of this blade that no harm shall ever come to Lydia at my hand, word or deed."

Hunt gazed upon the blade for a time before he nodded and gestured for Brodie to put it away.

"Very well, you have my permission to court her. But you will say nothing of her trip to Scotland with you. I expect you to agree to whatever my wife says with regard to how you know my daughter and where she's been of late. Is that understood?"

"Yes."

"Good. Then present yourself at the assembly rooms tonight. My family will be there. You may make your intentions known to her then, and we will both abide by her decision." He held out his hand to Brodie. "I shall see you this evening."

Brodie shook Hunt's hand and took his leave. He would be counting the minutes until he could see her again and hopefully win her back. It would be the most important battle of his life.

❦

LYDIA STOOD IN ONE OF THE ASSEMBLY ROOMS OF Bath, watching the couples twirl in a lovely pattern. Lysandra was talking beside her, but the words floated past Lydia rather than through her. Since she'd left Scotland, she hadn't been herself. She had been more subdued, listless, and she'd had quite a bit of difficulty focusing on what people said to her. Her mind was far away, and her heart was with it.

Lysandra gently nudged her elbow. "Lydia? Are you all right?"

"What? Oh yes, I'm sorry," Lydia apologized. It had been such a whirlwind returning to Bath and meeting the rest of the Russell family so they could hear the news of the hasty marriage uniting the Russells and the Hunts. But the news had been well received by the Russell brood, even if they had been quite surprised at it. She had become a sister to all the Russells overnight, as had Portia. Jane had come up with a clever lie to cover any scandal, and not one word was breathed of Lydia's sudden disappearance from Bath.

Portia had taken the news well, but something was bothering her, and she would not confide to Lydia what it was. She'd simply withdrawn from everything and everyone. Everyone except Isla. The orphan had taken to Portia in a way that had surprised everyone. She'd crawled into Portia's lap and handed her doll to Portia to try to make her feel better, and the two had quickly bonded.

Even now, much to Lydia's continued amazement, Portia had passed on the chance to dance and meet eligible men. She had remained at home, caring for Isla so the child would not be lonely.

Lydia's life had change drastically since returning from Scotland. Her father was no longer so accommo-dating and tolerant with Portia, and Lydia, who had been so often overlooked, was now consulted frequently by her doting stepmother. It was going to take some getting used to. She rather felt like Cinderella. But all the good changes in her life didn't make a difference when she thought of Brodie and how brokenhearted she was. Fanny had settled in working as a lady's maid for Portia and the two had struck up an unlikely friendship.

"Lydia," Lysandra murmured. "You look very pale. Perhaps we should go home. I'll tell Mama and Mr. Hunt."

"Yes, perhaps that's a good idea," Lydia agreed. Lysandra left her alone to go seek out their parents, who were on the opposite end of the room.

The current dance ended, and Lydia watched the couples disperse. As they did, she looked across the room and, her heart jolted at the sight of a man in a dark-blue coat and tan breeches who was watching her. He was beautiful in a wild, untamed way. His dark hair was tousled and his gray-blue eyes were turbulent. Lydia dared not let her heart fill with hope again, yet she could not look away as he crossed the room toward her.

He stopped within arm's reach and made an elegant bow.

"Miss Hunt, would you do me the honor of a dance? If you have any available?" Brodie spoke so gently, so earnestly, that she wasn't quite sure it was him and not some kind of daydream.

"I . . ."

"I'd prefer a waltz, lass, to better hold you in my arms."

Now she knew she had to be dreaming.

"A waltz?" she echoed as he took her wrist and examined her card. He made a soft tsking noise as he saw she had no dances yet claimed. He took the pencil attached to her card and wrote his name down on every line for every dance. Then he held her hands for everyone to see.

"Lydia, lass. I wish to claim every dance for the rest of our lives." He stepped closer. "What do you say? Will you give me that honor?"

"Every dance for the rest of our lives?" Was this truly happening?

"I daresay the poor Scot is trying to propose," a familiar voice said nearby.

Lydia spotted Rafe not too far away, watching them with amusement, a puckish smile hovering on his lips. She turned back to Brodie.

"Are you?" she asked, her entire body starting to tremble.

"Aye, lass. In my own way, I am." He put an arm around her waist, and several gasps from nearby matronly ladies made Lydia's face burn with mortification.

"Oi, you lot can stop your bloody gasping," Rafe growled, making their turbans quiver.

"Well put, Mr. Lennox," Jane said as she and Mr. Hunt approached them. Jane fixed the matrons with a withering glare. "Mr. Kincade and my stepdaughter have been secretly betrothed for a year. He's merely reaffirming their pledge, aren't you, Mr. Kincade?" Jane lied so smoothly that even Lydia believed her.

"I am," Brodie agreed, and he met Lydia's gaze.

"What do you say? Have pity on a man who loves you fiercely. Tell me you'll be my wife, my love, my *everything*, lass."

Lydia glanced hastily at her father, who did not look entirely pleased, but he also didn't object. He gave her a small nod instead, while still scowling a little at Brodie.

"You truly love me?" she challenged Brodie, matching his quiet tone as another dance started up behind him.

"Aye, far too much to be wise. I love you blindly, madly."

Lydia's throat tightened as she tried to calm her racing heart. "When did you know?"

"That I loved you?"

She nodded.

"That first night I carried you away in my arms. I couldna hate you, even when I thought you were your sister. You enchanted me, lass. And in time, you showed me I wasna a broken man."

Brodie squeezed her hands, and she saw the adoration in his eyes.

"So long as you love me, lass, I will fight the world to keep you."

Lydia squeezed Brodie's hands back. "Yes."

"Yes?" His eyes gleamed with excitement as she nodded again. "Then dance with me."

Brodie swept her onto the floor, and they danced throughout the evening. The master of ceremonies had to turn a blind eye to the succession of dances after Jane frowned at him quite sternly.

Word of Lydia's secret engagement to Brodie took Bath by storm that night, but Lydia didn't care at all. The only thing that mattered was that she was dancing with the man she loved, and they would go on dancing together the rest of their lives.

EPILOGUE

A Scottish wedding was always a magical event. Lydia entered the old stone kirk on Castle Kincade lands. She clung to her father's arm as he walked her to Brodie, who stood proudly at the altar, his plaid kilt showing off his legs in a way that made her blush. Her father paused at the front of the church with her, and the two men shared a look of understanding before Brodie nodded at him.

Her father kissed Lydia's cheek, and she blinked away tears as she joined Brodie before the altar. The ceremony was a blur of smiles and happy tears for Lydia as she spoke her wedding vows. She only had eyes for Brodie.

When it was over, they gathered in the kirkyard with their friends. In that moment, Lydia felt as though she could ask for nothing more of the world. She had a family who loved her and a Scottish rogue who worshipped her. It was as though every dream she had buried in her heart had been brought back out into the light.

Brodie curled an arm around her waist and leaned in to kiss her cheek. "Happy, my love?"

She gave him a smile that could barely contain her bursting happiness. "I don't think it's possible to measure my happiness," she confessed.

Brodie turned her fully to face him as he cupped her face, his eyes searching hers. "My love for you rivals the depths of the seas and extends beyond the stars themselves."

It never ceased to amaze her how much he had changed in the weeks leading up to their wedding. He'd become a happier man, a true romantic, and yet he was still that same wicked rakehell in their stolen moments together. The ghosts that haunted him from his past were starting to fade, leaving behind a man who enjoyed life.

Lydia curled her fingers into his cravat and pulled his head down to hers to steal a kiss.

"Dance with me tonight?" he asked.

"Where?" Lydia giggled.

"Anywhere." His eyes smoldered as he added, "How about our bedchamber? I would love to see you dance like I did that night in the inn, for me and me alone."

Lydia grinned. "Will it tempt you, my darling Scot?"

"Aye. *Always.*"

RAFE WATCHED BRODIE AND LYDIA WHISPER TO EACH other in the kirkyard. He wasn't one to applaud marriage as a rule, but in Brodie's case, the man sorely needed it.

"Papa?" Isla's voice broke into his thoughts. Isla stood next to him, wearing a pale-blue satin gown with an orange sash tied into a bow at her back. Her hair was only partially pulled back by ribbons. She'd been over-joyed to attend the wedding in the fine new clothes that he'd purchased for her.

He took her small hand in his. "Yes, kitten?"

"Can I truly call you Papa?" Isla asked. It was perhaps the tenth time this week she'd asked that same question.

Rafe had spoken to Lydia and Brodie two weeks before and had asked them if he might take the child as his ward. It had surprised them, and they had raised concerns about why a single gentleman who'd never been married would want to raise a little girl. He had replied that he had plenty of interfering relations who would no doubt be more than happy to help him do the thing properly. They ultimately agreed, so long as Isla wished for it too. And she had.

"Yes, Isla, you may call me Papa. Or Uncle Rafe. Whatever you prefer."

Isla swung his hand back and forth in hers as she seemed to think it over. "I want you to be my papa, but I already have one."

Rafe turned and knelt before the little girl. "You may have another papa. Just as Lydia now has a new mama. You will always have your first papa and mama." His inexplicable connection to the child was soul deep, and he had a strange feeling that Isla's parents, wherever they were, were watching over him. He didn't want to let them or Isla down. For the first time in his life, someone depended on him. It was unsettling, but also exciting.

"Oh, Rafe, there you are." Ashton and Rosalind joined them in the kirkyard. Rosalind took Isla by the hand and led her away to admire the wildflowers growing at the edges of the yard.

"How fares the child?" Ashton asked.

"Well enough. She misses her parents." Rafe followed the child with his gaze, wanting to make sure she was safe and well.

Ashton stroked his chin, and Rafe could feel his older brother's gaze upon him. "Rafe, are you certain you can care for this child? I'm happy to set aside a trust with plenty of funds for her, if you'd like."

"No, I will not take money, Ash."

"Well, that's a first," his older brother mused. "But if you need it, I will give it. I must admit, I've seen quite a difference in you these last few weeks. Dare I say you're leaving your rakehell ways behind?"

Rafe chuckled. "I prefer to think that I'm redirecting my focus in life. Keeping that girl entertained can be a challenge. But I may have a bit of devilry left in me yet."

Ashton laughed. "So long as you keep it far from that child, you'll be fine."

"I promise nothing," Rafe said with a smirk. "Other than to vow to never see her hurt."

"What is it about her that draws you?" Ashton asked. "She is a lovely child, of course, but you've never shown interest in children before. They used to terrify you."

"They've never terrified me," Rafe protested. "I simply . . . have trouble relating to them."

"And what makes her different?"

Rafe smiled as Isla gathered a bouquet of flowers and presented them to Rosalind.

"She's thoughtful and wise for a child. She thinks of others more than herself, despite her hardships. Doesn't a child like that deserve to enjoy life? And who knows more about enjoying life than your dearest brother?"

Ashton smiled, but it was one that betrayed his doubts. "Yes, who indeed?"

TWO MONTHS LATER

Aiden stared out at the cliffside landscape that draped into the sea off the coast of North Berwick. He urged his horse to race down the coastline, feeling free for the first time in days. He had left Castle Kincade to allow Brock and Joanna some time alone, and he had agreed to meet Lydia and Brodie as they returned from their honeymoon on the Continent.

He was bound for the distant docks of North Berwick. He would likely have to wait a few days, perhaps a week if the ship carrying his brother and sister-in-law was delayed, but he was glad for the time alone.

Too often of late he'd been reminded that he alone of the Kincade siblings had not married. He likely never would. But that was something he chose not to dwell on, when at all possible. The past had caused him too much pain, and he could not expose a woman he loved to the nightmares and the scars he carried.

The sun set on the horizon. The orange orb dipped behind the distant mountains and bathed the world in fire. Aiden guided his horse down the smoother slopes to better admire the view of the brightly lit water along the sandy beaches. The whispering of the surf against the shore and the cries of seabirds were soothing.

Aiden watched the black-and-white birds overhead catch a current in the air and hold steady in the same spot for minutes before they tucked their wings in and shot down into the water like arrows, only to bob up seconds later with a wriggling prize caught in their beaks. Animals were truly magnificent. He always found peace when he was near them. They acted only out of need and never malice.

He cast his gaze out at the water again and noticed large pieces of wood floating and tumbling until they washed up on shore. Something had wrecked out at sea.

Poor souls. It seemed that whatever had happened, there may have been no survivors.

Aiden rode closer to the water, examining the flotsam and jetsam as it appeared more frequently. Then he saw a body, draped over what looked like part of a mast. Long, dark hair was plastered to a red gown. It was a woman!

Aiden leapt off his horse and dashed into the surf, just as a wave carrying the woman rolled over and crashed into him. The breath was knocked out of his lungs as he struggled to catch the woman's body. They tumbled in the waves before slamming into the sand. As the water receded, he dragged the woman up the shore a ways before he rolled her onto her back. He expected to see the hallmarks of death, a face ravaged by sun and sea. Instead, he saw an exquisite beauty, almost perfect delicate features that would make an artist weep for wanting to paint her.

He bent over her, pressed his palms on her chest in a rapid succession of beats, and then covered her mouth, breathing into her as he'd seen a man do once when a boy had been drowning near their village in a small loch. He continued to do this until her body spasmed and she expelled the seawater from her lungs. Long, dark lashes fluttered and revealed honey-brown eyes. It was like seeing a ghost. It was the woman from his dreams, the fairy princess he had known in his mind and heart for as long as he could remember.

She coughed, and her glassy gaze began to fix on him before her eyes widened.

"You. It's *you*," she said in a light accent that he couldn't place, and then she passed out in his arms. Aiden stared at her and then the sea, watching more wreckage wash up on the shore.

"Who are you, lass?" he whispered. He lifted her up and carried her toward his horse. They would find the nearest doctor at North Berwick, and hopefully he would uncover who she was there.

But whether she was simply a woman or a fairy princess, Aiden knew he held his destiny in his arms.

THANK YOU SO MUCH FOR READING NEVER TEMPT A Scot! The next two books in the League of Rogues series will be **The Earl of Morrey** (involving Gillian's half brother and James the Earl of Pembroke's sister Letty), and **Lost with a Scot** where Aiden Kincade will finally have his happy ever after!

UNTIL THEY RELEASE, CHECK OUT MY LATEST

historical release ***Devil at the Gates*** a lush, gothic historical romance! Turn the page to read a sneak peek about the daughter of a famous fencing master who's on the run from an evil stepfather and stumbles into the path of a dark and brooding lord who doesn't want to be tempted to love again...

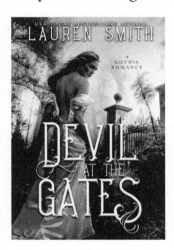

DEVIL AT THE GATES

PROLOGUE

Dover, England - 1793

The Duke of Frostmore stirred fitfully in his bed. The sheets that clung to his skin were damp and fresh with terrible dreams that had jolted him awake. He'd never slept well when it rained, even as a boy when he'd simply been known as Redmond Barrington. There was something about the sound, the way it plinked against the windows as the wind whined through the cracks in the stones of the large old medieval manor house.

He rubbed his eyes and squinted at the darkened bedchamber. Something had awoken him, something outside his door. A soft cry came, echoing through the gloom. Redmond turned in his bed to see if his wife had been disturbed. But the bed was cold, empty.

The duchess was gone.

He shoved back the covers and pulled on his dressing gown.

"Millicent?" He wondered if she'd perhaps gone to her bedroom, which was next door. He'd agreed to the tradition of allowing his wife to have a separate room, but he'd told her from the start that he longed to share his bed each night with her. She'd been hesitant, like many a new bride, but he'd cajoled her into agreeing at last to share in the intimacy of remaining in his bed after they'd made love. Whatever had drawn her from his bed tonight? Had she fallen somewhere, gotten hurt while walking in the dark?

The stones beneath his feet were ice cold, but he didn't mind. He liked the cold, liked the way it stirred his senses and kept him alert. He cracked open his bedchamber door and peered out into the corridor. The sound came again, but he saw nothing to indicate where it was coming from. He eased farther into the hall, still listening. Finally, he traced the sound to a bedchamber down the hall, the one belonging to his younger brother, Thomas.

"Thomas?" Redmond rapped at the door and pressed his ear to listen. There was a rush of hushed voices, followed by silence. Redmond's heart fluttered as his mind made the terrible connection as to his missing wife and the voices coming from his brother's room.

"Red?" Thomas finally asked as he opened the

bedroom door. His hair was mussed, and he was only half-dressed. "What are you doing up? It's late..."

"Are you alone? I heard a crying sound. I'm worried Millicent is hurt. She wasn't in bed when I awoke. Will you help me find her?"

Thomas swallowed hard, and his gaze darted to the left as he began to craft a lie. Redmond had practically raised his younger brother and knew right away when Thomas wasn't being truthful. Which meant...he knew where Millicent was.

Redmond's heart hardened as he faced the betrayal by his own blood.

"She's with you, isn't she?" Redmond's veins filled with ice as he spoke what he hadn't wanted to admit had been true for months.

It hadn't been a cry of pain he'd heard but one of *passion*. A sound he'd never been able to coax from his wife since they'd married six months ago. She'd remained gentle and still beneath him in bed, and each time he'd tried and failed to excite her. Most of the time, he'd given up and rolled away from her, his heart pained by his failure.

Thomas's eyes refused to meet his. "She is."

Redmond kept his rage reined in, but barely. He loved his brother, but Thomas was a fool who would follow his heart right into the bed of a married woman, even the wife of his own brother.

"Redmond, please...let me explain," Thomas began

again, but unable to find the words, he sighed and stepped back, letting Redmond enter the room.

Millicent peered around the edge of the changing screen in the corner of the room, her eyes wide with fear.

"Millicent." Redmond spoke her name softly, and even that gave a stab of pain to his chest.

"I'm sorry," she whispered. He saw the truth glimmering in her pretty blue eyes as they filled with tears. "I love him, Red. I think I've always loved him."

"Yet you accepted my proposal?" Redmond rubbed at his temples as a headache began to pound the backs of his eyelids. How had he been so bloody blind to let this slip of a young woman fool him into thinking she cared about him? Because he'd wanted to be loved, to be cherished for himself and not his title.

"My father said I had to accept you...to have a duchess in the family. He...he was so proud of me." The words trembled on her lips.

Thomas stepped between them. His stance was casual, but Redmond knew his brother was ready to protect Millicent should he fly into a rage. But the rage that brewed inside him was not directed at her. The pretty young woman was only nineteen, married to him less than six months and clearly too young to make a decision that would affect the rest of her life. No, Redmond was furious with himself. He was twenty-five, old enough to know he should have sensed Millicent's attraction to his title and not to him.

My damnable pride, he thought darkly.

Redmond walked over to the crackling fire in the hearth and braced one hand on the marble mantel. His thoughts raced wildly until they jerked to a halt. He turned around to face the exposed couple. Thomas had his arm around the girl's shoulders, and tears streamed down her face.

"You want Thomas?" he finally asked. Each word cost him much to even speak. A world-weary sorrow began to leach into his anger, eating away at him until he felt nothing at all. He was as hollow as the old dead trees in the woods beyond his estate.

Millicent nodded, the girlish hope in her gaze only deepening the emptiness inside him. She'd never looked at him that way, with hope.

"Then I give you my blessing. I will contact my solicitor tomorrow. We will have to demand an annulment which won't be easy. But know this—once this is settled, neither of you must return here ever again." He couldn't bear to see them, even his beloved brother. The pain would be too great. To annul a marriage meant he'd never consummated his love for his wife, but he had. Everything was built upon more lies now.

Thomas's lips parted as though he wished to speak, but then he seemed to reconsider and answered with a nod.

"Thank you, Redmond... I...," Millicent started, but her words died as Redmond stared at her.

"Don't," he warned before she could say another word. Redmond stalked from the room. He could not stand to listen to her thank him for letting her break his heart.

He didn't go back to bed. There would be no sleeping now. He headed to his study and sat in the moonlit room as he retrieved a bottle of scotch from his liquor tray by his desk. He didn't bother with the glasses. He simply drank from the bottle until his stomach revolted and he choked on the liquid. Then he leaned back in his chair and stared out the tall bay window overlooking the road that led to the cliffs. The sea would be harsh this time of year, the fall winds giving way to icy winter. He could simply go, walk out into the night and head to the cliffs. No one would see. No one would stop him. No one would care.

Thomas would become the Duke of Frostmore, and all would be well. Thomas had always been the favorite, the more handsome, more charming, more likable brother. He'd heard the whispers all his life: *Why couldn't Thomas have been born the first son?* Even his own parents had preferred Thomas. Redmond was quiet, intense, gruff at times, and not everyone understood him. Now it had cost him what little happiness he had carved out for himself.

Why had he ever thought Millicent would choose

him when Thomas was at his side? From the moment he'd met the girl, her laughs had been for Thomas, her smiles, even her cries of passion. Redmond had never stood a chance.

Because I wanted to be loved, fool that I am.

He stared out at the cliffs a long time before he made a decision. A divorced man would have few options—no decent woman would ever be enticed by his title to become a second duchess after such a scandal broke. There was only one way to end this. He rose from his chair and grasped the bottle of scotch, taking another long, burning swallow.

"I never wished to be a bloody duke anyway," he muttered as he walked unsteadily out the door of Frostmore, his ancestral home. "Good riddance."

He stumbled a little but kept walking toward the cliffs until he could hear the crashing sound of the waves. There was nothing more beautiful or haunting than the sea when she was angry. Rain lashed his face and blinded his eyes to all but the lightning splitting the skies overhead. He moved numbly across the cold grass until he felt the rocky ledge was beneath his feet, and he wavered at the edge, his breath coming fast and his head spinning from grief and alcohol. All he wanted in that moment was for it to be over, to lose himself in the dark violence of the sea below. Then he took that final step toward the craggy abyss...

CHAPTER 1

FAVERSHAM, ENGLAND - SEVEN YEARS LATER

The bedchamber in Thursley Manor was dark except for a few lit oil lamps. The wind whistled clearly through the cracks in the mortar in between the stones. Harriet Russell tried to ignore the storm outside as she clutched her mother's hand. This old house, with its creaks and groans in the night, had never been a home to either of them, yet Harriet feared it would be her mother's last resting place.

"Harriet." Her mother moaned her name. Pain soaked each syllable as her mother coughed. The raspy sound tore at Harriet's heart.

Harriet brushed her other hand over her mother's forehead. "Rest, Mama." Beneath the oil lamp's glow, her mother's face was pale, and sweat dewed upon her skin as fever raged throughout her body.

"So little time," her mother said with a sigh. "I must

tell you..." Harriet watched her mother struggle for words and the breath to speak. "Soon... You will be twenty. Your father..."

Harriet didn't correct her, but George Halifax had *never* been her father. No, the man who held that title had died when she was fourteen. Edward Russell had been a famous fencing master, both in England and on the continent. He'd also been a loving man with laughing eyes and a quick wit whom she missed with her whole heart.

"Yes, Mama?" She desperately needed to hear what her mother had to say.

"George is your guardian, but on your birthday, you will be free to live your life as you choose."

Free. What an amazing notion. How desperately she longed for that day to come. George was a vile man who made her skin crawl whenever she was in the same room as him, and she wished every day that her mother hadn't been desperate enough to accept his offer of marriage. But fencing masters, even the greatest ones, did not make a living that could sustain a widow and a small daughter.

"Mama, you will get better." Harriet dipped a fresh cloth in clean water and placed it over her mother's brow.

"No, child. I won't." The weary certainty in her mother's voice tore at her heart. But they both knew that consumption left few survivors. It had claimed her father's laugh six years before, and now it would take her mother from her as well.

The bedchamber door opened, and Harriet turned, expecting to see one of the maids who had been checking on them every few hours to see if they needed anything. But her stepfather stood there. George Halifax was a tall man, with bulk and muscle in equal measures. The very sight of him chilled her blood. She'd spent the last six years trying to avoid his attentions, even locking her door every night just to be sure. She may be only nineteen, but she had grown up quickly under this man's roof and learned to fear what men desired of her.

"Ah...my dearest wife and daughter." George's tone sounded outwardly sincere, but there was the barest hint of mocking beneath it. He moved into the room, boots thudding hard on the stone. He was so different from her father. Edward had been tall and lithe, moving soundlessly with the grace of his profession in every step.

"Mother needs to rest." Harriet looked at her mother, not George, as she spoke. Whenever she met his gaze, it made her entire body seize with panic, and her instincts urged her to run.

"Then perhaps you want to leave her to rest?" George challenged softly.

Harriet raised hateful eyes to his. "I won't leave. She needs someone to look after her."

"Yes, you will leave, daughter." He stepped deeper into the room, fists clenched.

"I'm not your daughter," Harriet said defiantly. His lecherous gaze swept over her body.

"You're right. You could be so...much...more." He paused between the last three words, emphasizing what she knew he had wanted for years.

"George...," her mother, Emmeline, gasped. "No, please..."

"Hush, my dear. You need your rest. Harriet and I shall have a little talk outside. About her future." He came toward her, but Harriet moved fast, despite the hampering nature of her simple gown. She'd been trained by the best to never be caught flat-footed.

"Stop!" George snarled and grabbed her by the skirts as she ducked under his arm. With a sudden jerk, she hit the ground, her left shoulder and hip hitting the pine floorboards hard. A whimper escaped her as he dragged her to her feet and slapped her across the face.

Her mother made a soft sound of distress from the bed, and she heard the whisper as though from a vast distance away.

"Harriet...go...*run!*"

Harriet kicked George in the groin as hard as she could. He released her to clutch himself.

"Get her!" George shouted in rage.

Two hulking men she didn't recognize from among the household staff of Thursley Manor rushed into the room. She tried to dodge them, but they trapped her in the corner and dragged her from the room by her arms.

"Lock her up!" George's shout followed them down the corridor.

Her mother called out weakly for her, but no matter how Harriet screeched and fought, they wouldn't let go. She was taken to an empty bedroom and shoved inside. The door was locked with a clack of cold iron. Shivering hard, her shoulder and hip still sore from her fall, Harriet threw herself at the door, but she was too small to break the sturdy oak.

Her mother's warning had come too late. She wouldn't turn twenty for another month, and George was already taking control of her, just as she feared he would. There was nothing he couldn't do to her, stranded as she was at Thursley. They were too far from the town of Faversham for anyone to come this way except on purpose. She had no friends, no one who would worry about her, which she now suspected with dread was what George had wanted all along.

The dark bedchamber was bracing in its chill. No fire had been lit in the small hearth, and she knew no one would come to see to the task. There was only one small oil lamp on the side table next to the bed. She dug around in the drawers of the side table until she found a pair of steel strikers. She used the strikers to light the lamp. The light blossomed into a healthy glow, but it offered no warmth. Outside the storm seemed to build as rain joined the howling winds.

She had to escape. Harriet attempted to pry the windows open, but nails were driven deep into the wooden frames. She even studied the lock of the door, trying to use a hairpin to see if she could twist the tumblers in a way that would set her free, but nothing worked.

A few hours later, footsteps echoed in the corridor. A key jangled in the lock, and a latch lifted. She tensed, her muscles tightening as she expected to see her stepfather or one of his men. But she saw only the cook, Mrs. Reed.

"Thank God you're all right, lass." The tall Scottish woman placed one hand on her bosom. "I was worried to death when I found out he had locked you up." Mrs. Reed spoke in a whisper and glanced down the darkened hall behind her, as though fearful of being overheard.

"Mrs. Reed... My mother... Is she...?" Harriet choked on the words.

"No, not yet, lass, but there's no time. You must go. *Now.*" The cook came into the room and cupped her face the way Harriet's mother used to. "I know you dinna want to go, but you must."

"I can't leave Mama here, not with him."

"You can and you will. Your mother told me when she fell ill that she feared she wouldna be around to protect you. She made me promise that I'd help you escape," Mrs. Reed insisted. "The master has plans for you. Plans I cannot abide, you ken. He means to hurt you, to use you like a..." She shook her head as though the rest of what she might have said was too awful. "He wanted me to drug you. But I drugged him and his men instead. We dinna have long." The cook put an arm around her shoulders and dragged her back down the servants' stairs and into the kitchens. A scullery maid named Bess was cleaning a pot and looked up at them as they entered.

"How are they, lass?" Mrs. Reed asked the girl.

"Still asleep," Bess whispered, her eyes wide with fear. "Mr. Johnson has the coach ready. He thinks he can take Miss Russell as far as Dover, despite the storm."

"Dover?" Harriet repeated in shock. That was so far away.

"Aye, lassie. You'll take this." Mrs. Reed pulled a leather pouch of coins from a pocket in her dress. "Buy passage to Calais."

"France?" Harriet trembled. To travel alone as a single woman was to invite trouble, possibly even danger.

"France will be safe. The master could have you tracked from here all the way to the bloody Isle of Skye in the north. 'Tis best if you leave England."

Harriet swallowed hard and nodded. She knew some French and could learn more when she was there. Her father had relatives in Normandy, second cousins.

Perhaps she could reach them and find work. She tried to do what her mother had taught her, which was to focus on a plan of action rather than let fear freeze her in place.

Mrs. Reed pulled a heavy woolen cloak off of a nearby coatrack and wrapped it around her shoulders. "We have no time to delay." She led Harriet to the servants' entrance, which took them to the back of the house where the stables were. George's coach stood waiting, and the driver huddled near the horses, which pawed the ground uncertainly.

The rain came down in thick sheets, and Harriet splashed through the mud to the waiting coach.

"Take this." Mrs. Reed followed her and handed her a basket of food before she climbed into the vehicle.

"Mrs. Reed..." There were a thousand things she wanted to say, and a dozen new fears assailed her at what her life would become now as she fled. But only one thing truly mattered above all the rest. Her mother was still dying, and Harriet was abandoning her.

"I know, lass." The cook squinted in the rain and squeezed her hand. "I know, but you canna stay here." She turned to head back to the servants' entrance.

"Take care of my mother. Tell her I made it to a ship and sailed for Calais," Harriet called out from the coach as Mr. Johnson, the driver, shut the door, sealing her inside. She wanted her mother to believe she had escaped, even if she never made it. It might be the last comfort anyone could give her. Harriet's bottom lip trembled, and she fought off a sob.

Mrs. Reed waved at her and then ducked back inside the house. Harriet began to shake as the wet woolen cloak weighed her down. An extra chill settled into her skin from her soaked clothes.

The coach jerked forward, and the basket of food in Harriet's lap nearly toppled over. She set it down on the floor and closed her eyes, trying to calm herself.

"Oh, Mama... I wish I didn't have to leave you."

But if she had stayed, the horrors she would have endured were unthinkable. And to suffer a life trapped beneath George's control... She knew he wouldn't honor her twentieth birthday—that must have been what her mother wished to tell her. That she would be free of him as a guardian, but she would need to escape him before he could stop her. Harriet collapsed back onto the seat and silently sobbed for her mother, for the life of the last person she'd loved in the world.

"Dry your eyes, kitten." Her father's voice seemed to drift from the past as old memories of her childhood came to her. She closed her eyes, imagining how he used to find her when she'd fallen and scraped a knee. He'd curl his fingers under her chin and gently make her look up into his smiling, tender face.

"Papa," she breathed, feeling more like a child now than she had for years. She clung to the vision of him inside her head.

"You are my daughter. You do not cower when life becomes difficult. Face every challenge with courage, and refuse to accept defeat."

Harriet's eyes flew open as she thought for a moment that she felt a caress on her cheek. But the ghost of him vanished just as quickly as it had come. She wiped her eyes and tried to steady herself, lest she burst into tears again.

She remembered how her father used to counsel the young lords he taught fencing. Harriet used to hide behind a tall potted plant, tucking her skirt up under her knees as she watched her father move about the large room with a dozen young men wielding fencing foils. He would call out the positions, and the men would fall in line, raising their blades and performing. When they began to tire, he would call out, *"Clear eyes, steady hands, you shall not fail."*

She would need that advice and more to find a new life in Calais.

She leaned against the wall of the coach, listening to the rain and wondering what the dawn would bring.

CHAPTER 2

Rain whipped at the coach windows as Harriet attempted to catch a few hours of sleep. Thunder shook the road so hard that more than once Harriet was jostled awake in fright. She rubbed her eyes, fatigue hanging heavy in her limbs. It was close to midnight, and they still had a ways to go before they reached Dover. In good weather it would take at least two hours, but with the roads muddied and visibility hampered, that time might double.

With a quiet sigh, she wrapped her black wool cloak tight about her shoulders; it was freezing in the carriage. Her toes were already numb and her fingers icy as she twisted them beneath her skirts to try to keep them warm. She turned her thoughts to what would happen when she reached Calais. Harriet was completely alone and had no one to help her find her way, but surely with

her passable French she could find a coach to Normandy.
With the coins Mrs. Reed had given her, she should be
able to afford a room at an inn before she journeyed
ahead.

Caution would be crucial, however, because she
knew she would be a target for men. Alone, and just shy
of destitution, she would be easy prey if she wasn't careful. Harriet's only hope now was to trespass on the kindness of her father's distant cousins until she could find
suitable work. She'd attended a finishing school for
young ladies until her father had died, and she'd been a
prized pupil of the instructors there. Perhaps she could
find her way as a governess? If that didn't work, she
might have a chance to be a seamstress. She wasn't
completely useless with a needle and thread.

The storm only worsened as midnight passed, and
the rains flooded the road. More than once, Mr. Johnson
slowed the coach to allow the horses to walk through
deeper pools of water that had gathered on the road.
Harriet pressed her forehead against the coach window
and peered into the darkness. She glimpsed nothing
until a flash of lightning lit up the roads, and she was at
last able to see what obstacles the horses were facing.

The poor beasts, they were risking their lives to save
hers. They didn't even have the comfort of stopping
here, because the countryside around Dover wasn't a
safe place, at least according to the gossip she'd heard in
Thursley Manor.

Harriet prayed that they would make it to Dover's harbor without a reason to stop. They were passing through the Duke of Frostmore's country, and Harriet feared meeting up with him. Redmond Barrington was known as the Dark Duke or the Devil of Dover by the servants at Thursley, and rumors followed his name like shadows cast by gravestones.

Harriet knew all the stories, of course. The duke feasted on naughty children who did not abide by the wishes of their parents; he stole the virtue of unsuspecting maidens foolish enough to travel alone in his lands. Perhaps the most gruesome tale was that he had killed his younger brother, Thomas Barrington, in a duel after Lord Frostmore discovered his brother bedding his new bride. They said he cast his wife off the cliffs before he shot Thomas in the stomach and watched him slowly bleed to death. Harriet knew that the younger brother was in fact dead, according to parish records, but no one knew the truth of how he'd met his end other than that he had been shot.

George had often bragged at dinner that he was well acquainted with Lord Frostmore, and that only made Harriet's fears of being caught in Dover that much stronger. What if the duke discovered she was here and returned her to George?

Regardless of the veracity of the grim tales, Harriet knew it was not wise to be caught alone on the duke's lands, especially when the cliffs of Dover were so close.

Flights of imagination led Harriet toward visions of carriages plummeting over the cliffs and crashing into the sea below.

She shuddered at the notion of gasping for air and breathing in only icy seawater. Harriet tried to dismiss her fears as much as she could, and instead focused on thoughts of her father. She was almost asleep again when the carriage suddenly lurched and toppled onto its side.

Harriet's head struck the wall of the coach when the carriage overturned, and something warm began to trickle into her eyes. For a long moment she was paralyzed with pain and confusion as her vision blurred. Finally, her sight cleared enough for her to get up. Her right arm felt oddly numb after a violent pain. She lay against the window of the coach, which was now pressed into the muddy ground. Broken glass cut her palms as she tried to rise, and she winced as her shoulder suddenly flared with fresh pain.

"Mr. Johnson?" she called out.

There was a cry, muffled beneath the crash of thunder. Harriet shoved at the door above her so she could climb out of the side of the carriage, now the ceiling. Her hem tore as she jumped from the carriage, and her arm twinged as she braced herself to land. She sank almost instantly into several inches of oozing mud. The road was dark; moonlight was unable to pierce the storm clouds. In a brief flash of lightning, she saw Mr. Johnson clutching his leg, his face twisted in pain.

Harriet ran over to him, hunching over to get a better look.

"Are you able to ride, Mr. Johnson?"

"Afraid not, Miss Russell." Mr. Johnson winced as he tried to stand, but fell back to the ground. "You should take a horse, ride to find help. I'll stay with the coach."

"We have to get you to a doctor," Harriet insisted. Lightning tore across the sky, and in the distance a mountainous edifice was momentarily revealed. "What place is that, Mr. Johnson?" She pointed in the direction of the distant building.

The driver's face darkened. "That is Lord Frostmore's estate."

"The Dark Duke?" Harriet's heart jumped in her chest.

"Yes, miss. I know you to be a brave lady, but you mustn't go there." Mr. Johnson grasped her arm as though to prevent her from going for help.

Harriet pried his fingers off her arm gently. "Is there nowhere else close enough to reach?"

"Not in this weather," the driver admitted.

"Then I must go to the duke."

"Miss, please...," the driver protested, but she shook her head.

"Do not worry about me, Mr. Johnson. Now come, let me help you up. You can rest inside the carriage until help arrives. You mustn't catch a chill in this storm."

Harriet forced him up and got him inside the

carriage with some difficulty. After Mr. Johnson was secured, Harriet loosed one of the horses and pulled herself up onto the beast's back, grasping the long reins. She hadn't ridden a horse since she was a child, and while she was uncertain as to her skill now, she knew Mr. Johnson depended on her.

Her torn and muddied skirts split easily as she straddled the horse. Wrapping the reins tight around her fingers, she kicked the horse's sides. It didn't need any other urging to fly across the soaked road toward the distant estate. Her cloak flew out behind her as she dug her muddy boots into the horse's flanks again, spurring it toward the dark, shadowy edifice she'd glimpsed moments before.

Harriet rode the horse hard all the way to the gates. The heavy wrought-iron structure was open just enough for her horse to pass, but Harriet lingered at the entrance, taking in the sharp spiked tops of the gates and the stone carved with the name of "FROSTMORE" near the gates.

A pair of devilish gargoyles crouched menacingly on either side of the entrance pillars. And when the lightning flashed over them, Harriet nearly screamed as she swore they moved. More pain lanced through her shoulder, and she cried out, clutching her injured shoulder.

The large mansion lay in the gloom beyond. There within its walls was the Dark Duke. Could she pass these gates and brave the risks? Harriet thought of Mr.

Johnson and his injuries, and she remembered her father's fencing lessons. She was capable of defending herself if it came to it, assuming he wasn't like her step-father, with men hired to trap her, so she spurred her horse again and rode through the gates, ready to risk her life in order to help her driver. But she would do her best to beg for help from the servants who would answer the door, and hopefully they wouldn't share with their master that she was here. It was a small hope, but she clung to it, nonetheless.

The manor house was dark; only a few lights were lit near the main entrance. She abandoned her horse and ran up the stone steps, beating on the heavy oak door with the knocker. After a few minutes, a middle-aged man with a somber face opened the door. He was in his nightclothes, with a candle raised near his head. His bleary eyes focused on her in surprise and confusion.

"Please, sir. My coachman is injured. Our carriage overturned on the road to Dover. He cannot walk or ride without assistance!" Harriet blurted out quickly.

The man took in her dirty, drenched appearance and opened the door wider. "Come in, my child. Quickly now," the man whispered in a soft tone. Harriet followed him, and he led her through darkened halls until they reached a small sitting room. The man lit fresh kindling under the logs in the hearth with his candle and turned to her.

"Now, more slowly, tell me exactly what has

happened." He gestured for her to sit on the settee. She did her best to recount the accident on the road.

"I will see to his retrieval and care at once. Please remain here. Do not leave this room—it is better that no one but myself and a few others know you are here," the old man warned. There was a shadow of concern in his eyes that urged her compliance. He must wish to hide her arrival from the duke, and that was quite fine with her. But if the carriage was broken, she had no way to reach the port of Dover...and George may already be looking for her.

After the butler left her alone, Harriet stood up and walked to the fire, holding her hands out to warm them over the meager flames. Her shoulder still ached with a dull, agonizing pain, but she didn't want anyone to know she'd been hurt. Weakness in a woman traveling alone was even more dangerous.

A few minutes of dead silence passed with nothing but the ticking of a grandfather clock before she heard a stirring in the hall. She looked up to see a large black dog standing in the doorway. The silhouette of the creature was startling, like the interruption of a dream by a hellhound. It let out a low growl, its white teeth bared. It was nearly as tall as her chest. The dog took a step toward her, its growl deepening to a deadlier tone.

Harriet brushed her hood back and shoved wet locks of blonde hair away from her face so she could better make eye contact. Her stepfather had several mean-spirited hounds back at Thursley, which she'd had to defend herself against more than once. She did not back away or show fear. She braced her hands on her hips and leaned menacingly toward the dog. The dog took another step forward, its brown eyes boring into her blue ones. It let out a snarl and trotted toward her.

"Sit!" Harriet shouted in a commanding tone.

The massive dog froze, the growl dying in its throat. In mild confusion, it slowly lowered its back haunches so it now sat two feet away from her. For a long moment she continued to glare at the beast, which as she got a better look at it appeared to be some kind of hound...a schnauzer? But she had never seen one this large. It had a noble black beard, a strong and well-formed body, and a glossy coat.

Harriet carefully extended her hand to the creature, who craned its neck forward, brushing its wet black nose over her fingertips in a cautious but friendly manner. It snuffled loudly but made no move to bite her as she stroked its great head. The hairs on the back of her neck rose, and a sense of being watched prickled along her skin, sending little tremors down her spine.

"You are the first person Devil hasn't bitten upon first meeting," a cold voice said from the doorway.

Harriet's head flew up, and she saw a tall man leaning in the doorway. His head was afire with deep-red hair that was cut a tad too long, and his hazel eyes gleamed with the fire's distant glow like topaz. His face was carved with perfect masculinity, but there was a hint of cruelty that hung about his sensuous lips, and anger radiated from his eyes. She bit her lip and tried to still the trembling of her body as she took *him* in. There was no question—this was the Duke of Frostmore.

He was not pretty, as some men tended to be. There was certainly nothing angelic about his face or form to bring forth a sense of natural charm. Instead, he seemed to exist in a singularly masculine way that made her sit up and take notice. Fear and curiosity warred with each other as she continued to stare at him.

"Devil?" It was a foolish thing to say, but no other thoughts in her mind were coherent enough to say. The effect George had on her paled in comparison to this man. Fighting George, had it come to that, would have been difficult, but she could tell with one look that attempting to resist this man would be impossible. She swallowed hard and resolved to be pleasant, but not overly so, lest he think she was a woman he could take to his bed.

"Yes, my black-haired companion here. I spent a summer in the Bavarian Alps two years ago and brought him back with me. He's a rather new breed of dog, a giant schnauzer. Devil seemed a fitting name for the brute. He's torn many a throat from a careless man and even a few careless ladies." His tone was serious, but she thought—or rather hoped—she saw the glint of teasing in his eyes, a dark, cruel teasing.

"If that is so, perhaps the fault lies not with the beast but with his master," Harriet replied, meeting his gaze with courage, despite the fact that deep within she was quivering.

He's no different than George. You can handle him.

She tried to instill within herself a sense of confidence, but her right arm ached fiercely, and her head was pounding with a headache that made even the light of the fire sear her eyes. She had dealt with men like this, the kind who took pleasure in striking fear into a woman's heart. But Harriet was not so easily shaken.

Lord Frostmore crossed his arms and leaned lazily against the doorjamb, preventing her from escaping. She felt his eyes rake over her, as if he wanted to rip her clothes clean off her body and ravage her.

But much to her surprise, the power of those eyes was enough to send a whisper of a dark, forbidden thrill through her as well, something she'd never felt before. George had only ever disgusted her when he looked at her like that, but with this man...something was different. The anger and disdain mixed with lust in the duke's eyes seemed different. And there was something else in his gaze...shadowed not by evil, but rather by pain. Pain was something she recognized all too well.

The man snapped his fingers, and Devil trotted out of the room, leaving his master and Harriet alone.

"Might I ask, Miss...," he began.

"Russell, Harriet Russell." She blurted out her real

LAUREN SMITH

name without thinking, but it was too late. She couldn't take it back. She could only pray that if this man indeed knew George, then George would never have had a reason to discuss her, let alone call her by her name.

"Miss Russell, what are you doing in my house at this *ungodly* hour?" His lips curved upward as he said "ungodly," as though sharing some private joke. So she'd been correct in her assumption. He was the Dark Duke, the infamous Devil of Dover.

"My carriage overturned, and my driver was injured. I sought help from the man who answered the door." She took a small step back as the duke entered the room and shut the door behind him. She heard the sound of a key turning in the door before he faced her again. Harriet gripped her wounded arm to support it, while also attempting to look relaxed, lest she betray her wounded condition.

"So my man Grindle let you in, did he?" The duke leaned back against the locked door, eyeing her with increasing interest.

"Your Grace, I did not mean to intrude, but my driver is terribly injured, and the storm is worsening."

Thunder rumbled as if on cosmic cue, shaking the house around them. Harriet tried to remain calm as the duke came closer. He wore buff breeches and a loose white lawn shirt that billowed open at his chest, revealing broad shoulders and a sculpted chest so breathtaking the angels would have wept. His state of relative

424

undress had escaped her attention while she'd been so focused on his face and his dog.

Harriet took another involuntary step back, her body warning her of the danger that emanated from him. She should not be left alone with him. Daring to look around, she tried to find a bell cord to pull that might summon a servant to protect her if her strength failed her.

"Are you all *alone* this night, Miss Russell?" The duke was only a foot from her now, peering into her eyes.

He cupped her chin, raising her face up as he studied her. She tried to retreat, but the settee was right behind her now, her calves pressed against the base of the cushions. Lord Frostmore reached up with his other hand to undo the clasp of her cloak at her throat. The thick fabric collapsed at her feet in ebony waves of coarse wool. Harriet felt suddenly naked beneath his gaze, despite the pale-pink muslin gown she wore.

"I am alone, save for my driver," she answered. He would know the truth in her eyes if she tried to lie, and she refused to be cowed by him. The duke's hand at her throat dropped slowly to her chest and then to the rising flesh of her breasts. His fingertips traced a burning line over her skin before he withdrew his hand.

"You should *never* travel my roads alone." Lord Frostmore released her chin and turned to face the fire, no longer looking at her.

"I am not afraid," Harriet declared boldly.

He chuckled softly. "You will be before this night is through." He said this to himself, as if his words were not a warning but a dark promise.

"You would not dare touch me." Harriet's tone remained steady, despite her rising concern. She wanted to convince herself that he would do her no harm, not with Mr. Grindle and the other servants as witnesses. The duke turned back to face her, a cruel kind of delight shining in his eyes.

"I would do more than *dare*, my dear. Do you not know in whose house you stand?" He returned his focus to the fire, but she knew his attention was still upon her, as though he waited for her to scream or faint dead away like some ninny of a girl.

"You are Redmond Barrington, the Duke of Frostmore." She did not think it wise to mention his other names. The duke gave a wide smile as the firelight played with shadows on his face. Had she made a mistake in coming here? But what choice did she have? She couldn't leave Mr. Johnson injured in the midst of a dangerous storm. She'd face this devil and do whatever she had to survive the night.

WANT TO KNOW WHAT HAPPENS TO HARRIET AND THE Duke of Frostmore next? Grab the book HERE!

OTHER TITLES BY LAUREN
SMITH

Historical
The League of Rogues Series
Wicked Designs
His Wicked Seduction
Her Wicked Proposal
Wicked Rivals
Her Wicked Longing
His Wicked Embrace
The Earl of Pembroke
His Wicked Secret
The Last Wicked Rogue
Never Kiss A Scot
The Earl of Kent
Never Tempt a Scot
The Seduction Series
The Duelist's Seduction

The Rakehell's Seduction
The Rogue's Seduction
The Gentleman's Seduction
Standalone Stories
Tempted by A Rogue
Bewitching the Earl
Seducing an Heiress on a Train
Devil at the Gates
Sins and Scandals
An Earl By Any Other Name
A Gentleman Never Surrenders
A Scottish Lord for Christmas

Contemporary
The Surrender Series
The Gilded Cuff
The Gilded Cage
The Gilded Chain
The Darkest Hour
Love in London
Forbidden
Seduction
Climax
Forever Be Mine

Paranormal
Dark Seductions Series
The Shadows of Stormclyffe Hall

The Love Bites Series
The Bite of Winter

His Little Vixen

Brotherhood of the Blood Moon Series
Blood Moon on the Rise (coming soon)

Brothers of Ash and Fire
Grigori: A Royal Dragon Romance

Mikhail: A Royal Dragon Romance

Rurik: A Royal Dragon Romance

Sci-Fi Romance

Cyborg Genesis Series
Across the Stars

The Krinar Chronicles
The Krinar Eclipse

The Krinar Code by Emma Castle

Buy these books today by visiting www.
laurensmithbooks.com
Or by visiting your favorite ebook/paperback book store!

Lauren
SMITH
TIMELESS ROMANCE

ABOUT THE AUTHOR

Lauren Smith is an Oklahoma attorney by day, author by night who pens adventurous and edgy romance stories by the light of her smart phone flashlight app. She knew she was destined to be a romance writer when she attempted to re-write the entire *Titanic* movie just to save Jack from drowning. Connecting with readers by writing emotionally moving, realistic and sexy romances no matter what time period is her passion. She's won multiple awards in several romance subgenres including: New England Reader's Choice Awards, Greater Detroit BookSeller's

Best Awards, and a Semi-Finalist award for the Mary Wollstonecraft Shelley Award.

To Connect with Lauren, visit her at:
www.laurensmithbooks.com
lauren@laurensmithbooks.com
Facebook Fan Group - Lauren Smith's League
Lauren Smith's Newsletter

Never miss a new release! Follow me in one or more of the ways below!

facebook.com/LaurenDianaSmith
twitter.com/LSmithAuthor
instagram.com/Laurensmithbooks
bookbub.com/authors/lauren-smith

Made in the USA
Monee, IL
13 January 2022

88764691R00256